The Wolf's Name

Raelyn Teague

THE WOLF'S NAME

Published by Outland Entertainment LLC
3119 Gillham Road
Kansas City, MO 64109

Founder/Creative Director: Jeremy D. Mohler
Editor-in-Chief: Alana Joli Abbott

ISBN: 978-1-954255-25-8
Ebook: 978-1-954255-21-0
Worldwide Rights
Created in the United States of America

Editor: Gwendolyn N. Nix
Copy editor: Alana Joli Abbott
Proofreader: Tara Cloud Clark
Cover Illustration: Raelyn Teague
Cover Design: Jeremy D. Mohler
Interior Layout: Mikael Brodu

Printed and bound in the United States of America.

Visit **outlandentertainment.com** to see more, or follow us on our Facebook Page **facebook.com/outlandentertainment/**

PART I

— INDUCTION —

June 15th, 1883

Lucas kept his word. His front-page advertisement in the paper brought half of New Westminster to my show. On the outdoor stage, a simple suggestion from me had Mr. Richards howling at the late afternoon sun and pawing at an itch with the toe of his muddy shoe. The air filled with laughter, and the eyes in the crowd glittered so bright I thought they were diamonds.

They wouldn't have grinned if they'd known how the Power could enslave them. If I only knew how to wield it. If I let it enslave me first. Oh, how it wanted to.

At dusk I had my usual drink with Lucas at the printing press, but this time he'd invited Joseph and brought twice the whiskey to celebrate. Lucas kept my glass filled and promised to finance more shows if I'd teach him a few tricks.

We'd downed a few too many when Mr. Richards barged in on us. He'd had too many himself. I reminded him he was the one who'd demanded to come on stage, but from his slurred rambling, I realized he wasn't angry about me embarrassing him at the show. Then I thought he'd come to pester me again to sell him the farm, but, no, it was something else… Something about wild dogs in the woods I could "magic away."

Lucas managed to escort Richards away without protest. He has a magic all his own, but Richards would give anything for the last word. Perhaps it's still coming.

Once they were out of earshot, Joseph leaned in with a warning. "Don't be swayed by Lucas's promises," he said. "He can afford his schemes, but when it fails, you'll be the one to pay."

But to have the O'Connor name remembered with diamond eyes instead of— Well, I might even sell myself to the Power.

God forgive me, I know I would.

— CHAPTER ONE —

NATHANIEL

The hum of magic through Nathaniel's body made him feel like a god and less than human all at once.

As he ran, the damp Canadian autumn chilled his lungs, but his skin baked under the heat of the Power sizzling about him. His senses became heightened with it. His prey had left footprints he shouldn't have been able to see in the night and shadow, but even with the Power's aid he barely heard the scamper of feet through the woods ahead.

He won't escape this time. Not this time!

Movement flashed at the edge of Nathaniel's vision. The beast darted under an arch of skeletal firs, their branches entwined in a gateway to some unknown hell, and it disappeared down an overgrown path. Nathaniel vaulted over felled trees and unearthed roots in pursuit. The path broke into a narrow clearing where his quarry halted, turning from flight to fight. Nathaniel dug in his heels.

Given up on its escape, the beast stared him down with bloodied teeth bared. It backed toward the door of an abandoned cellar half-hidden in the wisps of tall grass, unwilling to abandon its only refuge. Nathaniel had the animal cornered, which made it more dangerous. Even to him. His finger curled around the trigger of his old Model P pistol for courage.

"Caught you." Nathaniel's voice carried the tickle of the Power instead of weariness from the chase. "Don't you try to run again."

Naked but for the mud on its skin and a haystack of orange hair, the beast showed no weakness to the cold night. It snarled with the craze of a rabid mutt but walked upright on the balls of two human feet. Instead of paws, it flexed scythe-like fingers with ragged nails. It was skinnier than the last time Nathaniel had seen it. Far too skinny. A sack of bones and bloodlust abandoned to death and damnation.

Little remained of the foolish boy he'd first met, but there was enough. Enough to make it right.

"Keith," Nathaniel said, "come back to your senses."

With a ravenous growl, the beast charged.

Instinct alone called the Power to Nathaniel. It crackled around him in a shield of sapphire light. Out of habit he searched for the flicker of a Name around the creature, but he found none. It didn't matter. The boy's true identity was etched into Nathaniel's memory like a scar.

The beast leapt. Nathaniel threw out his arm, striking the animal with a hammer of raw energy.

"Regret!"

The sound of its Name knocked the creature from its feet. A light the colour of decayed leaves flared over the treetops and slammed into the creature, a dying star striking the earth.

Keith sucked in a breath as the sickly fire of his Name entered him. His arms and legs jerked toward his centre. When he recovered from the blast, a sputtering yellow glow emanated from him. He groaned, the sound broken but recognizably human. The beast had vanished, but there was nothing Nathaniel could do about the monster left behind. Trying had only made everything worse.

"Y— you—" Keith said as though he'd never spoken the word before. Nathaniel offered a reluctant hand, and the young man, barely more than a boy, eyed his palm with suspicion. "I—"

"Welcome back to humanity," Nathaniel said. Warily, Keith accepted Nathaniel's hand, and he hauled the boy to his feet. "Horrid, isn't it? Men are fouler than dogs."

Keith's legs wobbled once the support of Nathaniel's hand was gone. He snaked his arms around his naked chest, his shoulders tucked up to his ears. "Why'd you help me?"

"I'm not helping *you*." A poison roiled in Nathaniel's gut at the thought. "And I have my reasons."

"Yes." Keith shook his head as if to clear up space in his mind. "Yes, your sister. I think I remember…"

He remembered too much.

"There's no time; he'll already know you've got your Name again." Nathaniel tapped his pistol against his leg to be sure Keith knew it was there. "Tell me the truth. Where's the other mutt?"

"Mutt…?" Keith wrinkled his nose in confusion. "Ah, Sheridan! He was turned—"

"Yes, yes. I know that already. Tell me where he is so I can deal with him."

Keith chuckled darkly, the sound fractured between the shivers that rocked his body. "He's in these woods, but you won't find him."

"You'd better pray I do. Pray hard. *Regret*."

At the command, Keith's light left his body and streamed into Nathaniel. He hated this part—where another's Name left its stain on him. Keith's brought a bitter taste to Nathaniel's mouth that reminded him of rotten potatoes and the pain of hunger. All of Keith's regrets felt like his own: the heartache of a sister's death and the loss of a home and country he barely remembered yet could never forget. Luckily, Keith's light had weakened in the time it had been away from him. With so much regret of Nathaniel's own, it would have been easy for him to be consumed by it.

Drained of his light, Keith's shivers diminished again. His arms dangled like twigs from his shoulders, and his vacant eyes stared forward.

"Forget." Nathaniel sent the command on tendrils of the Power and let them seep under Keith's skin. It was too good a punishment for someone like him, too merciful, but Nathaniel no longer had the right to judge him. "Forget your life as a dog and go back to the Brotherhood. Convince them to return to Washington. For good."

The command given, Nathaniel released the boy's light for the final time, and as the rays emptied from his body, the bitterness on his tongue subsided. Keith's regrets faded and left only the ones Nathaniel had earned for himself.

When the boy's aura descended back upon him, Keith's eyelids fluttered, but he didn't seem to see Nathaniel. With glazed eyes locked forward, he limped noisily into the trees, pulled by an invisible rope.

How long before his memories return? How long will I have?

Hanging above the clearing, Orion's belt dimmed as the first gestures of dawn lightened the sky.

Sheridan will already be in hiding.

Nathaniel released the Power like a long sigh and let it weaken until he no longer felt even a spark of its allure. His hearing deadened. His vision dimmed. Tremors now moved through his body, and as he stumbled through the shadows of the woods, the wheeze of his breath made him feel less of a devil.

One more day. Sheridan could wait one more day.

— CHAPTER TWO —

THE WOLF

Forward.

Backward.

Pain.

Back and forth. Chains dragging. Chains biting skin and bone.

Voices through the ground above.

"Regret!"

Voices gone. Wolves alone again.

Back and forth. Forward. Backward.

Alone.

— CHAPTER THREE —

NATHANIEL

Hidden in a thicket, Nathaniel recovered his strength while the day wore on. He lay on a bed of dirt and cedar and listened to the nostalgic mooing of cows on a nearby farm. He'd never imagined he'd miss that sound—never thought his gut would twist with longing for a place he'd spent most of his life wishing to escape.

When the shadows cast by the trees grew long toward the east, he hid his pistol under his coat and found a trail that wound toward New Westminster.

Time for a final farewell.

For as long as he could, he stuck to the woods and kept his distance from the sleepy farmhouses, their windows now lit with a soft amber glow to keep out the evening. By the time he'd crept to his destination, the sun had almost disappeared; it peeked through scarlet clouds and hung low toward the western sea. Farther on, the city stirred as people hurried home by foot or creaking wagon, but those sounds were dim echoes on the outskirts where the cemetery lay still. Sombre. Only Nathaniel's breath and the whisper of unkempt grass in the breeze broke the silence left by the dead. He stole toward a pillar of stone looming straight and white against the darker hillside. A year of mucky springs and livid storms had dirtied the roses carved into the stone's pale face, but he didn't bother to clear the filth from the name etched among the roses. He remembered it well.

"Hello, Lucas. Wherever you are now."

He should have brought a better token to set by his friend's gravestone. Cow dung, maybe. All he had was the letter tucked into his coat. He pulled the envelope out, his hand folding it into his fist.

"That fire at the printing press. How convenient." Nathaniel muttered each sour word slowly. "I've waited for this for a very, *very* long time, but I bet you thought this day would never come."

Bile chewed a trail inside Nathaniel's chest. He stared into the falling sun until it burned the memory of pain out of him and tickled his throat. With a damp cough into his ragged sleeve, he looked down his nose at the swirling letters chiselled into the pillar.

"It's over, or it will be soon. Soon the world will know what happened, and they'll know what a coward you are."

Footsteps rustled the grass. Nathaniel felt beneath his coat for his pistol.

Down the line of weather-worn headstones, a young woman with a baby in her arms made her way toward a lowly stone. She choked on her sobs and seemed aware only of the grave at her feet.

Just a widow. Still, better not give her a fright.

Part of him wanted to hold onto his anger and to the letter in his fist, but before the woman could spy his face, Nathaniel set the envelope at the base of the gravestone and pinned it under a stray pebble. Stifling another cough into his sleeve, he turned his back to the widow and tiptoed down the hillside. His last day as a dead man. After he'd taken care of Sheridan, he'd face the dogs' master on even ground. Then they'd see who had the better tricks.

Then they'd see who'd end up here in the cold, dead earth.

— CHAPTER FOUR —

THE WOLF

Dark.

Forward and backward.

Wood creaks above. Roof opens. Master comes with shadow. Dark. Blurred. Looks human. Smells of blood.

"You know what to do, my dogs." Master's voice hurts. Burns. "Don't disappoint me."

Master waves his hand. Shadows rise. Devour.

Legs weak. Falling. Falling into the black.

"Sleep." Master's voice fades in the distance. "Soon we hunt."

— CHAPTER FIVE —

MATILDA

Matilda O'Connor pointed her rifle to the ground and leaned over the Brunette River. The water roiled, thick with red-bellied salmon splashing upstream toward their birthplace, and warned her away from the river's edge.

Where did she go?

No moon reflected in the salmon-churned waters below, but it watched her from the twilight heavens, full and ashen on a bed of timid stars. If it could see her target, the moon kept it secret.

I can't lose another one.

Swallowing her doubts, Matilda cupped a hand around her ear. A gust of wind carried the salty taste of the sea but none of the sounds she'd hoped for. Instead, she heard the bickering of her younger brother and sister. The ruckus they made rattled through her ears, reckless children unaware they were swatting a hornet. And Matilda felt ready to sting.

"Do you think the cow went for a swim?" Elliot cut off one of Olive's complaints and joined Matilda on the river's bank. "Why are you staring at the water?"

His attempt to joke now of all times shattered the last of Matilda's composure. "I wouldn't be out here at all if you'd mended the fence as I asked instead of waving fists at other boys!" She tried to sound parental like Nathaniel. He'd been good at that, but for all her nineteen years, she felt like a child pretending to be mature. "We'll be looking all night."

Turning from the river, she gave her brother a scowl. The vanishing day had washed the bronze out of his skin, but the play of light from his kerosene lantern flooded an ochre glow over his cheeks that hardly made him look repentant.

Elliot adjusted the coils of frayed rope at his shoulder and jutted out his chin like he was taller and much more important than a boy who'd barely begun to shave. "Give me the rifle," he said, blowing a tangle of hair off his forehead. Like Matilda's, his hair was the shade of singed oak and never wanted to stay put. It fell back over his brow and cast shadows across his eyes. "Your aim went off while you were working at the manor. I'm the better shot."

"Not in the twilight, you're not," Olive said. A year older than Elliot, she had more than an extra year's worth of maturity, but her small frame made her look the youngest of them all. Instead of the others' dark hair, waves of honey gold slipped loose from her ribbon as she hugged her shawl to her body. The excess of cloth around her emphasized her dainty form, and she clutched Sable's rope leash as though the whimpering hound was all that protected her from goblins in the night. "Let's go home. We'll get lost ourselves if we wander too late. The cow will return on her own."

Matilda couldn't count on that. She could count on precious little these days. "She won't if she breaks her leg on a muddy slope," Matilda said and brushed past her siblings, heading back into the thick of the woods.

"Or if we're all eaten by Mr. Richards's dogs," Olive mumbled.

"That's why I brought this." Matilda raised the rifle just enough to draw attention and signalled for the others to follow her into the southern grove. "Stay behind me and listen for that cow."

"Besides," Elliot said to Olive, his voice dropping the way it did when he was about to get himself into trouble, "it's not dogs that should worry you, it's ghosts and trolls. Tonight's the kind of night they hunt for scared little girls."

"Stop it!" Olive said.

"There are no trolls in the woods," Matilda said as much to herself as the others. She hated to admit it, even to herself, but Elliot was right. Now that dusk weighed heavily on them, the night reminded her of her father's stories of bean sidhe or of the Little Folk who stirred the autumn leaves. Long ago she'd stopped believing in magic and heroes and fathers, but with the last grey haze of daylight sifting weakly through the trees, she remembered she still believed in monsters. "Stop trying to give your sister more nightmares, and both of you be quiet. You'll spook the cow before we find her."

"Maybe not trolls," Elliot mumbled. He dragged his feet as he followed behind Matilda. "Just Fenians."

Matilda stumbled in her tracks, her blood freezing more than the swiftly fading sun could explain. She whirled around to face her brother. "What did you say?"

Elliot's eyes bulged when he realized his mistake, and for a moment he lost his daring. "I didn't mean— It's what I heard," he said, avoiding Matilda's gaze. "Junior said his father heard Irishmen in these woods. There's talk of another raid. Like befo—"

"I'm surprised you're capable of conversation with Junior Richards that doesn't involve bloodied knuckles," Matilda said, her own knuckles turning whiter as she tightened her grip on her rifle.

She'd heard enough of Fenians to last her through Judgement Day. Angry at English misrule of their once homeland, the Irish nationalists thought they could take their motherland's sister colony hostage and negotiate Ireland's freedom. They were hopeful fools, but they were fools who caused more heartache and terror whenever they reached for their goal. And, oh, what reach they had. Mother had abandoned everything but her children to escape the damage the Fenian raids had wrought in their Manitoba home. So many lives lost. Their husband and father branded a traitor, and the disdainful whispers that hounded his wife and children any time they showed their faces in public.

What reach the Fenians had indeed for Matilda to hear their wretched name these long years and miles away from that life.

"You know Junior's drunk of a father has his eye on our farm," Matilda said. "Either of them would say anything to get us to leave, so why would you listen to a word of it?"

"Because if he'd wanted to pick a fight, he'd have just hit me!" Elliot's brief moment of weakness gone, he planted his feet wide apart and thrust his lantern at her like it was a fist. "Junior doesn't know that Father helped the raiders or why Mother brought us here without him. You're the one who won't forget!"

Olive moved between them and wrung Sable's leash between her hands. "Stop it, please! Let's calm down and go back home."

Matilda massaged her forehead and the headache pounding there, her exposed fingertips cold against her skin. It didn't help the ice in her veins, but the unspoken rebukes in her chest fled her with a sigh. Somehow her voice came more calmly now. "Junior is wrong. We left all that behind us. Half the country separates us from those devils now."

"Then why won't you let the past go?" Elliot muttered as he marched by her and Olive on the path.

Matilda fought back a frustrated scream and followed the light of his lantern as the shadows it cast prowled through the woods.

Please, just let us find the cow.

A deafening boom cut Matilda's prayer short, and her heart seized in her chest. A brief pause followed, and then another boom crackled through the sky.

"Richards," she groaned between her teeth. She pressed the heel of her hand into her ribs to restart her heart. "Someone ought to take away that man's weapon."

"He's shooting at those strays that killed our hens." Elliot raised his lantern and peered deeper into the trees toward their neighbour's farm. "He's doing us a favour for once."

"It was probably *his* dog that killed our hens," she said. "That man is blinder than a body in a grave. He couldn't tell a mongrel from his own son."

"Nobody can," Elliot said.

She'd run out of stern looks to give her brother, but she waved impatiently to him, motioning for his rope. "He'll be shooting at our cow, no doubt," she said. Elliot shrugged out of the rope, and Matilda looped it over a shoulder to leave her hands free to cling to her rifle. It was only a small comfort in the night. She nodded her head to Olive. "Take your brother home. Much as I'd like one less belly to feed, I'd rather not give our neighbour the satisfaction of shooting an O'Connor."

Sable stood alert at the end of her rope, ears propped forward and tail stiff behind her. Olive held the dog back and clutched her shawl around her throat. "What about you?"

"I'm going to get our cow," Matilda said. "Now go home, both of you."

Elliot grabbed Olive by her elbow and frowned at Matilda. "Watch your feet if you go onto Richards's land. Junior and his pa have been setting traps for the strays."

All the more reason for me to hurry and find that cow.

For all she'd begged them to return to the farm, Olive dragged her feet as Elliot pulled her and Sable away. She gave Matilda a last, worried glance over her shoulder before she disappeared into the woods with her brother.

With the rifle under one arm, Matilda hiked her skirts and weaved between the trees toward her neighbour's farm. Branches clawed at her, blending in with the nightfall now that Elliot's lantern had gone. She should have kept it.

A third shot roared through the skies, closer than the first two. As it rang through her ears, she ducked and covered her head, spilling the rope.

That fool is going to kill me!

"Richards!" She reached for the rope and strung it back over her shoulder one-handed. "Don't shoot!"

Movement at the edge of her vision drew her eye. She squinted into the trees, hoping to discover her lost cow, but whatever had been there had disappeared without a sound.

Dogs? She released her skirts and took her rifle in both hands. *I'm not afraid.*

"Matilda?"

The whisper came from behind her. When she whipped around, she found only trees and darkness encircling her. She must have imagined the sound of her name on the breeze, but all thoughts of the lost cow vanished. Matilda lowered the rifle, its weight too much to bear with the tremble of her hands. *I know that voice. But how?*

"Nathaniel?"

She barely dared to speak the name. Countless times she'd imagined her brother returning to her, as though the last year without him had been no more than a nightmare. In her imaginings she'd always embraced him readily, but always the dreams ended with her waking to a world without him.

Nathaniel ran away. He left us.

"Matilda, you can't be here." The voice came again, bodiless through the trees ahead.

The illusion refused to vanish like dreams should, and it was horribly detailed. Though her eyes strained into the hollows between the trees and found nothing, the voice was a perfect replica of her brother's—more perfect than her memories could conjure. The youthful tones, the soothing depths that made her think of warm cider and sunlight over the meadow. It was all there, all as known and right to her as sliding her feet into her own slippers, except now it carried a strange hint of tension behind the words. Harsh. Rushed.

"You have to go home," the voice said.

"Is this…?" She blinked to ease the sting behind her eyes, but it worsened until everything seemed to sway around her. No matter how many times she'd woken from this dream to the agony of real life, she could never stop herself from giving in to the dreams' cruel lies of hope. "Are you real?"

Before her brother could answer, a spitting growl cut through the evening and raised the hair on the back of Matilda's neck.

What was that sound?

"Go *home*." There was nothing soothing in the voice now, nothing but command as harsh as a slap on her cheek, but it was drifting away from her.

Nathaniel was leaving like a dream after all.

"No." She stretched her hand toward the voice. "Nathaniel, wait!"

Matilda hobbled as quickly as she could manage through the night. She staggered through underbrush and over uneven ground, an arm thrown up in front of her face to protect her from unseen branches, but she couldn't catch up with her brother. Still she followed the path his voice had disappeared from until she stumbled under two dead firs that tangled above her. A branch snagged her sleeve. Her arm was yanked painfully backward, and her rifle flew out of her grasp.

She fought her way free from the branches and felt for her rifle in the mud. As her fingers brushed the cold metal of the barrel, a black shape slipped through the shadows ahead.

Nathaniel?

No. Not him.

A strange creature faced her. It crouched low to the ground by the base of a tree, its form almost human, but when it raised its head, it let loose a snarl so wicked it could only belong to a hell hound. Matilda froze, hoping the thump of her heart wouldn't rile the animal.

A gasp of wind carried the scent of muck and wet hair. She blinked, trying to distinguish the creature's figure from the background, but what she could make out of it was too enormous for any normal dog. Her heart raced faster.

There are no trolls or wolves in these woods. A chill swept over her and prickled the skin down her back. *You're too old for stories, Matilda. Time to grow up. There are no wolves.*

The creature's legs bent, ready to attack.

She aimed her rifle for something that looked vital. *I've no time for fear. Nathaniel is out there.*

BANG!

Another ear-splitting gunshot blasted through the woods, but the wolf darted into the brush, unharmed. Her bullet had missed its mark. No, her finger hadn't pulled the trigger of her carbine at all. The shot had come from another weapon.

Richards.

She growled more fiercely than the wolf. "I said *don't shoot at me!*"

— CHAPTER SIX —

THE WOLF

B*ANG!*

Loud. Fear. Pain. Scent of blood and death.

Run!

Trees. Scraping, hurting. Run!

Stop. New scent. Demon scent. Close.

Must hunt. Must obey.

— CHAPTER SEVEN —

MATILDA

Nathaniel!"

Matilda scoured the woods and listened for any trace of her brother, but she found only the continued threat of oncoming night. In a confused zigzag she moved through the trees and held the rifle ready for more wolves.

"Nathaniel!" she called again. "Come back!" She couldn't stop searching—couldn't allow a moment for reason to catch up with her.

I can't wake from this dream again. Not again.

She freed herself from the clutches of another tree and broke through the woods. Ahead of her, the wide fields of the Richards's farm slumbered under moonlight that washed the clearing with ghostly silver. The corn stalks quaking in the breeze were barren, but from the other side of the clearing where hogs lazed near the barn, the stink of the mire filled her nose.

So did the scent of gunpowder and blood. Matilda stumbled to a halt and held her breath until the pain in her lungs matched the dread closing in on her.

A warning flared at the back of her mind—something Elliot had said about going on Richards's land—but the bay of hounds broke

Matilda out of her stupor. Three hounds burst out of the Richards barn and cut through the field in her direction.

"Stay back!" She clung to her rifle but shuffled away, circling toward the cover of the corn field. Before she reached it, her heels thumped into something big across her path. She crashed to the ground hard, winded.

Teeth bared and glinting like knives, the dogs snapped at her ankles. She jerked them out of their reach and across the thing that had tripped her. At first she thought it was another dog or an escaped pig, but it lay as if asleep, and Richard's hounds gave her no time to spare a thought for anything but survival. The animals circled around her, their growls promising her a savage and excruciating end. They sought an opening—an unprotected back or throat. Her heart slammed against her ribs, but she stared the beasts down until another gunshot rang through the air and a drunken voice called the animals to their master.

"Get back 'ere, you lousy mutts!"

Even from across the fields, Jacob Richards's voice felt like hot tar rolling down Matilda's back. But, grumbling, the dogs slunk back toward the farmhouse and left her unscathed.

The thunder of the gunshot still echoed in Matilda's ears as she caught her breath and lowered her eyes to the heap across her path.

Her heart lurched.

A man with golden hair lay sprawled on his stomach. Clasped around a pistol, his hands were raw and tattered, and he smelled of sweat, alcohol, and something coppery. She scrambled to his side and heaved him onto his back.

"Nathaniel!"

He was a shadow of himself. Too skinny. Too many hard angles. She felt his body for movement but found none. A gaping hole cut through his throat, and she pressed her hands into the wound to stall the bleeding. Warm scarlet wet her palms and soaked into her skirts. So much blood. Too much.

"No! Don't you dare leave me!"

Nathaniel gave no response to her cries. No assurances. No soothing words. His chest was frozen without breath; his blue eyes stared at the moon, lightless and cold.

Matilda collapsed atop her brother, her trauma stealing her own breath from her. She laid her cheek upon him, crinkling a folded paper tucked in the pocket of his waistcoat, and begged her mother to send him back.

June 18th, 1883

A surprise met me when I arrived at the printing press this morning—Miss Kovacs waited outside the building. I've been dreading the sight of her since the night of my show. Her nose is as good as ever, because she knew it was me when I tried to sneak past. She grabbed me by the ear with her wrinkled hand like she did the day she realized I'd discovered the Power.

The Christmas I was fourteen, the year there was a lot of Winter Fever going around, Mother thought it was her Christian duty to bake bread for half the city. And that it was my *Christian duty to deliver it.*

I couldn't help it. Ever since I learned I could, I'd been slipping into the trance so often it had become habit. I wanted to see the glow everyone had. To know what the shift in their colours meant. What the whispers meant. When Miss Kovacs opened her door, I went into the trance without thinking. For the first time, those whispers gave me a Name.

Until I felt the pain Miss Kovacs wrenched through my ear, I didn't realize I'd called out to her Soul Name. It hadn't answered my call, but she'd recognized the prickle of the Power.

Mother's Christian duty meant I'd spend many, many more afternoons with the city's witch. Miss Kovacs demanded every spare moment I had so she could bring me under her heel and cure me of my "treacherous curiosity." While Mother thought I was helping an old, blind woman repair her fence, I was enduring Miss Kovacs's lectures. Learning of mesmerism and so much more until the folks at church questioned if I'd made a deal with the devil too.

Today's lecture was little different. "I told you not to go through with that nonsense!" she said. "A public performance? For the greed of money?"

It wasn't greed. I need the money. I have a family to care for.

She told me I should count myself lucky to have a family. She'd told me before about why she left her fiancé behind in Hungary. I know "family" is a sensitive subject for her, but it isn't my fault she renounced hers.

I knew better than to say that, but the way she frowned, I swear she heard my thoughts. No wonder the folks at church are superstitious.

She reminded me she only took me as an apprentice because I'd have gotten myself "up to my nose hairs in trouble" otherwise. She accused me of messing with things I didn't understand. She said my "whole being" screamed it at her. She could smell it.

But I didn't do anything wrong. That show was harmless. And I never lost myself in the Power. Never stepped too far. I have more control than she believes.

I don't think I'll ever understand why she's so afraid of what I can do. Well, what I could *do if she'd teach me more. I've barely scratched the surface of my potential. She can't hold me back. She should thank me for putting on my show. Another one or two like that, and people would throw themselves at her feet too. My mentor. Instead of "witch," they'd call her "wise."*

She sighed, and I don't think I've ever heard a sound from her like that before. "You're a fool boy. I made an oath. Don't force me to break it."

I told her I wouldn't, but I'm not sure it was the truth.

Maybe she can smell that too.

— CHAPTER EIGHT —

MATILDA

Matilda, my dear sister, I can't bear the things I've done. The Fenians… I thought I was doing the right thing when I joined them, but I was as foolish as Father. No. I was more foolish, because I already knew the pain I could cause. I can't anymore.

God forgive me for what I've done; I can't ask you to do the same.

Despite the days she'd had to confront her pain, Matilda couldn't believe the lies of the wrinkled note in her palm, but the cursive letters scrawling over the page were in Nathaniel's unmistakable hand. The ink bled where her tears wet the page.

Suicide. That's what the officers who'd come to the Richards's farm when she'd run for help had told her, no matter how long she'd screamed at them that it wasn't true. She'd wailed about the hole in Nathaniel's throat and Richards's gun until she lost her voice, but they'd stared at her with stony, blank faces, as if they couldn't see what was right before them.

Only one of the constables had offered answers. Joseph Harrison—Nathaniel's old friend and Matilda's former employer at the manor—had veiled his own grief long enough to give her this crumpled note taken from Nathaniel's pocket. He'd said Richards's dogs must have discovered the body before Matilda, but the killing blow had come from Nathaniel's own weapon.

Suicide.

She couldn't look suicide in the face and curse its evil. Joseph couldn't lock suicide in prison. It didn't punish Richards, and he deserved to be punished. Though she knew little of what had happened that night, of that much Matilda was certain.

The Fraser Cemetery lay on a wooded hillside midway between the city's reaches and the O'Connor homestead, up a narrow trail through the brush. Nathaniel's grave was far from Mother's, though there had been ample space next to her amid the scattering of tidy, new headstones in the cemetery's most recent clearing. He was too far away to keep Mother company. Too far to keep any God-fearing Christian soul company. Alone. A flat, impersonal stone adorned with neither date nor name marked his final resting place in the unconsecrated ground at the farthest edge of the clearing. The gravestone of a traitor. Like Father.

Matilda couldn't think of this as her brother's resting place. The grave belonged to a *Fenian*: an extremist who'd betrayed his new homeland to seek revenge for a home he'd left behind.

But Nathaniel had been Olive's courage when she couldn't find her own. He'd taught Elliot to look after his sisters, and it was the only thing anyone had taught the boy that had stuck. When Matilda had earned her first few dollars working at the Harrison manor, Nathaniel had been so proud he'd kept a twenty-five cent piece from what she'd sent home. He'd pierced it and worn it around his neck so often he'd had to replace the cord twice.

When Matilda had cradled his ragged body, the coin was missing.

So whomever this man—this Fenian—in the unmarked grave was, he wasn't her brother any longer. He was a stranger.

"Why would you do this, Nathaniel?" Matilda asked his blank headstone as she stood in the rain-soaked, yellowing grass before it and crumpled the note in her palm. It wasn't her brother's confession, no matter her familiarity with the hand that had written it.

"Don't follow questions that lead to dark places," said a male voice, deep and calming.

On any other day Joseph Harrison's voice—one of the most beautiful sounds Matilda had ever heard—would have carried a hint of roguish charm and sent just the right kind of shivers down her spine. Now she only shivered with the wounds her brother's deceitful note had scraped across her being.

Joseph had left behind his stiff policeman's uniform and wore a dark, fitted coat with buttons that reflected the grey heavens. His bowler tucked under one elbow, he linked arms with his mother—a portly woman with her white-streaked, chestnut hair neatly swept under her hat. Mother Harrison kept her eye on Elliot and gently rubbed Olive's back with a hand Matilda only now realized was tightly bandaged. She couldn't bring herself to ask about it now.

The four of them hovered at a respectful distance from this bleak corner of the cemetery, just close enough to offer Matilda the comfort of their presence. It was testament to her grief that she'd almost forgotten them. Mother Harrison had been the O'Connors' friend and guardian since long before their own mother had lost the battle against her illness, and ordinarily Matilda's thoughts drifted to Joseph at the slightest invitation—to his fair locks, the reach of his long legs, or the suggestion of a smirk that on happier days lived in the corner of his mouth.

And it was a testament to its heaviness that the striking silver of Joseph's eyes didn't send her heart into flutters.

"My dear," Mother Harrison said. She slipped out of her son's grasp and crossed the cemetery grounds toward Matilda, arms outstretched. Apart from the straight back and shoulders of a piano teacher, everything about the woman was warm and soft. Her voice like a lullaby, her sad smile a potent comfort, and her arms like downy blankets, she hugged Matilda against her bosom as though she was a child. Matilda never wanted to leave, but there was something about Mother Harrison that felt ... old. Old in a way a heroine and saviour never should be.

"You mustn't despair. You have us to help you through this." Mother Harrison held Matilda at arm's length once more. "I hope you know that."

Matilda tried to smile, but from the consoling look in the woman's grey eyes, she hadn't succeeded. "I know."

Mother Harrison patted Matilda's shoulder. "Take a moment, but don't stay out in this chill too long, dear." She wrapped Matilda in one more hug before she reached for Olive's hand. "Come along, Olive, Elliot."

As the three of them made their way down the hillside and through the older, moss-covered headstones, Matilda clutched Nathaniel's note in her hand. She waited for Joseph to follow the others, hoping he might not witness her so enfeebled by her sorrow, but instead he remained, looking as statuesque as the chiselled stone angels that guarded some of the graves.

"She's right, you know. You aren't alone." That playful smirk wasn't on Joseph's mouth today, but his steady gaze felt calming until he dropped his eyes to the note caught in her fingers. His lips pinched together just enough for Matilda to notice. "I hate to ask, but about your brother's note—"

Matilda shook her head, guessing at his request. "I won't mention anything to your mother."

The O'Connors weren't the only ones who'd left their old life behind after the Fenian raids back east. In the same raid that had cost Matilda a father, Mother Harrison had watched her husband's hospital burn to the ground. Doctor Harrison never escaped the building, and his wife and child never escaped the memory. Matilda knew better than to cut open old wounds. Apparently, Nathaniel didn't.

"I don't remember Ireland. Olive and Elliot have never seen it." Now that Matilda had admitted one pain to Joseph, more poured out of her. "Even Nathaniel only remembered the weeks he spent seasick after our ship departed. Canada has always been our true home. He never said it, never aloud, but he hated our father even more than I did. Only your family and mine knew of the stain on our name. Why would Nathaniel do this when we'd finally found peace?"

"Mourn for your brother," Joseph said, "but don't chase his ghost. You deserve to have your peace, Miss O'Connor."

He was as polite as he was oblivious to her affections, but something about the way he'd said her name felt powerfully intimate. She'd probably imagined it. He glided to her side, and though he didn't touch her, the warmth of his kindness embraced her.

"It may not seem like it now, but you'll recover from this," Joseph said. "I still remember the girl who nearly broke my arm when I threw mud on her dress."

But I barely remember the boy with the horrid temper.

Joseph had changed much from the boy who'd once made Matilda fear going to school, especially this past year. He'd grown up to become a considerate and respectable gentleman.

But she was still the little girl in a muddy dress.

"I haven't grown up much, have I," Matilda said.

Joseph's lips parted like he wanted to laugh but couldn't find the strength. "I'm glad to hear it. There's no rush for either of us to grow dull and grey." He gestured across the cemetery toward the rough trail that led through the woods and back toward the city. "This place is affecting us. We'll feel better after a warm meal."

Matilda slid Nathaniel's note into her coat and tore herself away from his grave. Rather than have to make conversation, she read the names on the desolate markers as they walked side by side along the row of graves. Many crosses dotted the lower stretch of the hillside, etched beside names or standing on pedestals that towered over the wilted grass. She read the names of old men, mothers lost in childbirth, and then another name on a marker that called to her from memory.

She paused in front of a stone thrusting up from the ground like a spear, a pillar of white bronze so ornate it could only mark the grave of someone either wealthy or very important. Carved roses bloomed at the base, and knotted vines crowned the top where the four planes of the pillar came to a point. Cradled by more rosebuds, a bold script read:

In memoriam
Lucas Theodore Wellington
Loving brother and son
Born January 23rd, 1864
Died July 12th, 1884

"Lucas Wellington," Matilda read. "Nathaniel's best friend." Only twenty years of age when he'd died. What a terrible shame.

"You remember him?" Joseph said.

"I never met him, but Nathaniel spoke of him often." It grieved her to think of it, but Mr. Wellington had been a better support to Nathaniel after Mother's death than she had, and he'd been the only friend Nathaniel had made time for between working the farm and caring for their siblings. Every Saturday night after seeing Olive and Elliot safely to bed, Nathaniel would head for the Wellington printing press for a late-night smoke and friendly drink. Not even Joseph held the same honour.

She'd attended the young man's funeral, hoping Nathaniel would make an appearance. Now she only wished Mr. Wellington had lived to tell her every story of Nathaniel she'd forgotten or never heard.

"I met him a few times." Joseph's voice seemed thin, far off in memory. "Lucas was a bit of a dreamer, I gather—always making grand schemes and promises that came to ruin for one reason or another—but he deserved a different end. After the fire, his brother sold everything and left the city. I can't say I blame him."

Painful, year-old memories bore down on Matilda. Memories of Olive and Elliot waking her in her bedroom at the manor, their eyes bloodshot with worry because Nathaniel had never come home. Memories of ash and smoke over the printing press. The nightmare of a victim pulled from the rubble. The body was singed beyond recognition, but an engraved pocket watch caught in the corpse's ribs had identified young Mr. Wellington.

Others assumed Nathaniel's remains were also lost in the ashes. The ladies at church still gave Matilda pitying looks the moment they thought she wouldn't notice, but she preferred the explanation she'd given Olive and Elliot: that Nathaniel had run off to seek the adventure he'd always wanted.

Someone else had visited Mr. Wellington's grave recently. A crumpled letter lay before it, held in place by a pebble, and the handwriting on the envelope's face had been so spotted by morning dew Matilda could barely guess the recipient's name. How quickly time tried to erase the dead.

"Come." Joseph must have sensed her darkening mood. He draped her in a mournful expression and gestured away from the gravestone. "Let's leave this dreary place."

It was hard to leave the Wellington boy's gravestone behind. Matilda felt its pull even as she turned her back and followed Joseph across the yard. It wasn't until a slurred drawl sounded ahead of them that whatever hold the gravestone had over her snapped.

"Let me by, woman!" The voice, like the sound of stone scraping over stone, made Matilda cringe, but it was the belittling tone she recognized first.

Richards.

A middle-aged man with a scowl that twisted his whole face tried to totter past Mother Harrison and into the graveyard. Olive and Elliot safe behind her, Mother Harrison held her bandaged hand out to barricade the man's path. The man spat curses from under his bushy moustache. Even from a distance Matilda smelled the heavy scent of drink upon him and noticed the damp spots on his shirt where he'd spilled his bad habit all over himself.

The muscles down Matilda's back tensed. She couldn't help checking Richards's hands for his firearm, but for once they were empty.

How *dare* he come here!

"Go home, Jacob." Mother Harrison held her ground with the tenacity of a badger. "I won't have you bothering these children."

"Even if Father..." Richards said between hiccups, his lazy drawl slurred all the more by the liquor on his tongue. "Even if 'e gave my inheritance to your boy, Jo doesn't own this place. So get outta my way!"

Joseph slowed his pace. "Uncle Jake's been at the drink again." The others hadn't seemed to notice their approach yet, and Joseph held out a hand to stop Matilda. "Wait here while I—"

Matilda brushed past his hand and stormed forward, her fists clenched. "Richards!" The name felt like vomit on her tongue, but it got the man's attention. After all he'd done, he dared to glower at her. It'd only make her feel better when she clawed that wretched mouth off his face. "You vile, drunken—"

A hand clasped around her wrist, gentle but too strong for her to wrestle free. Joseph gave her a sympathetic look but shook his head. "This isn't the way." He kept his voice low, private, but his soothing tones washed over Matilda like the waters of a deep river. It was almost enough to cool her rage. Almost. "You saw Nathaniel's note for yourself."

I don't care about the note. It isn't true! Why couldn't Joseph understand that?

"He killed Nathaniel!" Her insides boiled, burning away the calming effect of Joseph's voice. She thought she'd cried all her tears, but new ones rimmed her eyes as she turned back to Richards. She tugged at Joseph's hold, a rabid dog at the end of her leash. "Why? We wouldn't sell our farm to you, so you thought you'd kill us off? I saw the marks! I know you and your vicious dogs killed my brother!"

Richards shoved past Mother Harrison and waddled Matilda's way on bowed legs. He licked his lips like a toad after a fly. Olive scampered out of his path, but when Richards spat his tobacco near Matilda's shoes, Elliot looked ready to join the fight, even as Mother Harrison tried to usher the children away.

"My dogs?" Richards's eyes dissected the cut of Matilda's figure—whether with lust or something deadlier, she couldn't tell, but she felt the movement of his gaze over her like talons tracing her skin. "My dogs keep the woods safe from you squatters."

"That was *not* helpful, Uncle," Matilda heard Joseph mutter behind her.

Mother Harrison threw up her arms. "Jacob Richards, that's enough out of you. Go on home, now."

At last Richards's gaze left Matilda. He looked over his shoulder at Mother Harrison, and the motion sent him swaying until he replanted his feet in a wide stance. "You'd no right to give my—" He gave another hiccup and wiped spittle off his chin. "You'd no right to give my inheritance to those brats. I'll get it back."

"By murdering us?" Matilda said, pouring into her question every drop of revulsion that churned in her belly.

Richards made a sound more animal than human. It started with a hiss leaking through his teeth, then the deep slur of his voice raised into a high-pitched moan. He sounded ill, but his lips pulled back to reveal his teeth. He was *laughing*.

"If anyone killed the boy," he said, "it was his Fenian friends."

Joseph's hold on Matilda tightened.

Mother Harrison's face drained of colour, and the fight left her body. She stumbled back a few steps until Olive lent a hand Mother Harrison barely seemed to notice. "Fenians?" she said, her voice weak.

"Uncle Jake," Joseph said as he finally released his hold on Matilda, but he swept toward Richards before she had her chance to lunge. Taking his uncle by the shoulder, Joseph directed him away with more strength than his slender build implied. "You really do need to leave. Now."

"I heard them in the woods." Richards tried to remove Joseph's hand from his shoulder, but his clumsy fingers couldn't get a firm hold. "Them and the O'Connor boy. There'll be another raid like the one that killed your father."

"That's *enough,*" Joseph said, a hard edge replacing the gentle tones of his voice. He pushed against Richards's shoulder, and, swaying on his feet, Richards was no match for a sober Joseph.

Her rage not yet gone, Matilda started after them, but a slim, cool hand wrapped around hers. Olive looked up at her with pleading red eyes. "Look," Olive said, and she pointed to Mother Harrison, who hid her face behind her hands as her shoulders racked with sobs.

Matilda's gut twisted with guilt. She should have known better than to provoke Richards in front of Mother Harrison, but he should have known enough to keep his mouth shut. *What a thoughtless fool.*

Even now Matilda's rage refused to vanish. It burned at the bottom of her belly, eager to flare up, but she stamped it down for now. She went to Mother Harrison's side and took one of her hands between her own. It was her turn to be a strength to the woman who'd always been there for her.

"He's gone," Matilda said. "Joseph's taken him away. It's time to get you home."

— CHAPTER NINE —

MATILDA

It had taken most of the ride for Mother Harrison to stop sobbing, but she didn't seem aware of her surroundings. Only when Joseph halted the buggy in front of his house and reached for his mother's arm did Mother Harrison show any responsiveness. She blinked rapidly at Joseph's touch, as if she wasn't certain who he was, but she accepted his aid and slid out of her seat. Elliot hurried to open the door for them and, abandoning horse and buggy in the yard, they all climbed the porch steps toward the Harrisons' home.

Kerosene sconces lit up cream-and-gold wallpaper as they stepped into the parlour, the soft glow a welcome reassurance. Joseph led his mother past her mahogany piano, its ivory keys scarlet under the light of the flames crackling in the fireplace, and helped her into a chair with clawed feet and cushions of red and pearl. Mother Harrison slumped and stared vacantly into the fire, its dancing light hypnotic.

Who'd fed that fire while they were at the graveyard? And what was that Matilda smelled on the air? It mixed with the scent of the logs burning in the fireplace until she couldn't tell the scents apart.

Olive and Elliot shrugged out of their coats but huddled together, too quiet. They shouldn't see Mother Harrison like this. Matilda collected their coats from them and pointed them toward the hallway. "Why don't you two find something to read in the library," she said.

Ordinarily Olive would have leapt at the offer to drown herself in the Harrison's vast collection of books, but she shuffled slowly down the hall as if she'd forgotten her love of the written word. Elliot's groan was expected, if weak. He hurried after his sister.

Joseph fetched a spare quilt from the closet under the stairs and laid it across his mother's knees. He took great care to drape the hand-stitched blanket cosily around her, but his hands gripped the quilt with too much force.

"There you go," he whispered as he knelt in front of his mother's chair. He pulled her hands out from under the blanket and placed them in her lap, especially gentle with her bandaged one. "You're warm and safe again."

That bandage on her hand... Has she had other fits?

"Should she see a physician?" Matilda asked. She laid her siblings' coats over the chesterfield across from the chair and stood behind Joseph. Mother Harrison paid her no attention. The woman kept her eyes on the fire, but Matilda knew the only fire Mother Harrison saw was the one that had stolen her husband from her.

That's all she saw in any fire—the printing press fire, the cooking fires of the indigenous Musqueam's camps along the river, or even the tranquil flicker of a candle's flame. She couldn't forget the past. She couldn't let go.

Joseph tucked the corners of the blanket around his mother, tying her snugly in place. "She's been to one already. There's a decanter of brandy in the kitchen, if you wouldn't mind?" Joseph's voice fell quiet. "It's the only thing that numbs the bad memories."

"Yes, of course."

A year away from the manor hadn't dulled Matilda's memory of the place. Her feet found their own way toward the kitchen while her thoughts focused on the medley of smells that wafted down the hall. She should have paid more attention to her feet. When she turned into the kitchen, she collided with a cloud of steam and a strange man with a platter of buttered corn.

"Oh! What are you—" A gasp shot into her chest and cut her short. The man rebalanced the platter, not spilling a single drop of butter, and she took in the sight of him.

Not much taller than her, he was maybe a handful of years older. He wore a grey waistcoat that matched Joseph's taste in fashion, but his obsidian hair grew long, gathered into a tail that wagged halfway down his back. That, as much as his black eyes or terra-cotta skin, marked him as foreign.

"*Who* are you?" Matilda stepped back. *Joseph replaced me with a Chinaman*?

"I cook and clean," the man said, answering Matilda's silent question. His clear English surprised her, but his voice carried a heavy accent that sparked memories of shouting and violence. She didn't want to entertain those memories—not today of all days. He laid the platter on the counter next to the stove, and she forced the memories back down where they came from. "You are one of the guests?"

"Yes, I—" She stepped into the kitchen but kept close to the wall, never taking her eyes off him. "I'm looking for the brandy."

The servant swept by her. She flattened herself against the wall, but he glided past a bubbling saucepan on the stove and opened up a cupboard on the other side of the kitchen. He pulled out a tray with Joseph's decanter of brandy and a single, crystal glass. The man didn't bother to fetch more glasses or ask Matilda if she needed them. It was as if he already knew the brandy was for Mother Harrison alone.

She'd been right, then. Mother Harrison had had these fits before.

Measuring a *very* generous serving into the glass, the man returned the decanter to the cupboard and approached Matilda with the tray in hand. She tried to keep a distance from him, but the wall already pressed into her back. He paused in front of her, his strange eyes narrowing slightly, and thrust the tray toward her.

"The brandy," he said, as if the fruity scent rising from the glass didn't make that obvious.

Matilda hated that the tray rattled when she took it from his hands, but if he noticed, he ignored it. He returned to his work in the kitchen and left her a path to escape to the hall. She took it gratefully and hurried back to the parlour.

Still kneeling where she'd left him, Joseph smoothed a loose lock of his hair back into place and took the glass from the tray. "Thank you."

Mother Harrison barely looked conscious, but she downed the drink in long, slow sips as Joseph tipped the glass to her mouth. Matilda set the empty tray next to Joseph's pipe on the side table and lingered at a comfortable distance, the way he'd done for her at the graveside.

Her heart clenched to watch them both so sullen and still. Joseph should have that handsome smirk on his face, and Mother Harrison's cheeks should be rosy from laughing, not from crying.

When his mother had finally drained the glass, Joseph set it down on the tray and rose to his feet with a sigh. "I need to see to my horse, but—"

"I'll stay with her," Matilda assured him. "Take your time."

Joseph nodded—a simple motion that was full of gratitude. He crossed the parlour without a sound until he clicked open the door and stepped outside. Matilda settled across from Mother Harrison, sitting on the very edge of the chesterfield so she could take her guardian's injured hand carefully between her own.

The brandy helped. Even before the drink had time to take full effect, a touch of awareness sparkled in Mother Harrison's eyes. Maybe the routine of her drink was comforting enough to calm the darkness that had overtaken her.

"Are you feeling better?" Matilda asked when she saw enough of Mother Harrison's old self returning. She rubbed circles in the back of the woman's hand to help ease her return to her body and home.

Mother Harrison blinked moisture into her dry eyes and watched Matilda's hand move across her own. She offered Matilda a tiny smile but looked confused and more than a little ashamed. "I'm meant to be cheering you today, not the other way around," Mother Harrison said.

"Nonsense," Matilda said. "You've been a godsend most of my life. It's time I repaid you."

The smile on Mother Harrison's mouth deepened a hair, at least until a whisking sound travelled down the hall, reminding Matilda of the man in the kitchen.

"Did you see the houseboy?" Mother Harrison's smile twisted into a thin-lipped frown, and her hand tensed between Matilda's palms. "Can you believe Joseph would hire him after what happened with the last one? Do you remember, dear?"

Better than I want to.

The memories Matilda had stifled in the kitchen returned without permission. Her recollection of her last night at the manor was mostly shrouded in fog, but the face of Mr. Gän, the Chinaman, who'd come looking for new work after the railway jobs ended, refused to be forgotten.

Woken from hazy dreams and unsure how she'd gotten to the bottom of the stairs, she'd stood frozen in terror as Joseph struggled for his life a mere few steps away. Mr. Gän had straddled him on the floor and pummelled his face. She couldn't remember with what or how Joseph had fought the man off—the details had thankfully been lost in all the confusion—but she remembered Joseph's bloodied nose and someone yelling for her to run. She had first thought the old servant kindly, but no matter how muddled her memories of that night, the horror and sense of betrayal had never quite left her.

All because Joseph had confronted the man about some missing silverware.

Early the next morning, before dawn had had a chance to chase away the terrors of the night, Matilda had learned of the destruction of the printing press and Nathaniel's disappearance. It was too big a hole to tear through her heart after the night she'd had. Too big a hole to mend.

"My son swears this one is trustworthy," Mother Harrison said, pulling Matilda out of her horrifying memories, "but you never can tell, can you?"

No, you can't.

For a long moment the only sound was the whisper of the fire and the noises escaping from the kitchen. Matilda kept Mother Harrison's hand warm while the woman recovered strength of mind and body. Then Mother Harrison cleared her throat and straightened her back.

"I must apologize for my brother's vulgar behaviour earlier." Mother Harrison's voice came much stronger now, steadier, but there was a cautious shadow behind her eyes. "Is what you said true? Did my brother... Did he—?"

At the mention of that wretched man, Matilda's stomach tightened with fury. Mother Harrison would believe her about Richards, and it took everything for Matilda to keep from telling her the truth. She needed *someone* to believe the truth.

But that wasn't what Mother Harrison needed. Instead, Matilda forced her anger to fall back for now and gave Mother Harrison's hand a gentle squeeze. "Never you mind that."

Mother Harrison stared at the patterns in the crown moulding above the fireplace. "Maybe he's right, though," she said. "Loath as I am to give my brother what he wants, maybe it's time you sold the farm." Matilda mashed her lips together to hide a scowl, but when Mother Harrison's gaze returned to her, she laid her uninjured palm across Matilda's hand. "I only meant you have to think of your future now that...now that Nathaniel is gone. My dear, look at these callouses and wounds on your poor hands. That farm is too much work for you to do on your own." Now she took Matilda's hand between hers and clasped it with a strength she hadn't had moments ago. "You should work here again. Heaven knows I trust you with my silverware more than that Chinaman. Bring Olive and Elliot with you. Perhaps with all of us together, you and Joseph could..."

Heat flushed in Matilda's face. It was a tempting offer: beds warmer and softer than the ones back home, just enough work to keep Matilda from getting bored, and the chance to sneak glances at Joseph when he joined them for supper. No more lost cows or hens. No more wolves in the woods. No more Richards.

But...

"Think on it, dear." Mother Harrison patted Matilda's hand and leaned back in her seat before Matilda could answer her. "Until then I suppose I'll have to put up with the houseboy."

The conversation lulled again, and when that far-off look threatened to return to Mother Harrison's eyes, Matilda called Elliot into the parlour to distract their guardian with a request for a piano lesson. Then, needing space and fresh air to sort her thoughts, Matilda stepped outside onto the porch.

Evening hadn't yet arrived, but already the moon glowed silver in the sky. The air cleared her head but chilled her fingers, and she tucked her hands under her arms. As she thumped down the steps and into the yard, the same rains that had dampened the morning now made the grass bow around her. Not even the manor was immune to the day's melancholy.

Return here? For good?

It wasn't a real manor—Mother Harrison had once tended to house and garden by herself—but the place felt distinguished and peaceful compared to the O'Connor homestead. When she'd lived here, Matilda had spent many hours on the quiet window seat of her second-floor room, looking down at the springtime flowers beneath the maple tree and wishing in her foolish fantasies that Joseph would pick one for her. Now the flowers slumbered beneath a dusting of scarlet leaves.

"You're out here?"

Lost in her own thoughts, Matilda hadn't heard Joseph's approach. He peered across the yard and through the window of the parlour as if to check on his mother, but the muffled sound of his mother's voice and Elliot's discordant piano notes seemed to satisfy him.

He winced as Elliot plunked a sharp key like he was chopping logs for the woodshed. "I've never heard the hymns played so expressively." A note of humour coloured Joseph's voice, but as he turned to Matilda the amusement left his face. The contrast of his fair skin and hair with the black of his clothes was both beautiful and grim. Matilda imagined if she ever met the Angel of Death, he'd look as lovely and sad. "I apologize," he said. "Today's not a very good day to jest. Thank you for your help with my mother." Joseph strolled to Matilda's side and brushed a lone bit of straw off his sleeve, making his coat pristine once again. "Kāi tries to help, but she won't let him near her."

Kāi? Was that the servant?

"I didn't know she'd had more fits since last year." Mother Harrison hadn't left her house for days after the incident at the printing press. She'd handled the thieving servant's attack on Joseph far better than the sight of that building in flames.

"It's been getting worse for a long time. The truth is, I'd like to have someone here to watch over her." Joseph slid a handsbreadth closer to Matilda. A strange mix of jitters and certainty warred in his eyes, but in the end, certainty claimed victory. "There's a place for you here, if you want it," he said.

Matilda groaned. She'd meant it to be a laugh, but she didn't have any mirth left in her body today. "Did you and your mother plan this? Not five minutes ago she asked me to come back to work here."

A tender warmth lit Joseph's eyes. She could have lost herself easily in that soft, grey heat, but the thinning line of his lips made her hesitate. What was so hard for him to say?

"That isn't what I meant. I've had something to say to you for some while, but it was never the right moment. Today is worse timing, but I fear to let another chance slip by." Joseph released a long sigh in a puff of white mist. How could a man be born with a voice so captivating that even a sigh had her spellbound? "I'd like you to stay here as my wife," he said.

The heat in Joseph's eyes blazed over Matilda and burned through the air in her lungs, leaving her tingling and breathless.

"I know it must come as a surprise," Joseph said, recovering from his confession quicker than Matilda, "but I want to be there for you. *Here* for you. And I want you to be here for me."

She inspected him for the telltale glint that crossed his eyes when he was in a playful mood, but she found only the steady burn of his gaze. All those stolen glimpses she'd taken when she'd thought he didn't notice her...had he been watching too?

Why now?

"But...the farm."

This wasn't the way her fantasies of this moment were supposed to go, but the words came out on their own.

"Leave it." Joseph stepped closer. His scent intoxicated her—the faintly sweet smell of his mother's brandy and the slightest traces of tobacco and cedar. "Leave the bad memories behind."

The daydream shattered. Matilda backed toward the maple tree behind her. *He usually has such a way with words.*

The *bad* memories? The memories of Mother's lullabies or the smell of Nathaniel's eggs in the mornings?

"You mean the memories of my brother," she said. "You believe what they say about him."

"I—" Joseph said. She'd seemed to catch him off guard, and he took a long moment before answering. "Don't you?"

"You were Nathaniel's friend! How can you think he was a *Fenian?*"

It stung her even to say the word, but it was Joseph who flinched. The heat in his eyes shifted, burning hotter, but no longer from passion.

"You hate the Fenians," she said. Joseph hid his ire better at her second mention of the rebels, but not so well she didn't notice the way his brows pinched together. "Then you must hate Nathaniel."

"My father died because of them," he said. Sometimes Matilda forgot Joseph was a man and not truly an angel. He was always so poised, so equally full of wit and tenderness, it was easy to forget he'd once been a boy ruled by an anger he couldn't find a place for. Now he let that anger boil under the surface where it couldn't scald anyone but himself. "Sometimes I hate them so much I wonder if there's room in me for anything else. I'm trying to show you there is, Matilda."

Matilda.

The sound of her name on his tongue should have made her greedy to hear it again and again, but it twisted her in knots.

"The note they found is wrong," she said. Thoughts that had been jumbled in her head since that night in the woods pieced together on their own. "Nathaniel's coin was missing when I found him. He *always* had it on him. And his hands were bloodied as though he'd been fighting for his life. Why would a man desperate to live kill himself before the wounds had time to heal? It was Richards who killed him. He must have framed him."

Joseph's lips pressed together while he took in her questions. She could see him weigh each one in his mind until she mentioned his uncle. "Uncle *Jake*? He can't keep sober long enough to get out of bed in the morning; he couldn't have written a false note. I know your brother's hand, and I think you know it too."

Matilda pressed back into the maple tree until the knots in the trunk bruised her. The constables who'd come to her farm hadn't believed her, but Joseph's disbelief wounded deeply.

"Richards killed my brother." She raised her chin and tried to maintain control when all she wanted was to strike at something, anything. "I'll prove it."

She ducked under a low branch to escape Joseph, but he caught up with her and stepped into her path. Unable to meet his gaze, she stared at the line of polished buttons at his chest.

"Please." Joseph's voice was quiet and unguarded. He raised a hand toward Matilda's face, long fingers uncurling toward her chin. They never quite touched her, yet her head lifted, called by his magic hold over her. "Don't take on the burdens of a man who carries them no more."

His plea wrenched at her heart. "I'm sorry," she said. "Until I stop my brother's murderer, I can't give you what you want."

What I've *wanted for so long.*

With a headache and with her journal lying open on her chest, Matilda woke beside Olive in their shared bed. No morning light crept in through the window yet, just an icy draft, but the memories of last night hounded Matilda: refusing Joseph's proposal, sitting across from him at supper but unable to look at him, and the awkward ride home next to him in his buggy.

Matilda bookmarked the unfinished entry in her journal and pulled her covers up to her chin, but the frost inside her wouldn't thaw.

I'll prove it to him, Nathaniel. To all of them.

She only wished she knew where to start. Why had Nathaniel gone to Richards's farm? How had Richards known he'd be there when no one had seen Nathaniel since he'd disappeared? *Why* had he disappeared?

Maybe Richards had something to do with that too.

Elliot had once tried to teach Matilda a little of what he'd learned about hunting, about following an animal's trail, but Matilda didn't know how to retrace Nathaniel's steps. He'd only had Joseph or Mr. Wellington to turn to—and Mr. Wellington was dead—so where had Nathaniel hidden for the last year?

Olive moaned and thrashed against the net of covers, yanking Matilda out of her thoughts with a start.

"Olive." Matilda poked her sister in the arm and found the girl's nightdress damp with sweat. "Olive, you're having another nightmare."

When her sister gave another moan, Matilda grabbed her by the shoulders and shook her until Olive gasped. Her eyes darted around the room as Matilda squeezed her in a tight hug and lent her what warmth and comfort she had left to give.

"It felt real," Olive blinked away the terrors; her voice sped faster with each word. "I couldn't breathe, and I—"

"Hush." Matilda hugged Olive closer. "I'll take you to see Miss Kovacs again."

Miss Kovacs! Why hadn't Matilda thought of her before? If anyone could tell her anything about Nathaniel's disappearing act, it'd be the woman who'd taught him every mind trick he'd learned.

She didn't know how far on Nathaniel's trail that put her, but at least it was somewhere.

"You don't need to." Olive pulled away from Matilda and rolled over so her face was hidden. "I'll be all right."

I'm sorry, Olive.

"No," Matilda said, "I think we really must go."

August 4th, 1883

Mother's cough is worsening. I thought the new windows the money from my show paid for would keep out the breeze so she could rest better. I thought the new wagon would make her rides to the general store and to church more comfortable.

Since moving here, I thought her coughs were from the dust around the farm.

I should have realized she was hiding her infirmity even before I saw her cough up red. Every hug she gave felt more desperate, and yet weaker, than the last. Her hands are as raw from washing them as mine, but instead of the ink that was on my hands, she'd been washing the blood that speckled hers.

She was so tired last night she mistook me for my father. She speaks of him with longing when she's too exhausted to realize what she's doing. It makes my skin itch. I can't help but feel his memory is the true illness wasting her away. The memories of that Fenian raid back east, of the hospital they'd set alight… Mother Harrison's wails when she realized her husband was inside. It's enough for my anger to give me a fever like Mother's. The memory of father's betrayal is enough to make me choke on my own breath. The thought of the monster he became, like the creatures from the bedtime stories he used to recite—it's enough to make me taste blood too.

I let myself look at Mother's Soul Name for the first time in years. It's still the colour of a new dawn, but weaker. Like someone scooped a little sunrise into a jar and filled the rest with water. The physician said fresh air and exercise will help Mother, but that's all she's had since we came to New Westminster.

I could make her Name strong again. All I'd need is time to learn to control the Power.

Miss Kovacs will have my head, but I don't think I can keep my promise.

— CHAPTER TEN —

MATILDA

The nightmare hadn't left Olive's eyes by morning, and the frightened look she carried with her worsened as the day wore on. When they finished their afternoon chores, leaving Elliot to mend the pasture fence, Matilda hitched the family mare to their wagon and all but hauled Olive into the seat next to her.

There was only one road a wagon could travel from their farm to the city, and it skirted the penitentiary grounds and the secluded asylum. The structures stood back from the road where the imposing walls and barred windows could observe travellers from a distance, but the demons that haunted both buildings followed the wagon even after they'd rolled out of sight. By the time they arrived outside Marta Kovacs's home, only Matilda's need for answers restored some of her mettle. She stepped down from the wagon and offered a hand to Olive.

"I— I've decided I don't want to go after all. Elliot says she's a…" Olive's voice fell to a whisper. "A witch."

Matilda almost wished it was true. A real witch could give her a spell or potion to make Richards confess.

"She's a mesmerist," Matilda said, but she couldn't help but feel vulnerable in front of the home. "She does tricks like Nathaniel."

Only tricks.

Miss Kovacs's property of wild grass and dead leaves offered no warm invitation. A crooked fence with rusted nails snagged newspapers out of the breeze, the ink erased from the pages by rains and summer sun. The papers crinkled against the fence posts and whispered hexes, but it was the house itself that filled the soul with disquiet. The roof sagged. The walls shed their skin of paint in ragged, grey chips. Amber slits for windows squinted at passers-by from behind the corpses of gnarly apple trees. Once, after Nathaniel had spent one of his lessons stranded here during a storm, he'd told Matilda of the ghostly moans the house made.

Reluctantly, Olive accepted Matilda's hand and followed her to the door. "You know Elliot was only teasing you," Matilda said. "You used to let Nathaniel practise with you all the time, and Miss Kovacs taught him everything he knew."

Allowing gentle, trusted Nathaniel into her head was a far different thing than volunteering mind, body, and every secret vulnerability to the whims of a cold-blooded harpy.

"I won't let her turn you into a worm," Matilda said, giving Olive's hand a squeeze. "I promise."

Olive's mouth thinned into a line, but her grip on Matilda's hand softened. At the doorstep, Matilda raised her fist to knock, but before she could, a woman's thick, Hungarian accent croaked from the other side of the door.

"If you're going to come in, then do it."

"Do you see?" Olive said, then mouthed the words, *a witch.*

And she's in a lovely mood.

Matilda pulled open the door for her sister and cringed at the whine of hinges. She'd been inside the mesmerist's home before, but each time she felt she'd stepped through a magical doorway into the wrong house.

Instead of the mouse droppings and sticky cobwebs she always expected, every corner of the floor shined. The walls stood bare of decor—not even a cross sanctified the house—but the rose-blossom wallpaper showed no peeling edges. Placed out of the way, the old woman's maple cane leaned near the door, and the home smelled of apple and cinnamon.

Miss Kovacs emerged from her kitchen in a white apron and stood in the hall like the stump of a felled tree. Her grey hair swept so tightly toward the top of her head that the wrinkles on her face almost disappeared, except where they framed her ever-present scowl. Only the way her walnut eyes stared vacantly through Matilda's chest marked the old woman as less than whole.

"The O'Connors, by that old barn smell. I've been expecting you." Miss Kovacs huffed and clasped her hands behind her straight back, her chin raised with authority. "Come along, then."

After hanging her apron on a hook near the kitchen, Miss Kovacs led the way to her sitting room, her hand stretched toward the wall to feel her way. Matilda took her sister by the shoulders, guided her after the mesmerist, and tried not to think of Olive as a human shield.

"Don't forget what you promised," Olive said. She pushed back against Matilda with a cornered look in her blue eyes. "You'll stop her if she does anything strange."

"I would have been chased out of the city if I turned every child into a worm, Miss Olive," the old woman said.

Olive jumped halfway to the ceiling, and Matilda's cheeks flushed with heat. *Those ears of hers!*

"I only transform the especially horrible ones, and no one misses them." With a stiff hand, Miss Kovacs gestured to a brown chesterfield across from a fireplace with red coals. "Now, sit down."

Matilda and Olive crossed the room with the care of scouts in enemy lands. On the mantle above the fireplace stood several jars filled with concoctions of oil and herbs, strips of bark, or slices of dried fruit. An intricate wave of fragrances washed over them. One jar with an open lid held the apple rings and cinnamon Matilda had smelled on the apron in the hall. As she breathed it in, it left her placid in a way that should have been alarming.

To a blind woman the scents must have been stimulating, but to an imaginative child the jars were no different from potions, maliciously distilled and bottled for use on hapless boys and girls.

"It's the nightmares again, isn't it," Miss Kovacs said. She moved in front of Olive, taking the girl's chin in her talons. Olive flinched but faced the woman with as much bravery as her small body could fit. "Close your eyes and do exactly as I say."

"Y— Yes, ma'am."

Once, years ago, Nathaniel had performed on stage when Mr. Wellington had sponsored him, giving him a glimpse of a life as an entertainer. Nathaniel had worked his tricks with the same disarming voice he'd used to comfort Olive or Elliot when they couldn't sleep. That voice made others trust him without fear and without question, fully and completely. They eased into a welcome trance, yearning for him to take control long before he ever did.

Miss Kovacs employed different methods.

Her voice commanded obedience. Demanded it. *Received* it. Without choice, Olive shut her eyes. Soon her breath deepened with a false sleep. It unnerved Matilda to see Olive so malleable in anyone's care but Nathaniel's, but no other treatment had ever soothed the more troubling consequences of Olive's imagination.

"Speak." The old woman released Olive's chin. "Tell me of the nightmares."

"I— I see it..."

With stumbling words, Olive regaled Miss Kovacs with descriptions of dreams so harrowing and vivid the girl could only be reliving them. She spoke of a shadowed entity that overtook the farm, its vile energy devouring the woods and meadow while, alone, she watched from the bedroom window. The cows bellowed in the pasture until, one by one, the energy sucked them into nothingness. The homestead's floorboards dissolved from under Olive's feet as the house and everything she knew sank into the earth.

"Enough," Miss Kovacs said.

Whether she was speaking to Olive or to the entity in the dreams, Matilda didn't know. She waited for the reassurance or instruction Miss Kovacs always offered before she ended a trance, but the mesmerist gave nothing but a tap on Olive's forehead and another command.

"Awaken," she said.

Despite the awful visions Olive had described, when she opened her eyes again, there were fewer cares in them. Matilda had seen Nathaniel's mind tricks hundreds of times, but the magic never dulled.

It worked. Somehow it worked.

"Wait in the wagon for me; I won't be long," Matilda said as she helped Olive out of her seat. Once she'd heard the squeal of the door shutting behind her sister, she checked her reticule. She hoped she had enough, but the coins in the bag made more noise rubbing against the fabric than they did clinking against other coins. "About payment..."

"Even I know not to take money from mud-faced orphans." Miss Kovacs waved her hand dismissively. "Buy your sister a new dress instead. The one she has smells repugnantly of wet straw and cow dung."

We wash the laundry regularly... Matilda raised her wrist discreetly and couldn't help but sneak a whiff of her own dress. It smelled embarrassingly like saddle oil and the family mare.

"It won't work for long this time," Miss Kovacs said, the set of her frown rigid but the crease between her sparse eyebrows smoothing. "I can ease Olive's fears, but I can't cure the cause of them. She's lost too much for a girl her age—first a father and mother. Now her brother." Miss Kovacs traded her usual bark for a more solemn tone. "Yes, I heard of Nathaniel. Can't go anywhere in this city without some fool wondering if there are Fenians in their backyard. Nathaniel and I had our quarrels, but for what it's worth, he didn't deserve that end."

Consoling words were a rare gift from Miss Kovacs. They felt strange to Matilda, but she welcomed them. "Thank you," she said, then cleared her throat. *Now, Matilda. Do what you came to do.* "Did he… Before Nathaniel disappeared, did he say anything to you about why he was leaving? Did he tell you where he planned to go?"

The crease between Miss Kovacs's eyebrows returned. And deepened. It made Matilda wonder if she'd imagined that brief moment of kindness. "You are asking me if I knew he survived the fire and withheld that knowledge from his grieving family," Miss Kovacs said.

A frigid stillness followed the woman's words. "No," Matilda said, and she couldn't help stepping closer to the low flames in the fireplace. "I didn't mean to—"

"I'm a miserable woman, so by your reckoning I must be a cruel one as well," Miss Kovacs said. She didn't need to shout; her gravelly voice whipped like the branch of a willow, and when Matilda attempted to interject, Miss Kovacs cut her short with another wave of her hand. "You've had a rough go this last year, rougher of late. I know better than most how difficult it is for a woman to find her own way through this world. I locked the girl I was away and became the headstrong crone I am to survive, and you have done the same."

Matilda could barely stomach the comparison—the accusation—even in her thoughts. Only yesterday she'd lamented her immaturity to Joseph, and already she'd become a *crone?*

Of course Matilda had changed. When a need for money had driven her to work at the Harrison manor, she'd given up school and any budding dreams for herself beyond raising her siblings and finding a suitable husband. After Nathaniel's disappearance, she'd learned to be tenacious when the grocers intended to pay less for the cows' milk than they'd paid her brother. And however Elliot teased her about her perfectly sufficient aim, she'd taken to her rifle as well as any man to protect her home and family. She couldn't deny being headstrong.

But a *crone?*

"I'll pardon your misstep," Miss Kovacs said, as though she hadn't made one herself the way she'd trampled over Matilda with her observation, "but let me assure you, if ever I harboured any secret, I did so only because knowing was worse than not."

It took a great effort for Matilda to swallow her pride. "I meant no offence," she said, though part of her now wished she had. *A crone, indeed.*

"Never mind that now; you're here for your sister, not Nathaniel," Miss Kovacs said, and Matilda felt a slight twinge of guilt for her mixed motivations. "I can't fix your sister's problems forever, so it's time you learned to fix them yourself."

Fix them herself? What magical hold did Matilda have over another's thoughts? She couldn't even get Elliot to eat his potatoes at dinner unless they were sandwiched between beef steaks. "But I'm not a mesmerist," she said.

"Who said anything about that?" Miss Kovacs stared blankly through Matilda's middle, but the twist of the wrinkles around her mouth gave the old woman a sneer. "Olive needs stability and a chance to be a child. If you can't give her that, find someone who can."

I rejected him.

The thought hit Matilda like a bout of nausea. She'd gone almost the whole day without reminding herself of Joseph.

"Now, shoo!" Miss Kovacs fluttered her hands at Matilda, giving her no time to mourn for her shattered dream. "It's almost supper time, and I don't care for guests."

Before Miss Kovacs could swat her away, Matilda made for the door and winced again at the squeal of hinges. "Good day," she said, holding the door open. Across the yard, Olive sat in the wagon with the reins in hand, looking eager to leave. "Thank you for helping my sister."

Miss Kovacs dismissed Matilda with another wave of her hand, grabbed her apron off the hook on the wall, and shambled into the kitchen. When Matilda heard the clank of a pot and the whoosh of the stove lighting, she paused in the doorway, recalling what the woman had said about Nathaniel. Miss Kovacs hadn't truly denied keeping secrets. Why should she decide if Matilda deserved to know them?

Matilda caught Olive's gaze from outside and mouthed, *one minute*. She let the door creak shut and tiptoed farther into the house, barely daring to so much as breathe. From the *chop chop chop* of a kitchen knife, Miss Kovacs was too occupied to hear Matilda's return to the sitting room.

There must be a clue somewhere in this house.

Whatever she was looking for, she couldn't seem to find it. The cushions of the chesterfield hid nothing beneath them. If there was evidence in Miss Kovacs's potions, the scents made her head spin too much to find it. Only a modest bookcase in the corner of the room connected this place to Nathaniel. Several thick tomes lined the shelves, and a few of them had titles Matilda had seen in her brother's room. Miss Kovacs probably hadn't cracked their spines since she'd still had the use of her eyes, but Nathaniel had devoured every word in his copies until he'd had to have them rebound.

How is this supposed to tell me where Nathaniel was?

Begrudgingly, Matilda turned from the shelf. This had been a silly idea. She pushed herself off her knees, careful not to make the floor creak, but when she turned toward her escape, Miss Kovacs stood at the edge of the sitting room with her hands in the pockets of her apron.

"You won't find Nathaniel in those books," Miss Kovacs said without a hint of surprise in her voice.

Had she known the whole time that Matilda hadn't left?

"It seems I wasn't blunt enough when I said I don't have answers to give you." By the jut of her chin, Miss Kovacs had a few more things she'd like to be blunt about, but she took her hands out of her pockets and smoothed her apron. When she finished, a fragment of the sympathy Matilda had detected before returned to Miss Kovacs's features. "Nathaniel was no more a Fenian than he was a blushing maiden," she said, "but he must have been hiding for a reason—trouble, if you ask me. You shouldn't go looking for it."

"I have to." Matilda clenched her skirts in her fists. "I have to stop him before he hurts one of us again."

The few hairs of Miss Kovacs's eyebrows sank low on her face. "Stop who?"

Richards.

Matilda kept the name to herself. If even Joseph, who'd known Nathaniel almost as well as Miss Kovacs and knew his wretched uncle far better, couldn't believe what Matilda knew in her heart, Miss Kovacs would only scoff at her. "Olive is waiting for me," Matilda said. She made for the door sincerely this time, but before she left the sitting room, Miss Kovacs blocked her path.

"Hold." Miss Kovacs hadn't used the same command in her voice that she did when she had someone in a trance, but Matilda's feet glued to the floor of their own will. "You watch your family, girl. I may not believe that nonsense about Nathaniel being a Fenian, but others will. Some might do something about it."

Her cautionary words were the most tender Matilda had ever heard from her, but they still scalded. It had taken years to rebuild the O'Connor name after Father destroyed it. How easily a single lie had made them into traitors again.

They're wrong this time.

Matilda let herself out, shutting the door solidly behind her to let the woman know she'd truly left. The burden of unanswered questions weighed her down as she dragged herself across the overgrown yard and back to the wagon. She climbed into the seat next to Olive and crossed her arms over herself.

Olive's eyes gave Matilda a quick inspection, likely looking for warts or other symptoms of a witch's curse. With nothing to find, Olive gave a soft rap of the reins. "Come on, Duchess," she said to the mare, and she drove the wagon toward home, leaving Matilda to her thoughts.

If Miss Kovacs can't tell me about Nathaniel, who can?

Matilda's chilly mood seemed to freeze time itself as they travelled home. Few signs of life beyond the sleepy evergreens or the yap of a farm dog accompanied their journey, and the wagon rolled past the asylum with nothing but the sound of the dirt road cracking under the wheels. Daylight faded quickly behind the clouds sagging over the land, but once they neared the turn to their homestead, a loud whistle broke through the sky.

Matilda sat up, alert. Something about that whistle cut through her. "That's coming from the meadow. Olive, move faster."

Olive clicked her tongue. "Go, Duchess."

With a spirited trot the mare took the wagon over bumpy terrain. Muffled shouts and the rumble of hooves followed another whistle, and when the trees parted to reveal their homestead, riders galloped around the meadow on fierce horses.

Whooping and howling, three boys carried hatchets and raced their knife-footed mounts around the field. Elliot guarded the pasture with only Sable cowering at his side, but alarmed moos revealed the cows had busted a new hole in the fence. The riders charged at them, and the cows scampered into the woods.

"Hey!" Elliot raised his hammer and chased after the horses. "Get away!"

The riders circled their horses around Elliot, laughing and unafraid.

"Traitor!" one boy called.

"They'll trample him!" Olive said. She snapped the reins again, urging Duchess into a gait the wagon wasn't meant for, but she drove straight toward the other riders.

"No! To the house!" Matilda gripped the dash and sat on the edge of her seat. "Hurry!"

The moment Olive halted the wagon, Matilda jumped from it and darted inside the house with a crash of the front door. Her rifle waited eagerly by the entrance, but when she returned with it locked against her shoulder, the riders had already vanished down the road. Only their voices rose over the treetops.

"Fenian dogs!" they shouted. "Go and die with your brother!"

— CHAPTER ELEVEN —

MATILDA

A single cow huddled near the shelter of the barn and backed skittishly into the fence. It lifted split hooves as though to flee and moaned for its companions.

By lantern light Matilda examined the breaks in the fence. Most of the wood was scattered over the ground in jagged fragments, snapped by the cows' stampede, but many of the fallen pieces carried the grooves of the boys' hatchets.

Sable leaned into Matilda with her head bowed. She whined and wagged her tail repentantly.

"What use are you if you don't guard the cows?" she asked the dog.

Elliot stomped around the pasture. "That was Junior and his pals. I'll beat him until he turns purple."

Matilda had half a mind to join him, but the rest of her felt depleted. "Find some wood to fix the fence," she said, unable to hide the fatigue in her voice.

Elliot, muttering oaths beneath his breath, stamped toward the woodshed and returned with two boards dragging behind him. He dropped them near the broken fence and assessed the work before him. "Maybe we shouldn't bother." He nudged one of the boards with his toe, and his voice dropped, forlorn. "Fixing this, I mean. Mother's gone. Nathaniel's gone. There's nothing worth staying for."

Not you too.

When Nathaniel had first built the fence, it had been proud and sturdy, but for a long time since the posts had leaned unsteadily. Now the rotten pieces barely held together. Maybe that was all Elliot saw when he looked at their home: a run-down bit of wood and earth.

"Do you remember what Mother looked like?" Matilda asked.

"Of course," Elliot said. "Her portrait hangs over the fireplace."

Matilda shook her head. "That was painted when she was sixteen. Do you remember the grey streaks in her hair or the way she'd hide her face in her hands when she laughed?"

Elliot didn't answer.

"Sometimes when I hear Olive hum her old lullabies, I remember. Mother used to do the same when she'd wash our clothes. Right there." She pointed at an area of ground past the barn and pictured Mother rubbing aches out of her wrists after a wash. "Do you remember the day Nathaniel brought Sable home?"

"She cried all night until I let her sleep in the bed," Elliot said, sounding distant. "Nathaniel slept on the floor because there wasn't room left."

"Every blade of grass is a memory." With her shoes on, Matilda couldn't feel the grass between her toes, but she ran them over the ground anyway. "Mother and Nathaniel are here. I won't give them up."

Elliot scratched behind his ear, more for the feel of it than because of an itch, it seemed. After a moment, he picked up one of the boards at his feet. "We're almost out of lumber," he said, not looking at her. "I'll miss a few days of school and cut more."

She patted her brother on the shoulder. "Your schoolwork is poor enough without missing lessons. I'll find a way to do it myself."

I have to find a way.

After she'd seen to Duchess, Olive joined them with several coils of rope looped over her arm and another lantern hoisted before her.

"We should split up. Elliot, stay and fix the fence as best you can." Matilda took the longest stretch of rope from her sister. She pointed south toward the Fraser River. "Olive, you head that way with Sable. Can you do that for me?"

Despite the tremble in Olive's lower lip, she nodded. Patting her thigh, she called Sable to her side and made for the southern woods and the sound of the river.

"Run straight back if any of Richards's dogs are wandering out there," Matilda called after her as she fetched her rifle from where she'd leaned it against the fence.

Balancing the rope and lantern with one arm, Matilda tucked her rifle under the other and headed west.

Each breath brought the crisp scent of the evergreens. It kept her awake when the soothing rush of the Fraser and Brunette rivers made her want to nestle against a tree and dream of better days. The distant moos of a cow beckoned her toward Richards's farm. She gripped her rifle tight.

The woods thinned, but the brush at her feet closed about her like carnivores circling prey. Then a shrill animal cry pierced through the trees and set her heart thumping.

Richards's dogs are loose again. Good thing she'd warned Olive.

But the sounds weren't right. The bellows were panicked, not aggressive, and thuds far too loud for a dog's soft paws pounded on the earth somewhere ahead of her. It made her think of the wolf from the night she'd seen Nathaniel.

I need to find those cows!

Snapping twigs and the rustle of frantic movement through the trees caught her ear, and as she stepped over tangled roots and brush onto a game trail, her lantern revealed a giant, black creature writhing on the forest floor. Her cow. It smelled of fear and blood.

The beast lay on its side, and its hooves carved wounds into the earth as it moaned in pain. Blood soaked the cow's front leg where a rusty hunter's trap snapped above the hoof. In its flight to escape the boys, the animal had ensured its death.

No. Oh, no.

The cow breathed erratically. It made a whine she'd never heard from a cow before and looked at her with white-rimmed eyes that begged for help.

Matilda gave it. She steadied her rifle in both hands. It took only one shot.

She sank to her knees beside the empty carcass and released the breath she'd held to stable her aim. It shuddered as it passed her lips.

Another cow dead.

Another hole in the fence.

Another wet, gloomy winter ahead of them as well as the ill will of their neighbours.

"Nathaniel, why did you leave us?" She closed her eyes and imagined her brother before her, giving ear to her struggles as he always had. He smiled at her with freckle-dusted cheeks and straw-coloured hair barely long enough to brush his ears. Instead of the nauseous scent of pain around her, she pretended she smelled the morning dew and the scent of the smokehouse always caught in his clothes.

The vision in her mind burned clearer than daylight, right down to the glimmer of Matilda's twenty-five-cent coin at his throat.

Even imagined, Nathaniel gave her comfort, but something behind his eyes twisted Matilda's heart—something that had always been there but she'd never wanted to notice: exhaustion.

Nathaniel had given up everything after Mother's death. If he'd kept his partnership with Mr. Wellington, by now he'd be travelling far and wide to bring laughter to the world.

Instead he'd given up *his* whole world to bring laughter to three pitiful orphans.

Why would he give everything up for us if he was only going to leave?

The memory gave no answer, and his image faded from her mind, leaving her with only a bloodied carcass and the embrace of darkness for company.

BANG!

The boom of a rifle blasted her despair away and turned it to rage. She rushed to her feet and knocked over her lantern, plunging her in dark.

If Richards kills another of my cows, I'll shoot the man myself!

— CHAPTER TWELVE —

THE WOLF

B*ANG!*

Fire. Pain. More fire.

BANG!

Fire bites skin and bone. Blood and pain.

Run.

Over rocks. Into water. Water cools. Water numbs.

Falling. Drowning. Dying.

Swallowed in dark.

— CHAPTER THIRTEEN —

MATILDA

"Richards!" Matilda shouted. She hiked her skirts up to a scandalous height, held the rifle under her arm, and marched as fast as she dared through the darkness.

It was foolish, staggering toward Richards when he had a weapon. Part of her hoped he'd use it. Then no one would blame her if she shot back.

Following the gunshot took her out of the wood's oppression and down to the banks of the Brunette River. Had she come so far already?

A cough broke through the night. In the heavens, the moon peeked through the clouds and trickled liquid silver over the ripples in the river. Touched by the light on the shoreline, a shadow moved upstream.

The creature struggled over the riverbank, half submerged in the mirror of water until it collapsed with a splash.

Not another cow!

She ran toward it, but as she neared the fallen creature, she knew it was much too small for a cow. When she drew close enough for the spill of moonlight to identify the animal, she stumbled over her own feet.

A man lay in the water.

A *naked* man.

"Oh!" She threw her arm up over her eyes and staggered backward. "Sir?"

When he didn't answer, she lowered her arm slowly. Face down, most of him lay hidden under black water. His fingers had clawed tears in the mud, but his chest was still.

"Sir, are you all right?" She abandoned her rope and rifle on the ground and knelt in the icy water at the man's side.

Moonlight lit the stubble on his jaw and the long, water-soaked veins of black hair stuck to his skin.

Is he…dead?

She reached toward his shoulder, but before her fingers brushed him, he groaned. The sound blew thinly through his lips, but it shook her to her centre. Something was wrong. He weakened every second, but something venomous and wicked infected his groan.

"You're letting the dark get to you, Matilda," she told herself.

Her timid fingers reached toward him again, prepared for the cold, unnerving feel of coming death on his skin, but they didn't find it. His body *burned.*

She heaved the man onto his back and found him covered in blood and silt. Water had washed some of the blood away, but now that she'd moved the man, it flowed freely from a graze wound at his temple and flooded from a hole in his chest. Far too much blood.

He needs a surgeon!

She tore cloth from her underskirt and pressed it over the wound on his chest. Beneath her hands he felt hard and brittle. As she applied pressure, he gave another groan, high-pitched and agonized like her cow's final sounds. Then he went still.

"Sir?" She shook him and tried to get his eyes to flutter. "Sir—" His head rolled to the side; a small disk of metal slipped around his throat.

From a tattered cord barely clinging to his neck the object dangled free, dirty and scuffed but instantly familiar even in the low light. She felt the ridges of what she knew would be a wreath of maple leaves on one side and the face of the queen on the other.

"Nathaniel's coin," she whispered, "but why do you have it?"

His only answer was the shudder of his breaths, each one weaker than the last.

PART II

— SUGGESTION —

December 6th, 1883

All my efforts were in vain. I was too weak. Too late. Mother is gone.

Now the farm is my responsibility, as are my sisters and brother. Elliot throws tantrums. Olive cries until she makes herself ill. I don't know what to do about any of it.

Matilda does. She left for the manor today, though the Harrisons don't need another to cook and clean. I think Joseph knew we needed money but didn't want to hurt my pride. Matilda shouldn't have had to give up friends and school to help out. I should have been stronger.

Joseph forgot his newspaper on the table when he took her away. I saw the headlines. Fenians. Here. I won't go through that again.

Matilda is doing her best to protect the family. It's time I did too.

— CHAPTER FOURTEEN —

MATILDA

Matilda peered through the narrow window in the surgeon's door and pounded on the frame. The inside was as black and silent as the street outside it.

"Doctor, wake up!" she called.

Her heels scuffed over the boardwalk as she stepped out from under the awning. Curtains drooped behind the second-storey French windows. No light. No sound of footsteps answered Matilda's thumps on the door. She rushed back under the awning and beat the wood hard enough to crack skin.

"Please. You treated my mother! Someone's hurt!"

A click and the scrape of wood on wood sounded above her head. Over the candy shop next door, a white-framed window opened, and a wrinkled woman in a frilly nightcap poked her head outside with a scowl.

"Keep it down!" The woman flapped a shrivelled hand at Matilda like she was a filthy street cat. "He isn't home! He's gone to Surrey to see his new grandson. Now, *go on!*" The woman muttered a few insults just loud enough for Matilda to hear before she ducked inside and slammed the window shut.

Her mind raced, trying to recall the name of another surgeon, but her feet knew where to take her. They carried her back to her wagon, and after a snap of the reins, Duchess dashed through the street at a dangerous pace.

Please, let the mare keep her footing.

Let him survive.

Matilda's thoughts were a whirl of panic until Duchess careened onto a quiet street that led up a low rise. She couldn't remember how they'd arrived at the other side of the city, but the yellow house atop the hill was familiar and comforting.

Why did I come here?

Despite the black windows, the Harrison manor stood like a beacon in the night. Duchess trotted up to the house, and Matilda leapt from the wagon before the wheels had stopped turning. She flew up the steps to the porch and hammered on the door.

What am I doing here? I need a surgeon, not a policeman! Her instincts to seek her guardian angel were stronger than she'd realized, but what could Joseph do with a bullet wound?

Matilda wrung her hands together and waited for someone to answer. After twelve agonized beats of her heart, the door finally opened, but it was a slight man with coal-coloured eyes and the scent of dishwater on his hands who appeared behind it. The Harrison's servant stood on the other side of the portal, dressed in trousers and a pigeon grey waistcoat.

Not him!

"Mr. Harrison." Matilda dug her fingernails into her palms. "Find Mr. Harrison."

The man's eyes narrowed at her.

Doesn't he understand? There's no time! She stood on her toes and threw her voice past the servant. "Mr. Harrison!"

"He's gone." The servant's response came with such a dreadful delay Matilda almost shook him by his waistcoat to rattle the answer out of him. "A fight broke out at the saloon."

Matilda ran a hand over her tangled hair. She'd probably passed Joseph on her way here. She should have paid more attention!

I can't ask for Mother Harrison's help, can I? She shifted from foot to foot and bit back a frustrated scream. *But there's no one else.*

"Is someone hurt?" The servant's voice snapped Matilda out of her thoughts. He lowered his eyes to her sleeves. "You have blood on you."

Scarlet clung to her knuckles and stiffened her skin as it dried. Most of her dress was too dark to see the bloodstains, but she felt the weight of the river water in her skirts. It made her woozy to think of all the blood mixed with it. That man wouldn't live long enough for a surgeon.

"I am not a physician." The servant's jaw tightened as he battled with some unspoken question. Whatever answer he came to, he said, "I can treat minor wounds."

Her mind flashed with memories of Mr. Gän cracking Joseph's nose, but when she opened her mouth to refuse the servant, she said, "Hurry!"

Duchess mouthed the bit as Matilda turned the wagon around while the servant ran for his coat and hat. He hopped into the wagon bed a moment later with a small rucksack cradled in his arm. Before he'd found his seat, Matilda urged the mare toward home.

The man crouched in the back of the wagon, his face shielded by his woven, wide-brimmed hat. He stayed low and quiet until they'd escaped the city, passed the penitentiary, and left all onlookers behind. Then, his hat pinned down with one hand, he leaned forward.

"Who's hurt?" he asked. "What happened?"

"I don't know." Matilda thrashed the reins and poor Duchess threw herself down the road at a deadly pace. "I think my neighbour shot him."

"Shot?" The man's voice raised to an incredulous pitch. "With a gun?"

"I wouldn't have bothered looking for help if it had been a cannon!"

"Turn back." He gripped the back of the seat. "I said I knew a little, but I'm not a surgeon!"

"You are tonight. I wasted enough time searching for a surgeon. You'll have to do."

The servant muttered a string of words, none of them English or likely polite, but when he was finished, he gritted his teeth and sat back in the wagon.

At last the trees gave way to the O'Connor meadow. Elliot waved his lantern at her from outside the barn. Matilda let him take the mare by the reins when she pulled up and slid out of her seat. "How is he?" *Please be alive.*

Where the lantern light fell on him, Elliot's face shone with a pallid glow. "I don't know. Sometimes he opens his eyes, but I don't think he knows we're there. He looks really sick."

But he's alive, she told her skittish heart.

"Chinaman, hurry into the barn!" Matilda ordered, but when she turned back to the wagon, it was empty.

"My name is not 'Chinaman,' it's Kāi." The servant's jaded voice came from inside the barn, and, trusting Elliot with the mare, Matilda rushed inside after him.

When she entered, the servant—Kāi—had his back to her. Next to him, Olive raised her lantern high to flood the barn with light, but she shivered so violently the lantern swayed and sent shadows chasing each other around the log building. Kāi removed his hat, his braid trailing down his spine, and crouched over a stagnant form in the straw.

The stranger lay buried in woollen blankets, his eyes sealed shut. Under the light of Olive's lantern, his bloodless skin offset the blue of his lips and the dark, bloodied tear at his temple.

After he'd felt at the stranger's throat, Kāi pulled the blankets down to expose the man's wounded chest, and Matilda cringed at the sight of the man's body.

Now she knew why the man had felt strangely brittle and light when she'd pulled him from the river.

Little remained of him but skin and bone. Each rib dug hills and valleys in his chest, and knobby, twig-like appendages fell at his sides. His knotted hair hung, thin and limp, over sunken eyes and hollow cheeks.

Her hope withered. A strong man might have had the barest chance, but, starved and sick, this man had been on death's doorstep long before Richards's bullet had struck.

"I need clean water and fresh towels." Kāi fiddled with the sack he'd brought and leaned over the would-be corpse. The pungent scent of a mix of herbs Matilda couldn't identify filled the musty barn air as the servant loosened the sack's ties and pulled out some sort of medical kit. "Go!"

The command in his voice shocked Matilda back to her senses. She sprinted from the barn and into the house. By the time she'd found enough towels and returned with a pail of water, the servant had all of his herbs and tools—bandages, needles, and a narrow-bladed knife—arranged on a cloth within reach of his hand. "Bring those and sit." He snatched a towel from her and dipped it in the pail before she'd even set it down. "Do exactly as I say. Are you ready?"

She knelt at the wounded man's side and gripped a towel in each hand. "I have to be," she said, but Kāi already immersed himself in his work. He peeled the torn strip of Matilda's underskirt, now stained red, back from his patient's chest wound.

"Water," Kāi said, "and more light."

Olive brought the lantern closer as Matilda poured water over the wound and winced as it ran red. She'd escorted her ill mother to the physician many times, but she'd never witnessed a real surgery. How could she know if the servant knew what he was doing?

As much as he'd protested, Kāi didn't fret at the blood on his palms. Sweat dotted his brow, but his hands worked with a steady calm.

Matilda washed the wound clean whenever he asked and tried not to squirm when he inserted his narrow blade into the man's chest.

I've skinned rabbits and deer. This is no worse.

But they'd been animals and already dead. This was a man—a living, breathing human somehow connected to her brother. She shut her eyes and swallowed the sick feeling in her throat.

"The wound is not as deep as I thought," the servant said. "Clean it again."

Opening her eyes once more, Matilda dabbed a damp cloth around the injury. Kāi pulled the blade out of the man's chest and drew something from the wound. He dropped a bloodstained bullet, deformed from impact, onto the discarded rag at his knees.

Matilda kept her gaze turned while Kāi stitched the wound and laid a folded cloth over it. Afterward, he dabbed at the blood at the man's temple and got Matilda to help him wrap the bandages.

"That," the servant dipped his red-stained hands in the pail of water and rubbed them clean, "is all I can do. He needs rest. And a *real* physician."

He needs more than rest. With the bandages wrapped around his skeletal form, the man reminded Matilda of the lepers in the bible. He needed his own miracle now.

Olive lowered the lantern and rubbed her shoulder. "Will he be warm enough here?"

Her first winter on the farm, Matilda had survived far cooler nights than this. Back then the chill, humid winds of midwinter had found cracks between the logs of the little one-room cabin they'd built and tormented the family each long, spiteful night. But she'd had fire, flesh around her middle, and Mother's embrace to warm her.

"Fetch the extra blankets from the chest, will you?" she said.

Olive hung the lantern on the hook by Duchess's stall and left the barn.

Once Kāi had washed his tools and gathered his things back into his sack, Matilda rinsed the ruined towels as best she could. "Will he live?"

Kāi drew his sack closed and sat on his heels. A frown tightened his lips. "You know as much as me. Hope he isn't ready to meet his ancestors."

With nothing else to distract her now, exhaustion and the cold of her damp clothes seeped into her. She felt heavy and more tired than she'd thought possible. "When will we know?" she asked.

"You—"

"I know as much as you," she said. "I know."

Olive returned with the blankets and helped Matilda layer them over the stranger, covering him from his chin to the tips of his bare toes. When she arranged the blankets over his feet, she found what meat he had around his ankles was swollen. The skin had peeled until there was barely any left, only a band of rough, discoloured flesh. Similar rashes circled his wrists and neck.

What is this? Is it some sort of disfigurement?

After Elliot had rubbed Duchess down and locked the exhausted mare within the half-fixed pasture, Matilda sent her brother and sister to wash up and go to bed. Though Kāi offered to stay with his patient alone, she left the stranger's side only long enough to trade her wet clothes for dry ones.

What if the man woke but only for a moment? What if she missed her only chance to ask him of Nathaniel?

After an hour Kāi's head drooped. He folded his arms across his body for warmth and leaned back into one of the wall supports. Soon his breath made the slow, even sounds of sleep.

Matilda peeled the blankets back from the stranger's throat. Her fingers explored his neck until they found the leather cord. She untied it and drew Nathaniel's coin out.

It had lost its shine but fit into her hand the way it had when she'd given it to her brother. She ran her thumb over the embossed numbers and the ring of maple leaves. "My brother wouldn't have given this to just anyone," she whispered. She flipped the coin over in her palm and absently traced the contours of the queen's face. It couldn't be coincidence Richards shot this man only days after he'd murdered Nathaniel. "You knew my brother, didn't you? You know something about what happened to him."

The stranger's only answer was the slow rise and fall of the blankets as he breathed.

After tying the coin around her own neck, she settled the blankets back over the man and hoped each of his weak breaths wouldn't be his last. By now she trusted hope as much as she did Richards, yet hope was all she had to cling to.

Please, don't let this man die.

— CHAPTER FIFTEEN —

MATILDA

Dust tickled Matilda's nose. With the urge to sneeze, she drifted into consciousness to the smell of horse feed and leather. Her body had gone cold in the night, but when she readjusted her blanket, her fingers only sifted through straw. Begrudgingly, she cracked open her eyes. It was still dark but getting lighter, and shafts of faint light squeezed through crevices in the roof and walls. Instead of the spiderwebbed cracks in her bedroom ceiling, broad rafters loomed high above her.

The barn?

Already the cows wakened, softly mooing nearby. Something in the back of Matilda's mind rejoiced to hear them home safe. Had she lost them? She couldn't find them, but she'd found...

The man with Nathaniel's coin!

She shot up from her back with a gasp, spilling straw from her lap.

Eyes closed in what she hoped was sleep, the stranger lay exactly where she'd left him: underneath the weight of enough blankets to crush what remained of his body.

What if he's dead? Is he breathing?

"He lives."

Matilda barely suppressed a shriek before it jumped out of her. A foreign accent shaped the strange voice. She'd forgotten about the Chinaman, hidden away in the corner where the early morning light couldn't reach him.

Her face burned enough to thaw her frozen earlobes. *I spent the night alone with two strange men? Mother, forgive me.*

She tucked her legs beside her and reclaimed what dignity she could while picking straw out of hair that was flecked with mud and smelled like fish. "Is he in danger?"

"He should be dead," he said. "I thought I was going to treat a dog bite or broken nose."

"But you saved him." It hardly seemed true, but, at least for now, this servant had saved her last hope. It hadn't even cost her silverware.

Not that she had anything worth the trouble.

"How did you learn medicine, houseboy?"

"I told you I have a name." Through the dimness of the barn Matilda couldn't make out the servant's expression, but she heard a slight edge to his voice. "Kāimēin Mũn. Mr. Harrison calls me Kāi."

She frowned at his tone but tasted the peculiar name on her tongue. "Mr. Kei."

"Kāi," he said.

"Mr. *Kāi,* I'm—"

"Miss O'Connor," he said. "Mr. Harrison speaks of you sometimes."

Joseph speaks of me? The thought should have made her sing, but her stomach twisted when she recalled her last meeting with him. *He won't speak of me fondly anymore. I doubt he'll even want to see me.*

A disagreeable silence fell between her and the servant. *Kāi.* He seemed to dissect her as he watched from his dark corner. Testing her, she thought, but she didn't know why.

"I learned from my father; he was an herbalist once," he explained. "Sometimes when Mr. Harrison is out, I read his father's books. Your people's medicine is strange but sometimes useful."

Matilda blinked, confused by his admission, then she remembered she'd asked him for it.

Kāi came out from the corner and tended to his patient again, making himself too busy for idle talk. He drew the blankets back from the man's upper body and revealed a dark circle of blood in the bandage over the man's chest. Gently, Kāi peeled back the bandage and peered at the wound.

"Hmm." The sound hobbled through Kāi's lips as his eyebrows knit together.

"What is it?" Matilda pushed herself to her knees, ready to dash for more towels or water, and she edged forward for a better look. "Is it terrible?"

In better light the man's wound would probably have been a seething red instead of the deep grey it appeared now, and veined, black bruises infested the skin around the tear. Not even the bruise one of Richards's colts had given Elliot last year had looked so fierce.

"It's healing," Kāi said, though it sounded more like a question. "It's healing well."

Even the sight of the wound made Matilda's chest sore, but Kāi's declaration put a curl in her mouth. The smile felt unpractised on her lips but welcome. "Then he'll recover? That's good news!"

"No." Kāi covered the wound again. He sat heavily on his heels and didn't look the least bit pleased as he rubbed the back of his neck. "It's impossible."

Then it's a miracle. "What of the rashes?"

The same sense of danger she'd felt when she'd first found the man flashed through her again as she leaned toward him. For a moment she thought she saw movement in his face—a flutter of lashes or a twitch of his brow—but he lay still. She pushed the ill feeling aside and drew one of his arms from under the mound of blankets. His wrist remained red and chafed, but the swelling had disappeared during the night. "These marks are healing too."

"Marks?" Kāi shuffled through the straw and took the man's arm in both his hands, raising it in an attempt to get better light. He examined the mark from every direction, a glower spreading across his face, and set the man's arm back down. He pressed both hands into his forehead. "How do you know this man?"

"I don't," Matilda said. "I found him in the river."

"You brought a stranger to your home?" Kāi pointed to the other man's wrist. "He was wearing chains. He's a criminal."

"Chains?" A cold dread fell upon Matilda. She studied the injured man's wrist again, hoping to find evidence Kāi was wrong. He wasn't: the raw band of skin made sense only when she imagined the man shackled.

"He must have been shot when he escaped," Kāi said, "and you brought him here."

The stranger slept, not woken by their raised voices, but there was nothing about him that seemed peaceful. His hollow cheeks and his jawline, sharp enough to saw through a tree, would have better suited a body dug up from the grave. The skin sinking between every bone made her doubt he'd had a warm meal in months. Maybe years. "That can't be true," she said. "Look at him! A good lawman like Mr. Harrison could never starve a man like this. I won't believe it."

"Then bad lawmen did." Kāi put his hands on his knees and heaved himself to his feet. He fit his strange hat over his head and collected his sack. "I'm late, and Mr. Harrison won't like that I left without a word. I hope he's as fond of you as he seems."

He bowed his head to her and made for the door. Matilda abandoned the stained towels and tailed him out of the barn. The waking dawn stung her eyes as she stepped out into the morning, and the creak as the door shut behind her grated through her ears. "You won't tell him anything, will you?"

When the sting passed from her eyes, she saw her cows loose in the meadow and Kāi half-turned toward her with his mouth in a thin line.

"Mr. Harrison is fairer than most," he said, "but he will want to know why I didn't finish my work last night."

"You can't say a word to him!" Matilda said. "If Mr. Harrison knows a criminal—a *suspected* criminal—is here, I won't get my chance to question him before he's dragged away to prison."

"Question him?" Kāi scrutinized her like she was a medical text. "That is Mr. Harrison's duty."

Joseph believes Nathaniel was a traitor. He won't ask the right questions.

When Kāi turned his back to her again, it felt like he'd saved her last, fragile hope only to cut it cruelly short once more. She felt it wither inside her as he walked away, but she grabbed onto the traces of it and held tight.

"You knew my name," she said. "Did Mr. Harrison mention another name too? Did he mention Nathaniel?"

Kāi halted in his tracks. He seemed determined not to answer her as he tightened his straw-flecked overcoat around him, which was answer enough.

"Whatever you heard, it's not true." Matilda's throat tightened, and her eyes stung anew. "My brother was murdered, but not even Mr. Harrison believes it. That man in the barn, he knew my brother somehow. He's the only one who can give me answers."

At last Kāi turned to her, and she thought she saw a flicker of sympathy cross his eyes. "What if you don't like what he tells you?"

"I—"

A dry bark disturbed the rest of Matilda's sentence. At first she thought it was Sable somewhere in the meadow, but Kāi's gaze shot toward the barn door. Another weak bark sounded, then another. Coughing.

Matilda flung the door open with a scream of hinges and rushed into the barn.

The stranger groaned between rasping breaths. Bloodshot eyes flitted about the barn as he laboured to his elbows, a corpse rising from a shroud of blankets.

"Stay down." Kāi tramped past Matilda and toward his patient. "You'll bleed again."

The man ignored Kāi's instruction and tried to sit up, but his eyelids fluttered, and his head rolled on his shoulders.

Kāi knelt at the man's side and reached out to help him back into his makeshift bed, but before Kāi could touch him, a low rumble emanated from the stranger's chest. Dark, hostile eyes locked onto the servant, and his lips parted over white teeth. His nose crinkled with a scowl, his fingers formed claws that dug into the ground, and every weak muscle in his body tensed.

"We won't hurt you." Matilda displayed open hands in a show of peace and tiptoed closer. "He saved your life."

The stranger's rumbles raised a pitch, turning gritty. Matilda crossed her hands defensively in front of her. *He's acting like a wild animal!*

A dark feeling tingled down her shoulders. She stepped back. "I think we should leave." She spoke only loud enough for Kāi to hear. "Now. Slowly."

Kāi kept his body low until he'd put distance between himself and the stranger. Then, carefully, he eased himself to his feet. To Matilda's eyes he'd made no threatening movement, but the criminal snarled like a beast.

He lunged at them, teeth bared.

— CHAPTER SIXTEEN —

THE WOLF

Pain.

Man and woman come close. Too close. Man smells of blood and straw. Woman smells of…

The demon.

Pain. No escape. Demons.

Stop the demons!

— CHAPTER SEVENTEEN —

MATILDA

Matilda bolted. Kāi hurtled through the door behind her. Savage teeth and two dark eyes glinted at her before she slammed the door shut.

She threw her shoulder into the door and yanked the iron bolt into place. A weight thudded into the other side, and the door heaved against her. Kāi dropped his medical pack and threw his weight beside Matilda, but when the door heaved again, the blow shoved them both back.

Kāi grunted and readjusted his hold. "I think I know why he was chained."

Vicious snarls befitting a rabid dog threatened Kāi. The door heaved again.

"Don't speak," Matilda said, and another lurch of the door pounded against her in response. Pain throbbed through her shoulder. She thrust her back against the door, dug her heels into the ground, and shared a glance with Kāi. She dropped her voice until it barely sounded through her clenched jaw. "It seems to anger him."

Kāi shut his mouth. The door pitched against them again, and she heard fingernails claw into the wood. How could a man so wounded yet have so much strength?

How could a man who *wasn't* wounded have so much strength?

He's going to break down the door!

Another shove, then another. When Matilda didn't think her body could take another beating, the stranger gave a disappointed huff. His footsteps limped deeper into the barn.

Cautiously, Kāi released his hold on the door. Matilda kept a precautionary hand in place, but she peeked into the barn where a knot in the wood had left a gap between the boards. She raised herself on her toes and pressed an eye to the hole.

At first she saw only blurred shapes hidden in the dark, but once her eye adjusted to the dim light, she made out movement. Despite the chill of the early morning, the man ignored his blankets and hobbled through the barn completely bare.

Dear me!

Matilda jerked away from the peephole. She'd never seen a grown man so…exposed before, but now wasn't the time to be shy. Careful of where her eye strayed, she peeked through the door again.

Mother forgive me, but he's hurt.

She spotted him more easily this time. Straw stuck to his back and knobby shoulders, and at least several months of dirt browned his skin. Even last night's fall in the water had only left more muddy streaks. He cradled his head in his hands and swayed drunkenly on his feet until he crashed to his knees by Duchess's empty stall.

His emaciated features made guessing his age difficult, but Matilda placed him somewhere around thirty. His tangled black hair framed high cheekbones and feverish, wide-set eyes. Those eyes closed in a grimace of pain as he pressed the heel of his hand into the bandages at his chest. When he drew his hand away, it left a smear of crimson in its wake.

"He's bleeding again." She crept back from the door and moved a safe distance away. "He needs help."

"Yes." Kāi panted, still trying to catch his breath. "But not from me."

"I've never seen anyone move like that." *Or heard anyone growl like that.* Maybe he hadn't understood when they'd tried to calm him. "Do you think he speaks French?"

"No." Kāi stared at the barn like it was alive and pointed a shaky finger at it. "I don't think he speaks at all. The growling, and the way he moved— It was like a dog."

Or like a wolf.

That moment in the barn before he'd lunged, she'd sensed a cornered animal in him: wild, aggressive, and moved by instinct. It reminded her of the night she'd spoken with Nathaniel and the creature she'd found in the dark.

Kāi stood beside Matilda, but, by the distant look in his eyes, his mind was in a far-off time and place. "A little girl disappeared from my village once. We thought bandits took her, but she returned six years later, walking on all fours and snapping at anything that moved. My father tried to cure her, but..." Kāi blinked and brought himself back to the O'Connor farm. "She never spoke."

"No, he's not like the girl from your village." Matilda searched for an explanation, desperate. *He* must *tell me what he knows of Nathaniel!* "He's skin and bones now, but he must have been raised well. He walks on two feet, and you had as close a look at his teeth as I did. They're healthier than mine."

"Then someone took care of him," Kāi said. "He must have come from the asylum, unless you think he is someone's pet."

He said the comment in jest, but the thought made Matilda uneasy in her skin.

Then why is no one searching for him?

If the man really was the creature she'd met in the woods, he'd have been loose for days, maybe longer. There should be constables scouring the woods. There should have been whispers of a madman.

Matilda flattened her hand over her chest, and something hard pressed into her palm. Nathaniel's coin. Her brother must have filled it with his tricks, for when she clenched it in her fist, it assured her in a way no one but he could.

"It's no coincidence that man was shot so soon after my brother's death," she said, trying to control her features but feeling them contort with what must have been a woefully dismal expression. "So close to where he died."

Kāi collected his pack from the ground and dusted it off. "What does he have to do with your brother's suicide?"

Suicide. Matilda cringed.

"Nathaniel was murdered. This man knows something about what happened, I'm sure of it now." *Something worth killing for.* Matilda crossed her arms and levelled Kāi with a stare that would have given Elliot nightmares. "You can't tell anyone he's here. Richards is trying to cover up Nathaniel's murder, and the moment he knows this man survived, he'll try to kill him again. Mr. Harrison believes Nathaniel killed himself, so right now this man—"

"Needs you to hide him," Kāi said. "Even if you're right, you're asking a lot of me. I can't afford to lose my work if Mr. Harrison learns I've been hiding a criminal from him."

"I wouldn't ask if it wasn't important," Matilda said.

As his gaze clouded with old memories, Kāi's lips thinned. One by one past regrets tormented him until Matilda nearly felt she could name them. Whether it was pity for the village girl's fate or redemption he sought for his father's failure, he gave a resigned sigh that smoothed his doubts away and abated hers. "Are you certain?"

She nodded. "He needs me as much as I need him to tell me what he knows."

Kāi's fingers relaxed their hold on his pack. It hung limply at his side. "How? He doesn't speak."

Matilda raised her chin and felt a smile dance on her lips. This time it almost felt natural.

"Not yet," she said.

September 22nd, 1883

Lucas knew something was on my mind when I met him for our usual drink. He pays close attention. Maybe too close.

A few folks were working late, taking a break before loading a new roll onto the cylinder press. Smoking their pipes with all that paper around to drop an ember on, the fools. They didn't notice me pass by, but the moment I pushed open the door to Lucas's office, he gazed up from where he slumped behind his desk, drowning in account books and looking like he could have used a head start on the bottle of whiskey before him, to ask what was bothering me.

A few of the boys see Lucas's costly clothes and pocket watch or hear his mischievous humour and think him vain, oblivious, but no one else noticed my burden.

Drink after drink, my tongue loosened. I told him more than I meant to. About Mother. About how my "mind tricks" haven't done a thing to help her yet. About how I shouldn't have spent that money on windows. Me and Elliot would have survived another year of drafts. We could have found another way to warm the girls' room. If only I'd known Mother would need doctors and treatments.

Now she needs me too. On the farm. Mother hid it too well too long, but she's suffering, and Matilda can't attend school, mind Olive and Elliot, and *tend to the garden and cows.*

I'll miss the smell of ink and machine oil. I'll miss the feel of the metal type as I set and lock them into the bed, but I can't work at the printing press anymore.

Lucas tried to fix it. Told me he'd sponsor another show to raise money for Mother, though I know his father gave him an earful over spending his profits on our last "adventure in tomfoolery." If he's not careful, his own father will give him the sack.

It took all the soberness left in me to turn him down. I owe Lucas far too much already.

I asked him why he was so generous when his father already chides his impropriety of befriending a lowly employee like myself. Lucas merely shrugged, stared wistfully into his whiskey, and said, "I'm sure I'll find a way for you to pay me back."

I think he likes to be the hero too much. He dreams of adventure as much as I do, but now I must put those dreams aside. I hope for his sake Lucas doesn't dream too far.

— CHAPTER EIGHTEEN —

MATILDA

Matilda's fingers warmed the iron bolt of the barn door as she paused outside it. Close at her side, Elliot bent his knees and carried his hands open in front of his chest. Sable cowered behind him with her ears flat against her head while Olive waited with an enormous pot of broth steaming in her arms. The vapour drifted skyward with the scent of beef bone and salt, forming little droplets on Olive's lashes.

Ready? Matilda mouthed. After the first day, she'd learned to not so much as whisper until after they'd fed the beast. Wolf Man's hearing was as acute as his namesake's.

Olive squeezed her eyes shut, but she gave a curt nod. Elliot replanted his feet and dipped his head.

One.

Olive bowed forward, her eyes still closed.

Two.

Elliot sank deeper into his ready stance.

Three.

Matilda slid the bolt back and yanked open the door. Olive rushed forward and plunked the pot down just inside the barn.

"He's coming!" Elliot pranced in place. "Close it!"

Olive dove out of the way. Matilda slammed the door and thrust her shoulder into the wood, locking the bolt into place. Elliot threw his weight at the door beside her.

Furious snarls sounded before a thump from the other side of the door rocked them back. Wood lurched and hinges wailed, but the door held.

Sable cried and buried her muzzle in the ground.

When another blow to the door didn't come, Elliot brushed his palms off on his trousers and patted Sable's head until she stopped whimpering. "He's friendly today. Only one shove at the door this time. I'm still sore from trying to keep him in yesterday; I thought he was going to break through!"

"Well, it's not good enough." Matilda dug out a sliver of wood from her shoulder with a wince. "How am I to teach him to speak if he throws a fit whenever I look at him?"

Safe again from any unsightly views in the barn, Olive opened her eyes and dabbed steam off her face with her sleeve. "It's only been one week. I think being in the barn is driving him mad."

"He was already mad," Matilda muttered, "and we can't let him out until we know he won't hurt anyone."

Elliot made a sound somewhere between a cough and a chuckle. "We might have to wait until he's old and all his teeth have fallen out."

Even then he might be too dangerous. Why did I ever think this was a good idea?

Matilda nudged Elliot out of the way and found her peeping hole. Wolf Man lugged the pot of broth deep into the barn and tipped it to his mouth too fast to catch every drop. She curled her lip in disgust as he drained enough broth to feed three O'Connors and dropped the bowl next to the pile of cups and pots left from other feedings. The homestead sorely needed more dishes.

A week of rest—or whatever rest he'd gotten between their dinnertime battles—had done Wolf Man much good. The broth and porridge Matilda brought him each day had yet to fill out the skin hanging from his bones, but his rashes had faded, and the gash at his temple was already a scar carved into his hairline. Even the hole in his chest scowled less fiercely now that the bruises had lightened into greens and yellows. He couldn't stretch his shoulders without wincing yet, but he'd recovered some of his strength.

Which was a frightening thought. The barn door barely held against an *injured* Wolf Man.

It was all an uncanny miracle that the man's vicious wounds were healing so quickly.

But he's not a man. Not in his head.

When he'd left that first morning, Kāi had promised to keep their secret, but she couldn't stop wondering if Joseph would come to take her charge away. Every time Wolf Man banged on the barn door, snarled at them, or howled when they left him alone for too long, Matilda's gut felt like a string about to snap. Never mind if Kāi would keep the secret—how long would Wolf Man keep *himself* secret?

"Why doesn't Wolf use any of the blankets in there?" Matilda said with a sigh. "He'll catch a chill if he doesn't put on the clothes I left for him."

A pair of Nathaniel's old trousers lay over straw inside the barn, kicked about whenever Wolf Man got bored. Where the shirt and coat had gone, Matilda didn't know. The mornings and evenings were cool enough to turn her cheeks pink if she stayed long outside, but Wolf Man seemed bothered by neither cold nor his indecency. His only discomforts were his wound and her mealtime visits.

"He probably knows how much you like staring at him," Elliot teased.

Matilda pulled away from her peephole and gave her brother a glare. "It isn't like that. And I'm not *staring*."

"He needs a proper name, don't you think?" Olive's eyes fixed toward the heavens, undoubtedly considering several candidates. "We can't keep calling him 'Wolf.'"

"I thought you were afraid of him," Elliot said. "Now you want to name him?"

Olive frowned. When Matilda had warned her siblings of their new guest's malady, Elliot's morbid curiosity wouldn't be sated until he'd witnessed for himself how brutally Wolf pummelled the barn door, but Olive had scarcely left the house unless Sable had accompanied her, cowering at her side. Olive's fears hadn't stopped her from watching the barn from the bedroom window, though, and slowly Matilda had watched her sister's innate compassion temper her anxiety. "I am afraid," Olive said, "but he can't help the way he is. He deserves a nice, gentle, kindly name."

"He must already have one," Matilda said. "He wasn't born from a wolf. He would have had a mother and a name."

"Not one he's ready to tell us." Olive dusted dirt from her clothes. "He needs a new one."

"Yes, he does." Elliot surprised Matilda with his wide-grinned agreement. He bumped Olive with his elbow. "We should name him Cannibal. Or maybe Butcher."

"We're not naming him Butcher." Matilda returned to her peephole. At the very least Wolf seemed accustomed to his feeding ritual, even if he worked himself into a rage because of it. Now that he'd filled his belly, he no longer seemed to mind their presence; he simply paced around the barn, grumbling to himself and eyeing the walls like they were enemies. Olive was probably right about the barn driving him mad. Or madder. "We don't need to encourage his aggression," Matilda said.

"We should name him Lucky," Olive said.

"Lucky?" Matilda pulled her gaze from the peephole and studied her sister. "That's what you wanted to name Sable. It's not a good name for him."

"Junior has a cousin named Lucky," Elliot said.

Matilda resisted the urge to groan. "If the two of you could keep your hands to yourselves, you'd be the best of friends, you know."

"You'd hate it if we were friends."

"I would. He's a poor enough influence on you when you don't get along."

"But he *is* lucky, isn't he?" Olive said, ignoring the shift in conversation. "He escaped from something terrible and survived a bullet. Now he has a new home. I think it's a lovely name."

Perhaps a little too lovely for him.

"Go on, now." Matilda ushered her siblings away from the barn. "I have work to do. Hurry off to school."

"Aw," Elliot protested.

"And don't—"

"Don't say a word about Wolf to anyone," Elliot and Olive said in unison. "We know."

"Even if you won't say why," Elliot added.

After her outburst at Richards the day they'd buried Nathaniel, Matilda had been careful not to mention her suspicions in front of her siblings again. Let them find what peace they could for themselves. They were too young for the burden of finding peace for their murdered brother.

"Wolf might know why Nathaniel disappeared; that's all you need to know." She shivered at the thought of what might happen if the wrong ears heard of their visitor—what might happen to Wolf as well as to them if even one person passed along a rumour of a werewolf at the O'Connor farm. There'd been enough blood spilled by Richards here already. "He was one of Nathaniel's friends." *I think.*

"Then Nathaniel had strange friends," Elliot said.

And if Nathaniel had friends this strange, this dangerous, then how much worse were his enemies?

After another week of dismal days and nervous nights, Matilda peeked in on her charge after a Saturday-morning feeding. Olive busied herself with the hens, and Elliot took an axe into the grove to replenish the woodshed before the nights got colder. For now, Matilda faced Wolf alone.

With the skies overcast, only a few weak rays illuminated Wolf's shoulders as he gulped his breakfast out of a pewter jug. They'd solved their dish problem—a long rope connected the pitcher to Matilda's hand—but they'd never recovered any of the old dishes. She didn't think she'd ever want to eat out of them again anyway.

I hope his appetite won't keep growing. He'll eat through our winter stores before Christmas!

At least Wolf had gained flesh and a few sinewy muscles—still much too thin, but no longer a walking carcass. She could take solace in that at least, if not in his continued nakedness or the tangles in the beard now growing on his chin.

"How did your last caretaker look after you when you're so mean?" she wondered aloud.

He didn't snap at her when she spoke anymore. She'd caught Elliot spying through the peephole a few times, and even Olive sat at a safe distance and read to him from her novels each day. Wolf allowed them near without complaint so long as no one touched the bolt on the door. But the moment he heard a chance for freedom call…

"He must have been brave to put up with you."

Matilda's mouth turned bitter the moment she'd said it, and she only felt a small relief that Wolf couldn't understand her. Someone had chained and starved him—maybe Richards. If Wolf was a beast, then his captor was a monster.

Had Nathaniel been shackled too? Is that why he disappeared? The more Matilda learned, the less any of it made sense.

"What did he do to you?" She raised her voice and tried to catch Wolf's attention. "Hmm? What did he do to you, John?"

The name brought no more response than anything else she'd said. Swallowing the last drops of his meal, Wolf tossed the jug aside, and when she dragged it toward the door, he followed, curious. She left the door latched, and when the jug sat motionless too long, Wolf grew bored. He passed in and out of Matilda's constricted view, wearing a trail around the barn's perimeter.

"Not a John, then," she said. "How about William or Edward?"

Wolf passed out of her sight without a response.

She hesitated with her next attempt. "Lucky?" she said softly.

Wolf appeared within sight again and raised his head at the sound of the name. His eyes sought her through the peephole as though she'd summoned him.

"Olive has gotten you used to that name, hasn't she? But William is a better name. A boy named William used to tease me because of my freckles. It's a good name for someone like you. *William.*"

Yawning, Wolf resumed his march on the worn trail and disappeared from her sight.

"Lucky?"

Footsteps hurried back, but she didn't spy him until one large, russet eye filled the peephole, staring back at her just a breath away.

"Ah!" Matilda cried out and stumbled back, holding her heart in her chest with both hands.

Well, I suppose I called him, didn't I?

Warily, she eased her eye to the peephole again. Wolf remained by the door, head lowered to the hole, but he, too, had taken a startled step back.

"All right." She breathed deeply while her heart found a steady rhythm again. "Lucky it is."

For many nights in the first weeks of November, a breeze made the trees and grassy meadow rustle like restless spirits. At dusk the winds picked up and tormented Matilda's thoughts. No matter how little the cold bothered Lucky, no man could survive a Canadian December without fire or clothes.

He didn't howl anymore, but sometimes when the dark closed in at night, Matilda would open her bedroom window to hear Lucky tear around the barn in a panic. When Olive's nightmares had been at their worst, she'd wake up gasping and patrol the room in frantic circles, biting her nails until Matilda calmed her, but Lucky had no one to coax him back to his bed of straw and blankets. She wasn't certain he slept at all with the stale smells worsening in the barn. If he didn't gentle soon, she'd have no choice but to fetch Joseph whether she'd learned anything of Nathaniel or not.

One more day, she kept telling herself. *If it's not today...*

One morning he seemed to give up any hope of escape, and Matilda managed to give him his breakfast without any help. Wolf ripped into a loaf of bread and crouched on the other side of the door where she couldn't get a good angle on him from her peephole. "I know you want out of the barn," Matilda said. "I'll let you out once you convince me you can be trusted."

After so many weeks of the same routine, the words felt hollow even to her. How was she any better than Richards?

She'd avoided the man more than usual, but when she'd been unable to evade him, his sneers and meanspirited jests badgered her long after their meetings. The man delighted in cruelty. Richards must believe he'd gotten away with murder and abuse too terrible to imagine. It would only be proper for Matilda to prove him wrong—for the sake of both Nathaniel and Lucky.

What I'm doing isn't the same as what Richards did. Lucky isn't chained or starving now. He's simply not trustworthy yet.

Clang. The rope in Matilda's hand went slack. That hadn't taken long.

Lucky's face appeared on the other side of the peephole. His eyes begged for freedom, and Matilda's gut clenched. "I'm sorry," she said, "but this is best for both of us."

Turning away, Lucky shuffled across the barn and kicked Nathaniel's trousers out of his path. When he moved far enough from the door that she risked seeing more of him than was decent, she drew away from the peephole to give him his unappreciated privacy. "I wish you'd put those clothes on. You'd be embarrassed if only you understood."

Banging and a swishing noise at the back of the barn startled her, then a rustle of straw marked the approach of feet. *What is he doing?* Matilda checked her peephole again.

He neared the door with something filthy draped over his neck. Nathaniel's threadbare shirt, pierced with straw, hung in ragged curtains from his shoulders.

She squeezed her eyes shut until sparks flared behind the lids, but when she opened them again, the shirt still draped him in a cape, the sleeves about his throat and the body of it trailing down his back. It did him little good like that, but he *did* wear it.

At her command.

No, it's coincidence. He doesn't understand. He...

"Lucky, do you understand English?" It couldn't be true. Lucky had only imitated what he'd seen of their clothes, yet her heart beat a little faster. "Touch your nose if you understand."

Lucky jutted out his lower lip and gave a baffled frown. He narrowed his eyes, tilted his head to one side then the other, and kept his hands at his sides.

"Never mind," Matilda sighed. *Of course he doesn't understand.* "I don't know what I thought would happen."

He shifted his weight, and, wearing that look of confusion, he raised one bony finger and brushed the tip of his nose.

She breathed in a gasp of cool air, but her chest filled with giddy warmth. "You did it!" she praised. "You do understand!"

He didn't smile the way a human would, but something replaced the confusion in Lucky's eyes. Pride? Was he pleased at her approval of him?

"Yes, you did well." She turned from her peephole and looked up at the dreary skies like she could see heaven. "He understands, Nathaniel. He understands me."

And soon he can tell me what happened to you, my brother.

— CHAPTER NINETEEN —

MATILDA

At church on Sunday morning, the Holy Trinity Cathedral overflowed despite the gloom and clouds outside, or perhaps because of it, but even with so many other faces in the congregation, Matilda's seemed to attract the most glances. It'd been that way since Nathaniel's death. The same biddy grandmothers who'd given her sympathetic looks after his disappearance now gave her unbridled scowls and whispered about Fenians. Matilda bounced her knee in her usual pew and stared through the elegant windows to avoid crossing gazes with her old schoolmates.

Sundays were the one day of the week Matilda couldn't escape Richards. He trudged into the chapel after everyone was already seated, smelling like his hogs and with his children following the trail of mud he tracked down the aisle. For one relieved moment, the scrutiny Matilda had endured diverted from her. Flushing a humiliated red, Junior took both of his little sisters by the hand and hurried them quietly to a row near the front. The lanky youth ardently ignored the gawking looks sent his way, even Elliot's frown, but Richards ambled by Matilda's pew with a leer reserved for her. His own pew too full for his tastes, he ordered an old widow to relocate to the row behind and dropped onto his bench with a *thump.*

When Matilda should have been focused on the lectionary or the reverence of the hymns, she stared at the back of Richards's head until she threatened to give herself a headache. Only when she let her mind wander back to the homestead could she feel the veins in her temples stop throbbing.

Lucky understands English.

As her eyes meandered during the service, they fell upon Joseph where he sat with his mother in the front row, his head pointed calmly toward the altar. Matilda appreciated the striking form of his shoulders and the way his golden hair gleamed in the light, but her jitters worsened with each stolen glance.

Will I ever be able to look him in the eye again?

After the sermon and Sacrament, Joseph laughed casually with a few of his fellow constables, but Matilda hurried out the door before he could take notice of her. She helped Olive into their wagon and let Elliot take the reins.

At the end of Carnarvon Street, he turned south to find the mucky road that would take them out of the city. The closer the wagon rolled to the Fraser River and the busy Chinese shops on Front Street, the more men with woven hats and tails of black hair wandered past the clusters of parishioners headed home from church. Memories of Mr. Gān tried to pollute Matilda's thoughts, but when a slight Chinese man in a western coat like Joseph's crossed the road ahead, all thoughts of the old man vanished.

That's Kāi!

"Let me out," she said. Kāi didn't know what she'd learned about Lucky. If Lucky could already understand English, perhaps Kāi could give her insight into how to free Lucky's tongue. Snatching the reins from Elliot and halting Duchess by the boardwalk, Matilda stepped down from the wagon. Unlike the worshippers at the cathedral, none of the tawny men who passed her seemed to care two whits about her, but she lowered her voice anyway. There was no need to let *all* of Kāi's fellows know of the boarder she harboured on her farm. "Head home without me, but don't visit Lucky until I get back."

Olive pouted, but Elliot shrugged and clicked his tongue at the mare.

Kāi had disappeared toward the waterfront by the time Matilda sent the others on their way. She hurried the way he'd gone and soon found herself on Front Street, the place brimming with too much traffic and noise for a quiet Sunday. Looking for Kāi's velvety coat in the crowd, she rushed past the tailors and general stores until the shops around her bore names unpronounceable to her tongue.

The air around the Chinese shops carried the pungent aroma of fish, unfamiliar herbs, and the cleaners used in the laundry shops. An alien language flooded her ears from every corner, and down the street a crowd gathered outside a shop with the name of Võng above the door. From somewhere inside the crowd, a pair of dissonant voices sparred. Matilda eyed the commotion warily as she approached.

Võng's teashop drew the ear more than the eye by the way its narrow windows discouraged curious onlookers, but the place buzzed more than a hornet's nest. Rumours of this place had even reached Matilda's ears. It was the sort of place Richards would like, if he cared for tea or Chinamen. The exotic serving women, however, were exactly to his tastes, and it was the one place in the city where Chinese women were readily found.

More shouts resounded outside the teashop, cracking like a storm. Planted next to the shop door, two Chinamen argued hotly, and Matilda felt a weight hit her stomach when she recognized Kāi's coat.

Walled in by the crowd, Kāi stared down a squat man with grey-streaked hair. Even from across the road, Matilda saw that the coals in Kāi's eyes were ready to spark.

The older man posed outside the teahouse in cascading silks of plum. His wrinkled face sat no higher than Kāi's chin, but he had a command that marked him as a man of station among his own people. He scowled, jabbing a finger in the air with vitriol.

Mr. Võng, Matilda assumed by his attire.

Lingering behind Mr. Võng, a young woman stood framed by the open door, looking like a silk-screen print. Obsidian hair adorned with combs swept back from a porcelain face, and her embroidered silks shimmered in scarlet. Her painted lips betrayed no emotion, but her eyes darted between the quarrelling men with concern and, Matilda thought, anger.

The dispute escalated, both men gesturing to the woman in the doorway, and though neither Mr. Võng nor Kāi shouted a familiar word, Matilda thought she understood. Matilda would never know the heartache of a father who disapproved of a man she loved. The thought both relieved her and cut her deeply.

Waving his daughter back into the shop, Mr. Võng ducked inside himself and slammed the door in Kāi's face.

"Mîfä!" Kāi thumped on the door. "Mîfä!"

Two scruffily-dressed Chinamen peeled Kāi from the door and hauled him into the street. The younger one patted Kāi on the shoulder with a pitying look, but the other glowered and shoved him away. Right into Matilda's path.

Kāi noticed her in time to avoid knocking her over, and he jerked back, his eyes bulging at her.

Anything she'd prepared to say abandoned her. "Mr. Kāi, I—"

Kāi turned on his heels and strode away.

"Mr. Kāi!"

She caught up with him, though he didn't make it easy, his strides too long for even him as he attempted to outpace her. When she pulled up even with him, he shot her a defeated look out of the corner of his eye and slowed his gait. "If you need a surgeon, find someone else," he said.

"I came to speak to you," she huffed, trying to catch her breath.

He wore a reluctant expression, but he gazed up the busy street, watching the flow of the crowd. "If it's about your guest, we shouldn't speak here."

In a narrow alley within sight of her church, Matilda and Kāi found a private space. The chapel door muted choir voices practising Christmas melodies and a few carriages rolled lazily by the sandstone building, but no one paid Matilda or Kāi any mind. Still she turned her face away from the street. The last thing her reputation needed was rumours about her alone in a dim alley with a man.

Now that they were here, Matilda didn't know where to start. Kāi didn't seem to know either. They stood in the alley and listened to a soprano's warble until, finally, Matilda asked, "Who was the woman in red?"

"No one," he said too quickly, but when he met Matilda's sceptical stare, he yielded. "She is Mîfä. Our parents chose us for each other when we were children, but..." An old pain crossed Kāi's eyes; he ran his tongue over a dry lip.

Her father changed his mind.

Matilda turned from the street again as another driver rattled his wagon past the church. "But you're determined to have her."

"She's the woman my parents chose," was all he said in answer, but she thought she saw a smile tease his lips. It was small and half sad, full of youth and years in the same moment. He cleared his throat, and the smile vanished. "Never mind that. I kept your guest secret, but if he's hurt again..."

"No," she said. "Lucky is well."

"Lucky?" Kāi wrinkled his nose.

"I know the name doesn't suit him, but he won't respond to anything else." When the song ended and the church doors flung open to let the choir out to their buggies, Matilda signalled for Kāi to follow her deeper into the alley. "Lucky understands English."

"You taught him how to speak." It wasn't a question. It wasn't even a proper statement. The words fell from Kāi's tongue, hollow and dry. "In less than a month."

"He doesn't speak it, but he understands it. What does that mean?"

Kāi gave half a shrug. "Why would you think I'd know? Why tell me any of this?"

"I—" She paused. Why *was* she telling him? She had already placed perhaps too much trust in him, but by saving Lucky that night, Kāi had become her partner in a secret too significant to bear alone. "I have no one else I can speak to about this, and you mentioned that wild girl from your village. I thought you might have advice."

"Advice?" Kāi's voice darkened, raising the hair on the back of Matilda's neck. "Someone tried to kill that man for a reason—he's dangerous—but if you're right about your neighbour, he's worse." Kāi gave her an appraising look that said he wanted to believe her but feared what that meant. "My father couldn't help the girl from my village," he said. "I'm as confused about this as you, but there is one thing I do know: Lucky, and anyone who knows he survived, is a target now. I hope you know what you're doing, because neither Lucky nor I can help you if we're dead."

— CHAPTER TWENTY —

MATILDA

Faceless villains haunted Matilda for many nights after meeting Kāi, but when her nightmares were at their most soul-crushing, the visitor in her dreams wasn't faceless at all. He called on her wearing a visage she knew better than her heart.

Nathaniel appeared to her covered in blood and with eyes dead but not empty. Bitter, blue irises held the fear and fury of someone thrust into an unjust hell, resenting her more each day she failed him.

I'm trying, Nathaniel.

Icy toes against her calf jerked her out of nightmares. Olive rolled onto her side with a sleepy grumble and stole precious blankets and warmth. Cold enveloped Matilda like a tomb, and a breeze rattled the bedroom window.

Shivering, she slid her feet into her slippers. The window seemed closed, but she tiptoed across the room to ensure it was sealed tightly. She opened the drapes and peeked at the world outside.

Clouds emptied a deluge of fat raindrops over the meadow as the wind whistled a listless tune. In the pasture below, Duchess huddled with the cows near the barn, their backs soaking up the barrage. Poor things. With Lucky sealed away in the barn, the animals couldn't even seek warmer shelter under the barn's leaky roof.

Oh, Lucky!

In a frenzy, Matilda stole the last spare blanket from the bedroom chest and raced downstairs. She threw on her coat and gloves, traded her slippers for her boots, and sprinted into the night with a lantern.

Her knees bounced high to clear the suction of mud beneath her, and the assault of every raindrop stabbed cold into her skin.

He'll be frozen to death!

A lake puddled in front of the barn door. She splashed through it, but when she found her peephole, she saw nothing but black. She heard nothing but splatters of rain hosing through clefts in the roof.

She envisioned Nathaniel's vacant eyes and imagined Lucky with the same lightless stare.

All but dropping her lantern, she unbolted the door. When she heaved it open, the stale odour of old straw met her.

So did Lucky, standing in the doorway.

She dumped half the blanket in the mud. "Don't startle me like that!"

Lucky looked unapologetic. Rain sprinkled his shoulders and the top of his head, but he stood relaxed as he observed her through the doorway. Through the *wide open* doorway.

She threw the door shut in Lucky's face and rammed her shoulder into it, but a blow never came from the other side. Nor did the sound of claws against the wood. Nothing. Her breath caught in her throat, Matilda slivered the door back open.

"Are you all right?" she asked, shuddering with the chill seeping through her nightdress. "Are you cold?"

Are you going to eat me?

From behind her, the lantern light flowed past her and illuminated half of Lucky's face. His skin shone pale amber from weeks away from the sun and contrasted sharply with his unkempt hair and beard, but deep, brown eyes watched her with a sparkle of intelligence.

No matter how she looked into those eyes, she couldn't see madness. Behind a curious gleam lived fear—a fear that had once turned him as vicious as a rabid wolf—but there was no lunacy in the soft warmth of his gaze. No cruelty.

How is he not shivering?

"Kāi is wrong about you, isn't he?" Half hidden behind the door, she searched for some answer in the embers in his eyes. "You aren't going to hurt me, are you?"

Lucky breathed out a puff of air down his beard.

Thankfully Matilda's own shadow covered most of him from the light. One dirty shirtsleeve draped over his shoulder, but the rest of him remained bare. A tingle of heat even the November rains couldn't overcome passed through her cheeks.

"Here." She turned her face away and stuffed the blanket through the door. "Wrap this around yourself."

With a rustle, the blanket pulled out of her fingers, and a flutter of air fanned the heat in her face. When she turned back, Lucky wore a new cape of green and brown patches.

A bubble of sound popped out of Matilda's throat. A laugh. It felt new and unfamiliar. "Aren't you cold?"

No goosebumps covered his skin. Matilda's arms dug into her sides for warmth, but Lucky's posture was relaxed, as though his body didn't know cold.

"Please wear the blanket properly," she begged. "You can't survive winter with only your skin." *He can't, can he?*

Lucky stared at her as though she'd spoken in Kāi's native tongue.

"I know you understand me. So why don't you…understand me?"

Her question received another puzzled look. *This is pointless. I'm running out of time.*

The blood and suffering from her dreams burst anew through her mind. Shivers quaked through her as she remembered

Nathaniel's cold eyes, lost and waiting. She was failing him. *Lucky* was failing him.

"How much longer are you going to be like this?" Her bemusement vanished, and the words fused together as they rushed out of her mouth. "You've been here for weeks."

No, not weeks. One month exactly.

She'd forgotten her brother even as she'd obsessed over his death. "One month ago today my brother died," she whispered. Her throat constricted. Something was wrong with her eyes. Everything blurred, and tears spilled from them, pooling into the raindrops on her cheeks.

Heat brushed her face, soothing but sudden. She jumped back and slapped a hand to her cheek where the feel of another's touch lingered. Lucky leaned back from her, his hand hovering uncertain between them.

"What are you doing?" she asked, barely able to voice the words as she stood as unmoving as steel.

When she made no more protest, he reached cautiously toward her again. She leaned her head away, but his reach was long. He traced her tears with a finger, his eyes wells of confusion and childlike concern.

Self-conscious, she wiped her face with her gloves, but his touch had melted away more than the chill. Her heart felt lighter. Warmer. "It's all right. I'm not hurt."

She blinked back the rest of her tears and brushed his hand aside. Even through her gloves she felt warmth emanating from him. *He should be half frozen.*

"Your skin..." she said, at once both tempted and afraid to grab his hand and steal a little of his heat for herself. *This isn't right. This isn't normal.* "What are you? A fairy? Or... Are you a demon?"

Lucky's head perked up, alert, and wiry muscles tensed beneath his skin. He looked like Sable in the moments before she bolted after a rabbit, but his movements weren't playful.

"No, Lucky—"

A snarl ripped out of his throat. Teeth flashed. He dipped his knees, ready to spring.

Matilda banged the door shut and rammed the bolt into place.

Crack!

The door pitched into her, barely holding. "Calm down!" she shouted.

What happened? What did I do?

Lucky scraped at the door, then his footsteps scrambled away. Not pacing. Hunting. He hurtled around the barn's perimeter, testing for a weak spot to tear through.

Matilda rubbed at her chest, trying to revive her heart. "What's the matter with you? You were getting better!"

His antics spooked the animals in the pasture, and in the distance Richards's dogs yapped.

Is that what riled him? He heard the dogs even before the cows did? How is that possible?

The barking drew nearer, and Matilda's unease turned to rage.

If those dogs so much as set foot in this field, I'll…

She sprinted to the house for her rifle and returned, sloshing through mud as she raced past the barn. Lucky growled and ran alongside her on the other side of the wall until he ran out of space to follow.

Halfway between the barn and the woods, she planted her feet and stripped her gloves from her hands with her teeth. She dropped them on the ground and locked her weapon against her shoulder, her eyes skimming the tree line.

Without any sound or warning, a dark shape emerged from the woods and cut through the meadow toward her. Spotting her, it dropped low to the ground. It made no sound but walked upright with a recognizable, masculine form.

A beard and bushy hair hadn't seen a comb or a wash in ages, and his clothes wore thin at the elbows and knees. With a hunched back and dragging arms, the man crept barefoot through puddles toward her.

"Sir, are you all right?" she called across the distance. He looked like a beggar, but not one she'd seen before. A drifter? Had he been attacked by Richards's dogs? She lowered her rifle, but as she watched the man's skulking, her finger glued to the trigger. *Something is wrong.*

The man answered her with a deep, beastly moan. He shrank lower toward the ground, gaze fixed on her.

Somewhere behind her, Lucky hammered on the barn door.

"Sir?" Her voice was less sure this time. "Can you hear me?"

Again the man answered her only with that chilling moan. Hair raised on the back of her neck. The man stole toward her, a mountain lion stalking a fawn.

Not a lion. A wolf.

"Stay back!" She snapped the rifle back into place at her shoulder. "I'll shoot."

Teeth bared. A vicious growl rumbled, and the creature broke into a run straight for her.

BANG!

The butt of the carbine battered into her shoulder. The creature zigzagged. Her shot missed its mark, and the beast charged.

Swallowing smoke and gunpowder, she yanked the rifle's lever and returned it to place against the stock. A new cartridge slid into place. Too slow. The wolf already lunged for her, close enough for her to glimpse its emaciated features and something black and metal about its neck.

No! Olive and Elliot. Nathaniel. They need me!

Crack!

The sound of splitting wood exploded from behind her, and as she knew she was about to die, the wolf man dropped to all fours and reversed direction. He scampered back toward the woods, faster than any man should move.

With a growl low in his throat, Lucky sped past her and gave chase.

"No! Lucky, come back!"

Matilda ran hard enough to churn the puddles into steam, but the wolf man already disappeared into the woods. Right on his heels, Lucky dove after him.

"Come back!"

She crossed the meadow and plunged into the trees, stung by cedar needles and whipped by low branches. Under the dark of the trees, she couldn't run, and her skirts tangled in underbrush. She gasped for air and dragged herself onward, but the territorial growls vanished.

How many wolf men are there in these woods?

One wolf man could be dismissed as an escaped madman or even a feral human, but two? Two deranged men on the loose and not even a word about it in the city?

Someone did this to them. The thought would have been absurd if she hadn't once seen Nathaniel make Richards believe he was a wolf. It had all been for show then, harmless. Had Richards found a way to do something worse? It wasn't enough to kill Nathaniel, he had corrupted a talent that had been so beautiful in Nathaniel's hands. Was this Richards's way of getting payback?

Was he here in the woods now?

Matilda's blood froze, and her eyes flitted across the blackness as claws of cedar and fir stretched from the shadows toward her. She turned back toward the meadow before ghouls or terrors could sneak upon her.

"Lucky," she whispered, too afraid to attract the other monsters in the woods. "Lucky, please come back."

Every tree that creaked or twig that snapped under her feet set her on edge as she bumbled through the dark. When she found her way back to the meadow, she felt torn, longing for the warmth and safety of her house but agonizing over Lucky's escape. Would he be lost or captured again? Killed?

When Matilda returned to find the barn door torn from its hinges and scattered in splinters over the ground, she realized she'd been a fool to think she could contain Lucky. He'd only stayed as long as he had because of his injuries. There was nothing to bring him back now.

Shivering and exhausted, she collapsed to her knees beside her lantern.

"Lucky," she said again, quivering as rain pelted her head and back. "You can't leave."

Something splashed behind her. She wheeled around, her numb fingers fumbling with her rifle.

Lucky trotted leisurely toward her as though he'd returned from a walk, holding the gloves she'd abandoned.

"You came back!" She dropped the barrel of the rifle, her eyes widening until they pained her. "Are you hurt?"

Forgetting any fears or propriety she once might have had, she jumped to her feet and snared his chin in her hand, turning his face from side to side and feeling it for injuries. He permitted the abuse, and she found only what felt like an old scar on the bridge of his nose. She felt down his arm to the tips of his fingers but discovered no blood or torn nails. Just more warm skin.

She breathed a sigh of relief. The other wild man might still be out there, but Lucky hadn't become a murderer.

He tugged free of her grasp and disappeared inside the barn. When he returned, he stood over the broken door without remorse. Perched atop the remains of his vanquished wooden enemy, he wore his cape of grey and brown patches over his shoulders and gave her a proud look.

Matilda stared at the ruins of the door with a mixture of regret and awe.

"Well, you didn't eat me," she said. "That's a start."

— CHAPTER TWENTY-ONE —

MATILDA

"This way."

Matilda backed into the house, beckoning with a finger, but Lucky hesitated outside. Ankle-deep in muck and wearing nothing but the blanket she'd finally gotten him to wrap around his waist, he seemed more at peace with the downpour than the thought of more walls.

She held the door wide. "You'll like this place better." Paws padded behind her, and Sable nuzzled against her leg. "See? Sable likes it here."

Lucky didn't budge.

"Why did you get out of bed?" Olive said. Matilda glanced over her shoulder to find her sister yawning as she tiptoed downstairs. "And why is the door open? You're letting out the heat."

"I'm trying to get him inside," Matilda said. She patted her leg, but Lucky wouldn't respond.

"Him? Who—" When Olive spied Lucky beyond the door, she froze mid-yawn with her eyes about to fall out of her face. "In—Inside? But he—"

"He won't hurt us. He's calm." *Mostly.*

Olive fiddled nervously with the neckline of her nightclothes. "He's still a strange man."

"Ha! He's not a man." Matilda set her rifle by the door and slipped her reddened fingers under her arms. "He's barely *human.* Now, stop standing there and help me get him inside."

With a doubtful expression, Olive joined Matilda's efforts. They offered gentle words and promises of reward, but Lucky only mashed his lips together and let the wind scatter raindrops into the house.

Feeling a tension in her jaw that worsened each moment she stood in the doorway, Matilda stamped fists onto her hips. "Enough! I don't care if the rain doesn't bother you; it bothers the rest of us. Come inside *now.*"

Matilda bellowed the last word, and Lucky lowered his head and rushed into the house. She could almost imagine a tail tucked between his legs.

"Good boy," she said.

The wind breathed against the windows after she shut the door, but she stoked the coals in the fireplace until they burned with new flames and worked at drying her coat sleeves.

"Where will he stay?" Olive wrapped her arms around herself and joined Matilda at the fireplace. "There's no extra bed."

"I don't think he minds." Matilda wiggled her fingers above the fire and felt tingles as they thawed, but she kept a watchful eye on Lucky as he explored the room, Sable following curiously at his heels.

Lucky gripped the blanket at his waist and let the excess trail behind, giving a brusque growl to Sable whenever she stepped on a corner. Testing his place in the hierarchy. Sable lay on the floor with a whine, and Lucky returned to his wandering.

He studied everything from the wood creaking beneath his feet to the texture of the tabletop. He raised his nose, sniffing some scent Matilda couldn't detect, but when he came to investigate the valleys of mortar between the stones of the fireplace, another scent she couldn't ignore buried her in a thick cloud. Lucky carried on him the sour odour of the barn. She pinched her nose as he leaned over her and ran his fingers along mother's painting on the wall.

"No, don't touch that!" She swatted his hand away from the portrait.

Lucky jerked his hand back, stunned. The frame fell from its hook, but Matilda caught it before it crashed to the floor. Barely.

She shot him a disapproving glare, but he'd already discovered his next curiosity: a twiggy broom Olive had forgotten to put away.

"We'll worry about sleeping arrangements later." Matilda fanned the air in front of her nose and returned Mother to her place of honour. At least the painting hadn't been damaged. Her mother's hair sill haloed her head like a crown of daffodils; her young, vibrant smile glowing.

I know you wouldn't approve, she told her mother, *but he's going to help Nathaniel join you in peace.*

She turned from the painting before she could imagine her mother's scolding. "Elliot, wake up!" she shouted up the stairs. "Olive, will you get us better light?"

Olive gave Lucky a wide berth as she made for the broom closet.

Lucky's attention passed from object to object, from pots and pans hanging above the wood stove to the dusty curtains and the wonder of the foggy window. He pressed a hand into it and watched streaks of water race each other down the glass.

"See?" Matilda said. "I said you'd like it here."

After he'd marvelled at his own palm prints in the window, he found his way back to the door and to the rifle in the corner where it gleamed wickedly under the firelight. Grabbing the end of the barrel, he raised it to his face and peered in.

"No!" Matilda screeched. "Drop that!"

Lucky dropped the rifle to the floor and stumbled back, wide-eyed like she'd struck him. She snatched the weapon away and locked it safely under her arm.

Calm down. He doesn't know how to use it.

"You must never touch this. It hurts people. Like this." She pressed a finger gently to the crater in Lucky's bare chest and at the scarring at his hairline. His eyes lost some of their roundness, and a memory of pain flickered in them. "You understand, don't you? It could kill someone."

"Don't give it to me, then." Elliot's footsteps thumped down the stairs. "I'm in the mood to use it. The sun isn't up yet, why am I?" He dropped down the last step with a lumbering *thud* and blinked away the last of his dreams. "What's *he* doing in here?"

"He desperately needs a bath," Matilda said. "Warm some— On second thought, don't bother with warm water. He won't mind. Just show him what to do to get rid of this horrid smell."

Elliot clapped a hand to his chest and grimaced. "Me? No!"

"Do you think Matilda or I should bathe a grown man?" Olive returned with the lantern she'd found and enticed a little more light out of it as she set it on the table.

"She's the one who's bothered by his smell," Elliot said, though he pinched his nose against the stink, "and she's already peeked at everything he has to hide anyway."

I have not!

Matilda's face burned hot, but she bit back her protest and tapped her fingers threateningly over the barrel of the carbine. "You have two choices: you can show Lucky how to bathe and dress himself, or you can spend the entire afternoon cleaning that stench out of the barn."

Elliot's face paled to a sickly white. "Lucky, come to the bath."

— CHAPTER TWENTY-TWO —

LUCKY

Water. Everywhere.

The boy rubs Lucky's head.

"Hold still. Ugh, disgusting!"

Water falls over Lucky. Stinging. Eyes burn. Lucky growls.

"Lucky, no! I said hold sti— No! Ah!"

— CHAPTER TWENTY-THREE —

MATILDA

By the time Matilda had set a steaming pot of porridge on the table and Olive had seen to the cows, the puddles outside glowed pink under clearer skies and the new sun. From the room by the stairs, Elliot barked orders that Lucky answered with grumbles and chaotic splashes. Elliot gave an aggravated groan, and Matilda and Olive shared a chuckle.

When Elliot stomped out of the room and dropped into his chair at the table, muttering incoherently, water drenched his night-clothes and dripped onto the floor.

Lucky emerged after him, his hair tangled but clean. At the root it grew thick and healthy, but ratty ends dripped pools into one of Nathaniel's old shirts. The buttons fastened in the wrong holes, and his trousers ended too far above his ankles. Tugging uncomfortably at the fabric around his legs, he trudged into the kitchen with a violated frown.

"You'll be used to them in no time," Matilda said. "Come and eat breakfast."

Table manners were another skill Lucky had never learned.

He dug his fingers into his porridge and slopped it over his lap. After he'd knocked Olive's bowl off the table and eaten both his *and*

Elliot's breakfast, Matilda set his porridge on the floor where she wouldn't have to look at his mess until she was done eating.

Now I suppose I must teach him table manners as well. I've gained a third child!

Olive swallowed the last of her rescued porridge and observed Lucky on the floor. "He doesn't smell, but he's still scruffy. Someone should clip his nails and cut the mats out of his hair."

Matilda kneaded her forehead, fighting off the threat of a headache. "No more fuss this morning. I'll do it later."

"Why are you complaining?" Elliot said. "Your morning hasn't been half as bad as mine!"

Why, yes. Apart from the wolf man who tried to kill me, my morning has been splendid.

Matilda pursed her lips. In the chaos of getting Lucky settled in the house, she'd almost forgotten about the wolf man, but now her mind had time to recall the unsettling and ferocious man-beast. Lucky had chased him away for good, hadn't he? Olive didn't need another reason to have nightmares.

"I'll do it," Olive said, interrupting Matilda's thoughts. "I want to help." She pushed her empty dishes away and rushed upstairs.

Timid Olive wanted to help? With *Lucky?* An hour ago she'd been terrified of him!

Matilda warmed wash water for the dishes and sent Elliot to market for supplies to repair the barn door. "Don't go near the woods," she warned him. "And take the rifle with you."

Elliot crammed his feet into his boots. "Why?"

"Richards has been worse than usual," she said after a moment of consideration. It was the truth, if only part of it, and Elliot wouldn't question her. "Stay on the road, and turn Duchess back if you hear dogs."

Elliot gave a scoffing grunt. "I'm not afraid of him or his dogs," he said, but he grabbed the rifle before heading out the door.

When Elliot had left, Olive came back from upstairs with an armful of towels, combs and brushes, and a pair of scissors. She pulled a chair out from the table and patted the seat to encourage Lucky to sit. "Come on."

It takes more than a few gentle words to get him to listen, Matilda thought, but before Olive had a chance to say anything more, Lucky heaved himself up from the floor and nestled in the chair. Matilda shook her head. *That rascal.*

Olive carefully explained to Lucky the purpose of the brush in her hand and what she intended to do to him. Matilda doubted he understood much, but he watched Olive with interest and let her do as she wished.

"Sit still," Olive said.

Working the brush through the net of Lucky's hair, Olive chattered at him with none of the fear she'd shown before, and her hands moved confidently with their task. She treated Lucky little differently than she would Sable, but the smile beaming on her face while she hummed Mother's lullaby was new and wonderful.

Matilda returned to her own duties, gathering the dishes from the table and scrubbing the bottom of the porridge pot while she listened to Olive pause her humming to issue a string of directions.

"Tilt your head. No, the other way. Yes, like that. Now, keep it there, and I'll..."

Clip. Clip. Thump.

Matilda finished with the dishes then cleaned up the floor where Lucky had eaten. As Matilda wiped the last drop of porridge off the floor, Olive said, "Good boy." Matilda peeked over her shoulder, and her jaw dropped. Lucky sat in the chair while Olive glided around him, snipping the last few unruly hairs.

At least Matilda *thought* the man in the chair was Lucky.

Once dull, shoulder-length hair now ended at brow length, licorice black and full of life. It softened as it dried and swept across his forehead with a slight, playful curl at the ends. His knotted beard now lay in bunches on the floor. A few dark hairs stuck to Nathaniel's shaving blade on the table, but Lucky's jaw was almost as smooth as her own. He was much younger than she'd first thought—with his youthful skin filled out again and the ratty hair gone, he looked barely older than herself.

A thin, white line crossed the bridge of his nose, but the scar was old. Where Olive had shaved him, no cuts marred his skin. He'd sat perfectly still for her.

He'd been shaved when I found him too, she remembered. *Why would Richards shave Lucky when he couldn't be bothered to feed or dress him?*

Why did he keep the wolf men? For some dark circus? For mad experiments? And *where* did he keep them? For both wild men to have shown up in those woods, they must have been kept somewhere close. Perhaps Kāi wasn't far off when he'd suggested Lucky had come from the asylum, but, as much as Matilda might like to imagine Richards locked away there himself, she could think of nothing to connect him with that place. The only other possibility she could think of was that the second wild man had followed Lucky's trail to her farm. She shuddered at the thought.

He won't come back. Lucky will keep him away.

"See?" Olive ran her fingers proudly through Lucky's hair to be sure she'd snipped everything. "Now he's handsome enough for church."

Matilda draped her washcloth over the sink to dry. "He can't come to church with us."

"Why not?" Olive asked, her voice wounded.

Because Richards would kill him and probably the rest of us too. With his rifle, his vicious mongrels, and his disregard for where his property ended and hers began, he'd plagued Matilda with enough threats to her safety when all he'd wanted from her was her home. If Richards knew she now sheltered a threat of her own, a swift death would be preferable to whatever torments he'd given the wolf men.

Drying her hands on her apron, Matilda faked a smile. "There are enough rumours about us without adding Lucky to them. Now hurry on with the rest of your chores."

Elliot returned from the market later than expected, setting the rifle in its place by the door and seeing to Duchess, but his hammer resounded through the valley when Matilda stepped outside with Lucky on her tail. The barn door lay in pieces, half-buried by mud, and Elliot stood away from it where he could contemplate solutions without the stink of the barn tainting him. He blew warmth into his hands, then knelt by the door and tapped another nail into place.

"They wouldn't sell the nails for a fair price. They didn't want *Fenians* in their store." Elliot ripped a bent nail from the door like it was a neck he wanted to strangle, and he didn't seem eager to say more about his trip.

They won't want to buy *from us next milking season either.* Matilda hid a frown. "We'll manage." *Somehow.*

"I didn't think to buy new hinges," Elliot said, seeming desperate for a change in conversation. "How did he break the door? It's twice as thick as my arm!"

"He must have worn it down," Matilda said.

"Maybe." Elliot didn't sound any more convinced than she was.

Lucky refused to approach the barn and crouched in a dewy bed of grass at a safe distance, watching her and Elliot with a mix of curiosity and apprehension.

He'd come out without shoes, not that there were any in his size. At least the thistles and cool muck between his toes didn't seem to hurt fairies or demons or whatever manner of being he was.

"What did Olive do to him?" Elliot scrunched his eyebrows as he spotted Lucky. "She's turned him pretty. You can't tell he's a lunatic now."

"You shouldn't say that." She stepped past Elliot into the barn. "You know how sharp his hearing is."

An acrid miasma drifted over the pile of dirty bowls and blood-stained blankets, soaking Matilda with a month-old, foul perfume as she moved toward the back of the building.

She tied her scarf over her nose before searching for the shovel she normally used to muck out Duchess's stall. She found it with the other tools—not placed neatly where she'd left them but on the floor of the tack room, kicked and scattered about the place.

Lord, give me patience, she prayed when she discovered the wheelbarrow tipped on its side and Duchess's saddle tossed on the floor.

"He can't help it, you know," she said to herself as much as to Elliot, choking on her scarf and the smells it couldn't entirely disguise. "Mr. Kāi says he might have grown up without parents or brothers to look after him."

Elliot was silent so long Matilda worried he'd abandoned his chores already, but she found him where she'd left him, his shoulders hunched and his hands thrust into his pockets.

"I don't have parents or a brother." He sounded almost sympathetic until a scowl twisted his features. "But I'm not a monster."

"*Don't* say that!" she said, even though she'd thought the same thing many times. Lucky hadn't moved from his spot in the grass, but he tilted his head at her raised voice. She dropped it low. "Names have power. Say that enough and he might believe you. Then we'll never learn what he knows of Nathaniel."

Elliot's eyes reddened more than his rosy cheeks. His fists pulled free of his pockets and quivered at his sides. "Nathaniel was a bad man like Father," Elliot said, his lip trembling, "and he killed himself. I hate him."

Matilda dropped her shovel next to the pile of dirty bowls. "Take it back."

"No," he said and gave her a mutinous glare.

"Take it back!"

"No!" Elliot kicked his hammer, plopping it into a puddle with a spray of brown water, then stomped out of her sight.

"Elliot!" She ran to the door and craned her neck around the corner.

Lucky stooped in the grass and watched Elliot trudge by. Olive returned from the chicken coop, her arms laden with a now-empty feed bucket, and Elliot stormed past her and across the meadow.

Matilda yanked the scarf from her mouth. "Come back here right now!"

"No!" He broke into a run toward the tree line.

"Elliot!"

Olive set the bucket on the ground. "Let him go, or you'll make things worse."

"Don't you mean *he'll* make things worse?" Matilda stomped out from the barn but winced from a blow of pain when her toes smacked into the corner of the broken door. She bit her lower lip and rubbed her toes against the back of her calf.

And now he's left his chores for me.

"You work on the door," Olive said, and she gave Matilda a charitable look. "I'll muck out the barn."

"You don't have to do that," Matilda said, straightening her toes with another wince. "It's a horrid mess."

"I want to do it." Olive's smile appeared genuine despite her ridiculous statement. She tied her worn scarf over her nose and hiked into the barn, and a moment later, the squeak of the wheelbarrow and the rustle of fetid straw accompanied her work.

Picking the hammer out of the puddle and brushing the worst of the grime off the handle, Matilda tore the warped hinges from the door.

By midday, she'd barely reassembled half of the structure, but Olive escaped the barn with a full wheelbarrow, filthy but triumphant.

"There." She clapped her hands together, ridding herself of dust and straw. "Once the dishes and dirty blankets are washed—or burned, maybe—no one will be able to tell a wild man lived here."

A wild man. Matilda slammed the hammer over a nail with an unsteady blow. It glanced off the head and dented the wood. *A wild man! Elliot!*

She jumped to her feet. Her gaze followed the canyon Elliot's footprints had dragged through the mud, but nothing but more mud and a wall of trees filled her sight.

"He hasn't come back yet," Matilda said.

Olive brushed bits of straw from her skirt, not sensing the concern in Matilda's voice. "He won't come back until the anger is gone. I think it embarrasses him."

Matilda threw the hammer down and scattered her pile of nails. "We have to find him. Now."

"You really should let him come back on his own."

"I can't," Matilda said. "There's another wild man in the woods. Elliot's in danger."

— CHAPTER TWENTY-FOUR —

LUCKY

"Elliot is in danger. Fetch the rifle. Quickly!"

Shouting. Small Female runs. She smells of rotten grass and fear.

"Lucky!" Alpha Female calls. Loud.

No. Hates the cage. Hates it. Hates it! Won't go back. Lucky hides in the grass.

"You're not in trouble." Alpha Female speaks soft sounds. "I need your help."

— CHAPTER TWENTY-FIVE —

MATILDA

Lucky bolted across the meadow faster than a stag. Matilda sprinted after him with Olive close behind, but he leapt into the woods and out of sight.

"Wait!" Matilda shouted. "Stay with us!"

Olive gasped for breath when they entered the woods and were forced to slow their pursuit. "Do you think he understands?"

"I hope he does, because I don't know which tracks to follow."

Matilda's footprints from that morning littered the patches of bare ground between the trees and brush. Elliot's prints criss-crossed with hers, blending trails until she couldn't tell whose wandered left and whose right. Only a barefooted set of prints were clear—their owner raised on the balls of his feet to leave distinctive forms in his wake. She followed their trail and hoped the prints didn't belong to the other wolf man.

"What if the wild man is still here?" Olive huddled so close to Matilda she threw her off her step.

Matilda thought of no comfort to give Olive that wouldn't feel hollow. "I have the rifle," was all she said. She clutched the weapon tighter and tried to keep more fear from creeping upon her.

"We should tell Mr. Harrison," Olive said.

Green, dagger-like needles on the trees and the girls' own quivering breaths were the only signs of life in the woods. Matilda kept her eyes on the prints in the mud. "We can't. He'd take Lucky away from us."

"But what if this wild man hurts someone?" Olive said. "What if he kills someone?"

"He—" Matilda shut her mouth, unable to argue. *But what if telling Joseph gets Lucky killed?*

"Keep Lucky secret if you think you should," Olive said, "but tell Mr. Harrison of the other man. Nathaniel wouldn't want anyone to be hurt while you help his friend."

Olive fell into fearful silence then and left Matilda with wrestling thoughts. *Is the wild man here? Can he hear us?*

Matilda kept alert as the breeze muttered threats to them, but her heart pounded in her ears. It nearly exploded when Olive grabbed her by the arm.

She squeezed Matilda's arm tightly. "Stop," Olive said. "Do you hear that?"

At first Matilda heard nothing but the flow of the Fraser in the distance and the murmur of the breeze through the trees, but then she *did* hear something: a voice. The woods muffled the words, but its tone rose angrily. She turned her ear toward the sound.

"Stop!" the voice commanded. "Go away!"

Olive's teary eyes brightened with relief. "It's Elliot! He's safe—" The smile in her eyes vanished as Elliot's protests raised higher.

"Let go!" Elliot shouted.

Thump. Scratch. Thump.

The sound drew nearer, but they were the sounds of a struggle.

"Let me go! What *are* you?"

Matilda forced her fears back into submission and threw herself toward her brother's shouts. "Elliot!" she called.

Elliot's complaints turned more desperate. Matilda buried her feet in the muck and wedged the rifle against her shoulder, ready to fire at whatever came through the trees. *What if it only angers the wolf man? What if I hit Elliot?*

Branches snapped and flung raindrops from their needles before two figures burst from the trees.

Elliot was draped over Lucky's shoulder, pummelling his fists into his kidnapper's back, but Lucky barely seemed to notice the assault. He set Elliot down before her, looking as pleased with himself as a bird dog dropping a duck at his master's feet.

Elliot rubbed his hip. "I only went for a walk!" he protested. "What's wrong with him?"

Matilda lowered her rifle, pressed a hand to her stomach, and breathed out the tension in her. "He's obedient."

Elliot oozed sour glares until Matilda explained about the wolf man. Then he returned to his chores, far too quiet for the rest of the day, and went to bed an hour early.

Matilda took one of Lucky's blankets—washed twice, though she'd liked Olive's idea of burning them—from where it was drying by the fireplace and stretched it over the floor with Nathaniel's old pillow. "You stay here," she told Lucky, pointing to the nest she'd made for him. He stood at the window, his back illuminated by the flames near Matilda's feet as he watched the shadowed night outside. *Did he hear me?*

When she turned toward the stairs with a yawn, Lucky pulled away from the window and followed behind her, eyeing the steps inquisitively as they creaked under his weight.

"No," Matilda said firmly. Even a step higher than him, she still had to look up to meet his gaze. She raised herself another step and gained half a head on him. That was better. Authoritative. "Stay."

His eyes melted into a pitiful sulk.

"It won't work. Olive's got sadder eyes than you, so you won't sway me so easily."

But Olive's delicate blue eyes always kept a distance from others, resisting human connection at the same time they craved it. Even when she spoke with Matilda, that brittle shield sometimes raised over Olive's eyes—a look that said she waited for the day Matilda abandoned her too. Matilda thought with a pain in her throat that the claws Elliot lashed out with were made from the same uncertainty.

Lucky's eyes were different, and without the barn door to shield Matilda from them, they were...*stronger.* Despite the trauma hidden deep in them, his eyes met hers with an honesty and welcome so overwhelming they swallowed her up before she knew she was falling into their depths.

That desire for connection was the one thing she saw in him that was recognisably human, and it was so compelling she felt herself bowing under the pressure.

"Stay." She turned away before those eyes could break her resolve, but even with her back turned, she felt the weight of his gaze on her as she climbed the rest of the stairs. No creak of the steps followed her this time, but the touch of Lucky's soulful stare clung to her skin long after she'd turned down the hall.

He's safe and warm down there. She tried to shake the feel of him off her. *Let him be.*

Sable dozed outside her bedroom door, and she stepped over the dog and into the room. Olive sat on their bed and combed her river of hair. The yellow locks had lost some of their summer sheen, but they still cascaded around her in soft curls. She looked like a mermaid as she hummed softly to herself, her tune beautiful and sentimental.

Matilda dropped heavily to the bed and released her own dark, dull hair from its twist on her head. Olive motioned for her to turn her back and eased the comb through Matilda's knots.

For a while the only interaction between them was Olive's touch on her hair. Holding in another yawn, Matilda slumped with her elbows on her knees and felt the gentle tug of her hair as Olive weaved it into a braid.

"Elliot doesn't hate him, you know," Olive said with the softness of a feather. Matilda didn't need to ask who she'd meant. "We never had a chance to say goodbye or tell Nathaniel how he hurt us when he ran away. We never got to tell him we love him. Elliot's angry."

But he's angry at the wrong person.

Matilda pursed her lips and took her nearly-finished braid from Olive, working a ribbon around it. Switching places with her sister, she parted Olive's waves into sections and laced them together.

"What if Lucky never learns to speak?" Olive asked.

Matilda's hands paused with her sister's hair caught between her fingers. The locks unravelled from her hands when Olive turned to face her.

"Or..." Olive lowered the shield from her eyes for a moment, leaving them vulnerable and unguarded. "What if you don't like what he has to say? Will you let Nathaniel go then?"

Matilda's fingers knotted together in her lap. "Could you?" she asked.

The look on Olive's face was bittersweet. She shuffled close, looped an arm through Matilda's, and leaned her head on her shoulder.

Tired enough to sleep where she sat, Matilda closed her eyes, but a muffled thump disturbed her respite. Then a jarring clang made her cringe. "What was that?"

"It's coming from downstairs," Olive said.

"If Lucky is getting into the taffies, I'll—" Matilda leapt from the bed and burst out of the bedroom. Sable now lay at the top of the stairs, watching below.

Crash!

Matilda rushed past the dog and down the steps, but in the flicker of firelight, she barely recognized her own house.

Overturned chairs cast crawling shadows around the room. Two of Matilda's best pots rolled on the floor, and the candy jar lay in scattered ceramic shards and taffies. Lucky paced around the room and knocked over anything in his path. Back and forth; back and forth.

"No!" she shrieked.

Back and forth—Lucky didn't stop.

Jumping over the broken jar, Matilda rapped his shoulder hard enough to get his attention. He halted, giving her an offended look.

"No! Bad do— I mean bad Lucky!" *Look at this mess!* She kicked a chair and a pot out of the way and cracked open the front door. Clammy air chilled her skin. "Go! Sleep in the barn tonight."

Lucky's shoulders sagged.

"Out." She gripped the door so hard she almost believed *she* could break it off its hinges.

He hunched his back and stepped out into the damp and dark.

"But it's cold outside," Olive said.

"He'll be fine." Matilda turned to find Olive gliding down the stairs then shut the door behind Lucky. She stomped toward the window to be sure he did as told. The moonlight could barely pick him out from the rest of the night, but even as a shadow he looked crestfallen. "He doesn't feel the cold."

Olive joined her at the window. "What if he runs away?"

"He won't," Matilda reassured her.

"How can you know?"

"Strays don't run away once you feed them."

Lucky's shadow looked small and fragile before the cavernous barn devoured him. Matilda felt a twinge of guilt, but it disappeared the moment she turned back to the mess he'd left behind.

Another night out there, and maybe he'll learn to behave himself.

"Help me clean up this jar, will you, Olive?"

Olive ran off to find the broom and Matilda stayed by the window. Her eyes begged her to close them and drift into sleep, but she blinked at the barn and imagined she could see Lucky inside it.

"When are you going to realize you're human?" she said.

A dark thought responded.

If he is *human.*

October 2nd, 1883

A heavy gloom has lingered in the house since yesterday. Elliot tussled with Junior. I know those two have been itching to fight for months, ever since Junior laughed at Elliot's maths score.

Richards came over to holler at me. Brought his drink with him. No one blamed him for taking to the bottle after his wife passed, but no one thought he'd be inseparable from it these past years either. It has brought out his worst qualities. And probably invented a few more. I suspect it's the reason Junior has been lashing out so much lately. He's much too young to raise himself and his sisters alone.

No matter how I tried to calm him, Richards wouldn't leave until Matilda came outside with the rifle. I don't think I've ever felt such guilt in my life. She shouldn't have to know how to use a gun. She wouldn't *have to if I hadn't left her to fill my shoes as guardian so I could seek glory and adventure. And fail to find either.*

I fear she made a mistake. Richards won't take kindly to her threat, but at least for now he's gone.

There have been strange sounds coming from his property, though, and I don't like any of it. I know he bought himself a few pups to guard his farm, but the way they wail sends shivers down my spine.

I hope Elliot's temper won't make today's fight a regular occurrence. Richards already holds enough grudges against us to do something about it, and he's losing his fear of the consequences.

— CHAPTER TWENTY-SIX —

MATILDA

Before daylight peeked through the bedroom window, Matilda dragged herself out of bed to tend to the animals, and the skies flushed a soft rose colour by the time she adorned her Sunday dress, grabbed yesterday's leftover loaf of bread, and went to the barn.

"I brought breakfast." She stepped into the barn, braced for a terrible odour, but the night had cleared out the building quite well. The air was crisp and cool. Quiet.

And empty.

Lucky's path wore a trail along the inside of the walls, but he wasn't on it. He didn't seem to be anywhere.

"Lucky?"

Panicked, she turned over every corner of the barn. Duchess's stall stood vacant and the door closed. Searching through the straw in the loft turned up nothing but a long-abandoned owl's nest. Even the tack room remained as tidy as she'd left it yesterday.

"Lucky?" she called again, her pitch rising with concern as she stood in the tack room doorway.

A tuft of black hair was just visible above Duchess's saddle in the corner. Wedged behind it and the wall, Lucky sat with his knees against his chest.

She pressed a hand to her throat and stepped into the room for a better view of him. "I thought you'd run off."

His shoulders barely fit between the saddle and wall, and they scrunched up to his ears as he rested his forehead on his knees. At first, she thought he was dozing. His arms held his legs close, and for a moment he seemed more like a frightened child than a dog or a man.

Why does he hate the barn so much?

Whatever it was, it was more than itchy straw and locked doors. The nightly pacing and the way he huddled here in the corner, making himself small and hidden—something about this place disturbed him.

"The house doesn't seem so horrible now, does it," she said, her voice soft. He set his chin on his knees but refused to look at her. "There's no need to pout. Here, eat this."

She presented the loaf of bread to him but lamented the thought of her ever-diminishing sack of flour. Begrudgingly, Lucky accepted the loaf and nibbled the end of it.

Such a child.

"You can leave the barn now, but stay on the farm, understand?" she said. He kept his eyes stubbornly on his loaf of bread but tilted his ear toward her. "Don't go on the roads or into the woods. Stay hidden and don't let anyone see you while the rest of us are gone."

To be safe, she repeated her instructions twice more, taking Lucky by the chin until at last he looked at her.

"Be good," she said. "We'll be back before long." She remained with his chin in her hand and searched his eyes for some assurance he planned to obey her, but when she found herself admiring the amber flecks in them instead, she yanked her hand away and trudged out of the barn, clearing her throat.

As soon as the O'Connors had finished their eggs and buttered toast and Matilda had readied Duchess and the wagon, she herded her siblings out of the warmth of the house. Olive took the reins, and Matilda watched the barn get smaller as the wagon rolled toward the city. Lucky came to the doorway of the barn to watch their departure.

He understands, doesn't he? He'll be safe on his own.

The wagon rocked along the bumpy road. Matilda watched Lucky until the road bent around the trees and he disappeared with the rest of the farm.

— CHAPTER TWENTY-SEVEN —

LUCKY

Gone.

Alpha Female told Lucky to stay. The pack left him. Where did they go? Why did they leave? What is "church"?

The meadow is empty. Lucky's chest hurts. The old wound is scarred, but beneath the scar it hurts.

Stay.

She told Lucky to stay, but the meadow is empty.

— CHAPTER TWENTY-EIGHT —

MATILDA

The Holy Trinity Chapel's sandstone walls shone almost like glass in the morning sun, but the buzzing of gossip and cheerful banter outside the building hushed when Matilda arrived with her siblings.

A few of her old classmates carried babes in their arms or bellies and sent her biting looks as their husbands helped them down from their buggies. The men barely glimpsed at Matilda at all, avoiding her like they would a vagrant. Three widows in pretentious, feathered hats squawked by the chapel door and weren't as quiet with their remarks as they pretended.

"Fenians," one croaked.

"Traitors," said another.

Nasty old harpies, Matilda silently chided.

Olive hooked her arm through Matilda's and squeezed until Matilda's fingers turned numb.

Though the chapel's polished, wooden pews quickly filled, the worshippers shunned the O'Connors' usual seats as though God had marked them for the damned. Elliot slid in first, his stare fuming but kept to the patterns in the wood of the pew ahead. Matilda took her seat by the aisle last, and Olive slumped between them and distracted herself with the wrinkles in her skirts.

The chatter died in the chapel, but the sideways glances lived on. Matilda did her best to ignore them, but one pair of eyes attracted her attention. The way they always did.

Joseph sat in the first row with his mother, his bowler hat removed for the service to reveal his starlight-gold hair, but he looked over his shoulder and locked eyes with her the moment hers crossed over him. His silvery irises mesmerized her until she remembered their last encounter. She snapped her gaze down to her lap and immediately felt silly.

I can't avoid him forever, and Olive is right: he should know of the wolf man.

"Ah, the O'Connors."

A drawling voice and the suffocating scent of whiskey enclosed Matilda and banished all concerns of Joseph. She steeled herself, her teeth clenched.

Richards stood in the aisle with his hollowest grin and his children at a distance behind him. His twin girls clung to Junior the way Olive held fast to Matilda.

Junior threw Elliot a sour look, but for once Elliot ignored the older boy altogether. Disappointed, or maybe relieved, Junior led his sisters to the second row.

Richards remained like a bad smell. Matilda focused ahead at the chapel's ornate altar. *Leave me be, Richards.*

"Sit up front with the pious folk," Richards barked. He sounded almost sober but was unmindful of his volume, and one worshipper cleared his throat disapprovingly. Richards frowned but lowered his voice. That only grated at Matilda more as he leaned in, pouring the scent of tobacco and whiskey over her. "I hear God welcomes all sinners back to His church."

She waved his stench out of her face and snapped before she could get hold of her tongue. "If you're here, that must be true."

Elliot disguised a chuckle and coughed into his hand.

Richards didn't laugh. "Still pretending to be made of iron?" All decorum gone, he dropped his voice even lower, mumbling only for their ears. His filthy teeth bared like a wild man's snarl. "You're only flesh and bone like the rest of us, and bones are real easy to break."

With his voice low and gritty as it oozed between his teeth, Matilda heard his ruthless cruelty in every word. The retort on her lips withered. *Foolish girl! Don't encourage the butcher.*

Elliot stopped coughing, all traces of laughter smothered under his steely glare. He leaned sideways in his seat with his arms tense at his sides. "Are you threatening us? Here?"

Matilda reached across Olive's lap and pinched Elliot's thigh. He shut his jaw tight enough to make the muscles jump, but Olive had to push him back in his seat.

"Just being neighbourly." Richards poured what he probably thought was pleasantness into his voice, but the patronizing stab of his glare spoiled it. "There's all kinds of dangers in those woods. Animals. Madmen."

Madmen? Visions of the wolf man rushing through her head, Matilda stiffened. Had Richards been in the woods the night Lucky had chased the wolf man from the farm? Had he seen Lucky?

"It sounds like you've been drinking," she said, thankful her voice hadn't squeaked.

Instead of another scowl or hurled insult, Richards laughed with some cruel joke. The sound made her skin itch. "No amount of whiskey would change what me and my nephew saw the other night."

"Mr. Harrison?" Matilda sat straighter. *Joseph knows? Did Joseph see Lucky too? Oh, please no.* She could barely breathe as she spoke. "Mr. Harrison knows of the wo— I mean, he saw this madman as well?"

Richards looked self-satisfied by her interest. "He didn't just see it. I called him out to track the man, but the lunatic tried to kill me." He pulled his collar down around his thick neck. Four lines marred the skin like claw marks, shallow but raw. "Joseph was a real man for once. Took him down with one bullet."

"How much does he kn—" Matilda's words caught in her throat as she took in what Richards had said. Shot. Joseph shot the wolf man. *Joseph.* "Did he get away?"

"Get away?" Richards scratched his moustache. "No man gets away from a bullet between the eyes. He's cold and dead now."

Dead?

Afraid she might vomit, Matilda put a hand to her stomach. One month ago that wolf man could have been Lucky—lost and afraid. She imagined Lucky's soft brown eyes glazed and vacant. Dead from Joseph's bullet. Her throat tightened.

"You take care of that little farm of yours." Richards licked his lower lip with a fleshy tongue. "Wouldn't want anything to happen t'you."

He tipped his head to her, but the gesture was full of malice. Matilda held her breath until he'd joined his son and daughters in their pew.

Dead. She rubbed her palms into her knees, leaving wrinkles in her skirts. *Dead.* Nathaniel. The wild man.

Richards had something to do with the appearance of the wild men, so why had he told her about them? Was he testing her reaction—to see if she knew of the wild man who'd gone missing? *He's looking for Lucky.*

And if he—or *Joseph*—found him, Lucky'd be as dead as the others.

She mumbled through the hymns and prayers, but her thoughts spun around the wolf men, Richards, and Joseph. When the service ended, Elliot and Olive rushed out of the chapel, but Matilda struggled to her feet.

Well, they can't have Lucky. She turned into the throng leaving the chapel, carried along in its flow, but she chewed her lip when she realized she'd stepped in line with the Harrisons.

"Oh, Matilda," Mother Harrison said. "It's been too long."

She strode at Matilda's side, her arm hooked through Joseph's. Dark circles hung under his eyes, but Matilda's attention dropped to his hands, searching for blood. His long fingers were white and washed clean.

When she realized what she was doing, so much guilt and shame filled Matilda's chest it hurt to look at Joseph. What right did she have to judge him when she'd stood in his place that night—her rifle pointed at the beast?

Fearing he'd see her thoughts, she turned to Mother Harrison instead, but that only gave her another shock.

Mother Harrison had circles of her own digging deep, dark wells beneath her eyes, and her cheerless dress drooped around her arms and middle.

She's wasting away!

"Dear." Mother Harrison gestured for Matilda to come closer and took Matilda's hand in cool fingers. "You've been too busy to visit an old woman like me, have you?"

She said it with a teasing smile, but Matilda's gut wrenched. She clumsily explained about the fence they were rebuilding and placed her other hand over the woman's bony fingers. She warmed Mother Harrison's hand and tried desperately to find in her something of the fierce guardian she remembered.

The three of them walked at Mother Harrison's pace, which moved too slowly even to be called leisurely. Mother Harrison's heels dragged on the floor, but Matilda pretended not to notice.

No one dared threaten or slight Matilda while she walked with the beloved Harrisons. There was no welcome in their eyes, but the men acknowledged her with a curt nod of their heads and the women kept their criticism locked behind fake smiles. Oh, the power of the good Harrison name!

Stepping out into the sunlight, Joseph donned his hat and helped his mother cross the muddied ground.

"Good day," Matilda said as Joseph assisted his mother into his crimson buggy, but he didn't let Matilda leave so easily.

"Hold on," he said. "I'll escort you to your wagon."

"I—" Matilda couldn't get another word out. The delighted gleam in Mother Harrison's eyes as she saw Matilda and her son together shone too brightly for Matilda to refuse.

After he'd settled his mother into her seat and made sure she was warm enough, he gestured to Matilda's solitary wagon farther down the street. Once they moved out of his mother's earshot, he said, "She misses you, you know. Even if only for her sake, there's no need to avoid me."

"I wasn't."

"You were." He didn't sound angry, not that he ever did. He even gave her a fragment of a smile, though it strained almost as much as his mother's had. "If I'd known I'd frighten you away, I'd have made sure you were completely charmed before asking you to marry me."

I was completely charmed. I still am.

Couldn't he see the effect even the sound of his voice had on her? Didn't he hear the way her heart thumped in her chest even now—the way it ached to see him hiding his pains behind jokes and smiles? "I didn't know how to face you," she admitted.

"There isn't a way you could face me that would disappoint." The compliment should have made her blush, but he seemed elsewhere with heavy thoughts. She wished she could tear his burdens away and let him breathe again.

"I heard about the wolf— I mean the madman," she said, testing Joseph's receptiveness with her confession.

His attention returned to her with a sharp turn of his head and an incredulous stare. "How did you know? Ah, of course. Uncle Jake." His teeth ground together. "Even he should know better than to gloat about something like that."

Seeing the way Joseph tensed at the memory, Matilda felt another twist of guilt in her gut. How could she have blamed Joseph for even one second? "You saved your uncle's life," she said, trying not to sound dissatisfied. "Are you all right? It must have been a shock."

"A shock, yes. To put it mildly."

He gave her a hint of a frown but said no more until they almost reached her wagon, Olive and Elliot looking pale and fiddling with something in the back. Before they got too close Joseph stopped, and, as though tied to him by an invisible string, she stopped too.

His countenance was serious and his gaze piercing. "I know you're determined to stay on that farm, but will you promise me something?"

One little promise—one more string tying her to Joseph when she should be letting go. But how could she ignore any request that came on a voice like his? She nodded.

"I'm sure your biggest threat is my uncle," he said, "but after what happened the other day, I don't like the thought of you alone out there. If anything happens—if anyone troubles you—you'll tell me, won't you?"

His gaze was so intense Matilda almost confessed about Lucky to him right there. She wanted to let Joseph take all her secrets from her, but in the back of her mind she knew she couldn't give Joseph any more worries when she couldn't even give him her hand.

"I know where to find you," she said, and she let him believe it was a promise, but she struggled to hold Joseph's bewitching gaze. It made her feel unworthy.

"Thank you." At last another smile warmed the cares in his face.

Olive and Elliot seemed eager to leave when they finally reached the wagon, but they made no complaints. In the front, Olive perched with her mittened hands clutching the reins. Elliot reclined against the canvas-covered lumber he'd left in the bed of the wagon and stared at his knees. Both pretended not to notice Matilda or Joseph. Had they been quarrelling?

"Good day, Mr. Harrison." Matilda accepted Joseph's hand as she climbed into the wagon. "Tell your mother it was lovely to see her."

"Only her?" Joseph said, turning his charm back on. It suited him so well she worried she'd be beguiled and forget the weight of the struggles he carried. Maybe that's what he wanted.

She hoped she wasn't smiling like a fool. "Was there someone else?" she teased as she slid next to Olive.

Something moaned. No, not moaned. *Growled.*

Elliot dug his elbows into the lumber and glanced over his shoulder at Olive.

"Oh." Olive slapped one mittened hand to her stomach. "I should have eaten more this morning."

Matilda furrowed her brow. *Odd. Olive ate as well as usual.*

"Ah, Olive is hungry." Joseph leaned on the side of the wagon and offered Olive a friendly grin. "You'd better hurry home before she withers away. She's pretty just as she is."

Elliot groaned, rolling his head back. "Now you've done it! Now Olive is going to write your name all over her journal like Matilda does."

"I do *not.*" Matilda's face burned, and she wished she could turn invisible. *I can't believe he said that to Joseph.*

"Elliot," Olive protested under her breath.

"Don't upset your sisters," Joseph said for the girls' benefit, but he bent toward Elliot with a sly look. His voice dropped, secretive. "Does she really write about me? What does she write?"

"Mr. Harrison, don't you encourage him," Matilda said.

"I'd never dream of it." Joseph tipped his hat and winked at Elliot playfully. "Good day to you all."

"Good day—"

The words hadn't fallen from Matilda's mouth before Olive turned Duchess into the street. The wagon jerked left. Joseph jumped right to avoid it, and Matilda grabbed the dash to keep herself from sliding out of her seat. Olive snapped the reins and raced Duchess down the road.

"Olive, slow down." Matilda held her hat on her head. "*You've* no need to be embarrassed, and besides that, Mr. Harrison is out of sight. Slow down!"

"She can't." Elliot shoved his weight awkwardly into the pile of wood at his back as though holding the pile down. He didn't seem comfortable at all.

"What are you hiding?" Matilda asked.

He pressed his lips together as she reached for the canvas, but he didn't try to stop her. "Careful."

Taking the corner, Matilda peeled back the canvas and peeked under it. Sprawled awkwardly between roughly-hewn logs and Elliot's elbows, Lucky stared up at her.

What is he doing here? She threw the canvas back over him and craned her neck in every direction. *Did anyone see him?*

The city smelled of fish and breathed with lively voices, but the only people who paid the O'Connors any mind were those who got caught in the spray of mud and puddle water as Olive sloshed the wagon by. Too occupied with sending dirty looks or brushing off the mess on their clothes, none took any care for the stranger hiding under the canvas.

"You brought him with us!" Matilda accused, turning to her brother.

"Why are you looking at me?" Elliot asked. "You know as well as I do we left him at home."

"He was already waiting in the wagon when we came out of church." Olive drove past a gentleman in a long frock coat, spraying mud on his shoes. "S-sorry!" she shouted into the street, but she only urged Duchess on faster.

Lucky was outside the church the entire time? In the open? "Did Richards see?" Matilda gripped the dash until she got flakes of paint under her nails. *What if he recognized him? What if he tells Joseph?*

"I don't know," Elliot said. "I don't think so."

Olive snapped the reins again, and the wagon lurched forward. "We shouldn't have left him by himself. He's lonesome."

"Why?" Elliot asked with disbelief. "Sable was there with him."

"He's not a dog, and somewhere inside I think he knows it." Olive took a tight corner and jumped in front of a black cabriolet, startling the matching bay geldings that pulled it.

"Olive, slow down or you'll only draw more eyes," Matilda said.

"How do you plan to keep him home?" Elliot asked Matilda as Olive slowed the wagon. Barely. The shops and buggies still flew by them. "He broke down the barn door, remember? Are you going to chain him?"

A grumble of protest rippled the canvas under Elliot.

"Of course not." Matilda directed her answer to Lucky more than her brother. The stirring beneath the cover stilled. "Someone will have to keep him company while we're gone."

"I'll do it," Elliot offered eagerly.

"You won't." Matilda thought of the way her old classmates had glared at her in the chapel. "None of us can afford to miss church. They'll think they've frightened us away. I won't give them the satisfaction."

"Who else is there?" Elliot asked.

"There's one person," Matilda said. *Just the one.* "Olive, turn the wagon around."

Matilda felt like a child, sneaking up to the Harrison manor and throwing pebbles at the attic window. She hid as best she could, blocked from the door by the twiggy maple. She tossed two pebbles at the glass without consequence. Had Kāi gone somewhere?

Mother Harrison's calm voice and Joseph's jaunting tones emanated from the house. They'd be in the sitting room, sharing a rare moment when Mother Harrison was in a joyful mood and Joseph had time to relax. He'd probably be smoking, and she'd be telling stories Joseph had heard hundreds of times but always pretended were new.

Matilda crept toward the gravel drive to find another handful of pebbles, but as she searched for lighter stones that wouldn't damage the window, her gaze followed the trail toward the stables behind the house. Joseph's polished red buggy stood visible within, the building's doors open wide. With the melody of Joseph's voice chiming from inside the house, Matilda took her chances with the stables.

Instead of must and oil, the Harrison stables smelled crisply of young pine, and the straw under Matilda's heels gave a pleasant crinkle. Joseph's horse politely nickered at her from where he stood hitched to a post. He was handsome, with graceful legs and glossy, white fur. As well-mannered as Joseph too. He stood placidly as Kāi appeared with a bucket of clean brushes and almost dropped them at the sight of Matilda.

"Why are you here?" Kāi asked. He recovered quickly, rebalancing the bucket before choosing a curry brush from it and setting the rest down. The gelding half shut his eyes as Kāi focused on massaging him with firm circles of the brush. "Mr. Harrison is inside."

"I know," she said. Even before she'd become more brazen to defend her farm and siblings, Matilda had never been skilled with subtlety. She wished she'd had more time to prepare a convincing speech, but she suspected Kāi might have seen through her anyway. "You're working? When I stayed here, the Harrisons gave me free time on Sunday mornings."

"I have nowhere to go. I can't go back to the teahouse without causing Mîfä trouble." Kāi raised his head from his task and narrowed his eyes at her. "Why do you ask?"

His admission chimed more beautifully to Matilda than the chapel choir's hymns.

"You're smiling." Kāi's eyes narrowed still further. "Why do I think you're about to ask for another favour?"

"I wouldn't ask if it wasn't important," Matilda said.

By the time they returned to the meadow, Olive's stomach genuinely grumbled for food. The moment the log farmhouse came within sight, Lucky elbowed his way out from under Elliot and hopped to the ground. He raced home but kept the wagon always in his sight.

Winter had brought shorter days with it, and they ate their supper by the light of the fireplace and two dripping candles on the table. After supper, Matilda sent Lucky to clean the beans and sourdough crumbs from his face, and Olive retrieved the family Bible. While she read aloud, Elliot cleaned the dishes, Matilda stitched a tear in her brother's coat, and Lucky sprawled on the floor at her feet and kept her toes warm. When Olive's eyes strained too much to read more, Matilda sent the children to bed. She spread Lucky's blanket on the floor in front of the fireplace again, pulling the corners to straighten it.

"No more pacing," she told him as he crouched beside her and watched. "Understand?"

Firelight intensified the red and gold flecks in his eyes. Cleverness shone there as clearly as the fire in the hearth, but some barrier Matilda couldn't break kept it trapped away. He didn't answer her. Maybe he never would.

No, he will one day. He must.

After she'd tugged the wrinkles out of the blanket, she repeated her orders with a shake of her finger. "No pacing."

She made for the stairs and heard the soft padding of toes behind her. When she climbed the first step, she turned on her heels and blocked Lucky's passage.

He pulled back at the last moment, sparing her from a collision. Again, she found herself looking up at him. She climbed another step.

No. Stay here.

She'd meant to say it aloud, but when she met his longing eyes, different words fell from her tongue. "All right." She threw her hands up in defeat. "Stay in Elliot's room, but don't expect good company."

Elliot already floated on the edge of a dream when Matilda knocked on his door and informed him Lucky would be staying. Her brother glared with sleep-clouded eyes, mumbled something certainly offensive, and rolled his back to her. She pushed Lucky inside the room and shut the door behind him.

Olive, too, already dozed when Matilda stepped over Sable in the hall and slipped into her room. Her sister had braided her hair by herself and curled up with a mountain of blankets. She made the peaceful hums she sometimes did when her dreams were comforting.

Sleep warred with Matilda's eyelids as she worked at her hair and changed into her nightclothes in a stupor. She climbed into bed and jotted only a few words into her journal. *There. I didn't write Joseph's name even once this time.* Leaving the journal on the side table, she pulled the covers up to her neck, put out the bedroom lantern, and let the waking world fade.

She last remembered the creak of Elliot's door and footsteps tiptoeing into the hall.

I told you he wouldn't be good company, she thought, and then her own dreams carried her away.

October 20th, 1883

Mrs. Wellington called her sons home for a family visit, so after supper with the Harrisons, I took Joseph out for a few drinks instead of heading for the printing press. It's about time I congratulated him on becoming a constable anyway. I'm already hearing talk around town about how impressed people are with him.

Strange how we've grown up. Used to be you couldn't keep us from talking with our fists, and now we can tolerate each other's company. Even enjoy it. We should have known when we were boys we had more in common than not. Both of us suffered at the Fenians' hands, if for different reasons. Both of us changed forever by that raid. Both hiding anger. Both without fathers.

The only difference is he still loves his.

My gaze slips into the trance at times. It used to be from curiosity, but now it's from need. Mother needs a miracle only Miss Kovacs can give, and Miss Kovacs has made her stance clear. That leaves me to become Mother's miracle, but I haven't been able to hear her Name. I can't call it. Can't heal it. Mother is little more than a skeleton and barely leaves her bed. Who knows how much time she has to wait on me?

It wasn't the proper time or place to practise, but once we'd downed enough drinks to excuse the blank look in my eyes as I fell into the trance, I let the Power flow through me.

I've wondered if those without knowledge of the Power can sense its presence. If Joseph sensed it, he must have thought it was merely a shift in temperature. He scratched his neck but said nothing, and his aura responded to mine only for a moment before it went still. Composed, like him. A cool grey today, not clouded like the night I'd first seen it. The first night I'd seen any Name.

I think I was eleven. I don't even remember what the fight was about, but we'd gotten into one again on a night after supper at his house. Gotten into one so hard we'd ended up falling off the porch, both of us hitting our heads on the way down. It so confounded me I remember feeling like I was floating. The trance fell and surrounded me easily, like it had been there all along and I'd never bothered to notice.

I thought we'd both died when I rolled over and saw the stormy grey of the light surrounding him. It was so hazy at first. Only faintly there, but it made me angry to think that he must have become an angel to glow that way.

At times while I recovered, I saw more lights: Mother's peach, Matilda's burgundy, or my own tidal wave of blue. I didn't tell the physician about the colours in case he'd have me sent to the asylum, but I couldn't stop myself from searching for them. From learning to read their shifts in hue the way most people read faces.

Joseph and I have both learned to control our tempers better now. No, to fuel *our tempers into our work. I've met enough constables to know Joseph takes his role as keeper of the peace to a different standard. He keeps an eye out. An ear open. People trust him.* I *trust him more than myself.*

He asked about Matilda. He's too proper to say it, but I think he might be sweet on her. He could give her a better life than I, but he better not try to charm her until she's grown up and finished school.

— CHAPTER TWENTY-NINE —

MATILDA

Nathaniel visited Matilda's nightmares again. He called to her through an impenetrable mist, his words impossible to understand but his voice piercing her so severely with horror and pain she thought it would kill her. She ran through the fog, aching to find him, but she couldn't find her way through it. The mist crashed over her like an ocean sweeping a rowboat out to sea. She crumpled to a ground she couldn't feel and drowned in the waves of her brother's pleading voice.

She woke with her covers crushing the air out of her lungs. She kicked them off and sat up with a gasp. The morning crept into the bedroom in a dreary glow, warmer than yesterday. Instead the cold Matilda felt came from within.

She blinked away the worst of the dream. Opening the nightstand drawer, she pulled out Nathaniel's coin from the back corner where she'd hidden it after she'd decided to keep Lucky. The chill metal in her palm felt like touching a piece of Nathaniel's soul from beyond the grave.

Soon, she told him, willing her thoughts to find her brother in that dreadful mist. *I'll free you from that place as soon as I can.*

Once her hand had warmed the coin until she no longer felt a connection to her brother's spirit, she tied the cord around her neck and slid her feet into her slippers. She arranged the blankets over Olive's shoulders and stepped out of the room.

Two shapes stretched across her path in the dim hall, and she stumbled back to avoid tripping herself. One shape she recognized as Sable, snoring with her head on her paws. The other was a Lucky-sized form at her feet. He lay on his side, his knees bent slightly and his head resting on an arm. He breathed slowly, lost in dreams of his own. As she listened to the soft, regular sounds of his breath, the fears from her nightmare released a little of their hold on her.

It was only a dream.

She fetched a blanket from the cedar chest and draped Lucky in it, wondering only after she'd tucked his toes under it why she'd bothered. He didn't need it. She tugged the blanket up to his chin anyway and headed downstairs.

Though she'd calmed her fear, the dream infected Matilda's thoughts long after the sun had brightened the world and Olive and Elliot had left for school. She couldn't quite lose herself in her chores. The cold isolation of the mist tainted her even while she sweat by the heat of the oven to replenish their store of bread.

The stairs creaked, and a moment later Sable nuzzled the back of Matilda's knee. She wasn't alone in the mist after all. Matilda glanced down at the dog but found Sable wasn't the only one behind her.

She barely kept herself from leaping into the oven. "Lucky! Don't sneak up on me!"

Unruffled, he watched over her shoulder as she returned to her work. She kneaded a second, over-sized batch of dough, and he leaned close enough for his breath to tickle the back of her neck and tingle down her spine. She nearly burned herself when she slipped the first batch out of the oven.

Once Olive and Elliot returned from school in the mid-afternoon, Matilda's work went faster. She left the freshly-baked bread to cool on the counter and washed the mixing bowl, but after she'd put it away, she discovered two of the loaves missing.

A trail of crumbs led to the corner by the fireplace where Lucky sat and licked his fingers.

Groaning, she shook a finger at him until he looked remorseful and retrieved the mixing bowl again. *Better make a third batch.*

When daylight began to fade, she helped Olive see to the cows for the final time that day, and everywhere she went Lucky followed. She and Olive spoke to him as they worked, recounting the Irish tales Mother had told them as children.

He responded best to the dramatic changes in Olive's storytelling. He leaned in with awe when her voice dipped secretively, and his face contorted with surprise when, in a sudden burst of excitement, she revealed shocking twists in her tale. Matilda watched the subtle shifts of emotion stream across his features and marvelled at the depth and mystery of the thoughts locked inside him.

At last Elliot completed repairs on the barn door, fastening the iron hinges Matilda had found in Nathaniel's box of tools. It took all three O'Connors to lift it into place while he secured it. How had Lucky taken it down? She looked over her shoulder, expecting to find him at her heels as he'd been all day, but there was only the farmhouse and field.

Where had he gone?

She couldn't spot him in the meadow, but when she heard the cows fussing in the pasture, she left Elliot and Olive to finish fastening the door and hurried to the pen.

Kicking up mud as he broke through the herd, Lucky chased Duchess and the cows around the pasture. They scattered when he rushed at them, and their hooves churned the ground into a bog. Lucky didn't snarl or snap; he frolicked about the field and got muck all over Nathaniel's clothes. The beasts seemed more annoyed than frightened by his play, but Duchess's ears flattened. She'd kick him soon. He'd deserve it.

"Lucky!" Matilda called. At the rebuking tone in her voice, he dropped lower to the ground and tried to hide from her behind the herd. "Come here!"

With his head sinking into his shoulders, Lucky plodded toward her.

He spent an hour repenting in the barn, but as Matilda found clean clothes for him in Nathaniel's old dresser, she stared out the window and ran her thumbs absently over the stiff collar of her brother's shirt.

One month ago he would have killed the cows. Maybe he's finally ready.

The next afternoon Olive and Elliot scribbled math equations at the table, wearing mismatched expressions of concentration and boredom, and Matilda sat Lucky down next to them for his first English lesson.

She tested his ability with writing and, as expected, found he had none. It took her a half hour to get him to hold the pen properly, and when she tried to teach him the alphabet, he scribbled wild lines on the paper and spilled Olive's ink.

Maybe we should start with something simpler.

Matilda cleaned up the ink stains as best she could and took Lucky around the house, naming everything she saw slowly, deliberately.

"Wall," she said. "Waaall." She ran her fingertips over the panels and studied Lucky's reaction. He glanced only briefly at her before he switched his interest toward the window. Matilda stomped her foot, catching his attention again. "And this is the floor."

Lucky observed her with blank eyes.

"Try it. Open your mouth."

He did, widely and showing every glistening tooth.

Matilda's lip curled back in disgust at his open maw. "Not like—Oh, never mind. Now say it. *Floor.* I'll give you a taffy if you do."

Lucky licked his lips hungrily then inhaled deeply. She leaned toward him, anticipating.

He released his breath with a huff, gave a disappointed glance toward the taffy jar, and moved to look out the window.

Matilda fell into the chair beside Elliot and propped her head up on her wrists. "I don't understand. He followed us all the way to church to be with us, but now he pretends I'm not here."

"He's smart." Elliot folded his arms on the table and stared down at his slate, only the first line of his math equation written down.

"I think you're going about it all wrong," Olive said before Matilda could flick her brother's ear for his insult. She'd already filled in her slate and now scrawled spirals into the margins absently as she spoke. "Lucky already understands English. He'll speak when he's ready."

"I can't wait for him to be ready." *Nathaniel can't wait for him.* "He understands English, but he doesn't...*understand.*"

Elliot chalked a seven on his slate but smudged it off with his sleeve a moment later. "That makes less sense than these numbers."

"He understands, but I don't think he realizes he's not speaking," Matilda said. "He sees no reason to change."

Olive finished off an elaborate spiral with a flourish of her chalk. "Then you have to make him want to change."

"He's better the way he is," Elliot said. "Do you know anyone else who can punch through a door? I'd like to watch him try that on Junior."

Matilda ignored her brother. "How do I make him want to change when everything bores him?"

"He's not bored." Olive turned her head toward the window and drew her river of hair over her shoulder. "Look at him."

"I have looked at him." Matilda raised her chin from her hands and rubbed at her temple, but she passed her eyes over Lucky anyway.

Shy rays of light through the window caught the darting movement of his eyes. He watched something outside, probably a hare or a barn cat, and his back tensed. Every muscle tightened, unmoving but for his toes. Those he tapped rapidly but soundlessly on the floor.

"Maybe you should have let him play with the cows after all," Olive said. "He's been cooped up too long."

Elliot smudged out another wrong answer. "Are you saying he needs to be taken on a walk?"

"That," Matilda said, watching Lucky's toes bounce on the floor, "is not a bad idea."

Trees flew behind Matilda as she galloped Duchess up the road. Above them, a single, harmless cloud turned purple from the sunset, but the sound of thunder came from Duchess's hooves. No wind blew but the one they made with their flight.

Her eyes caught a flash of movement in the trees. Duchess galloped faster than any creature on earth, but Lucky kept pace from the cover of the woods. Now and again she spied a face or sprinting leg between the trunks.

"You're too slow!" Matilda teased.

Lucky raised his knees higher, flying over the ground and competing for the lead. He was an impossible blur of motion Matilda could hardly look away from as he pulled ahead of Duchess.

He thinks he can beat me!

A girlish giggle escaped Matilda's mouth, and she nudged Duchess even faster down the road. Somehow the mare complied.

When had Matilda stopped this? When had she given up play and excitement and *life*? Had she grown too old for it already or simply forgotten how it felt to laugh?

Before they caught sight of the road to Richards's farm, Matilda turned her mount and raced Lucky back to the meadow, but even after beating him there by a head, she didn't want to quit. By the excited gleam in Lucky's eyes, neither did he.

Reining the poor mare back to a relaxed trot, Matilda crossed the meadow and found a familiar trail through the woods. Only a few game trails weaved through the trees with enough room for a horse and rider, and Duchess bounced along them between the evergreens. Their energizing scent called to memories of Matilda's youth. She'd run down this same path as a child, screaming and laughing as Nathaniel chased her. She remembered days picking yellow wildflowers with Olive and the time Elliot had broken his arm falling from one of the bristly trees. Even now she could almost hear the lilt of Mother's voice calling her home for supper.

As a child she'd forgotten all her troubles in these woods. Strange that the trees now brought back everything she'd hidden away.

Lucky jogged barefoot behind her, immune, as far as she could tell, to any injury from rocks and roots under his toes. His breath came evenly, and his skin lacked any sheen of sweat. What a curious creature he was.

What would it have been like if she'd met him when she'd been a small girl in these woods—before her eyes had lost their wonder and her heart its sense of adventure? Would his lack of speech have bothered her then? Maybe they'd have been proper friends instead of…whatever they were now. Nathaniel would have loved every last one of Lucky's mysteries.

Nathaniel did *love him,* she reminded herself. *He must have if he gave him that coin.*

But why would Nathaniel have given Lucky something important to Matilda?

The rush of the Fraser filled her ears as the woods thinned and she drew nearer to the river's banks. Duchess slowed to a plodding walk, and once they'd escaped the tree line, Matilda pulled back on the reins and slipped out of the saddle. Lucky emerged from the woods behind her with windswept hair.

Soon ice would cover the Fraser, but for now a few boats dared the cold waters, their reflections marred by the rippling flow of the river. Matilda kept a safe distance. She tied Duchess nearby and found a dry stump to sit on. Lucky sat on the ground beside her, and together they watched the calming motion of the river.

She attempted another lesson, pointing out anything within sight. Boat. River. Grass and rock. Sky and cloud. Now that he'd had a chance to run off his extra energy, Lucky gave her his eager attention, but he didn't speak a word. He only watched with interest and kept his secrets locked behind his lips.

"I know you understand." She rubbed rosy fingers together and tucked them between her knees. "So why don't you speak? What's wrong with you?"

She'd asked the question with the best of intentions, only realizing how insensitive it was after it had escaped from her mouth. Lucky didn't seem offended. Maybe he wasn't capable of anger.

Fear, yes. He was capable of fear so ferocious it terrified even those around him. How could she forget the way he'd roared like a beast when he'd woken in the barn? That night seemed like another man and another lifetime, but it hadn't been anger that had driven him mad.

If his fear had made him violent, perhaps it also kept him silent.

"Are you afraid to speak to me?" Matilda asked. "I was once so afraid I couldn't move or speak. I've never told anyone of that night, so I suppose I could understand if you felt the same."

Lucky watched the boats on the river as they drifted out of sight toward the city docks, but his ear tilted toward her, catching every rise and fall of her voice. *He's always watching—always paying attention. Maybe he simply needs me to show him what to do.* "What if we each told each other one secret? Hmm? I'll tell you about that night, and you tell me something in return, agreed?"

Lucky shifted his weight, supporting himself on one arm and leaning toward her until they almost touched. For once his silence made her feel easier—like she could say anything and he wouldn't make light of her silly fears. She didn't have to pretend to be brave. She didn't have to pretend to be anything she wasn't. Swallowing her doubts, she took a deep breath.

"I don't remember much, only the feel of a fear so overpowering I lost myself in it. I don't remember what woke me up or even much of what happened after, but I stood there as Joseph struggled with the servant."

Matilda pulled her hands out from between her knees and hugged them around her body. She almost felt the same ominous air from that night press in against her as she recalled the visions she'd seen. The images blurred together, faces and forms all a haze. Only one image in her mind stood clear from the others: Joseph writhing beneath another man who bruised and battered him.

Lucky bent his elbow and closed that last, narrow space between them, his shoulder pressing gently into her thigh. It was a small touch that reminded her of Sable brushing up against her legs. His eyes pulled away from the horizon and closed as if imagining Matilda's words into being.

"Someone called my name. Joseph, I suppose. He begged me to run, but I couldn't move. What a useless mess I was." She pushed the images of Joseph's fight out of her mind, even the memory enough to make her ill. "The manor was supposed to be strong and safe, but that was the same night Nathaniel disappeared. I was suddenly supposed to be Olive and Elliot's guardian, but I spent my first night home terrified of the dark and noise. I'd forgotten how the wind breathed against the house. I kept thinking someone had broken into our home. I kept thinking I'd lose someone else. I don't want to lose anyone else."

She hadn't intended to tell him so much, but Lucky listened to it all. His eyes cracked open in a sliver of russet brown. She turned on her stump and bent over her knees toward him, squinting at him as though it would help her understand the workings of his head.

"Now you tell me a secret. Something simple to start. What's your real name? Hmm? Or how did you get that scar?" She brushed her finger over the line across his nose, but he said nothing. "How did you know my brother?"

While Lucky stared ahead as wordless as he always was, she tugged at the collar of his shirt. Elliot had been lazy with the buttons. Two at the top sat undone and gave her plenty of room to expose Lucky's neck.

The rash at his throat had vanished long ago, but she imagined the raw, peeling marks colouring his skin. Chains and collars.

Nathaniel's neck was torn when I found him... Maybe it wasn't from the dogs after all.

"What happened to you?" Matilda shook her head to banish the horrors of her brother's lifeless body. She took Lucky's face in her hands and turned his head until he tore his eyes from the river and his soft brown windows opened to her. "You know you can tell me," she said. "You know I won't hurt you, don't you?"

Lucky didn't speak with words. Gently, he stretched toward her and brushed his forehead against hers before she knew what he was doing. The touch lasted only a fleeting moment, but the surprise warmth of his skin against hers tingled all the way down to her toes. She went still, afraid to move and as empty of words as he.

He pulled away first, turning back to watch the last boat disappear from the river, but Matilda's body remembered the feel of his touch like a brand on her skin. She leaned back slowly, her hand rubbing circles over a heart that wouldn't calm.

What was that?

Sable had nuzzled her thousands of times to show loyalty or affection, but it had never awoken Matilda like that—never plucked the breath right out of her chest and kindled a flame there in its stead. Lucky showed only the loyalty of a dog to his master. Why should it make her heart flutter?

He hadn't spoken with words, but in that moment, she'd heard his answer to her final question as clearly as if he'd spoken it in her ear. It hadn't been the answer she'd hoped for, but this simple response tore a few bricks out of a wall between them she'd bruised her fists trying to break down.

I know, Lucky told her.

— CHAPTER THIRTY —

MATILDA

Morning trail rides through the woods became a ritual that calmed Matilda as much as sitting down to her journal, and they were the only thing that gave her the patience to survive the frustration of Lucky's stagnant English lessons.

She woke early each day, stepping over Lucky where he dozed outside her door. Once she'd seen to the animals and the sun peered over the east, she would saddle Duchess, whistle for Lucky, and fly down a beaten path. At the edge of the woods she'd sit on her stump with Lucky beside her, and they'd watch the crimson sunrise tickle the Fraser awake.

As the weeks passed, the river transformed from a roving swell of water to a glassy mirror of ice. Matilda had always thought winter a depressing, sombre thing, but watching the play of light over the Fraser each morning was a peaceful dream. She hadn't known how much she'd needed that peace until she'd breathed in the serenity with Lucky at her side.

Then, when she did pull out her old leather journal before bed, she had something worth writing.

As he'd promised, Kāi walked to the farm each Sunday morning, rubbing at the bluish pillows that coloured the skin under his eyes these days.

Matilda didn't dare ask if the bags were from sleepless nights thinking of his love at the teahouse or if he'd developed them because of Mother Harrison's poor health. Each week the circles seemed darker than the last.

For Kāi's first visit, he and Lucky had stared at each other with so much distrust Matilda had feared it might not be safe to leave them alone after all. The two men had weighed on her mind so heavily during the church service she'd barely noticed what was now the usual disapproving whispers and sidelong glances sent to her pew. When she'd rushed the family back to the farmhouse afterwards, Lucky had expressed his displeasure at being abandoned by wilfully ignoring everyone.

At least he had for a while. After less than an hour, his self-made isolation had driven him to loneliness. He'd promptly forgiven them and lay over Matilda's feet while she sat by the fire.

Despite their mutual misgivings, by the third Sunday Lucky had greeted Kāi at the door as a member of their odd little pack. Kāi had pretended not to be moved by it, but last Sunday he'd brought some sort of Chinese sweet for Lucky, and when she'd come home, she'd spied Kāi teaching Lucky how to shave.

For some reason the scene made her think of Nathaniel. She couldn't help thinking he'd have taught Elliot to shave with the same brotherly affection.

It stormed most of the Saturday before Christmas, the rain turning to ice against the windows until the sun rose high to battle the frost, and Matilda didn't take Lucky for his run until the clouds had emptied. Just before evening, she led the way into the grove with Lucky trotting behind Duchess. Gleaming under the raindrops that still speckled each branch or leaf among the brush, the woods felt mysterious and new.

Already the sun's light faded, and cold prickled Matilda's cheeks. After testing out a few new trails, she considered heading back before she got frostbite, but deep into the woods a familiar arch of intertwined trees loomed before her. She leaned back in the saddle and brought Duchess to a halt.

The trees stood bare of all but a few lifeless needles and a damp sheen that darkened their rough bark. They crooked high overhead, and beyond them a winding path overgrown with weeds cut deeper into the woods. A hare's tracks crossed the path up ahead, but it seemed too wide for a game trail. Perhaps it was an abandoned wagon route, long forgotten before Richards or O'Connor had set foot in the woods. Though the forbidding dead arch gave no welcome, the road's secrets beckoned to Matilda with the unknown.

Lucky paused beside Duchess, but his eyes followed Matilda's gaze. He stiffened with attention. Did his sharp eyes see something she couldn't?

"Shall we see where this goes?" she asked.

She nudged Duchess under the arch and down the path, but after a few beats of the mare's hooves, Matilda noticed the space on either side of her was empty. She pulled on the reins and twisted in her saddle.

Lucky stood under the arch where she'd left him, watching her departure with anxiety.

"Are you tired?" she asked. "That's not like you."

He made a low, uneasy grumble in the back of his throat, conflicted. His expression said he longed to follow, but something greater than desire barred him. He raised a foot only to retreat again mid-step.

"Why are you nervous? Is something out there?" The road forward lay in a hush, hardly frightening. Duchess's ears rolled back and forth, listening to sounds in the woods Matilda couldn't hear. The mare shook her head, relaxed, but Lucky had sharper hearing than a real hound. Maybe he heard something the mare couldn't. Maybe something waited out there.

A shiver crept down Matilda's spine. Any creature that could frighten Lucky was reason enough to turn back.

She reined Duchess toward home and kicked the mare into a run.

— CHAPTER THIRTY-ONE —

LUCKY

Dead trees ahead. The dark place beyond.

Matilda calls. She wants to go, but Lucky hates that place. Hates it. Fears it.

Matilda comes back.

Safe.

For now.

— CHAPTER THIRTY-TWO —

MATILDA

Christmas arrived with more frost and a few drifting snowflakes in the dark of morning. Elliot emerged from his bed first and pounded on Matilda's door until she crawled out from the covers in a daze.

When the family arrived downstairs, they discovered their humble Christmas socks emptied on the floor. The apple pastries Matilda had wrapped and placed tenderly in each sock lay strewn across the front room, but the taffies she'd stuffed into the toes were missing.

Lucky hid under the table with sticky fingers.

Chest puffed out, Elliot sent Lucky to the barn before Matilda could utter a word.

While he paid his penance, they did their morning chores, feeding the animals and breaking the thin ice that covered the water trough. After Olive had gathered the morning's eggs, she fetched Lucky from his corner in the tack room, and once he'd made friends with Elliot again, Matilda sat him down at the table and gave him the gift she'd saved half her pennies for.

Lucky looked inquisitively at the beige box set in front of him. It wasn't much to look at, even with the green ribbon Matilda had tied around it, but he studied it with interest and sniffed at it. Olive guided his hands to the ribbon and showed him how to pull it loose. He pulled the lid off on his own. Nestled in the box sat a pair of socks and two simple, brown leather shoes in Lucky's size.

Will he like them? As he stared over the lip of the box, his hair growing longer again and falling into his eyes, she stared at him and took note of every minute change in the look on his face. *Will he know what they're meant for?*

Blowing the hair out of his face, Lucky snatched the shoes from the box and excitedly tried to put them on the wrong feet.

"He knows their purpose!" Matilda cried out as she knelt on the floor to help Lucky adorn both socks and shoes. She modelled how to tie the laces on one shoe and let him try with the other.

He surprised her yet again by getting it right.

Only once. She pondered Lucky as he strode about the room, stepping hard so the heels of his shoes clacked splendidly on the floor. *He only needed to see it done once. He's getting smarter.*

"He wants to be like us." Olive peered over the pages of her new novel and watched Lucky from her seat at the table.

But he won't speak like us.

Next, Elliot and Matilda opened their gifts. Elliot delighted to receive the pocket watch he'd wanted, even if someone else's initials marked the tarnished silver, and Matilda's new hat matched her Sunday dress better than her old one.

She ran her fingers over the maroon ribbon decorating the hat. Olive must have added the ribbon herself, but it looked flawless. Lucky watched as Matilda admired the satiny feel of the ribbon on her fingertips. His eyes stared, half-lidded with concentration.

He wears that same look whenever Olive tries to teach him to smile. Why is he staring at me like that?

Her cheeks burned under Lucky's unyielding watch, so she turned from him and tried on her hat. As she adjusted it on her head, Lucky approached her again with a hand stuffed in his pocket. He pulled it out and thrust a closed fist toward her.

"What is it?" When he brought his fist closer to her and gestured with it, she peeled back his fingers. Four soft taffies and a few specks of lint fell into her palm.

Is he giving me a Christmas present?

"Is that my taffy?" Elliot crossed the room and swiped one of the candies from Matilda's hand. "I thought he'd eaten it!" He brushed the lint off the wrapper and dumped the sweet into his mouth.

Olive took hers and placed it on her tongue with more manners, and Matilda's mouth watered gratefully the moment the salty sweet fell on her tongue. She unwrapped Lucky's taffy for him, offering it on an open palm, but he closed her fingers around it.

"But you love taffies." She opened her fingers again and bared the molasses-coloured candy to him.

Lucky wouldn't take it. Instead he gave the grin Olive had taught him; it sat lopsided on his mouth, clumsy but honest.

"I'll eat it if he won't!" Elliot swiped the candy out of Matilda's grasp before she could argue.

"It's his!" Olive protested, but Elliot had already popped it into his mouth.

"He didn't want it!" he said, and he stuffed the candy into his cheek with a satisfied grin.

Sighing, Matilda rose to start breakfast, but as she slid her chair under the table, movement far outside the window drew her eye.

Brushing the curtain aside for a better look, she angled her head to see up the road. Beyond the frost-dusted field, a speck of a woman trudged through the crusty white sea on foot. As she strayed off the main road and followed the wagon-wheel trail toward the farmhouse, her destination was obvious.

"Were we expecting company today?" Matilda asked.

"I don't have any friends," Olive admitted openly, which made her admission all the more pitiful.

"You don't like any of mine," Elliot said.

The strange woman drew closer, bigger now against the white scenery. Swallowed by a thick grey coat and woolly scarf, she strode with a cane that picked her way between the wagon wheel tracks. Matilda couldn't see the woman's face through the coils of her scarf, but she recognized the cane and the austerity with which she wielded it.

"It's the mesmerist." Matilda leaned back from the window. "Why is Miss Kovacs here?"

"She must be lost." Elliot ran an admiring finger over the curves of his pocket watch. For probably the ninth time he breathed on the glass face and polished it with his sleeve.

For a blind woman, Marta Kovacs didn't wander very blindly. Except where she dodged unruly tufts of weeds, the path she cut across the meadow ran straight and determined.

"She must be half frozen!" Matilda said.

She spun toward the kitchen and her teapot, colliding painfully with a brick wall. A brick wall named Lucky. For all he'd clicked his heels moments ago, she'd heard no sign of him behind her.

"Not so close." She caressed the bump his chin had left on her head and pushed him back.

"Lucky..." Olive's eyes slowly widened.

Lucky!

"Oh!" Matilda said. "Elliot, take him upstairs. Quickly! Don't let him leave your room."

"Why? Miss Kovacs can't tell him apart from Olive."

Matilda shot Elliot a look more sour than milk left in the sun. Like she'd turned into a bear, he flattened his hands on Lucky's back and pushed him up the stairs in a hurry.

While Olive cleared the mess of gifts and moved them out of the way upstairs, Matilda put a fresh log in the stove. As she put water on to boil, a knock hammered on the front door. Olive sped downstairs again. Matilda rubbed her palms on her apron and creaked open the door.

As always, Miss Kovacs's commanding presence made Matilda feel as small as a child. When the mesmerist tugged her scarf down from her face, her mouth stiffened like a beak.

"Miss Kovacs," Matilda said formally, "is everything all right?"

"I believe you're supposed to wish me a Merry Christmas, Miss O'Connor, whether or not I'm tired of hearing it." Miss Kovacs's Hungarian accent sharpened the cut of her words. She rubbed her gloved hands together. "Are you going to wait until I'm as frosty as those weeds of yours before you invite me in?"

"Oh." Matilda glanced upstairs, but the way was clear. "Please come in."

She angled away from the door, and Miss Kovacs kicked the ice flecks off her shoes before stepping over the threshold. While Olive collected Miss Kovacs's coat and scarf, Matilda pulled a chair out from the table and arranged it closer to the fireplace, inviting the hypnotist to melt the winter out of her bones.

"I'll find my own way." Miss Kovacs refused Olive's offered hand and crossed the room with the use of her cane. She placed herself in the chair, removed her gloves, and spread wrinkled hands over the heat of the fire. "Where is the wild one?"

Matilda's heart thumped. *Lucky? How did she know?* Was Miss Kovacs truly a witch? Had she read Matilda's mind?

"Elliot is upstairs," Olive said.

Oh. *Elliot.*

Her throat suddenly dry, Matilda sought out her teapot while Olive pulled a chair for herself next to the fireplace.

Whatever reason had compelled Miss Kovacs to brave the awful cold, she said nothing of it. Only the fire made sound, crackling as it devoured the log Elliot had fed it. Matilda knew she should say something to fill the silence, but her thoughts concentrated on prayerful hopes that Lucky would stay quiet.

After a moment, Olive softly cleared her throat. "How was your Christmas morning, ma'am?"

"Ha," Miss Kovacs coughed out a hoarse, mirthless laugh. She folded her hands in her lap, and her shoulders tossed back, square and imposing. "I haven't celebrated Christmas in over thirty years."

Then why has she come here?

"Oh." Olive imitated the old woman's straight back and asked another polite question Matilda didn't hear. Miss Kovacs gave a grouchy answer—something about the children on her street allowing their dog to leave its mess on her doorstep. She'd used the words "crude," "mollycoddled," and "rapscallions" all in one breath. How *did* the woman work her magic as a mesmerist with a tongue like hers?

After the teapot whistled and Matilda prepared Miss Kovacs a hot drink, she, too, moved a chair to join them by the fire.

Miss Kovacs turned an ear toward Olive, even when Matilda spoke or when the three of them sipped silently at their cups. The expression on Miss Kovacs's face appeared as foreign as Kāi's mother tongue, but Matilda saw something working behind the woman's blank stare.

She clearly isn't here for the company. What does she want?

They downed their tea quickly, favouring the bitter heat over conversation. Matilda collected the empty dishes, but as she took Miss Kovacs's cup, a loud thump struck the floor above them.

Miss Kovacs raised her eyes as though she could see through the ceiling above. "What is that boy doing up there?"

"Oh, he—" Matilda could think of no explanation. "Would you like another cup of tea?"

"No." Miss Kovacs beat the offer away with a snap of her wrist. "I'd prefer to address the reason I braved that insufferable cold so I may return to the comfort of my own home."

"Reason?" Matilda feigned surprise as she set the teacups on the counter and returned to her seat.

Miss Kovacs intertwined her fingers and laid them firmly on her lap again. "You didn't think I came here for Christmas songs and gossip, did you? I loathe such trivial posturing and pretence. I'm here to see my patient. Olive has been absent from my sitting room for more than two months. Given her state the last time, I came to see that she had not gone hysterical."

"I see." Matilda offered Olive an apologetic look out of the corner of her eye. Olive stared at her lap. "Are you here to treat her, then?"

"I don't make house calls, but I know your family has..." Miss Kovacs ground her teeth together, searching for the right word or maybe biting it back. How unusual for her to be speechless. "In any case, I can say nothing about that ruffian upstairs, but I've been observing Olive since I arrived."

"You have?" Olive asked, though from the flat tone of her voice Matilda suspected she'd noticed the old woman's attention too.

Miss Kovacs twisted her wrinkled neck, staring over Olive's head. "You're different, girl. Changed. What have you done?"

"I've done nothing, ma'am."

"'I've done nothing, ma'am,'" Ms. Kovacs raised her pitch so she sounded almost as girlish as Olive. "Two months ago you'd have burst into tears at the sight of me on your doorstep. Now you're sharing pleasantries and absolutely dreadful tea with me."

Dreadful? Matilda bit her bottom lip and held in a complaint as Miss Kovacs turned to her.

"And what of that Elliot?" the old woman asked. "Is he as hot-tempered as I remember?"

"Well," Matilda began, "he—"

A *thud* resonated through the house followed by the slam of a door upstairs. Elliot's voice rang out in an urgent command. It carried clearly to their ears downstairs.

"Stop! *Get back here!*"

Footsteps pounded along the upstairs hall then squeaked down the stairs. Every muscle down Matilda's back tensed.

No. Not now!

She jumped to her feet like a fish leaping onto the shore and spun toward the stairs, but Lucky already closed in with Elliot behind him.

Lucky circled Miss Kovacs and appraised her. He passed so close to her there was no way even the blind woman had missed his presence.

One of Miss Kovacs's eyebrows rose. Her eyes settled in the middle of Lucky's chest, narrowed into slits.

Spying Miss Kovacs, Elliot's face paled. He grabbed Lucky by the elbow and tried to persuade him back upstairs, but Lucky wouldn't have it. Stamping in his new shoes, he dragged Elliot behind him as he moved around the unfamiliar woman in the house. Perhaps judging her to be a friend or intruder.

Matilda blocked Lucky's path. "Go upstairs," she ordered with a low voice, hoping Miss Kovacs's hearing had been dulled by her walk through the cold.

"I couldn't stop him," Elliot whispered to Matilda. "He's been fussing ever since he heard the knock at the door."

Don't growl at her, Matilda begged Lucky silently. *Don't give yourself away.*

"Who is this?" Miss Kovacs pushed her hands against her knees and lifted herself to steady feet.

The last to stand, Olive sprang upward and rushed to Lucky. "This is our cousin Lucky from Manitoba," Olive lied. Both guilt and gratitude battled in Matilda's chest. Fortunately, Olive's novels had given her a quick imagination.

Lucky allowed Miss Kovacs to approach him but watched her with tense caution.

"Lucky, is it?" Now standing almost inappropriately close to him, Miss Kovacs leaned her head as far back as she could, nearly locking gazes with him. "Is that your real name?"

"Lucky doesn't speak much," Olive said. "He's— Well, he just doesn't speak."

"Doesn't speak?" Miss Kovacs coughed another dry laugh, but this time it sounded amused. "If only more shared his condition. I might be able to help him, though. Sit down over there, boy."

Oh, no.

"You don't need to bother yourself with him." Matilda grabbed Lucky by the shoulders and tried to turn him around, but he was too strong. "Elliot, take him upstairs now."

"Nonsense." Miss Kovacs waved a hand in the air. She felt her way back to the side of her chair and patted the seat. "Sit down."

Tentatively, Lucky obeyed, taking one creeping step toward the woman then another. His eyes never blinked, and he sat stiffly in the chair, gripping the seat.

Miss Kovacs steered around Lucky's feet and stood directly in front of him. "Everyone be quiet now. Not a word!"

"Please, Miss Kovacs." Matilda grasped Lucky by the shoulder again, "I don't thi—"

"Hush! Or do you want him to stay mute?"

At least for the next hour, yes!

Bending forward until her head was even with Lucky's, Miss Kovacs matched her breath to his. Matilda thought of Nathaniel—of the way he'd go quiet and still, imprisoning you with his hypnotic gaze before he took control of your mind.

What if she can *help him speak?* Matilda took a step back and lowered her arms again, but her hands clenched at her sides. *Doesn't that help me?*

Almost without a sound, Miss Kovacs mouthed words quietly beneath her breath. Her tongue formed one word, over and over again, with an expectant pause between each utterance: Lucky.

Lucky heard his name but tensed at the sound of it on the mesmerist's lips. The moment Miss Kovacs's chant fell on him, his lips parted over clenched teeth. His eyes flashed. Animal. Wolf-like.

No, Lucky, don't!

"Stop!" Matilda shouted. "Stop, I say!"

Miss Kovacs's mouth turned downward. "As you wish," she said, but her tone darkened, offended. "But it seems cruel to keep him separated from his voice."

"He's fine." Matilda slipped between Miss Kovacs and Lucky, breaking the woman's hold. "He's happy as he is."

"*Happy?* A drunk fool can be happy while he drowns in his drink, but that doesn't mean you should leave him with the bottle. There's a reason this boy doesn't speak—trauma of some kind, I'd guess. He's unwell."

"He's well enough," Matilda said. She slipped her arm through Lucky's and pulled him to his feet, holding him protectively against her as she defied Miss Kovacs.

The room chilled. The fire crackled on the hearth, but where Miss Kovacs stood, a blizzard roared.

When Matilda was certain she'd be overwhelmed by the storm, the mesmerist said, "Olive, fetch my coat. I want to be home before the day gets any cooler."

Olive dashed away and arrived a moment later with a woollen coat she helped Miss Kovacs slip into.

"Are you certain his name is Lucky?" Miss Kovacs fastened her buttons and tugged her sleeves down to her wrists. "It had little hold over him when I spoke it."

Hold? What does she mean? "Yes, that's his name."

"Hmm." The woman wrapped her head in her scarf and reached for the door.

"Wait." Matilda crossed the room reluctantly, grabbing her own coat. "I'll get the wagon and—"

"No. I've cared for myself since before you were born." Miss Kovacs turned the handle, but kept the door sealed. "If your *cousin* decides he'd like to speak, bring him to me. I can help him find his humanity again."

Miss Kovacs gave a curt nod, then cracked open the door and stepped into the winter.

A relieved sigh whistled through Matilda's teeth once the door shut behind the woman. It cut short when she realized what Miss Kovacs had said, and again Matilda felt the blizzard surround her.

She can help him find his humanity?

Miss Kovacs had understood too much in that brief moment with Lucky.

She knew he wasn't human.

November 6th, 1883

*Mother's Soul Name is fading. It's dying—*she's *dying. I need more Power to save her.*

Miss Kovacs is going to need a new lock on her door. She leaves her house so rarely, but even a witch needs to go to the general store for some flour and sugar now and then. I watched. And waited. Desperation has turned me into a criminal.

I know it was wrong of me, but Mother's life is too dear to care about right or wrong now.

Regretfully, but not surprisingly, my blind mentor doesn't have my compulsion to commit her thoughts and sins to paper. After an hour of searching her house, I found no journal. Her books on mesmerism are the same titles as mine. For a moment I thought I'd broken the law and Miss Kovacs's trust and gained no knowledge in return that could spare Mother's life.

But I did find one thing, tucked away in a box of trinkets in the corner of Miss Kovacs's wardrobe. She didn't sever ties to her family as cleanly as she should have. Letters from her father were dated most recently from thirty-four years ago. The letters held nothing of use, and I'm certain I'll pay dearly for my invasion of privacy, but a timeworn book with browned pages that smelled of chamomile gave me the first glimpse of hope I've had since learning of Mother's disease. "Advanced Medical Telepathy," the first page reads.

My mentor has been withholding so much more than I realized, but not anymore. Not if there's a chance to save Mother.

— CHAPTER THIRTY-THREE —

MATILDA

Matilda waited for a mob to overwhelm the farmhouse until she felt sick to the stomach. Each night she peered out the window and looked for the rusty pitchforks and cold, hard guns to come for the monster in her home.

Miss Kovacs could hardly keep any opinion of hers to herself. She'd tell of the beastlike man on the O'Connor farm. Most of the city would think her a mad old woman, but Joseph…he'd seen how dangerous a wolf man could be. He'd believe the mesmerist's tales, and others would follow him.

And Richards would come to kill the beast that got away.

For weeks she waited, but each morning when she looked out the window, she saw nothing but the quiet meadow and evergreens. Each night the only torches she saw were those up in the sky: the stars Olive called "Orion" or "Polaris."

Perhaps I read too much into Miss Kovacs's words.

Matilda sat on the porch steps next to Olive, fighting off the January cold with her scarf wrapped snugly over her ears, and she watched the first proper blanket of snow scatter the afternoon light. It glittered like a sea of diamonds under the sun's caress.

Sprawled on his back in a drift, Lucky soaked in the sun with his hands clasped over his chest and his eyes closed. If he had any idea how dangerous it had been to provoke Miss Kovacs—how much danger yet remained—he didn't show it, and Matilda didn't know how to tell him. Looking at his peaceful face now, she didn't know if she *should* tell him.

Elliot rolled a ball of white between his hands as he knelt behind the fortress wall he'd built to shelter the army of knee-high snowmen and snow wolves he'd sculpted with Lucky all afternoon. He found a prone target, grinned devilishly, and launched the snowball at Lucky.

It struck Lucky's knee and exploded over him in heavy clumps. Lucky raised his head from its wintry pillow.

"Ha!" Elliot ducked out of sight behind his shelter, but when no retaliation came, he peeked over the fortress wall. "Aren't you going to fight?" he asked.

"He doesn't know what to do." Olive's hands nestled under her arms for warmth, but her face brightened. "Show him."

"Like this." Elliot needed no more persuading: he rolled another snowball and hurled it.

The ball broke on Lucky's head. He leapt up and blinked snowflakes off his lashes.

Olive left the porch. Taking one of Lucky's hands, she guided it through the wet snow at his feet and helped him form his own weapon. "It's a game."

Elliot should never have taught Lucky to build snowmen. Lucky took Olive's snowball and grew it into a massive boulder.

"Throw it," Elliot said. "I bet you can't hit me."

The boulder broke into chunks as it flew through the air, but all of them struck Elliot square in the chest and knocked him off his feet.

"Oof! No more free hits!" Elliot struggled to his knees and brushed the snow off his coat.

Soon, the meadow erupted into flying snow and laughter. Olive teamed up with her brother, and together they chased Lucky in a maze around the snowman army, though he dodged each of their attacks and landed each of his. Despite the losing battle, Elliot's war cries carried more cheers than threats.

Matilda memorized the toothy grin on her brother's face and the sound of Olive's delighted squeal when one of her balls finally struck its mark. Matilda wanted to remember it all—how Olive grabbed her hand and dragged her into the fray and how Lucky allowed Elliot to tackle him to the ground and bury him in snow when they'd played themselves into exhaustion. Even when Matilda grew old and her memory was a fragment of what it was now, she wanted to recall how Lucky had brought them light and laughter.

Let the mob bring their pitchforks and guns. She'd never let them take Lucky away.

January faded into February in what felt like a dream. March brought the calving season and spring sunlight but also enough rain and extra work that Matilda barely had any chance to enjoy the warmer days. When she rode through the woods with Lucky each morning, the trees bowed with the weight of the prior evening's showers, and Lucky returned drenched and muddy.

Over time he tired of the clouded skies, or perhaps he grew bored of running the same trails. Instead of keeping pace when they ran, he lagged behind Duchess. When Matilda would slow the mare, he'd tug on her skirt, asking to return home a little earlier each day.

On the last Friday in March, Matilda woke with a tickle in her throat and a headache. She rolled over in her blankets and moaned, but darkness hung outside the bedroom window. She nestled next to Olive and shut her eyes. There was time to sleep a few more minutes…

When she opened her eyes again, Olive had disappeared. The weather outside was pale grey, but sunlight peeked through melancholic clouds. She'd slept well past dawn.

She shot up in bed.

It's so late—

Teetering downstairs with an ache she couldn't rub out of her head, she looked by the door for her winter coat. Olive's and Elliot's coats were gone, but the scent of roasted onion rose thick near the kitchen. An abandoned pot on the stove oozed broth down the sides.

If they made their own breakfast, they'll have forgotten the animals.

She fastened her coat buttons and stepped out into the late morning. The air was humid, and dark clouds lurked around the sun. They looked eager to bring still more rains. Hadn't the skies yet had their fill of weeping?

Dizzy, she stumbled past the declining pile of logs in the woodshed and into the barn to fetch chickenfeed, but she couldn't find her egg basket.

Olive must have forgotten it in the coop yesterday.

When Matilda stumbled to the chicken coop, she found the basket there, but not because of Olive's mistake. In the middle of the enclosure, surrounded by softly clucking hens, Lucky supported the basket and five speckled eggs with one arm. He greeted Matilda with a brief flit of his eyes and brushed through straw in search of more treasure. The hens ruffled their feathers lazily, pecking at the feed someone had already left for them.

"Did you do this?" she asked. The hens were rarely so calm even when Matilda collected their eggs.

Lucky's strength and endurance had proved useful for chopping wood and churning butter, but Matilda had kept him away from the coop. How could she trust a fragile hen's egg to someone with such brute strength? Yet here he was. Gentle. Capable.

Grateful and perplexed, she watched him work for a moment before leaving to check on Duchess and the cows.

The animals gathered comfortably around a full trough, the cows' udders empty and their bellies full.

Did Olive teach Lucky how to do this?

Matilda supported herself against the pasture fence. It held her weight without any groan or creak, and she admired the supports Lucky had helped Elliot build. Elliot had shown him what to do, and Lucky could sink a nail to its head with a single, precise strike of the hammer.

Once the ground dried, Elliot could show him how to dig up the old, rotten posts. With Lucky's help they'd have a sturdy new fence in a matter of days. With his help, they might even be able to survive here. *Thrive* here.

I'm doing it again.

Sometimes Matilda caught herself thinking of a future where Lucky lived with them on the farm. One year. Two. Or ten. Sometimes she tried to imagine what he'd look like running behind her through the woods when they both had wrinkles and grey hair. Sometimes she forgot he hadn't always been there with her.

He can't stay forever.

Her throat prickled, and she coughed into her sleeve. Lucky approached with the egg basket now full and watched her with his mouth thinning into a frown.

"What is it?" Her voice cracked like thin ice. "Are you waiting to go on our ride?"

He tugged at the arm of her coat, trying to pull her away.

She brushed his hand off her. "No, tell me." *It's been five months. If he can build a fence and gather eggs, he can speak.* "Say what you want."

Lucky adjusted the basket in his arms. The concern in his eyes darkened, annoyed.

"Well?" she said, but the word ended abruptly in another cough. Her head spun, and she leaned harder into the fence.

Again Lucky reached for her sleeve, and, wheezing, she surrendered.

He guided her back to the warmth of the house and set the basket on the table, leading her upstairs to her rumpled nest of bed covers.

"I can't rest now," she said. "There are dishes to be cleaned and clothes to mend."

Lucky nudged her toward her bed and shut her alone in her room. The bed covers felt warm and soft and so inviting.

He did *see to the hens. Perhaps one more hour of rest…*

Elliot and Olive brought a dark mood home with them and woke Matilda with a slamming door. When she went downstairs she found Elliot with scuffed knuckles and Olive with her face hidden firmly in a book, refusing supper and conversation.

Matilda didn't ask what had happened at school. Sleep had eased a little of her headache, but she hardly wanted another one.

By Saturday afternoon, Matilda's cough had gone, but the black mood that had followed her siblings home from school had only worsened.

After supper, Matilda sat at the table and pointed to the lines of one of Olive's drawings for the third time. They depicted Duchess so flawlessly Matilda expected the mare to search for a cube of sugar in her apron.

"Say it," Matilda said. "What is this?" As she tapped her finger over the drawing, Lucky watched with glazed eyes and a pencil held limply in his hand.

"Write it down, then. I know you remember your lessons on the alphabet."

Lucky scratched his pencil across the paper. Matilda chewed her lip in anticipation, but when she checked his work, he'd only scribbled "LUC" in messy letters in the bottom corner.

A month of practising his own name, and he still couldn't get past the first three letters.

Is he trying anymore?

"You can do this," she said. "Even Elliot's schoolwork improves when he does his lessons."

"What's that supposed to mean?" Elliot sat at the table next to Lucky and stared toward the window, his chair wobbling on two legs.

Matilda had been right about yesterday's skies. It wasn't yet late, but the clouds chased away the day and spilled their burden over the farm in an unusually fierce storm. At first a delicate sprinkle, the raindrops grew fatter and more numerous with every passing minute until they'd shrouded the world in a false night and Matilda had had to serve supper by lantern.

"Olive, don't you think he does it on purpose?" Elliot said. Seated next to Matilda, Olive ignored her brother and hid herself behind her book. Elliot frowned at her over his shoulder then returned his gaze to the weather outside. "I bet Lucky knows you'd send him to be with the other lunatics as soon as he told you what you want. Even this place is better than that."

"You'll break that chair leaning on it like that," Matilda said. "Set it down."

"No."

"Elliot."

With a grumble, he dropped his chair onto all four legs and slumped in his seat. Matilda returned to her lesson, nudging Lucky's shin under the table to make sure he was paying attention, and jabbed at the drawing of Duchess.

"What is this? Tell me."

A muscle in Lucky's chin jumped.

"How about this one?" She cracked her stiff neck side to side and took the next page from the pile of drawings. This one showed fishing boats and reminded her of many serene mornings by the Fraser. She'd sit alone with Lucky as the waking sun's mirror image rippled in the water. Surely the drawing would also evoke some response from him. "Name one thing you see. You can do it."

Lucky ground his teeth together, and his eyes stared darkly into the corner of the room.

He's not even listening.

"Who's the one who isn't listening?" Elliot muttered. Had she said that aloud? "He doesn't want to do these lessons. Leave him alone."

Swallowing her temper, Matilda pretended she hadn't heard Elliot and took the next drawing. Lucky didn't respond to it either. She took the next drawing after it. And the next. She flipped through the pages, but with every new drawing Lucky's eyebrows dropped lower over his eyes until his expression could only be called a scowl.

You're not the only one frustrated with these lessons.

"We wouldn't have to sit here so long if you'd only say something!" Matilda slammed the drawing in her hand onto the pile and threw herself back in her chair. "If you're bored then tell me! Say *something*."

Lucky turned dark, obstinate eyes to her and crossed his arms over his chest like armour. His lip twisted back, exposing teeth.

"N— no," said a deep, unfamiliar voice.

At first, she couldn't believe what she'd heard. She'd thought for sure it must have been Elliot, but her brother barked a laugh. "Did you hear? I told you he hates his lessons!"

'No'? That's *what he—? 'No'?!*

Her throat clenched as she looked down at the pile of drawings. Her hands tightened into fists on the table.

He could have named any one of these! How long has he been holding back?

"You know how important this is!" Matilda shot Lucky a glare of her own. "I've tried so hard to help you, and all I want in return is for you tell me what happened to my brother, but *'No'*?"

"Don't yell at him!" Elliot said.

Matilda pushed against the table and rose to her feet. Her body felt too heavy. And too hot. "Don't you start, Elliot. He learned that word from you."

"How would you know?" Elliot lunged to his feet. His hands gripped the back of the chair and turned white. "You're so obsessed with Lucky's lessons you didn't even notice Olive crying yesterday. Junior locked her in the outhouse after school and told her he'd only let her out if she kissed him."

Olive's eyes welled with tears she couldn't hold back, and she covered more of her face with her book. The retort Matilda had planned tied itself into knots in her stomach.

Oh, poor Olive!

"So I hit him," Elliot said with defiance. "He wasn't going to get in trouble for it. No one wants *Nathaniel's* brother and sister at school anyway."

The words cut Matilda. She grabbed her apron and wrenched it between her hands. Why did Elliot have to say Nathaniel's name with the same anger others showed? He knew him. He knew better.

"Please," Olive squeaked. She looked up from the pages of her novel with bloodshot eyes. "Both of you stop!"

"No!" Elliot's stare turned darker than the storm outside, and he kicked his chair back under the table, hard. "She only cares about Nathaniel because she wishes he was here instead of us. But he's dead."

"I—" Too many thoughts battled for Matilda's voice, and her hands pulled the twist in her apron tighter. *Is that what he thinks of me?* "You know that's not true."

Elliot backed away from Matilda and snatched his coat from its hook. When he opened the door, rain swept in like the tide.

"Elliot, come back here!"

"*NO!*" He stomped onto the porch and slammed the door shut.

Matilda stepped through the lake her brother had let in and reached for the door.

"Stop," Olive said. Matilda turned back to the table to find her sister watching her with a sickly pallor to her face. "Leave him alone. Please. He needs a little time."

We both do.

"Listen," Matilda said wearily, trying but failing to smooth out the wrinkles she'd put in her apron. "About what happened at school—"

"I'll wash up first." Olive shut her novel and stole away, arms hugged around herself.

"Olive..." Matilda said, but her sister rushed away.

Matilda dragged her chair near the fireplace and plopped into it, watching the flames consume the wood in the hearth. Lucky didn't lay across her feet the way he usually did. Anxiously, he went to the window and waited for Elliot to return from the porch.

What a mess we've made.

When Olive finished her bath, her waves combed and braided, Elliot still hadn't returned, but the skies outside the window were black and threatening. Matilda left the warmth of the fire. *I don't care if he's angry. He can be angry all he likes inside.*

An assault of rain crashed upon her when she opened the door, and she shivered as it seeped through her clothes. "Elliot, you'll catch your death if..."

The light from the house fought a losing war against the gloom outside. Matilda could barely see across the porch through the downpour, but Elliot wasn't there.

"Elliot!" she called, but the pelting of the rain absorbed her voice. *He left?* "Elliot!"

A weight dropped in her stomach. The rains swallowed everything in sight! If she left the farmhouse she'd never find her way back. *Elliot* would never find his way back. He'd freeze to death.

"Elliot, please!"

I can't...

"Come here, Lucky." She threw on her coat and fetched a lantern. "Hurry!"

He must have heard the fear in her voice. He left the window and came to her side with no sign of challenge in his eyes.

"Elliot needs me," she said. "You have to take me to him."

Whether he understood her as a dog or as a human, Lucky plunged into the storm without wasting time on shoes or a coat. She hurried behind him.

Please let us find him; I can't bury another brother.

— CHAPTER THIRTY-FOUR —

LUCKY

Cold flows through Lucky instead of blood, but it burns the feet. It stings.

Elliot is gone. Lucky's friend is lost.

The black sky growls, but there are other voices in the dark—other breaths Lucky hears. Cows soothe their babies. Animals hide in the cover of the woods, and Lucky hears their heartbeats. One of those heartbeats weakens.

Matilda follows through the danger. Her skin is too soft against the wet cold. She will freeze. Lucky wants to tell her to go back—to tell her he'll find Elliot. The words break apart on Lucky's tongue, there only a moment and then gone before Lucky can catch hold of them.

She won't listen to wordless language. She can't hear it. The only way she'll go home is if Lucky finds the boy first.

The ground and sky attack with teeth and cold, but Lucky runs into the dark.

— CHAPTER THIRTY-FIVE —

MATILDA

The black and bedlam engulfed Lucky until Matilda saw little more than a white shirt getting farther ahead of her. She bowed herself against the assault of rain and carried her lantern into the night.

Water seeped through her clothes and into her skin, drenching her in a cold bath. What wind accompanied the rain had no chance to dry her. Instead it sent shivers wrenching through her body. Her shoulder hit a branch, and the tree dumped a bucket of water down her neck.

She shuddered as the rain ran down her chest. Her lantern gave scarcely enough light to reveal evergreens surrounding her and her footprints already flooded behind her. *We're in the woods?*

Surely Elliot wouldn't have gone so far. Did Lucky think they were on one of their rides? He moved strangely, slogging through the mud. Sure of his direction yet languid. Didn't he understand? Was he leading them to their deaths?

Trust him.

Another branch scratched her face. When Lucky noticed her trailing behind him, he returned to her side to lace his fingers through hers. Already her hands were too numb to detect any warmth he offered and her thoughts too frantic to feel anything but grateful for his bold, guiding touch. He pulled her away from more branches and led her to a mound of weeds and brush at base of another tree. The brush moaned.

"Elliot!"

Her brother lay face down in the weeds, his feet hooked over an unearthed root and his clothes more water than corduroy. She dropped to a knee and brushed sodden hair out of his face.

"Elliot, get up!"

She shook him. His eyes slivered open at her touch.

"...Tilda," he said. "Cold..."

Then his eyes shut.

When Matilda followed Lucky to the house with Elliot sprawled across Lucky's back, Olive awaited them in the front room, pacing back and forth.

"Elliot?" The bells of Olive's voice clanged, high-pitched and shrill. She stumbled to a halt and looked at Matilda. "You left me here without a word! I've been so afraid something terrible... Elliot— Is he all right?"

"Lay him by the fireplace." Matilda set the lantern on the table and shed her coat. "Olive, fetch some blankets."

Olive's face reddened with a tumult of anger and fear, but she rushed upstairs.

Lucky placed Elliot gently on the floor then got out of Matilda's way. Before she had Elliot stripped of his drenched clothes, Olive returned with an armload of blankets, and Matilda wrapped her brother in a cocoon.

Olive provoked the flames in the fireplace into an inferno. "I'll make him something warm to drink." She dashed to the kitchen, giving Matilda space with her brother.

He stirred as she warmed his fingers between her hands. He mumbled something incoherent, and apart from a few red scratches he'd picked up from his fall in the woods, he was so pale it made her think of— No. She couldn't think of how Nathaniel had looked, lying motionless in her arms. Elliot wasn't dead. He wouldn't die. He *couldn't.*

When she'd heated water, Olive brought tea. Matilda nudged Elliot awake, though he barely opened his eyes, and she pressed the cup to his mouth, spilling as much as he sipped.

"You'll be all right, won't you?" She handed the cup to Olive before laying Elliot down and sweeping hair off his clammy skin. His eyelids fluttered.

"Lucky?" Elliot's eyes cracked open, revealing murky blue. He looked at Matilda without recognition.

She squeezed his hand. "Hush. Rest now."

"Help her ... if you can." He mumbled the words until they barely sounded English. "Even if she leaves us. It's our fault she ... gave up everything."

"Be still." Matilda stroked his hair and felt her heart breaking all over. *What's he saying?* She squeezed his hand again. "None of this is your fault."

"You won't leave us, will you?" His voice went quiet and breathy like he stood on the verge of sleep. He mumbled something she almost didn't hear. "Everyone leaves."

I know. I'm sorry.

"Nobody's leaving you," she said.

The creases smoothed from Elliot's face, and his breath deepened with sleep. While Olive took Elliot's teacup to be washed, Matilda held his hand and hoped he felt comforted in his dreams.

"Oh no," Olive said when she returned from rinsing the teacup. "We have another problem."

"Not now," Matilda said. "I can't bear any more tonight. I only want to look after Elliot."

"But it's Lucky. He's shivering."

"That's nonsense," Matilda said. With effort, she turned from her brother. "Lucky doesn't get co—"

Lucky stood near the door in a pool of water, shoulders hunched up to his ears and arms wound tightly around his chest. From head to foot he dripped, and shivers quaked through his whole body.

Matilda tried to rush to his side, but her body wouldn't move. How was this possible? What was happening to him?

Olive hurried toward the stairs. "I'll find more blankets."

Matilda released Elliot's hand and at last came to her senses, scrambling to her feet. "Hurry this way. We've got to get you dry."

Lucky stepped toward her tenderly. His toes were blue, but over the floor they left smears of red.

Blood?

"Sit." She yanked a chair out from the table and slid it toward Lucky. He slumped into it clumsily, and as she knelt before him and raised one of his feet, he winced at her touch.

Red lashed the underside of his foot. Fir needles and blades of stone had torn into his skin and left him bleeding into Matilda's palms.

That's why he was walking strangely!

Why hadn't she paid attention? Why hadn't he told her he'd been hurt?

"This is why you need to speak." She found a rag and a basin large enough for his feet. "You should have told me you were cold and injured."

She left more water on the stove to warm and set the basin in front of Lucky's chair. He cringed again as she placed his feet in the basin, but he let her tend to him.

"Take off that wet shirt," she said.

Shaking, Lucky tugged at his shirt, but when it tangled over his head, she had to peel it from him.

He's always there, doing whatever I ask, and all I do is shout at him.

She laid his shirt aside. "I thought you were the one who wasn't listening," she said, "but I didn't listen to you or to Elliot."

Lucky hunched over his knees. His teeth chattered, but his eyes met hers with full attention, showing no resentment.

"If you have something important to tell me, do whatever it takes to make me understand. Do you hear me? Whatever it takes."

He sat close already, but he drew nearer and rested his cold forehead on hers the way he'd done that night by the river.

I will.

She heard his answer more clearly than if he'd spoken it. So close to him like this, he didn't feel like a wolf. To Matilda, he felt more human than she.

Before she knew what she was doing, she threw her arms around his neck and hugged him tight. Her sudden affection seemed to catch him off guard, but for once he knew what to do. His arms encircled her. He nuzzled his face sweetly against her neck. It was the coldest embrace she'd known, but a warmth like mulled wine flooded her chest. As they held each other—him smelling faintly of cedar and trembling from the rain and her trembling from some raw emotion she couldn't even name—all she knew was that Lucky fit perfectly in her arms. That comforted her more than anything else could.

I'm sorry I was so angry. Thank you for saving him. For saving all of us. It was all too much for her to say and yet not nearly enough.

"Good boy, Lucky," was all she managed.

She took solace in the feel of his arms around her and squeezed him tighter until she heard Olive's feet pad down the stairs. Reluctantly, Matilda broke away from him before her sister could misunderstand their embrace.

I'm just grateful, she told herself, but as she went to test the temperature of the water on the stove, she could still feel the impression of Lucky's arms around her.

— CHAPTER THIRTY-SIX —

MATILDA

The rain pattered against the house through the night, but when Matilda woke with pins and needles in her legs, the house lay quiet. She opened swollen eyes and wondered when she'd fallen asleep on an unforgiving floor with Olive on her shoulder and Sable across her ankles.

Elliot snored before the coals in the fireplace, and the horrors of the night returned to Matilda. She slid out from under Olive's head and scurried close to her brother. He had more colour in his cheeks, but his skin roasted when she laid her hand on his forehead. Was it fever? Was she just too cold after a night on the bare floor? He slept deeply and, she hoped, peacefully.

"Sweet dreams," she whispered. *Please be well.*

Next to Elliot, Lucky nested in a pile of blankets. The fire's heat had dried his hair, but his skin remained pallid. Matilda laid her wrist across his forehead and found him as scalding as her brother, but he opened groggy, half-lidded eyes at her touch.

"I didn't mean to wake you." She brushed his hair out of his eyes. "Go back to sleep."

Obediently, he nuzzled into his blankets.

While the others slept, Matilda reignited the fire and warmed more water on the stove. She stood close to the heat to fight the ice within her, feeling the tingle of blood returning to her toes.

Olive woke next, wisps of hair freed from her braid and red wrinkles in her cheeks. "Do you think they'll recover?" Olive said. She, too, laid her hand over Elliot's and Lucky's foreheads in turn, but neither stirred at her gentle contact.

"I hope so," Matilda said.

Allowing Matilda to focus on breakfast, Olive cleared some of the mess left behind in the night. She returned the chair to its place at the table and scrubbed at the smears of blood dried on the floor.

But for the first bubbles rising in the water on the stove and the sound of a wet rag bathing the floor, it was a silent and still morning. So when the door quaked under a heavy thud, Matilda's heart dove into her belly.

Elliot remained deep in sleep, but Lucky sat up, disoriented and spilling blankets everywhere. Sable wagged her tail and bounced over to the door.

"Who is it?" Matilda mouthed to her sister.

Olive glanced at the door and shrugged.

"Keep Lucky quiet while I find a way to get rid of them," Matilda whispered.

Dirty rags abandoned on the floor, Olive shushed Lucky and buried him under his covers again. Matilda tried to hide the emergency hospital behind her as she cracked the door open.

Kāi stood on the porch. He drowned in his coat, dressed like he'd arrived from an expedition in the arctic rather than a walk through a cool New Westminster spring. His hands tucked into his armpits and a yellow scarf wound tightly around his throat. The morning was grey behind him, and with the weakness of the sun, his hat cast no shadow over his face.

His lower lip jutted out, and he ran his eyes up and down her wrinkled dress. "You're going to be late."

Late?

"It's Sunday!" She opened the door wide for Kāi. "I forgot—Come in. I need your help."

"I'm doing well, thank you for asking," Kāi said ironically. He left his boots by the door as he stepped inside, but, seeing the mess of blankets and bodies by the fireplace, he stopped in his tracks and gawked at the mess of rags and blankets on the floor. "What happened?"

Matilda explained the fright of the evening before, and Kāi wasted no time in examining Elliot, asking details about how long he'd been gone and how coherent he'd been when she'd found him.

This time the fuss woke Elliot. He gave them each a drowsy but wicked glare. When Kāi squeezed Elliot's wrist and asked him if he remembered anything, Elliot only said, "I hate rainstorms." He snatched his wrist away and yanked his blankets over his head before Matilda could ask him what he wanted for breakfast.

"His temper is as healthy as before." Kāi frowned at the heap of blankets. "Feed him and let him rest. He was lucky."

Lucky. Yes. It was Lucky.

Through the barrier of Elliot's blankets, Kāi instructed the boy to stay in bed until his strength returned. Elliot groaned. Before last night Matilda would never have imagined she'd find that sound encouraging.

Kāi examined his next patient. Lucky's feet appeared better than before, though he flinched when Kāi unwrapped the bandages she and Olive had twined around him last night. The wounds in his heels and toes cut angry crevices, but she saw no swelling or sign of infection.

"Do you think Lucky might be sick?" she asked Kāi. "He's never gotten hurt or weak since I found him in the river."

Shrugging, Kāi covered Lucky's feet with the blankets again. "His injuries are normal for a man running barefoot through the woods."

That's what worries me.

— CHAPTER THIRTY-SEVEN —

MATILDA

Matilda departed for church alone only after Olive insisted and promised to help Kāi look after Elliot. With the dirt streets now a deep, uninviting bog, only a few other buggies waited outside the church. Matilda took her seat and bounced her knee in place when the service began.

She shouldn't have come here. She should be home with her brother. And with Lucky.

The more she thought about it, the more she realized Lucky's injuries weren't the only signs she'd misread. Instead of worrying that his appetite was half the size it had once been, she'd only been grateful to have her stores last until spring. She'd decided he must be bored with their morning rides, but what if his slower gait and diminished stamina were a symptom of something more severe?

Kāi's evaluation of Lucky's health had left Matilda feeling torn and uncertain. The weaker he became, the more danger he'd be in, but the more humanlike he acted, the closer she came to learning truths she so desperately needed.

He spoke. Even if he'd chosen the most aggravating word possible for his first, he'd finally taken that step. Now, to get him to start running…

She wasn't the only one who had come to church alone. Joseph sat at the front, the seats on either side of him empty, and the set of his shoulders looked forlorn, worried.

Where is Mother Harrison?

At the end of the service, Matilda mumbled apologies as she squeezed ahead of an older woman in the aisle. Others trickled out of their pews, and the air stirred with noise.

Whispers slid off every tongue. They slipped in and out of Matilda's attention, unheard, until one word broke through her thoughts.

"Fenian."

She halted in the aisle. There it came again. "Fenian." Everyone muttered the same horror.

Her teeth ached as she clenched her jaw. *Have they not accused me enough?*

But the voices murmured low and fearful, and instead of the sharp glances she'd almost become accustomed to, no one even noticed Matilda. Men and women moved timidly down the aisle, huddled together in a single mass. Sheep watching for wolves. Even Richards and his children bumped past Matilda without so much as a scowl.

"Fenians." Richards puffed out his chest. "I've been saying it for months!"

Matilda felt as though she'd been thrust back into last night's storm. She fell into a stupor, lost and jostled by the crowd until a strong hand pulled her from the throng.

Joseph didn't greet her cheerfully; instead he adorned the diplomatic mask she only saw when he wore his police uniform. Today that mask looked thin. While the rest of the congregation filed out of the church, Joseph led her back to her empty row, but even after the worshippers had left them alone, uncertainty clouded his expression.

"Is something wrong?" she asked when time wore on and he still didn't speak.

He laid his hand over hers. His affection should have felt scandalously welcome, but today it felt...mundane. She really must have lost her senses in the storm if the touch of Joseph's hand didn't melt her.

"I'm not sure how to tell you this," Joseph said.

The admission made Matilda nervous. Joseph always knew what to say. He always knew *exactly* what to say. She held her breath in apprehension. Anything that had him stumbling to find the right words couldn't be pleasant news.

"We think we identified the madman on Richards's farm," he said, his words uneasy. "He is—*was*—a Fenian."

"A—" Matilda couldn't say it aloud. That would make it real. That would make it real a *second* time.

It's a coincidence. Nathaniel's letter and now this... Coincidence.

Joseph met her gaze, his doubts still present behind his mask. "We've learned there may be a branch of the Brotherhood hidden somewhere near New Westminster. They call themselves 'Sceolan:' the hound of Fi— I'm not sure how to say his name."

"Finn Mac Cumhaill," she said hollowly. "My father used to tell me of the myths."

They'd been happy memories once—her and Nathaniel each on one of Father's knees while he told them fairy tales of Irish Finn Mac Cumhaill's strange adventures. She hadn't known then that her favourite childhood stories would become the symbol for Father's rebellion.

"Yes, that's it," Joseph said. "We think they're scouts. The hound sent before the hunter."

Joseph went on—something about the Fenians' likely target being the new railroad in Vancouver, a target that would knock a heavy blow to the entire country whether they chose to usurp the rail or sabotage it—but for once Matilda could barely listen to his voice. Thoughts of her own drowned him out.

Sceolan. Hounds. Wolf men.

That wolf man was a Fenian? Did Richards torture him?

Maybe Richards had set his traps for Fenians, not strays, and then he'd turned the men into real hounds. Or maybe the Fenians were twisted enough to do it to themselves.

But what did any of this have to do with Nathaniel's murder? Had he stumbled upon Richards's vile deeds and paid the price?

And what did this mean about Lucky? Was he—

Matilda shoved the thought aside. No. Lucky wasn't a Fenian. He couldn't even say the word!

Lucky, who savoured warm sunlight and Kāi's Chinese sweets, wouldn't have trapped himself somewhere between human and beast. He'd been terrified and hurt when she'd found him—locked up and corrupted into something dangerous by someone with less humanity than the monsters he created.

Richards was capable of such cruelty. So were the Fenians.

And somewhere between them awaited the answers Matilda needed.

"Are you listening?"

Joseph's voice and a tug at Matilda's hand brought her back to the chapel. She felt numb, like she didn't own her own body, and the feel of Joseph's hand on hers was distant.

"I said I'm worried about you alone on that farm." Joseph's voice was the only thing that felt real to her. Now that it had called her back from her thoughts, it fell over her like a warm blanket. "Between the Fenians in the woods and the people who think your brother led them here, you're in danger. I think you should stay somewhere safer until the fear dies down."

It felt like a terrible joke. All this time she'd been worried a mob would come to take Lucky from her, but when the mobs came, they'd be out for her blood. A *Fenian's* blood.

"The Fenians followed us across the country," she said. "Is there anywhere we can go they won't haunt us?"

Joseph slid closer, his knees brushing hers. "Must you ask?"

His question weighed heavily upon her. *Not now. I can't do this now.* "Mr. Harrison, we've discussed this."

"And I can be as stubborn as you." The corner of his mouth hinted at a smile and he raised an eyebrow that dared her to challenge him. "But I'd feel much more at ease to know you're not at that farm. So if you won't accept me as your husband, at least accept our old arrangement."

She looked down at their hands. His made hers seem small and feminine despite her callouses and rough skin, and more muscles than his slim build suggested made his hands strong. Competent. It'd be easier to leave all her cares in hands like his than to carry them with her own.

But what about Lucky? And Nathaniel? I owe it to them to learn the truth.

Matilda slipped her hand out of Joseph's. "I can't. Not yet."

Joseph nodded with understanding, though his eyes muddled with the hurts of a second rejection. "Well, if you know how to wound a man's body like you do his pride, I suppose you'll survive out there."

"I didn't mean to—"

"I know. Don't fret, I still have a lot of pride left." Joseph gave a half-hearted chuckle and pushed himself to his feet. "How does the saying go? 'The third time's a charm'? I'd better make my next attempt count."

She sensed the distance in his voice—the wall she'd put up between them again—but as usual his words had a way of making her smile. Even with the burdens she carried with her, she felt lighter. "Your methods are very persuasive. You only need to work on your—"

"Timing, yes."

He offered her help to her feet and escorted her out of the chapel and to her wagon. After he'd assisted her to her seat, she tried to take her hand back from him, but he held it tightly. The smile and laughter abandoned him, leaving his features with a grim solemnity.

"I know it's Nathaniel who holds you back," he said, setting her hand gently in her lap, "but he can't help your family anymore. I can, if you'll let me. I hope one day you will."

Joseph set his bowler over his golden hair and tipped his hat to her. Without another word, he returned to his own buggy and left her alone in the churchyard.

The sun peeked shyly through the clouds as if embarrassed to come out after it had let yesterday's storm frighten it away, but it gave Matilda little peace. Guilt stalked her journey home and clung to her as she brushed down Duchess in the barn.

Joseph wouldn't keep his interest in her forever, and Matilda hadn't missed the looks other unmarried women gave him. Young women with willing hearts and better tempers. How long would he wait while she chased demons?

She imagined a life for herself at the manor—full of pretty dresses and beds without lumps. She'd smell like garden flowers and honey instead of chicken feed, and instead of "Fenian" her neighbours would know her as "Mrs. Joseph Harrison." Elliot would learn proper manners. Olive could have as many paints and brushes as her heart desired. And Lucky—

Lucky wouldn't fit into Matilda's fantasy.

No matter how she tried to picture him curled up at her feet in the Harrison's parlour, he wasn't there. If she imagined herself waking in her room at the manor, no one waited for her outside her door. The manor was beautiful, peaceful, but for all the company and the ruffly dresses in her wardrobe, the manor in her vision felt…

Lonely.

Lucky can't stay here forever.

It didn't matter anyway. She couldn't rely on Joseph's good name to wash the stains out of her own. Until she found justice for Nathaniel and peace for her heart, a life with Joseph was a beautiful dream meant to vanish.

She left Duchess in her stall with a bucket of grain, and her mood brightened when she sloshed to the farmhouse. Elliot and Lucky huddled in their blankets by the fireplace, but they wore fresh clothes and sat in a circle with Olive and Kāi, playing a card game Olive had invented called "Wizards and Goblins."

"Play your griffin card, Lucky." Olive peeped at the cards messily arrayed in Lucky's hands. They each had ink drawings of fanciful creatures Olive had made when she was nine years old. Even then she'd had an artist's eye.

Lucky chose a card from the middle of his hand and laid it in the row of cards at his feet.

"That's a toadstool, not a griffin," Kāi said as he reorganized the cards in his hand.

Elliot peered over his hand at the army of mythical creatures Lucky was building, then checked the time on the pocket watch sitting loose in his lap. "Hurry him up. I'm going to win next play."

"Only because he doesn't know what a griffin is." Olive placed Lucky's toadstool back in his hand and added the correct card to his forces.

"You're both looking better." Matilda peeled off her coat and hung it on its hook. "Are you hungry?"

Elliot grimaced and nodded to a pot sitting on the stove. "Olive already forced us to eat the potato soup she made. Ugh." He ignored the frown Olive shot him and checked his pocket watch again.

"You need to eat to get better," Kāi said. He looked up from his cards and gestured to Matilda with them. "Want to join the next round?"

After grabbing a bowl of soup for herself, Matilda claimed one of the blankets and knelt between Lucky and Elliot while Olive dealt a new game. It had been years since they'd played, and Matilda had never fully understood the rules, but she squealed mentally when she found a wizard in her hand.

The game was a welcome distraction from Joseph and Fenians. Matilda started to wonder if even Olive knew the rules to her own game, but none of it mattered when Elliot cackled after another victory, sounding like his old self. Kāi proved he was a faster study than Matilda when he won the next two rounds before needing to return to the manor. Olive cheered when Lucky finally learned to recognize the griffin card, and Matilda only realized how many hours they'd passed laughing when she caught sight of the time on Elliot's watch. Already the sky darkened outside the window.

"We're late with evening chores," Matilda said.

"Just one moment." Olive watched over Lucky's shoulder and tried not to smile as he considered the cards in his hand. After a moment of squinting at his options, he chose one and added it to the pile at his feet. Olive erupted into applause. "Well done, Lucky! You have a goblin hoard!"

Elliot threw his cards in his lap. "He actually beat me?"

Olive beamed. "And all by himself."

He learned the rules faster than I did!

"Wait." Matilda glanced from Lucky's pile of goblins to her army of black cats and wizards. "I thought three wizards beat a goblin hoard."

"You only have two wizards. That one is a..." Olive studied the third card in Matilda's pile, and her face flushed. "A hag."

That explains why she looks like Miss Kovacs.

Matilda dumped her cards in a pile on the floor. "Come along, Olive. We'd better hurry if we want to finish before nightfall." As she rose from her blanket, she ruffled Lucky's hair and appreciated how silky his locks felt between her fingers. "Smart boy, Lucky. You won."

His gaze darted to the door. He abandoned his cards and strove to his bandaged feet.

"Don't!" She pushed down on his shoulder, but he was determined to follow her outside. "You shouldn't be on your feet yet. Olive and I will take care of the chores tonight."

He brushed her off his shoulder and stumbled toward the table, bracing his weight on it. The muscles down his back tensed and he bit back pain, but his eyes fastened to the door. No—to something beyond it. He growled, and his gaze hardened, vigilant and territorial.

She'd seen that look before—in the barn a moment before the Fenian wild man appeared. Matilda's breath caught in her throat.

"We'll be right back." Olive misinterpreted his grumbling and tried to soothe him. "You won't even have time to miss us."

"Hush!" Matilda fetched her rifle and hurried to the window, flattening against the wall. She peeked outside. "Do you hear that?"

A rumbling sound had her convinced of another wild man outside, but then other sounds broke through the din. The barking of dogs. Men shouting battle cries and curses. And then the roar of hooves and guns.

The hounds appeared first in a pack, feeding off the rage in the air and maddening with it. They zipped toward the farmhouse as a legion of horses brought men with rifles. Scarves covered the faces of the men but couldn't hide the hatred that fuelled them.

They thundered through the meadow. Weapons fired into the heavens as the hounds bowled through the chicken coop and snapped at the cows' heels. Axes hacked Lucky and Elliot's fence to the ground.

Drums pounded in Matilda's ears. She slid the butt of her rifle into place against her shoulder and ran for the door. *I don't care how many of them there are. I'll put a bullet in their kneecaps!* Her hand twisted the doorknob.

"No!" came a man's clumsy voice from behind her.

A scuffle in the house distracted Matilda from her righteous fury enough to disrupt the war drums in her ears. Olive and Elliot each held fast to one of Lucky's arms and dug their heels into the floor as he dragged them toward the door.

"No!" He growled through gritted teeth and tried to shrug off his extra appendages. Olive and Elliot clung to him, slowing his charge but unable to alter his course. Red seeped through the bandages on his feet. He limped forward. "No!"

"Please don't!" Olive begged.

Elliot dug his fingers into Lucky's arm. "They'll kill you, you fool!"

Matilda's hand tightened around the doorknob, her rage making demands she'd only satisfy with blood, but Olive and Elliot couldn't hold Lucky back without help.

She released the doorknob. "Upstairs. Now." She bolted the door and flung the curtains shut over the window. "Lucky, get upstairs *right now!*"

He resisted the command in her voice but eased his struggle toward the door. Between the three O'Connors they pushed him upstairs and barricaded themselves in Elliot's room. Matilda leaned her rifle in the corner, ready to reclaim it if the mob came to the house, but Olive and Elliot climbed onto the bed and wedged themselves against the wall. Elliot hugged Olive as she wiped away a torrent of fearful tears.

"No. No." Lucky paced at the door, each step limping and less steady by the second. "No."

"Sit down." Matilda guided him to the desk by the window and pushed him down into the seat. He fell into the chair heavily, but his eyes were steely as they met hers.

"No." Each growl came quieter than the last, but the sharpness in his gaze never dulled.

She ran her fingers through his hair again, calming them both. "I know. I'm angry too."

"No."

Knotting her fingers in his locks, she peered out Elliot's window. The mob pulled more planks off the fence and scattered the cows into the woods. Matilda counted every hen the dogs ripped apart. For each one of them she plotted a new and worse revenge.

"I don't care if Nathaniel was a Fenian," Elliot said, his eyes deadlier than the mob's guns. "They're every bit as bad."

Olive rubbed more tears away with her sleeve until her skin rubbed raw. "Why won't they leave us alone?"

Because we won't denounce our brother.

Elliot pulled his sister closer, but with every gunshot Olive shuddered and his scowl twisted viciously. They should both be happy and safe in their beds, but they hid in their own home from the threat of monsters Matilda'd ignored for too long.

It was my choice to stay here, not theirs. I can't do this to them anymore.

The coop and fence destroyed and the mob's wrath appeased, the men whistled for their dogs. They waved their guns at Matilda in the window, but they left the house alone and rode for the city with the last of the day's light.

"They won't bother you anymore," Matilda said. "Gather your things. Tomorrow you're going to stay with Joseph."

— CHAPTER THIRTY-EIGHT —

MATILDA

For weeks Lucky spent his time inside, waiting by the door for Olive and Elliot's return from school. They never came.

Joseph had been furious to hear of the mob, more so when he'd realized Matilda planned to stay on the farm alone, but he'd kept his anger hidden to make Olive and Elliot feel welcome.

He'd promised to investigate the attack, but she expected no closure. Those men would protect themselves, and Joseph was too honest to seek justice outside the law. But he'd keep Olive and Elliot safe. She could depend on him for that.

Over the days that followed the attack, all but one of her cows returned to the farm on their own. When his feet were less tender, Lucky laboured on a new chicken coop and fence during the days, but each evening, after completing her chores, Matilda ventured into the woods to look for the cow yet lost. After so long, she feared she'd find it dead. Still, she took Lucky with her in the hope his keen senses would lead them to the beast, but each time he only brought her too close to the Richards farm for comfort.

Rifle in hand, Matilda slipped into her burgundy spring coat. Lucky knelt on the floor and rested his chin on the table, watching

Matilda with sorrowful eyes that looked more like a pup's than Sable's did.

He knows they're not coming back.

"Don't look so sad," she said. "I'm still here. Come on."

Moving like he weighed more than the earth itself, Lucky heaved himself to his feet and shoved his toes into his shoes.

Matilda felt glad for the warmer spring days, even if they brought mosquitoes with them. When they stepped out of the farmhouse, her feet trudged across the meadow, but Lucky's only made light padded sounds and rustles through the grass.

"You know what to do," she said.

As he always did, Lucky headed into the woods. The soaring trees stifled the sun's heat but let a few delicate rays of light splash over their heads. A magpie squawked at Matilda like one of her old schoolteachers, and a fawn vaulted across the forest path. She didn't see the fawn's mother but felt watchful eyes on her.

They walked slowly, Matilda shuffling her feet and keeping her eyes open for Richards's traps. When the woods opened to his unploughed fields and pasture, her will faltered.

This is where I found Nathaniel. This is where he *killed him.*

She halted in the cover of trees, her heart warning her not to go back to that place.

A piercing whistle put her on edge. Richards's mutts dashed from the barn in a mad sprint, but they didn't charge at her. They broke through the herd of colts and raced toward the house far down the field. They were probably after table scraps, which meant the Richards family had recently finished supper and should all be inside where they couldn't jump out at Matilda from behind a tree. She hoped.

"Those are Richards's animals, not our cow." Even though the dogs had disappeared from sight, Matilda kept her voice low. "Are you losing your sense of smell too?"

Lucky gave her an insulted grumble.

This is pointless. The cow probably got swept down the Fraser. "We'll end up shot if we stay here." She pinned her rifle under her arm and turned from the pasture. "Let's go."

"No." Lucky's stubborn glare would have sat naturally upon Elliot's face. He tugged at her sleeve then bounced over the pasture fence.

"Are you mad? Get back here!" She backed away from the fence and hid behind a fir tree, but Lucky stood in the open, an easy target. "Richards is a killer. He killed Nathaniel, and he tried to kill you, remember?"

With a nod toward the Richards barn, Lucky inched toward it but waited for her to follow.

"No, I'm not going. And neither are you. Get back here!"

He doesn't have to be as headstrong as Elliot just because Elliot isn't here!

Lucky took another step back and paused, waiting.

"Get yourself killed, then!" She feigned indifference and marched toward home, but she didn't hear Lucky's footsteps join her.

When she looked over her shoulder, he was making his own march toward Richards's horses.

"Lucky!" She rushed back to the fence, found a foothold, and clambered over. "Come back. I mean it!"

His ear turned to her, but he didn't look back, and he didn't slow his march at her command. If anything, it spurred him on. She crept across the field after him, warning bells clanging in her head as he stalked toward the horses gathered by the water trough.

He'll spook them! What if we're seen? What if the dogs return?

A buckskin raised its head at Lucky's approach. A few pintos sidestepped away as he cut through the herd, but two black beasts remained at the trough and allowed Lucky to approach. As he'd seen Olive do back home, he stroked the neck of one, and he sent Matilda a look that, clear as day, said, "See? I told you."

The beasts at the trough weren't colts.

They were Matilda's cows.

"That— That's the cow I lost last autumn! She's been here all this time?" Matilda's fears competed for space inside her as a ball of heat raged through her stomach like a flame on a dry prairie. That weasel of a man was stealing her herd!

At least it explained Lucky's disobedience. *I did tell him to do anything he could to make me understand him.*

"See if you can find us some rope," she said as she set down her rifle and propped it against the trough. She eyed Richards's farmhouse. She didn't hear the dogs anywhere, but when she did, it'd be too late. "Hurry, but don't be seen."

Compliant once again, Lucky's only sign of disobedience was a displeased growl when he glared at the barn. He leapt over the fence again and disappeared behind the building while Matilda kept the cows from wandering away. He returned in a moment with coils of cold, heavy metal. Broken chains dangled from his hand, each with a dog's stiff collar suspended from one end.

"I suppose this will do," she said.

She took one of the chains and, fastening the collar shut, looped it like a noose around one cow's neck. The collar's rough leather scrubbed at Matilda's fingers as she adjusted the chain. She almost pitied the nasty mongrel that had worn it before. How the collar must have chafed its neck. It reminded her of something…

Lucky's rashes!

She dropped the chain like it had grown hot. It slipped from the cow's neck, but she left it and crawled over the fence.

Her breath quickened as she approached the barn. When she slipped past the door, rusted tools lined the walls—hoes, shovels and a rake with a broken handle. Under the shade, the tools seemed to levitate, ominous and deadly. The familiar aroma of straw, animal feed, and oiled leather filled her nose, but so did the pungent scent of whiskey and blood. In the far corner, several chains screwed into the wall. Near them, the bones of a devoured rabbit collected flies.

Don't jump at shadows. Any farm with a dog would look like this.

Unless it hadn't been a dog chained to the wall.

Lucky hates barns…

The enormous barn closed around Matilda, tightening, suffocating. She couldn't breathe; when she tried, she inhaled the scent of blood and death.

I found Lucky on Richards's land. And the other wolf man. They were here! Richards chained them like animals. Starved them.

She'd been trying to find proof of Richards's evil for months, but this… Matilda pressed a hand to her stomach and tasted bile.

Strong arms wrapped around her and dragged her into light and fresh air. She covered her mouth and leaned into something warm. Lucky supported her while she breathed in and cleansed herself of the barn's taint.

In the distance, a door's hinges squealed, and Lucky lowered them to their hands and knees, a faint growl in the back of his throat as he covered her with himself. Her head spun as she leaned over the ground, but she made out Richards toddling out of his house. Matilda tried to hold her breath and crawl toward the pasture and her rifle by the trough. It only made her stomach reel. Lucky pulled her back into him, and she squinted across the field, searching Richards's hands for his gun.

He'll kill us both!

Richards slammed the door shut and scratched his belly, revealing no weapon. He waddled over to the gelding he'd left hitched by the house, freed it from the post, and lugged himself into the saddle. With a rough kick of Richards's heels, the horse trotted toward Sapperton Road.

Matilda eased her breath between her teeth as Richards disappeared. He'd be headed for another night of drinking.

When the nausea faded and she gained enough presence of mind to put words together, she freed herself from Lucky's hold. He'd growled at Richards. Did he remember him? Did he remember those chains she'd seen inside the barn? She gestured to the barn's gaping maw. "Is this why you hate barns? Did he keep you here?"

"No." Lucky shook his head, his hair swaying across his forehead as he returned to his feet.

No? But where else could it be? He…

"No?" she said. Her nausea threatened to return when she stood too fast. "Then you remember where. Is it nearby?"

Perhaps Lucky guessed her intentions or maybe it was the memory of his former dwelling alone that filled him with dread. Whatever the reason, he warily gave a single nod, so small she might have missed it if she'd blinked.

She chewed her lip. A single light emanated from a room on the upper level of the farmhouse. Junior must be busy getting his sisters ready for bed. She didn't want her or her cows to be anywhere near here when he let the dogs outside again, but with Richards drowning in spirits for probably the next hour, she'd never had a better opportunity.

"It's all right," she said. She'd meant to reassure Lucky, but she needed comforting nearly as much. *It's all right, Matilda. There's still daylight; you're safe.* "I won't leave you there, I promise, but I need to know where he kept you."

"No." Lucky's voice was hard, but instead of defiance, it was fear that sparked in his eyes.

"It's important," she said. "Please."

Lucky avoided her gaze, but his shoulders sagged in defeat. Hesitant and dragging his heels, he led the way across the pasture. Matilda reclaimed her rifle, fetched the cows, and followed him.

He chose trails the woodland creatures travelled and weaved between the trees in what seemed a random pattern. It crossed Matilda's mind he might be leading her aimlessly in the hopes she'd tire or forget her purpose, but then he took her on a trail she knew well. Old prints of hooves and the toes of a man's shoes patterned the mud here. They used this path for their daily ride, but Lucky turned onto another trail where the prints all but disappeared. They'd come this way once before. Only once.

Two familiar dead trees speared upward from the earth and twisted into an arch of knotted branches. Mother would have called it a gateway to the faerie realm. Perhaps it led someplace worse.

Matilda released her cows from their chains. The beasts flicked their ears and headed toward the comforts of home.

Lucky faltered underneath the trees and stared beyond them with apprehension.

"Don't be afraid. I'm here with you." She stepped up to the archway and wondered what horrors waited ahead.

Don't be afraid, Matilda. Lucky is here.

She slipped her hand around his wrist and gave it a squeeze. "Show me the way."

His heartbeat raced beneath her fingertips, but he passed through the invisible barrier that had held him back before. They sneaked forward, side by side, but when the trail curved sharply to the right, Lucky pressed straight ahead on his own path. Matilda stored every detail of their journey in her mind—each dip and hill in the ground, each tuft of weeds that broke out of the forest floor, and the hollow tree with an abandoned robin's nest.

We're on Richards's land again...

They stopped in a narrow clearing, not big enough for a pasture or garden but wide enough for a tangled patch of grass to sweep over a low mound. A few old logs half-buried in the ground showed where a little cabin had once been. Now the foundation was overgrown and long forgotten.

"Is this it? But there's nothing here." Matilda climbed the rise for better view, but when she scrambled up the face of the mound, her toe thumped something solid beneath a covering of moss. A hard surface laid hidden underfoot.

She brushed aside the kindling and debris and peeled a sheet of moss off a wooden plateau. Her fingers felt along the planks and discovered a cold iron ring. *What is this?* She curled her fingers through the ring and heaved upward. The door groaned horribly from age and neglect, but it opened to a set of steps descending into the mouth of a black cavern.

"It's an old root cellar," she said.

The stink of rotten wood and enough alcohol to drown in wafted from the hole, but no sound drifted to her ear. This place felt old and dead. If Richards had kept wolf men here, she didn't think they were here now. At least none still alive.

She tested the first step with half of her weight. The stairs were steep but surprisingly solid. She put both feet down and gave a little bounce. The wood creaked, but no more than the stairs at home.

Still and tense, Lucky watched the doorway like it had grown teeth.

"You can stay here if it bothers you." Matilda eyed the pit below her. *It's just a cellar, nothing dangerous. I can do this.* "Wait for me."

Lucky's mouth opened as though to speak, but the skittish flitting of his eyes said the most. Matilda descended into the cellar. A second set of footsteps followed her tentatively into the dark.

The air grew only more dense and wet as she climbed down. It was difficult to breathe through it all. She clung to the railing, afraid to fall into the blackness below, and only when her heels clunked on a stony floor did she let go. She leaned her rifle against the railing and waited for her eyes to adjust.

She'd stepped into the dwelling of spirits. Instead of rows of shelves filled with stores of food for the winter, at the foot of the stairs stood four rustic chairs and a square table. An old glass lantern sat on its surface, along with eight or nine emptied whiskey bottles, a giant pot, and a hill of sooty tomes and crumpled notes. Someone had lived here once, if it could be called living, but only dust and the memory of ghosts remained now.

Tree roots broke through the ceiling and walls and dangled over Matilda's head with twisting fingers. She found herself fearing they'd strangle her, but as Matilda moved deeper into the room, she realized this was no longer a cellar.

It was a torture chamber.

At the back of the room stood a reinforced brick wall, newer than the rest of the structure and unmarred by the invasion of roots. Fastened to it, chains of iron thick as her arm snaked across the floor. Somewhere among the dust and whiskey she smelled old blood, and lots of it. It poured out of the walls and made her think of an abandoned butcher shop, the meats left to rot.

Each heavy chain ended in a solid cuff. Unforgiving, cold, and the right size to have left the rashes on Lucky's limbs.

"Oh, Lucky." She reached for his wrist in the dark, and he leaned in close. "I'm so sorry."

No wonder the barn drove him mad. How long did he starve down here?

Several sets of cuffs cluttered the ground. One set for Lucky. One for the Fenian. But there were others. Where were the others now? Buried in the woods? Fish-picked bones at the bottom of the Fraser? Anyone who could do this to a man, even to a Fenian, wasn't human.

Dread settled over her. This was too much. Too deep and too fast.

"We sh— should leave," she said. "I want to go."

He must have wanted to flee twice as much as her, but Lucky waited for her to lead the way on wobbly legs. She paused at the table to steady herself and leaned over discarded books and a sickly, warm draft of air.

Sunlight from above weakened every passing moment and only exposed half of the table before her. She stared at Richards's scribbled notes but couldn't read them without stronger light. Records? He'd kept records of this madness and cruelty?

Is this enough proof for you, Joseph?

With trembling hands, she gathered what notes she could carry, the touch of the pages like poison on her skin.

Thump!

Something struck the ground at her toes. She stifled a shriek, but it was only a few books she'd knocked off the table. She picked up one of them, and the feel of it made her mind itch with a clouded memory.

Under the twilight from above, she saw an old, leather-bound journal with a frayed red ribbon for a bookmark. Small enough to fit comfortably in one hand, she slipped the notes she'd gathered under her arm and flipped through the journal. Page upon page of scrawling cursive and bizarre symbols filled the book. The few she could make out made no sense to her, but instantly she knew them.

"This is Nathaniel's!" She couldn't mistake his mess of cursive, not even in the dim light. "He was here! He was down here!" She pictured her brother in chains, nothing but skin and bones and hollow eyes, and her excitement died. "Lucky, was Nathaniel chained here with you?"

Lucky gripped her shoulder as though to comfort her. It was such a normal thing to do it shocked her, but then the heel of his hand dug sharply into her back. Not a comfort. An urging. He pushed against her, encouraging her toward the stairs.

"Yes. Yes, you're right. Let's go home." She turned to reach for Lucky's wrist but knocked the lantern over with an elbow. The lantern shattered on the ground, but a memory of its heat warmed her skin.

Heat? Oh, no.

Lucky made a nervous sound in his throat and backed uneasily away from the stairs. Then she heard the voices.

They drew near and carried an accent she remembered from her childhood. From her father.

The Fenians! The Sceolan are here!

— CHAPTER THIRTY-NINE —

MATILDA

Keith, you fool. You left the door open."

"No," came a rasping voice—male, but high pitched and younger than the other. "I— I know I covered it up. You must have opened it again!"

The romp of Irish tones neared, and Matilda cowered from the shaft of sunlight falling on her head. *They'll kill us.*

"Quickly." She scurried about the cellar. *"Hide!"*

Chains. Crumpled paper. Dust and broken glass. Where could she possibly hide?

"What does it matter anyway?" came that raspy voice again. The other one had called him Keith. "There's nobody in these woods but that drunkard."

Wood creaked under a worn leather boot. Clumps of dirt and stray pebbles clacked down the stairs. Matilda grabbed Lucky's hand and spilled the notes under her arm.

Nathaniel's journal tumbled with them.

Matilda lunged for the book, but Lucky tightened his hand around hers and dragged her behind the stairs.

But the journal!

The steep incline of the stairs left barely room for two behind them. Wood dug into Matilda's arm and cheek. Lucky hunched over her, pinned between her and the wall. His heartbeat pounded against her shoulder and matched pace with the scamper of her own.

The older Fenian thumped down the stairs and almost stepped on Matilda's nose. His wide, stinking feet connected to ankles built for a giant of a man.

"Look at this mess." His voice boomed, gritty, and his accent ran thicker than even her father's had. It shaped the words until Matilda barely understood them. "You let in a windstorm."

"Sorry, Isaac," Keith said.

Keith's accent came watered down, the Irish gambol almost gone. A young man who'd spent more of his life in the New World than on the Emerald Isle. His feet trudged lighter down the steps, and the limp carcass of a hare swayed at his hip.

"My notes!" Isaac lifted his toes off the scattered pages and frowned at the muddy boot print he'd stamped over the ink.

"They're here, aren't they?" Keith said, more defensive than glib.

"Does a book make sense with the pages all scrambled? Get the lantern, lad, and clean it up."

Their backs to Matilda, the two men stripped off their coats and freed the rank smell of week-old sweat. Willowy with youth but every bit as rugged as Isaac, Keith crouched by the notes and helped the older man sweep the pages into a pile. Matilda tried to turn her head to look for Nathaniel's journal on the floor but couldn't get the right angle.

"Ah!" Keith snapped his hand back with a cry. He plucked a fragment of glass out of his skin and pressed the wound to his mouth. "The lantern broke."

Isaac smacked the other man on the arm. "That's the second one!"

"There's still one left," Keith muttered.

He moved behind the table, rustling and clinking. A light sparked to life and flooded the room from corner to corner, leaving rectangles of yellow on Matilda where it sneaked between the cellar steps. She pushed away from the light but could sink no deeper into Lucky. She shut her eyes and prayed.

Please don't let them see us.

"Skin that rabbit properly this time," Isaac said. "The last one barely had any meat on the bone."

Matilda cracked her eyes open again, she and Lucky still undiscovered. Isaac took the new lantern from Keith and set it on the table with the notes he'd gathered. He dropped into one of the chairs, banged his grimy feet on the table, and scratched at a black, sooty beard. She was surprised the chair held under the weight of his muscles.

"They barely had meat to begin with." Unlike Isaac, Keith only grew patchy hair on his chin, and under the flicker of light his hair glowed the colour of live coals. As skinny as he was, he looked barely more than a boy.

But he's a Fenian.

Keith pulled out a knife and took the rabbit tied to his hip. His blade ripped through skin and fur with sounds that made Matilda fear for her own belly.

I can wait. They must sleep sometime. Her body tied in an uncomfortable knot with Lucky's, but she didn't dare move. *We can wait.*

After he'd skinned the rabbit, Keith dumped it into the empty pot on the table.

"Well?" As Isaac sorted through his notes, he held each page up to the light and squinted at the letters. "You going to stew it?"

Keith rubbed his filthy hands on his trousers. "I cooked yesterday."

"And I'd do it tonight if you hadn't made a mess. It'll be hours before I've sorted these." Isaac pulled a hand-sized journal out from a pile of pages and set it atop of the tower of books on the table.

Nathaniel's journal!

Matilda's heart fell. She longed to feel the journal in her hands, to read her brother's thoughts, and to breathe life into his memory once again. Why had she let it fall from her grasp?

"All right, all right." Keith made himself even thinner to squeeze between the railing and the back of Isaac's chair. "I'll do it."

He bumped the railing as he passed, and something metal dropped to the stone floor with a clang.

"What's that?" Isaac asked. "Move it away before it takes off someone's nose."

"It isn't mine." Keith bent to pick up whatever had fallen and offered it to Isaac. "You know I only carry a pistol."

A spike of fear drove into Matilda's chest. *Oh, no.*

Isaac took Matilda's rifle and turned it about in his grimy hands. "Seems we have company."

With an ominous, petrifying slowness, Isaac dropped his feet to the floor and scrutinized every corner in the cellar. He stood, growing to the height of an ogre, and then his fierce, hard eyes pierced between the steps, straight to Matilda.

"You." Isaac gestured to Matilda with her own weapon. "Out. Now."

His deep voice thundered in her ears, and her whole body trembled with the echoes of the threats he'd left unspoken.

"Be calm," she whispered to Lucky, but her own voice wavered out of control. She shuffled from her narrow hiding place and into the low light, her arm tingling as blood trickled freely through her veins once again.

Lucky followed so close at her heels she almost felt his fear seeping into her back.

"What have we here?" the Sceolan leader said dryly. He picked up the lantern from the table and held it high. "Come for a secret rendezvous, did you? You'd better tell me who you are. Now."

Matilda raised her chin and hoped she looked brave. "If I tell you, you'll let us go."

As one, the two men laughed with a sound like the scream of unoiled wheels.

"Give us your names," Keith demanded, "or we'll have to make them up when we write them on your gravestones."

"Y— You wouldn't dare." Matilda knotted her hands in her skirts to keep them from trembling.

"Hold on." Isaac scratched his chin and raised the lantern higher to squint at Lucky. After a moment of confusion, his eyes bulged as though he stared into the face of one of the cellar's ghosts. "He's—"

"It's him!" Keith whipped his hand toward Matilda, snagged her by her coat collar, and yanked her toward him. "Get away from him, girl!"

He shouldn't have touched her.

Lucky darted around Matilda and broke Keith's hold on her, ramming a shoulder into his chest. Keith crashed backward into Isaac with a shout. Lucky barricaded Matilda from the other men, a snarl high in his throat. Vicious.

"Shoot him!" Keith shouted.

"No!" Matilda screamed.

She tore her way out from behind Lucky. The barrels of a pistol and Matilda's rifle gleamed dangerously, trained on them. Lucky bared his teeth, and light turned the red specks in his eyes into hellfire. Matilda threw her back into him. She might as well have tried to hold back a bull.

"Move!" Keith said.

"Don't shoot him!" Isaac took the words right out of Matilda's mouth. He kept the rifle pointed their way, but he threw a fiery glare at Keith. "Don't you dare pull that trigger."

Keith's pistol shook in his hands, which only made Matilda more nervous. "It's him! Last time he tried to tear my throat out!"

"Put your pistol down." Isaac growled almost as much as Lucky. "He's off limits."

They know Lucky? Then it's true. Lucky is— He was one of…

Keith glanced at Isaac with white-rimmed eyes. Slowly, he lowered the pistol, but he didn't put it away.

Isaac kept the rifle pointed at Matilda. "Now tell me, miss, what are you doing with our lad there?"

She pressed back harder into Lucky and spread her arms wide over him. "Are you the one who shot him?"

"Far as I know, that *drunkard* shot him." Isaac displayed a row of yellow teeth beneath his moustache, but his eyes were full of grief. "We tried to help him."

"And he tried to kill me for it!" Keith said.

"This place upsets him," Matilda said, "but if you let us go, I can calm him."

"*Calm* him?" Keith's voice cracked, and he staggered away from them. "There's only one who can control him, and he's the one who changed us in the first place!"

Us?

Keith was one of the wild men? But he wasn't now. Then that meant—

"How did you do it?" Matilda said. She took a step toward Keith before she knew what she was doing, but Isaac jerked the rifle, reminding her he had her in its sights, and clucked his tongue at her. She stepped back until she felt Lucky against her again, but she couldn't hold back her voice. "Tell me how to change him back!"

"Weren't you listening, girl? You can't! Only *he* can." Keith seemed either about to scream or weep, but Matilda couldn't tell which. "He cursed us to kill our own friends. I don't remember how I got away, but I remember O'Connor. He did this to us."

O'Connor?

Isaac stomped his foot. "Quiet!" he roared.

Lucky grumbled at Isaac's aggression, and Isaac's roar cut short. A brief silence filled the cellar as both Fenians watched Lucky warily, but Matilda kept him back as the taste of blood filled her mouth.

O'Connor. No. She'd misheard. "Do you...mean Nathaniel O'Connor?"

Isaac tore his eyes from Lucky and levelled them at her. "Know him, do you? Who are you?"

Something, perhaps instinct, warned her to be careful with her answer. "E— everyone calls him a traitor," she said, hating herself for suggesting it even to defend herself. "They say he was a spy for the Fenians."

"Ha!" Keith released a wheezing laugh but bit off the tail of it, eying Lucky. "*They* have it backward," he said with a squeak, though the muscles in his jaw tightening with every word said he was trying to keep his tone low and even. He raised his pistol again and tightened his grip around the trigger. "O'Connor spied on *us*. Turned us into beasts. Now Sheridan won't stop trying to kill us."

Sheridan. Does he mean Lucky?

Matilda felt the quick rise and fall of Lucky's chest against her shoulders and felt his breaths brush her ear. Everything about him told her he'd charge the men the moment she let her guard down. She searched Isaac for some sign that this was a scheme. A lie. He bit his lower lip and stared at Lucky, but not with hatred. With mourning.

"You're lying," she said. "This is a trick. You and Richards tortured Lucky. Nathaniel wouldn't hurt anyone."

"How would you know about O'Connor?" Isaac said. "Are you his wife or something?"

The look in Isaac's eyes felt like waking from a vivid nightmare only to find it had followed you into the waking world. The lines in his face deepened, and his mouth stretched into a smile that wasn't at all handsome.

"No," he said. "Look at those eyes, Keith. We're in luck! O'Connor's sister is going to help us."

"I won't help you," she said, though she didn't know if she had enough courage to resist. "I won't betray my country."

Keith spat on the floor. "This isn't about Ireland anymore. I'm not here for the Brotherhood!"

"I told you to quit blathering!" Isaac turned the heat of his stare to the other man, and Keith finally went more silent than if Isaac had sliced out his tongue. When Isaac turned back to Matilda, his bushy eyebrows wrinkled his forehead. "The only leverage I need is you. Pray if you know how to, girl, because you won't see the light of day until O'Connor gives my son back his mind."

His son?

"You'll be waiting until the Second Coming, then." Fear fluttered in Matilda's chest, but with it flared sparks of rage. "My brother is dead. He's dead, and it's your fault!"

The heat of her anger only made Isaac's burn hotter. "Liar. It took us a long while, but we finally tracked my son to this cellar. All we found were those chains and this journal."

He picked up Nathaniel's journal from the pile of notes and flipped to a page near the end. He displayed the open book to her, not needing even a peek at the entry he'd burned into his memory.

"'July 12th. Sheridan returned today. Alive but not himself. He tried to kill Isaac. He was so far gone he couldn't recognize his own father...'" Isaac paused. His jaw clenched so tight Matilda thought he'd break his own teeth, but then he went on. "'We did this to Sheridan. Changed him.'"

We?

And that name again. Sheridan. Lucky is... Matilda looked at Isaac more closely as he held the journal aloft. Broad shoulders. High cheekbones and black hair with just a little curl. Like Lucky. *Lucky is a* Fenian's *son.*

Isaac snapped the leather book shut and dropped it on the table, his head bowed with the weight of a painful memory. "I can't make sense of the rest of the book, but I'll force O'Connor to undo his magic if I have to."

Magic? Nathaniel had loved tricks of the mind, but magic? The fools had listened to too many stories of the Fair Folk.

"There's no such thing as magic," she said.

Keith thrust a pale finger toward Lucky. "Then how do you explain *him?*" Even when his squawks provoked Lucky to push harder against Matilda, Keith didn't—perhaps couldn't—lower his voice. She couldn't tell if he trembled with fear or rage anymore. "His strength and speed—no man is like that. Not before O'Connor gets to them."

"The magic wore off Keith, but *someone* controls Sheridan. If O'Connor won't trade my son for you..." Isaac nodded his head toward Lucky. "Well, then, he'll lead us to his master, and I'll tear out the blaggard's guts. Either way my boy will be free."

"Didn't you hear me?" she said, screeching now. Behind her, Lucky's body stiffened at her outburst. "Nathaniel is *dead*. I saw his body myself."

"Did you?" Isaac said. "Or did you see what he wanted you to see?"

"I—" Visions of the night Nathaniel died returned to Matilda. The dark obscuring his body. A gun in hand and a gaping hole in his throat. Lightless eyes. She'd only just spoken to him in the woods.

His voice. Had he used his tricks? Had he distorted her memory somehow?

But she wasn't the only one who'd seen him. Joseph and half a dozen officers had carried him away, and they hadn't heard Nathaniel's voice.

I felt his body and wounds. I felt the blood. She could almost feel her hands bathing in it now. She rubbed her palms on her skirts as she had that night. The dress still hid in the bottom of her dresser drawer, stained.

"He's dead," she said, and her heart broke all over again.

"We'll see, won't we." Isaac turned to Keith. "Quit your cowering and chain the girl. I'll watch him."

Keith seized Matilda by the arm, his fingers digging into her bones.

"Let go!" she said. She slammed her heel into his shin. Keith yelped and whipped his hand at her. Stars burst across her vision.

A snarl ripped from Lucky's chest, and he lunged at Keith before the man could raise his weapon.

Snap!

Keith flew. His pistol clattered to the ground, but he was hurtled into the wall with a howl and a rattle of chains. He slumped to the floor and cradled an arm that twisted the wrong way.

Matilda ran for the pistol, but Isaac turned on her with the rifle. She grabbed the back of a chair and hurled it at him.

It barely put a scratch on his enormous body, but it distracted him long enough for Lucky to collide with Isaac. They smashed onto the table in an explosion of shattering bottles, flying paper, and Nathaniel's journal.

Yes.

The book fell to the ground. Matilda dropped to her knees and reached for it.

The click of a pistol's hammer sounded behind her.

She froze. Lucky's growls and the sounds of a scuffle ceased.

Right arm limp at his side, Keith loomed over Matilda with his gun a hair's breadth from her head. She stared along the barrel toward the crazed look in his eyes. He *would* pull that trigger. She didn't doubt it for a moment.

"Call off the dog." Keith's breath hissed between his teeth. The gun shook more than before, but that didn't matter this close. "He listens to you."

Isaac lay on loose notes and broken glass, still but for the movement of his chest as he breathed. Lucky perched over him, but he watched the gun pointed at Matilda and pressed a fist into his chest. Into his scar. An old pain glinted in his eyes.

Her rifle lay on the ground, almost within her reach. All she needed was one second. Just one...

"I told you to call him off." Keith's voice rose, hysterical. "I'll shoot."

"I know." She met his stare with as much confidence as she could feign. She had an idea, but only one. "The moment you pull the trigger you're dead."

"How do you figure?"

"You only have time for one shot before he tears your other arm off, and you know one bullet won't stop him."

"Shut your mouth!"

"This is what's going to happen." Her heart slammed about her chest. She hoped Keith couldn't hear it. "You're going to put the gun down and back away. I'm going to take my things, and Lucky and I will leave."

Keith looked like a cornered animal. His finger arched around the trigger, and Matilda awaited the boom that would herald her death.

Click. He set the pistol on the ground and backed toward the wall and chains.

She snatched Keith's weapon and slid it under her coat. "Come," she said to Lucky as she grabbed her rifle and Nathaniel's journal. "Let's leave."

Lucky left Isaac sprawled on the table, and they climbed into freedom. She slammed the cellar door behind them and fled with Lucky into the cover of nightfall.

PART III
— SUSCEPTIBILITY —

July 12th, 1884

I've been a fool.

Sheridan returned today. Alive but not himself. He tried to kill Isaac. He was so far gone he couldn't recognize his own father. He's lost—a man, not a dog. We did this to Sheridan. Changed him.

Thought we were warriors. Gods, even! We're devils, the both of us.

I was wrong to give the Names away. Soon my partner in this unforgivable sin will twist them as he did Sheridan's.

No cause justifies what I've done. All I can do is fix what I broke.

Tonight, I go to the printing press. I must stop this before it gets worse.

— CHAPTER FORTY —

MATILDA

Somehow Matilda's legs held her weight as she ran, but she forgot to breathe until her lungs ached. She leaned against a tree and wheezed.

They were going to— We almost—

Darkness flooded the woods. She had no lantern to show her where to go, but Lucky knew the way. He took her by the hand, and they ran on.

She didn't remember fetching Duchess or the ride into New Westminster. All she remembered was arriving at the manor and telling Lucky to hide in Mother Harrison's bushes while she pounded on the door.

Joseph answered the door with a robe over his nightclothes, looking half lost in sleep. Everything tumbled out of Matilda's mouth in a mess of gasps.

"The woods… The cellar—"

"Miss O'Connor." Joseph rubbed at his eyes. "Come inside and calm down."

He led her to a chair in the parlour and sat her down between Mother Harrison's ivory cushions. Something hard pinched her lower back. The Sceolan boy's pistol, tucked into her skirt, felt cruel and dangerous against her.

"Is something wrong?" Joseph lit the lamp on the wall then returned to her side. "If you're here to see Olive and Elliot, they've gone to bed."

She shook her head. "The cellar—"

"You're injured!" Joseph traced the swelling on her cheek with tender fingertips. She'd forgotten about the sting of pain. Even his gentle caress reignited it. "Wait a moment. I'll find something for you to drink."

"No!" she said, halting him in his tracks. "Will you listen to me? I saw them!"

"Who?"

"In the woods. Fenians."

She said it before she'd thought of the consequence. At the mention of the Brotherhood, something dark flickered behind Joseph's eyes. It lasted only a moment, but even when the look passed, a sharpness remained in his features. He was the policeman now—not the one who patrolled the city with a smile but the one who knew his pistol better than the man who'd designed it.

"Where did you see them?" He knelt in front of her. "How long ago?"

"Half an hour ago, I think. Th— there's a cellar. In the woods southeast of your uncle's farm."

Joseph messed his hair as he ran his hands through it. He disappeared from the parlour, and when he returned, he'd dressed and brought a glass that he placed in Matilda's hand.

"This will help with your nerves," he said. "Drink it, tend to that bruise while I'm gone, and for heaven's sake *stay here,* do you understand me?" Without waiting for her response, he grabbed his coat and ran out the door before he'd gotten his arms through both sleeves.

The silence in the house rattled her, and she sipped from her glass, startled at the fruity taste of Mother Harrison's brandy. It had been slipped into her drink with less subtlety than one of Elliot's insults.

The drink poured down her throat in a warm stream, stealing some of the cold and fright from her body. Soon her heart pounded evenly instead of throwing itself against her ribs. Her thoughts muddled, soothed.

"Matilda?"

Olive stood outside of the room with a woollen shawl wrapped around her nightdress. Her sister blinked heavy eyelids and crossed the room. She sank into the chesterfield across from Matilda, leaning forward with her dainty fingers hooked through the knitting of her shawl.

"Something's wrong, isn't it," Olive said. "Is it Lucky? Tell me something!"

The night Mr. Gän had attacked Joseph had been one like this: sinister and too quiet, with the haunting sense that the same walls that should have protected her instead trapped her with no escape. Olive's eyes gleamed with the same fear Matilda had felt that night.

"Lucky is safe." Matilda set her glass next to Joseph's pipe on the table by her chair. She scooted to the edge of her seat and patted her sister's arm. She'd meant it to be reassuring, but Olive's skin was so warm Matilda's icy hand must have felt like the touch of death. "We learned something tonight. Nathaniel wasn't a Fenian. He was trying to stop them."

"Trying to stop them?" In the dim light Olive's crystal blue eyes looked black. "Are you certain?"

"Yes. They said—" Matilda shut her mouth. Better not to mention anything about the Sceolan. Instead she reached into her coat, feeling for her hard-won prize. "I found his journal. It's filled with...magic. I don't know what else to call it, but if I learn it, I might be able to get Lucky to speak."

She opened the book to a random page and ran her eyes over scribbled diagrams and words that held no other meaning to her than the familiarity of her brother's hand. Her gaze took in every sketch and letter, drunk on the pieces of himself Nathaniel had poured into each line.

Olive's fingers stretched toward the book, yearning. They drifted over the pages and traced lines over the ink. Then she slipped her palms behind the cover and snapped the book shut in Matilda's hands.

"I think you should stop now." Olive pulled hesitant hands away from the book.

Stop? "Didn't you hear what I said? Nathaniel—"

"Is gone."

Those two words were the harshest, coldest, most *ruthless* thing Matilda had ever heard come out of Olive's mouth. She drew back in her seat again.

"I care about him as much as you do," Olive said. When Matilda pulled away, Olive nudged closer, barely on her seat at all. "I loved him more than I've ever loved anyone, and it sickens me to hear what people say of him. I feel sick *all of the time.* I've decided I want to be happy now. Nathaniel would want that."

Olive didn't know the Nathaniel that haunted Matilda's dreams. He wouldn't be satisfied if she saved herself and abandoned him. He'd never let her go. So she couldn't let him go either.

"Mr. Harrison has been very generous to us," Olive said. "He's a good man, and I know you have feelings for him. Why have you held them back?"

Matilda hid Nathaniel's journal inside her coat and pressed it close to her chest.

How can I give Joseph a heart that's broken?

She removed her hand and stood. Or wobbled. Her run through the woods had caught up with her. Or was it the brandy? "Joseph expects me to stay, but Lucky is waiting for me. Think of an excuse, will you? Say... Tell him that I—"

"That you're a fiercely prideful woman?" Olive said.

Must that always be a bad thing? "Good night, Olive."

She sent her sister upstairs and returned her glass to the kitchen, but when she headed for the door, a shadow leaned against it.

Elliot must have come downstairs when Olive had, but he'd been awfully quiet.

"Is it true?" he crossed his arms over his chest and stepped toward her. "Nathaniel wasn't one of them? And he really didn't kill himself?"

She should have left without the drink. She didn't know if she could depend on herself to say the right words. "It's true," she said, trusting no other confession, but a burden on her tired heart eased to say it aloud. "I have proof enough for us, and, in time, I think I'll be able to find the evidence I need to declare it to everyone else."

Elliot dropped his arms to his sides, his hands balling into fists. "Olive's right. You should stop. I want you to stop, but they took him from us, and I…" His voice rose in pitch, losing composure. He sniffed back a tear she couldn't see in the dimness. "Whoever killed him, I'll—"

"Oh, Elliot." Matilda threw her arms around her brother, pressing him tightly against her. She shouldn't have come here. She'd sent her brother and sister away to be happy and safe. Why had she brought this burden to them? "Don't say it."

Her brother tensed in her arms, and when he spoke his words were the edge of a knife. "I want to hurt them."

"I know," she said, "but you're better than them."

She held her brother until his fists unclenched and he stopped trembling with an aimless rage. When she sent him upstairs to bed, he seemed older than he had any right to be, and she didn't know if she could ever bring back the little boy he'd lost.

Joseph, please look after them.

She'd held Elliot longer than she'd thought. When Matilda stepped into the yard, the city had gone even stiller, and the moon had sailed farther across the sky.

Without a gardener's care, Mother Harrison's bushes grew wild, and even within reach of them she couldn't spot Lucky hidden among the leaves. She smelled far too much brandy on her breath when she opened her mouth to call him, but before she could say his name, she heard him.

He growled at her approach, making the bushes shake and the hair on her neck raise.

Lucky grumbled to express displeasure at baths, thunderstorms, or being told not to chase the gulls in the meadow, but never like this—not since she'd let him out of the barn. Never threatening.

She turned to stone. "What's wrong with you?" More of the brandy wafted off her tongue. Too much. The scent made her sick.

The growl retreated back into Lucky. Mother Harrison's bushes rustled, and he withdrew from hiding, his head lowered in apology. He greeted her with an anxious bump of his forehead against hers.

"You're forgiven," she said. She let him pause against her longer than she should have. After the fear and panic of the night, he was the one thing that made her feel stable. "We're both a little sensitive. Let's go home."

Despite the dance of stars in the heavens, the journey home felt like crossing a battlefield. At every moment Matilda was aware of Nathaniel's journal inside her coat. She laid one hand over it. It had been too hard won to let slip away again, and every house she passed seemed to watch her. Once she led Duchess out of the city, Lucky strode unusually close to Matilda and bumped shoulders with her. That, and the feel of the pistol against her, made her feel more secure, but she kept her eyes to the woods stretching by the side of the road.

When they reached the meadow, the cows she'd rescued from Richards waited for her near the barn and a lantern turned the farmhouse window orange. The light enticed Matilda to hurry home and rub the aches out of her feet, and as she saw to Duchess and led her cows to the pasture, her anticipation built. She shivered from nerves and exhaustion, but when at last she and Lucky left the cows behind and approached the farmhouse with longing, something in the back of Matilda's mind warned her.

I didn't light a lantern.

She felt for the pistol under her coat, but Lucky already marched up the steps to the door.

"Wait—" She hurried after him, ready to pull out her weapon at the first sign of a threat.

Apart from the flicker of the lantern's flame, the house stood still and quiet. Lucky entered the sitting room, his posture relaxed and calm.

See? There are no Fenians in the house. She almost believed herself, but when she shrugged off her coat, the stairs groaned under someone's weight.

With the pistol, she ducked into the kitchen and took cover behind the cupboards. She peeked around the corner, aimed the weapon toward the stairs, and prayed it was loaded.

"I have a gun," she said. She steadied her arm against the counter. "Come downstairs. Slowly."

"Please, lower your weapon," said a young woman's voice. The words carried a foreign accent, but not an Irish one.

"Who are you?"

The light reached the stairs with weak rays, but a silhouette of a woman with raised hands glided down the steps like a swan over a lake. Her clothes barely rustled, and when she entered the amber light, her robes of silk shone crimson. But for lips the shade of her dress, her face was painted unnaturally fair.

The teashop girl? Matilda blinked, making sure she hadn't imagined the woman, and a sense of unease began anew in her stomach. She lowered her pistol but kept it at her side.

"Miss O'Connor?" The teashop girl lowered her hands and posed with the grace of a dancer. "I am Mîfä. I have come for a favour."

— CHAPTER FORTY-ONE —

MATILDA

Matilda blinked, but the woman didn't disappear. Lucky crossed the room and appraised the stranger, walking circles around her, and the woman dipped her head to him in greeting and showed no sign of fear.

"What favour?" Matilda asked. Whatever it was, she had a feeling she wouldn't like it.

"Kāi kept your friend secret," the woman said. "Now you need to keep my secret."

Matilda crossed her arms over her chest. "I don't know how much Kāi told you, but I've had enough of strangers and surprises today."

The woman opened her mouth to answer, but before she could get a word out, the front door swept open.

Matilda whirled around with her pistol, but it was only Kāi who stepped through the doorway. At the sight of her weapon, he uttered a string of Chinese and raised the sack he carried like a shield. It smelled like fried fish and onions.

"Don't startle me!" Matilda said. She set her pistol on the table before she could put a bullet in someone's leg, but her fingers itched to pick it up again. With the night she'd had, the next person who barged through her door might not be friendly.

Kāi lowered his sack with a relieved sigh. "*I* startled *you?*" He came the rest of the way inside and shut the door.

When his eyes found his lover across the room, he dropped his sack by the door and rushed protectively to her side. Touching the silk-clad woman only with his gaze, he fussed over her with words Matilda couldn't understand. Whatever Mîfä's response was, her answer had a calming effect on Kāi. He stilled his tongue but offered Mîfä a look that said she was far more to him than just the woman his parents had chosen, and Mîfä regarded him with a doting affection that made Matilda self-conscious, like *she* was the one who'd walked into someone else's house and was watching something she shouldn't.

Matilda flicked her gaze to Lucky. He'd already lowered his guard, seeming to trust Kāi's approval of the woman, and he perched on the bottom step of the stairs where he could watch the lovers' intimate display. Instead of embarrassment, he concentrated on them with curiosity.

Well, he might not understand the spectacle they were making, but Matilda felt uncomfortable in her skin. She cleared her throat. "Will someone please tell me why you're here?"

Kāi started at her voice as though he'd already forgotten Matilda was there. In her own house. "Mr. Võng banned me from the teashop," he said, "but sometimes we sneak away to see each other. The last time he followed us."

Oh dear.

If the girl's father had caught Kāi making eyes at her as he had now, or *worse,* Matilda was surprised he hadn't killed him.

"And you brought her here?" Matilda said as her insides simmered. What if they'd been followed again? Hadn't Kāi considered the danger Lucky would be in if Mr. Võng arrived unannounced? Didn't he realize how many people more dangerous than the teahouse owner Matilda was already hiding from?

"Yes," Kāi said, his tone rougher, "I have been a friend to you when you've asked for my help."

He made it sound as though she'd implored him to satisfy every silly whim that had crossed her mind. "I wouldn't have asked—"

"If it wasn't important, I know," Kāi said. "Why is it what you want is always more important?"

"It—" Matilda felt like Kāi had splashed cold water on her. A little heat remained inside her, but her temper had stopped boiling. "It isn't like that."

It isn't. Is it?

As a hush spread between Matilda and Kāi, the room took on an uncomfortable air. Lucky, relaxed only a moment ago, now flitted his gaze between her and Kāi, but Matilda wasn't sure what to say to mend the rift.

"I won't go back to the teashop," Mîfä said, and Matilda was so grateful for someone else to fill the silence she felt more relief at Mîfä's words than apprehension. "Mr. Võng was very angry when he found us." Mîfä's hand raised absently to her cheek, caressing a memory that stiffened her face. "I ran away. I won't go back."

Mr. Võng? Mîfä's troubles must be worse than appeared. Not even Matilda had disavowed her father so far as to call him "Mr. O'Connor." She studied Mîfä's face more closely. Even by the struggling light of the lantern she noticed the white paste on the woman's cheeks had been applied thickly. It hid every freckle and blemish. Maybe more.

She felt her own cheek where a man's hand had struck her, the skin still hot and swollen.

Kāi's eyes rested on Mîfä's cheek and hardened into black iron. He turned that unyielding stare to Matilda. "I kept my word to you..."

The threat left unspoken after his words rang clear, and even if Matilda thought he'd never betray Lucky, they'd already had too many close calls today. She turned to the teahouse girl. "Will Mr. Võng look for you?"

"Yes." Mîfä said, hard and honest.

A secret for a secret.

Matilda slid a chair out from the table and collapsed into it. Kāi was right: she did owe him a favour by now. "Then I guess it's fortunate Lucky keeps a good watch," she said.

Mîfä's dress had to disappear.

After they'd sat down to eat the fish Kāi had brought, he and Matilda mended a few of the injuries their quarrel had caused each other by trading updates on Lucky or how Mîfä had never eaten steak. Then Kāi returned to the manor late and left Matilda to find Mîfä a dress in a shade Mr. Võng wouldn't be able to see all the way from his teashop. Matilda's dresses were all too large, but Olive had left behind a dress with hems and elbows that had worn thin. It would have to do. Mîfä untangled herself from the curtains of embroidered silk, and Matilda hung it in the back of her wardrobe.

After she'd slipped into Matilda's old nightdress, wearing it like a tent, Mîfä removed the combs from her black hair and washed the paste off her skin, revealing ugly blues and purples on her cheek.

For the first time in thirteen years, Matilda felt the tiniest flicker of appreciation for her father. Of all his sins, he'd never laid a hand on his wife or children.

Once Mîfä laid her head on Olive's pillow and closed her eyes, Matilda hid the Sceolan boy's pistol in the drawer of the bedside table. Out of habit she reached for her journal, but she had too many thoughts to write anything of sense. She left her own journal on the table and instead retrieved Nathaniel's from her coat downstairs. She sat on the bed with the book open in her lap while Mîfä drifted into sleep.

Most of the entries were from a lifetime ago—Nathaniel's last week of school, the day he'd taken a job at the Wellington printing press, and his magic show in the park. The day they'd buried Olive's kitten. The day they'd buried Mother.

The memories, old and new, came to life in Matilda's mind and made her heart soar and crash all at once. To revisit the memories through his eyes and see his written hand—to hear his voice again in her thoughts—it was as if he'd finally come home.

Hungry for every drop of ink, she ran her fingers over the words he'd left behind. Words. Diagrams. Nathaniel's mind and soul in every brandished letter. Wanting to savour the words one by one but too eager at the treasure laid before her to stay on one page for long, she flipped through the entries until her eyes landed on a name that put a weight in her stomach.

Sheridan.

It was an entry written nearly six months before the fire. By the light of the candle dripping on the bedside table, Matilda etched the words into her memory.

> *I promised my partner Soul Names, but all I have is a headache from holding in the anger.*
>
> *Whenever I look at his Name, Sheridan thinks I've fallen asleep with my eyes open. It makes him nervous. He's smarter than the others.*
>
> *They poisoned Father and took away our first home. I won't let them take our new one.*
>
> *I see their Names—I see their colours, their very souls—but they won't yet answer my call. My partner waits. He doesn't know I already know the Names he seeks. I don't fully understand his plan and can't shake the feeling he's withholding part of it from me. That what he's withholding is more dangerous than hiding amid these wolves.*
>
> *I ask myself, "What does a farm boy know?" If he says this magic is the only way to stop a raid from happening here, then somehow I'll do it. The Sceolan think of themselves as war hounds. Let them learn what that truly means.*
>
> *And I will give my partner those Names, but only once I'm convinced the Power is as strong in me as it is in him. If my suspicions prove true, I can't afford any weakness.*

Unease settled over Matilda. She slapped the book shut and silenced Nathaniel's voice in her head. *It's true.*

Nathaniel's own hand told of being among the Sceolan and of… of *magic*. His writing cut into her. This wasn't the real Nathaniel. This was that stranger again—the stranger with her brother's face.

And that name. Sheridan.

Her hands had warmed the journal's leather cover, but it infused her with a chill. *No. I won't let it taint Nathaniel's memory.* She shut her brother's journal away with the pistol, crawled under the protection of her blankets, and blew out the candle.

Her dreams held no rest. The usual visions of Nathaniel plagued her, but new nightmares haunted her too. She ran through the bones of a dead grove, hunted by the Sceolan, but when they surrounded her, each of them scorned her with the same cold, blue eyes. Nathaniel's eyes. She woke with a gasp.

Beside her, a small form slumbered in Olive's place. Lost in the confusion her dream had left behind, Matilda thought for a moment it was her sister. But she'd sent Olive away. This was Kāi's lover. A stranger. Her presence in Olive's spot made Matilda feel more isolated than if she'd slept alone.

A scratching noise outside Matilda's door and a *thump-thump-thump* destroyed what calm she had left.

Who is it? The Sceolan? Mr. Võng?

A ghostly moan drifted through the walls. Matilda rolled over on the bed and felt for the ruthless metal of the pistol in the nightstand drawer.

She didn't bother sliding into her slippers and instead tiptoed barefoot across the cool floors. Turning the doorknob slowly enough to avoid the squeak of metal, she readied the pistol and opened the door.

The scratching sound grew louder, more immediate. Sable lay near Lucky in their usual place in the hall and peered up at Matilda, her tail beating the floor. *Thump-thump-thump.* The dog huddled closer to Lucky and rested her head on his chest. Protecting him.

Lucky lay asleep, but not peacefully. He twisted in his blanket and whimpered with the panicked, sleep-ridden moans of a boy lost in night terrors.

Running the pistol back to the drawer, Matilda returned to Lucky's side and nudged his arm. "Lucky." The nightmare imprisoned him too well. He wouldn't wake. She dug her fingers into his arms and shook him. "Wake up."

His eyes snapped open. He scrambled out from under her and backed himself into the corner of the hall. Rimmed in white, his eyes darted around the dark, and his chest laboured with breath.

"It's me," she said.

Cautiously, she crawled next to him and reached out a reassuring hand. He flinched away from her, but her fingertips found his tousled hair and slipped through the locks the way they did when she comforted Sable during thunderstorms.

"Shh. It was a dream. You're safe."

She stayed with him, stroking his hair and whispering calm words until her mouth turned dry. In time her efforts seemed to quell him. His breath evened. He tilted his head to accept her touch and comfort.

"You remember that awful place, don't you. You remember what happened to you there."

Her own memories of the cellar could provoke nightmares. Tough, merciless iron and the smell of blood. Snaking coils of black chain. The hair-raising misery haunting the stone and walls—the imprint left behind by the souls tortured and left to decay.

Lucky had *lived* through torments she could only imagine.

She wedged herself by Lucky and leaned into him. He leaned back.

Matilda remembered what the Sceolan had said of Nathaniel and shuddered. Had his magic touched Lucky?

He's not Lucky. He's Sheridan. A Fenian.

Matilda plucked her fingers free of his hair and jerked away from him, stung by her unwelcome thought.

A Fenian.

"Go back to sleep."

As she returned to her bed, she longed to pull out her brother's journal and read his thoughts again, but she *feared* to read them more.

If she did, she could no longer pretend Lucky was an innocent dog and her brother wasn't a monster.

— CHAPTER FORTY-TWO —

MATILDA

Matilda spread the old newspaper on the table. She flipped through the pages of crumpled articles and found a photograph surrounded by blocks of text. The headline read:

CANADIAN PACIFIC RAILWAY OPENS: VANCOUVER CELEBRATES.

The photograph depicted the festivities at the Vancouver railhead in black and white. Despite the celebration, the image looked tense, ominous. Several cold, imposing British warships supervised the crowd from the harbour, watching and waiting for the threat of a Fenian raid.

They're looking in the wrong place.

She pointed to one of the menacing ships. "What is this?"

Lucky glanced at the photograph only briefly before turning uninterested eyes away. He slumped in a chair across from Matilda and next to Mîfä, half-sprawled with his elbows on the table. Mîfä studiously chalked letters on Elliot's old slate. When she finished, she lightly tapped the slate before Lucky as if to gently remind him what he was supposed to do. Once again, Matilda had only been able to get him to write the first three letters of his name before he'd decided staring across the room and through the window was a better use of his time.

Why am I bothering with these lessons? I have the journal.

She hadn't touched the journal since that first night. She'd battled with her yearning for its words and her need to forget the ones she'd already read, but she'd not forgotten the Sceolan.

There hadn't been a whiff of them since Joseph had told her he'd found and burned the underground shelter. With their hiding place discovered, he'd assured her they must have retreated.

But Joseph hadn't seen their desperation. He didn't know she hid Isaac's son on the homestead. The Sceolan might have disappeared, but they'd track her down eventually. She'd be ready.

She kept Keith's pistol on her always, tucked into her skirt or a coat pocket, and wondered when the Sceolan would find her. Maybe they wouldn't have to.

Maybe Lucky would remember what he was and turn on her first.

Each lesson she fed him was another step closer to the moment he betrayed her, but for now he remained a dog. In fact, since that night at the cellar, he seemed more and more like one each day. He rejected human things—even things he'd once loved. He'd given up wearing his shoes though the ground hurt his feet. He no longer volunteered his help with her chores and took to chasing her last few hens whenever he thought she wasn't looking. Not even once had she heard him mutter the only word he knew.

It seemed as though the cellar had reminded him that a human soul lived inside him, and he feared to let anyone awaken it.

Matilda shared those fears.

"Boat." Mîfä filled the space Lucky's silence had left and revealed the tidy letters she'd written down. B. O. A. T.

Mîfä had proven to be a far more meticulous student than Lucky. Over time, the anger she'd brought with her the first night she'd come to the homestead had faded, and she'd replaced it with diligence in her studies and carefree, girlish smiles whenever Kāi visited. Her hold on English was stiffer than Kāi's, but she had a solid foundation to build from and the determination to perfect her skills.

"Yes, boat." Matilda flipped to another page and pointed to a photograph of a rotund man in a bowler hat. "And this?"

Lucky yawned, his eyes glazed with boredom. He stared toward the window as though he hadn't heard her.

Matilda's fingernails scratched lines into the paper. "You know what it is." She tapped the man's inky, black hat noisily with a finger. "Why won't you say it?"

She must have spoken more harshly than she'd realized. Mîfä raised an eyebrow, and Lucky crossed his arms and stared at the X they made over his chest.

We're getting nowhere.

Matilda folded up the newspaper, signalling the end of the lesson, and Lucky jumped to his feet the next moment, eager to be free. Mîfä followed him to the kitchen.

How much Kāi had explained to his love about Lucky, Matilda still didn't know, but Mîfä had taken to him faster than she had to Matilda. Mîfä couldn't know what kind of man Lucky had been. She didn't understand how that trickster lived somewhere behind those puppy-dog eyes. How liberating that ignorance must be.

As Matilda made for the stairs with the newspaper hugged to her chest, Mîfä fetched Lucky's after-lesson taffy from the candy jar.

"No, he hasn't earned—"

Mîfä offered the sweet to Lucky, and his bored expression lit up with his lopsided smile. He took the taffy happily from her tiny hands, and, as Mîfä lavished praises on him in her own tongue, he bumped his forehead against hers in gratitude.

Mîfä jumped back from him and pressed her hands to her cheeks.

Matilda's stomach burned with acid. *He likes* her *well enough.*

Well, Lucky could bump heads with anyone he pleased. The more human he became, the sooner he'd return to being Sheridan anyway. She didn't need his help anymore. If she could be brave enough, there was another way.

"It's a nice day," Mîfä said. "Should we go for a walk?" She left the question hanging, and it took a moment for Matilda to realize Mîfä was speaking to her. She took the empty taffy wrapper from Lucky and gazed across the room at Matilda with a friendly smile.

"Oh." After that catastrophe of a lesson, Matilda didn't feel much like being with company, but the sun outside the front window looked warm. Fearing the Sceolan, and fearing time alone with Lucky nearly as much—time to ponder the secrets she wished she'd never learned about him—she hadn't taken him out for their ride in some time. She'd only gotten any sun herself because of seeing to the livestock or her vegetable garden. But Nathaniel's journal called to her. "I suppose so. Perhaps after lunch?"

Mîfä's smile widened. She nodded, and Matilda plodded up the stairs. She threw the newspaper on her bed and slid open the nightstand drawer. Nathaniel's journal lay next to the pistol, its frayed ribbon marking her place in scarlet.

Be brave, Matilda. You have to get answers somehow.

For better or worse, she slipped her hand into the drawer and felt the textured leather cover under her palm. Sitting on the edge of her bed, she opened the journal to the bookmarked entry and slowly flipped a few pages ahead.

The later entries held more diagrams than words. Most of the writing she could find had been jotted down in a shorthand she couldn't decipher. She skipped through the drawings and symbols until a page that grabbed her attention flipped by. She thumbed back until she found it again.

Nathaniel had never had Olive's skill with sketching, but the ebony ink portrayed the recognisable figure of a man drawn inside a rough circle. Scribbled in bold, black letters, a name sat at the top of the page: Sheridan.

Down the page, whole paragraphs of shorthand almost completely filled the margins with ink, but the drawing itself had only two words scrawled alongside the figure of the man: "Anger" and "purple."

What does it mean?

Flicking through the pages, Matilda found three more sketches of men inside circles, one for each of the Sceolan men she knew. Each had the man's name, a colour, and one other description... an emotion? Her fingers hovered over what she assumed was the image of the man Joseph had killed. Dáithí Gallagher. His inscription read: "*Faltanas.*"

Is this Nathaniel's magic?

She flipped back to the beginning of the book, skipped over the entries about Mother or Nathaniel's work at the printing press, and searched for the first hints of her brother's secret life, but after an entry about Mother's death, Nathaniel's writings changed. The accounts of his days became fewer, interspersed instead with diagrams. Page upon page of charts and shorthand that seemed like the musings of a madman divided up chronicles of his life written weeks or sometimes months apart. Only a few more short entries appeared near the end of the book. She read one and hoped for some explanation that could give these strange records meaning.

> *It works! The Names—Faltanas, Anger, Bitterness, and Retribution—they now answer my call! I can only hold them a moment before they struggle away from me. The men wake up believing their blackouts are from too much drink, but I feel the stains their Names left behind on mine.*
>
> *It doesn't matter. I can call the Names now. It is only a matter of time before I can control them. Only a matter of time before I hand them over to my partner and let him bring an end to this.*

The trance. And those words again: *Faltanas,* Anger, Bitterness, and Retribution. Each word was capitalised.

They're titles, she realized. *No,* Names. *But what's the purpose of them? What do the colours mean?*

And this partner Nathaniel kept mentioning must be Richards, but why would he ever have joined forces with *Richards?*

She dove deeper into the journals and tried to make sense of Nathaniel's shorthand, but she could only make out a few references to other written works that tickled her memory. She'd seen them before. In Nathaniel's bookshelf.

Marking her place, she wandered to Elliot's vacant bedroom and knelt on the floor in front of the bookcase. She brushed off a layer of dust and read the titles on the spines.

There were books that mentioned mesmerists like Freud, and she recognized the books on magnetism and suggestion Nathaniel had studied when he'd trained under Miss Kovacs. He'd read them cover to cover again and again until half of the pages had fallen out. That had been a happier time before everything had broken apart.

She blinked back the melancholic thoughts and pulled out a fat book on someone named Braid.

There was another book behind it.

Not merely one. The top shelf had plenty of space for books, yet behind the row she'd glanced over, another row sat, concealed from any curious glance.

Nathaniel, what were you hiding? She pulled out the first row of books and exposed dusty texts that hadn't seen the light in years.

Maybe they should have stayed hidden. Matilda found books on topics that made her eyebrows rise: wolves, psychics from Europe, and even some titles with words she'd never heard before. Sandwiched between tomes on mesmerism and eye-fixation, she discovered a narrow book with an unravelling, hand-stitched spine. She slipped it out and opened it to the dog-eared pages. "Advanced Medical Telepathy," the first page read.

Medical telepathy? What is that?

Only about thirty pages of printed text formed the manuscript. Matilda turned past the title page and delved into the notes.

As far as she could tell, the author had been a mesmerist and a physician of some kind, though the language was too academic for a girl who hadn't finished her schooling. She crinkled her nose at long words and terms she couldn't pronounce let alone understand, but what little she absorbed surprised her. Riveted her.

If not for the technical nature of the script, she would have thought the book nothing more than a collection of fairy tales. The author detailed his research into children with strange and wonderful abilities Matilda could only ever imagine in one of Olive's novels: a boy who'd survived a stampede of elephants without so much as a broken toe, a little girl who could hear the sound of a spider weaving its web on the other side of a building, and a young man who could run from dawn until dusk with barely any rise in his heartbeat.

This can't be real, can it?

Elliot's door whined on its hinges. Feet scuffled close, and a body nudged her. Lucky.

He sat close enough to warm her skin. A thought tugged at her, a promise she'd made, but she pushed it aside before she could recall what it was. She scooted away from Lucky's touch, and her legs tingled sorely as blood flowed back into them. Had she been kneeling so long?

Lucky nudged her arm again.

"You're hungry, I know." She brushed him away. "Ask *Mîfä* for another taffy."

Moving to the desk chair, she turned to the next page of the essay and kept her eyes from straying to Lucky. *Let me be, please. I can't...*

After a moment, a rustle of movement and the creak of the door marked his departure. The feel of his presence didn't leave as easily, but with a little struggling, she evicted him from her mind. and returned to her task. Upon reading an account of five-year-old twins who never felt the chill of frost, the tone of the essay changed.

> *If such supernatural abilities appear in even a single human being, then it must be surmised the potential for it lies dormant in every man. To awaken such abilities would mean the end of*

human suffering. With more research, I am certain the Power can achieve this.

However, the Power's implications go beyond perfecting the human body. It may also be the answer to perfecting society. An accomplished practitioner could shape a civilisation devoid of war, pain, or sin.

A few handwritten words beneath the paragraph caught Matilda's eye. In a hand too feminine to be Nathaniel's, they read:

Or choice.

The words left Matilda feeling uneasy. "The Power," she said to herself. *These aren't the theories of a doctor. They're blasphemies! This can't be real!*

The Power sounded like some form of fantastical mesmerism, but Nathaniel had once told her a mesmerist couldn't force a man to do anything against his nature. This power, *the* Power, broke the rules. Not only could it force a man to do something, it could force him to *be* something.

The Power changed a man's nature.

Matilda stared at the page until the room darkened and the strain of her eyes gave her a headache. She let the pages close and glanced at the author's name.

The names of two authors adorned the page: Endre Kovacs and M. Kovacs.

M. Kovacs? Marta?

Olive's fears of the old woman had been right all along. Miss Kovacs was a witch.

Before bed each night, Matilda compared Nathaniel's books to the diagrams in his journal. She learned to make a little sense of his shorthand somewhere between milking cows, tending to the corn fields, and abiding Mîfä's invitations to walk with her and Lucky around the meadow—time Matilda mostly spent in her own head, piecing together what she'd learned from the journal.

Days blended together. Had it been one week since she'd found the cellar or two? Three?

Only Sundays stood apart in her memory. Those days she woke to hear Mîfä, already dressed and downstairs, humming happily while she practised her alphabet and waited for Kāi's arrival.

But no sooner than Matilda had thought she'd begun to understand her brother's journal, the entries darkened.

> *Sheridan returned today. Alive but not himself. He tried to kill Isaac.*

She sat at the table, her lunch barely touched. Mîfä rinsed her own plate before mumbling another invitation to Matilda. Matilda politely declined whatever it was and, as she returned to her brother's notes, did her best to ignore the crawling of her skin as she read.

> *I was wrong to give the Names away. Soon my partner in this unforgivable sin will twist them as he did Sheridan's…*
>
> *…Tonight, I go to the printing press. I must stop this before it gets worse.*

It was only a short entry, the rest of the page as empty as Matilda felt after reading the date scribbled at the top of the page. It was a date she knew better than the date of her birth: July 12th, 1884. The night of the printing press fire.

Wait… Matilda read the entry again and picked every word apart for meaning. *The printing press… Nathaniel didn't go there that night for a drink; he went to stop everything. Richards wasn't his partner—Mr. Wellington was!*

At least something made sense now: her brother's friendship with the man, their weekly meetings, and the show Mr.

Wellington had sponsored. He'd been scheming. Luring Nathaniel into his trap with power and promises.

Her gut twisted, and she ached with more questions.

But I don't understand. Richards was the only one there the night I found Nathaniel. He had *to have killed him, but…*

She delved into the penned lines on the facing page, the journal's final entry. It was dated the morning after the fire.

> *Lucas betrayed me. He promised he'd help me end this, but I guess Joseph was right about him after all. Now I'm the one picking up this mess alone.*
>
> *I don't think there's a way out. If I fight now, my sister will be the one hurt.*
>
> *I don't have the skill to face him anyway. Not yet. Until I have enough power to end this for good, I can't help her.*
>
> *For Matilda's sake, I must stay hidden where even the master can't reach me.*

At the sight of her name in Nathaniel's hand, pain flashed behind Matilda's eyes. For all the wrongs Nathaniel had done—for all his foolish, cold-hearted treacheries—in the end he'd wanted to protect her.

From what? From Mr. Wellington? What happened at the printing press?

Had Mr. Wellington refused to stop? With no other way, had Nathaniel set the fire to end his evil? Or had Mr. Wellington set the fire himself to throw Nathaniel off his trail? The knot in Matilda's gut pulled tighter.

"Wellington." She spat the name, and the sound of it made her insides boil.

But why had Nathaniel only mentioned Matilda's name? Why not Olive's or Elliot's?

She smoothed out the pages of the journal as if her touch could beckon more clues from them, and when she spread the pages, she found the tattered lines of paper that had once settled between Nathaniel's two final entries.

He'd written other accounts? She stared at the pattern of tearing, and somehow, with the feel of the journal under her palms, that tear reminded her of another tattered page with Nathaniel's words. She'd held it in her hand at the cemetery last fall.

She didn't have to run to her room and find her brother's suicide note in the drawer or lay its ragged edges along one of the torn pages here to know it would be a perfect match. She'd poured over that letter until she knew every crease and ink stain by heart.

If that page fit before her brother's final entry, then it had been written a full year before he'd been shot—before he'd made plans to fight Mr. Wellington.

I knew he didn't kill himself!

The stairs creaked as someone came down them, slowing as they passed near her table. "You're still reading?" Kāi's voice said.

"Hmm?" She wiped a damp spot from the corner of her eye and paid little attention to the voice. Far more important was the beauty of her name in Nathaniel's cursive.

"Names?" Kāi said. "Power? Is this what Olive and Elliot sometimes talk about at the manor? Your brother's tricks?"

Matilda stiffened in her chair. She turned to find Kāi reading the journal over her shoulder, and she flattened her hands over the pages. "Kāi! This is private!"

How much had he read? How much might he piece together?

"I apologize. I never see you without that book. I've been curious." He sounded sincere, but the way he stared through her hands across the journal with his eyebrows pinched tightly together, his mind was as caught in those pages as hers. Even when he brushed past her toward the door, ready to head back to the manor, his eyes had a harrowed look. "You should stop reading," he said softly.

"In a moment." Now that Kāi had interrupted her, her stomach grumbled fiercely, and she remembered her cold lunch pushed aside on the table. Had she eaten breakfast? Or supper last evening? She slipped the bookmark into place and closed the book.

Kāi's posture was as unnoteworthy as ever, but the way he scrutinized her, he might as well have crossed his arms and tapped his heel on the floor. "I meant you should stop reading it *at all*."

She set the journal on the table, but already she yearned to delve into its pages again. Now that she knew about Mr. Wellington, perhaps she'd unlock more secrets she hadn't noticed before. "Why should I stop reading?"

"What I saw in those pages looked dangerous," Kāi said, "and that journal is keeping you from your family. Your brother and sister never see you. You didn't go to your church today."

"The sooner I can solve my brother's business, the better." She slid her chair out from under the table but kept the journal under her touch. It's hold over her was astounding, like it held a magic as powerful as Nathaniel's. "Olive and Elliot understand."

"No one understands," Kāi said. "You're not yourself. You look sick, and Mîfä tells me you stopped giving lessons."

Her fingers tapped the leather journal, each fingertip rapping distinctly. *What a little spy!*

Where had Mîfä gone anyway? She wasn't in the room, and Matilda couldn't hear footsteps upstairs. Where was Lucky?

"She's grateful you let her stay," Kāi said more kindly, as though he'd heard Matilda's scathing thoughts. "I am grateful too, but she's worried."

The only thing that should worry Mîfä were those Sceolan, but they were all the more reason for Matilda to focus on the journal.

"There's nothing to worry over." It took all Matilda's willpower to let go of the book. "Where's Mîfä?"

Kāi frowned again and stared at the door. "He still needs to run, even if it tires him. Mîfä said Lucky had barely been outside in more than a week. She promised not to go far."

It isn't enough to give him taffies, she has to take over his walks too?

"She asked you to go with them, though you haven't noticed much that wasn't written in that book lately." Kāi twisted his mouth before speaking again. "If you've given up on looking after Lucky, you should get him the help he needs."

"You don't even know what he is. Well, I do." Matilda hoped her voice hadn't sounded as sour as it had felt coming out of her throat. "He's better the way he is."

"Better? He's better as your *pet?*" Kāi said. His hand grasped the doorknob tightly, but after a moment and what looked like conscious effort, he relaxed his grip. "He deserves more. I think you know that."

Lucky did deserve more–more than Matilda could give him, but the kind of help Kāi spoke of was more likely to burn away everything Lucky was to bring about Sheridan's rebirth.

What Sheridan deserved, Matilda couldn't bear to entertain thoughts of. She'd witnessed too much suffering already.

Kāi remained at the door, working his jaw back and forth as he silently considered something. After a moment, he released a long sigh. "I know you've sacrificed much for your family, but sometimes you are a..." He paused, sitting with his thoughts again. "A proud woman."

When Kāi opened the door, leaving Matilda in a stupor, he bowed his head to her as he ducked out of the house, but he shut the door with enough noise to make his objection plain.

A *proud* woman?

An hour later, Mîfä brought Lucky back. She wore a delicate, yellow blossom in her hair, and Lucky caught three weedy red clovers in his fist. Upon spying Matilda at the table, her lunch uneaten, he took the seat beside her and proudly showed her his collection.

"Yes, they're lovely." Matilda stuffed a carrot into her mouth so she wouldn't have to make conversation.

Grass-stained fingers peeled her hands from her plate, and Lucky pressed his flowers into her palm. He closed her hands around them, then left her to sprawl on the floor and let the day's heat seep out of him.

The stems tickled her skin, but she wondered if she'd imagined them. She looked to Mîfä. "Did you teach him to do that?"

As though she knew a secret Matilda didn't, Mîfä shook her head and smiled. "When he saw the patch of flowers behind the barn, he would not leave until he had chosen the best ones," Mîfä said as she sat in the seat across from Matilda, beaming. "He was very picky."

Matilda opened her palm to expose Lucky's gift to her. She'd dismissed them as weeds, but now she truly looked at them. The stems and soft leaves were a little damaged where he'd pressed them into her hand, but the petals formed perfect globes in a dainty mauve that, no matter how much she tried not to, made Matilda think of the many sunsets over the Fraser she'd watched with Lucky beside her.

Why would a dog give her flowers?

Don't do this, Matilda. Don't let yourself feel. You know what he is.

Mîfä's smile took on a wistful look. "Once, when we were younger, Kāi gave me some chrysanthemums from his father's..." She gazed at the ceiling as she searched for the right word. "The medicine shop. I had never told anyone how I liked them, but he noticed. Our parents had already chosen us for each other. I decided then that I would choose him too."

"What happened?" Matilda said. She hadn't meant to involve herself in their matters, but hiding Mîfä from her father meant she was already involved. The story Mîfä told didn't match what Matilda had seen that day outside of the teashop—Mîfä's father and Kāi, seeming on the verge of exchanging blows. What had changed her parents' opinion?

The smile on Mîfä's face waned. "Kāi told you of the wild girl?" she said, and Matilda nodded. "Against other's wishes, his father tried to help her, but...it ended terribly."

"What happened?" Matilda said again more quietly, uncertain she wanted to know the answer when her own experiments with Lucky felt one step away from the worst sort of disaster she could imagine.

"The little girl died," Mîfä said sombrely, and Matilda knew she'd get little more than that out of her, "and no one wanted to buy his medicines anymore. We call this place 'Gold Mountain.' Kāi came here to earn money to send home." Mîfä sucked in a deep breath and donned her smile again. Though it lacked the same cheer it had held moments ago, it was warm as she watched Lucky rub at the grass stains on his hands while he lay on the floor. "He likes you."

Matilda laid her clovers on the table. Part of her wanted to fetch a vase, though it seemed a silly thing to do for a handful of weeds. *She's wrong. He doesn't care for me in that way.*

And if he did, he wouldn't care for her once he remembered who he was. Once he knew who she was.

Perhaps Kāi had a point about getting Lucky help after all, though she'd never tell him that. No matter how Matilda and Lucky both tried to avoid it, Lucky was becoming human on his own. Wouldn't it be better for her to have it done with, to control the when and how before he confused her more?

Her fingers found their way to Nathaniel's journal again. If magic had broken Lucky, then magic could fix him. She only needed to learn how.

— CHAPTER FORTY-THREE —

MATILDA

The next evening, Matilda left Lucky and Mîfä watching the clouds turn the colour of wine, and she sneaked to her bedroom for privacy.

All day she'd scoured Miss Kovacs's essay and Nathaniel's journal. The essay called the magic "Power." Nathaniel sometimes called it a "trance."

I've seen the trance before.

Every time Nathaniel had helped Olive with her nightmares, she'd gone limp and quiet in a waking sleep. A trance.

That's why Mr. Wellington sponsored Nathaniel's shows. He was testing his skill. Looking for a partner. A victim.

She sat on the edge of the bed and felt for Nathaniel's coin at her throat, slipping it out from the neck of her dress. It didn't shine as it once had, but it reflected the sunset from the window with a subtle glow.

I've seen Nathaniel do it before. It seemed easy enough.

In later years Nathaniel hadn't needed help to put someone in a trance, but in the beginning he'd made Olive stare at a spoon dangling from his fingertips. It had swayed back and forth like a pendulum, catching the light and the eye.

Untying the coin from her neck, Matilda held it high overhead and concentrated on its fragile shine. She had an unwelcome thought as she watched the light play over the shape of the maple leaves.

What if Nathaniel hadn't kept the coin out of sentiment? What if he'd used the precious memory between them to hurt people?

Calm. I need to be calm.

She shut out all intruding thoughts, slowed her breath, and watched the sway and turn of the coin. One deep breath. Two breaths. Five. Twelve. Was something supposed to happen? She concentrated so hard she paid no mind to the footsteps in the hall.

"No, no," Mîfä said. She stood in the doorway, watching Matilda.

Blood rushed to Matilda's face. The cord slipped from her grasp, and the coin clinked on the floor between her feet.

Mîfä shook her head, but she wore no disapproval. She slipped inside the bedroom and knelt on the hardwood floor, beckoning to Matilda. "Like this."

Matilda remained on the edge of the bed. "You've seen this before?"

Mîfä fluttered her hand through the air. "Come."

Picking up the coin, Matilda clenched it in her palm and found a space on the floor by Mîfä. She imitated the young woman's folded legs and tucked chin.

"Close your eyes," Mîfä said. "Calm."

The wood floors were unyielding under Matilda's knees. She did what she could to ignore the discomfort, but after what seemed like an hour of nothing but kneeling and breathing, the folds in her skirt dug ravines into her shins and an ache formed between her shoulders.

"Relax," Mîfä said.

How could she relax in this position? She allowed her shoulders to slump and concentrated on her breath, matching her pace with Mîfä's even breathing.

In. Out. In. Out.

She imagined her breath flowing into her like water filling a glass vase. In her mind, she watched the line of water rising drop by trickling drop. As she exhaled, the pool's transparent surface rippled soothingly, and the ache between her shoulders eased. The bottom of her imagined vase seemed to stretch lower, deeper. The mouth of the vase widened until Matilda's consciousness floated above a tranquil, endless lake, and whenever a thought tried to grab her attention, she cast it into the pool and watched it sink into the depths below. Soon, any thoughts left in her head quieted, and all she had was the glassy mirror around her.

Somewhere outside her reverie, her legs tingled, but now the numbness in her toes felt almost pleasant. Her body felt both asleep and awake. Or neither.

The numbness spread through her. No, this feeling was new altogether. Warmth... An energy that started in her chest and tickled through her with the welcomeness of cider on a winter morning.

"Yes." Mîfä's voice sounded distant, phantom like.

Matilda cracked open her eyes and looked at Mîfä through a haze. She must have fallen asleep after all, because that was the only explanation for why Mîfä glowed. A dancing pink fire surrounded the woman, emanating from somewhere inside her.

What's happening to me?

A thrumming energy rode on the firelight toward Matilda. It spoke to her, a tapestry of voices mumbling words she couldn't understand.

When Matilda looked at her hands in her lap, another light frolicked about her in burgundy flames.

"Ah!"

She tumbled from her knees and shook the fire off her hands. The vision vanished, leaving her hands without burns, and the voices silenced as though they'd never been there. She clambered to unsteady feet and rubbed the itch out of her palms. *What happened?*

"Better?" Mîfä smiled and rose to her feet without any of Matilda's clumsiness.

"Wh— What was that?" Matilda asked. "Was that telepathy?"

Drawing her onyx braid over her shoulder, Mîfä sat on the bed. Her eyes glistened with confusion. "What is telepathy?"

"That." Matilda pointed to the floor where they'd knelt. "What is it called?"

Mîfä uttered a few uncertain words in her own language. "It's to clear the mind."

Nathaniel's coin dug into Matilda's palm as she tightened her fist. It didn't matter what the light was called. She knew she'd seen what the diagrams in Nathaniel's journal depicted—the circles drawn around the sketches of men. It was magic.

That glowing pink aura had been Mîfä's Name.

— CHAPTER FORTY-FOUR —

MATILDA

Nathaniel's magic was useless.

Each night Matilda knelt in supplication by her bed and invited that warm energy to fill her again. Even a little practice had strengthened her connection to the Power. Now it came to her readily and beat through her like a second heartbeat whether she knelt until her legs went numb or let her mind drift while she picked burrs out of Duchess's coat.

She didn't know where the Power came from or how her link with it had formed, but the more she used it, the more it became a sixth sense to her. In the same way she wasn't aware of her own breathing until she controlled it consciously, the Power was always present, imperceptible until she beckoned to it. Then she saw with a second sight. Heard what no one else could hear. Tasted things her tongue had never before tasted—like exactly which cupboard she'd stored the sugar in before she'd sprinkled it in her tea.

And yet, when it came to the one reason she needed Nathaniel's magic, it was of no help at all.

When she let her vision blur, the lights danced around human forms, subtly shifting tones with the person's mood. When Mîfä spied Kāi across the meadow on Sunday mornings, her colour changed from a dusty pink to a humming, vibrant rose. Matilda *saw* the aura plainly, but the voices that accompanied it hissed with scattered, incoherent syllables and withheld the identity of Mîfä's Name.

Worse yet, the magic didn't work on everyone. When Lucky sat at her feet in the evenings, Matilda's toes wiggled out from beneath him, her own burgundy flames burning low and murky, but no glow surrounded him. No taunting whispers called to her from him. Had she done something wrong?

Kāi hadn't given her any more of his *opinions* lately, but he couldn't hide his disapproval whenever he caught her with Nathaniel's journal in hand. She thought Mîfä might have told him about helping Matilda discover the Power. Mîfä didn't know much to tell, of course, but, since Kāi had seen Nathaniel's writings and heard tales from Olive and Elliot, Matilda worried he might be clever enough to piece more together than she was ready for him to know.

On the first Sunday in July, Matilda could barely go anywhere in the house without feeling Kāi's sideways glances at her. He and Mîfä had pulled out Olive's card game to play with Lucky, but all through the first two rounds, Matilda felt thorns in her stomach each time Kāi's gaze flitted her way. Desperate for an escape and some fresh air, she hid the journal in the nightstand drawer and left for church.

When Matilda arrived at the chapel, Olive and Elliot sat in the first row with Joseph and Mother Harrison. She took a seat next to her sister, who gave her a faltering smile but said nothing. Olive's eyes flitted away to stare intently at the altar, and she shifted closer to Mother Harrison.

Why is she so shy? Has something happened at the manor?

Poor Mother Harrison's skin hung from her face like the jowls of a bulldog, and no softness padded her bones. She wore too much makeup on her gaunt cheeks, but it was all that gave her face any colour today. "You're here today, my dear." Mother Harrison reached across Olive to pat Matilda's hand. As she stretched, her too-loose sleeve pulled back enough for Matilda to catch sight of a new bandage around her wrist. "We've missed you."

Elliot didn't look like he'd missed Matilda at all. With the humid heat around him, he slouched in his seat and dozed with his jaw slack.

Joseph gave a warmer welcome. Though the circles under his eyes had deepened, he smiled handsomely. "Good morning, Miss O'Connor."

Once the service began, it seemed it would never end. Like her brother, Matilda nodded her head to her chest—kept awake only by standing for canticles and psalms. When she sat still for the Bible readings, her conscious thoughts weakened.

And in those moments of weakness, the trance crept upon her like the tendrils of a dream.

She noticed the voices first. They breathed against her, wanting to share their secrets but speaking in a tongue she didn't know.

Then came the other sounds and smells as the Power heightened her senses. The fears and faith of the congregation were living things circling around her, intoxicating her. Dust floated through the air, and she felt each particle that settled on her skin. Stinking horse muck stained the shoes of a man at the back of the chapel. He was an old man. She *smelled* his age.

On the other side of the aisle sat Richards and his cinnamon-haired children. Halos of magic light emanated from each of them. Junior's sickly aura flickered between the shades of pumpkins and of dead maple leaves, and light the colour of a dark bruise surrounded both of his little sisters. Richards's aura swirled around him in a muddy foam that reminded Matilda of the drink she smelled on his breath even this far from him.

The magic *did* work. Why wouldn't it work on Lucky?

Glowing orange, white, coral, and teal played about the people around her. Today Olive's light shimmered the same timid blue as her eyes and smelled of youth. The deeper Elliot fell into sleep, the darker his blood-red light swirled around him. Mother Harrison's light barely rose off her skin and flickered like a candle flame near the end of the wick. It covered her in thick, oily black.

Poor Mother Harrison.

Joseph sat with his eyes forward, attentive on the sermon. His colour didn't shine as vividly as the others' lights. Instead it gleamed a steady, calming grey—a perfectly modest colour.

It's just like him. Stable. Dependable.

He must have felt her eyes on him. His head turned, and when their gazes met, his light changed.

The grey broke into other hues. It flecked with violet and red, the two colours lapping at each other and vying for space. Then a delicate, mossy green emerged between them, playing with the other colours whirling over Joseph. He gave her half a smile, and the display of red and violet bowed to that youthful green, letting it take control. It beckoned to Matilda, playful and invigorating; she longed to understand its fair whispers and return its call. Joseph was stunning, so beautiful it hurt to look at him.

I'm staring at him like a love-struck girl!

She turned forward and snapped out of the trance, blinded and deafened as the Power faded.

After the service ended, Matilda jumped from her seat, but the thought of returning to more of Kāi's glares made her feet reluctant to carry her away.

"Are you leaving again?" Joseph said to Matilda as he shook Elliot awake. "But Elliot has learned a new piece on the piano. He wanted to show you."

She wondered if that beautiful green was surrounding him now—but she didn't dare call the Power to her so soon. What if Joseph caught her staring at him again?

"Hmm? I— Piano?" Elliot groggily looked up at Joseph, and Joseph nudged him with an elbow. "Oh. I, er, piano. Yes."

"That sounds lovely..." But what about the journal? What about the magic? She needed a little more time to uncover the answers she sought. She was *so close.*

Olive took Matilda by the sleeve and looked up at her through the veil of her eyelashes. "Please come. Just for an hour."

Olive's eyes held a magic stronger than anything Nathaniel had ever done. Matilda looked into her sister's eyes and saw a young girl looking up at a stranger.

When was the last time I visited them?

She couldn't remember when she'd last said more than two words to her brother and sister. But Nathaniel... A *little* more—a little longer—and she could finally meet him in her dreams without guilt.

"An hour, that's all they're asking for," Mother Harrison said as though she'd sensed the conflict in Matilda. She accepted Joseph's hand as she struggled on weak legs. "Will you come?"

With four pairs of eyes harrying her, Matilda caved. "All right. One hour."

When they gathered in Joseph's parlour, Elliot played a hymn with a triumphant melody. It'd be years before he had Mother Harrison's skill, but he already had her feel for the music as he closed his eyes and let it guide him. Matilda felt it too, sinking into her skin as she sat on the chesterfield. The music's vibrations felt almost as thrilling as the Power until Elliot hit a note that fell flat. He hit the same note again a moment later, and she realized the mistake hadn't been her brother's.

Mother Harrison has let the piano get out of tune. Doesn't she play anymore?

"That was lovely, Elliot, but remember to...oh, I've forgotten." Mother Harrison drooped on the other side of the chesterfield with Olive snuggled against her shoulder, though her bony frame couldn't have been comfortable for either of them. "I think I should retire for the evening."

As Elliot began a new tune, Joseph pulled his pipe from his mouth and looked over the book he was reading. "It isn't yet noon, Mother."

"Oh, isn't it? But I—" Mother Harrison turned her ear toward the piano, and a nostalgic smile graced her lips as she listened to Elliot plunk out a reverent tune. "I adore this hymn, Joseph. It was your father's favourite. They played it at his…at his funeral."

Elliot ended the song in an abrupt clamour of notes.

Joseph snuffed out his pipe and dropped it on the side table. He jumped to his feet and took his mother by the arm. "You look tired, Mother. I'll take you to your room."

He led Mother Harrison from the parlour as she hid her sobs behind her hands.

Matilda pushed herself up from the chesterfield. "I'll—"

"I'll fetch the decanter." Olive hopped off the chesterfield and disappeared into the hall, and Matilda returned uneasily to her seat, unneeded.

Uncomfortable silence fell over the house. Now and again Joseph's muffled voice toned behind a closed door and carried down the hall. Though she couldn't hear a word, Matilda sensed desperation from him.

"She's worse every day." Elliot left the piano and dropped into Joseph's chair, a fearful look crossing his face. "A woman came here the other day. I overheard Mr. Harrison speaking to her. I think she's the director at the asylum."

Matilda swallowed dryly. *From the asylum? Surely he wouldn't do that to his mother.*

"Mother Harrison barely leaves her room anymore." Olive returned to the parlour, but she peered down the hallway with a sullen expression. "I used to take lunch to her because she threw tantrums if Kāi did, but now she only eats when Mr. Harrison sits with her. He can't watch her every minute of the day. He only wants Mother Harrison to be well."

Why didn't I pay attention to the circles under his eyes?

He offered Matilda friendship and even love, and she'd taken advantage of his generosity without a thought for how he suffered.

She stayed another hour longer than she'd planned, but still Joseph hadn't returned from his mother's side. "Look after him," she urged her siblings. "Both of them."

The sun climbed to its highest and hottest as Matilda slipped away from the manor, but even with sweat on her brow she couldn't shake the chill that clung to her. Once she'd brushed down Duchess and let the mare quench her thirst from the water trough, Matilda wiped a sleeve over her forehead and walked toward the house. No noise came from the building. Kāi must have already left. She thumped drearily up the porch steps and pushed open the door.

"You're late," Kāi grumbled. He leaned back in one of the chairs at the table but didn't look relaxed.

"I stopped at the manor." She ground her teeth together when a look both surprised and pleased crossed his face. He didn't have to be smug about it, but at least he seemed to forgive her tardiness. "Where's Mîfä?" she said.

She looked to the nook by the fireplace where Mîfä liked to sit, but only Lucky sprawled on his stomach there, his cheek squashed against the cool stone of the hearth.

"You forgot yesterday's laundry outside," Kāi said. "She's getting it."

"I suppose I've been distracted." Matilda fished her pistol from her reticule and deposited both on the table.

She felt Kāi's eyes upon her. "Are you going to keep that weapon? It's been months. The Irishmen are gone."

"They'll be back." She couldn't help glancing at Lucky. "They haven't finished what they came to do."

"Free Ireland from the British?"

"Look at him." She ignored Kāi's question and nodded toward Lucky. "Not a care in the world."

But as much as overheated, Lucky looked crestfallen as he slumped on the floor. Did the dog part of him still miss Olive and Elliot? Would that connection mean anything to him once he became Sheridan again?

"He has plenty of cares." Disapproval seeped into Kāi's voice again.

What colour would Kāi's light be? With his sour speech and glares lately, it was probably a sickening shade of green—not half as beautiful as the glimpse of leafy green in Joseph's. Even thinking about the way his aura had sparkled and shifted between colours healed the despair she'd caught at the manor. She felt almost giddy.

With that thought alone to beckon it, the Power poured over her in a tidal wave of energy. Her own light extended from her skin in a cloudy purple, and she felt the tingle of her blood in every vein. Kāi's heartbeat stomped like an angry bull, but through the thump of it, she heard the brush of Lucky's eyelashes when he blinked.

Lucky rolled onto his back like Sable asking for a belly rub, but no aura of light surrounded him.

Why won't it work?

"I'm going to be late," Kāi said, and she detected so many sounds on his voice her normal ears would never hear: the whoosh of his lungs releasing air into his throat, the sound of it moving over his tongue, and each minute change in pitch as he spoke. His ghostlike footsteps caused earthquakes in the floor. As he moved toward the door, a brilliant yellow aura surrounded him, sunshine glittering over solid gold. The light brightened, and the whispers that followed it called louder in Matilda's ears.

Kāi passed near her on his way to the door. The waves of his light drifted so close, and she reached her hand toward them, hoping to catch the rays between her fingers. The Power moved with her.

Like an extra appendage, a beam of her light extended from her arm and dipped into the ripples of Kāi's aura. His light brushed against her, and, as she leaned toward it, his light overflowed until Kāi disappeared and shining gold became everything she knew.

Then she heard the whispers. She grasped at the light with a flick of the Power at her fingertips. The golden aura bent in answer, and it formed strange shapes—letters—and the voices gave it a Name.

"Bāo-vì jēh?"

The golden light flowed into her at the sound of her voice, disappearing under her duskier purples. *Bāo-vì jēh.* It pressed against Matilda's mind and waited tentatively there—a stranger who'd heard his name called and paused to look for a familiar face.

She hadn't realized she'd said the word aloud, but Lucky raised his head, alert, and Kāi froze halfway through the door.

"Did you feel that?" she asked Lucky then turned to Kāi. "Did you feel it? Does that word mean something to you?"

Kāi didn't answer her. He didn't move at all.

"Are you all right?"

The frown on his face went slack. Daylight through the window fell into vacant eyes. Not *bored* eyes, but eyes that were open but asleep. This wasn't Kāi. It was only his shell.

His light swirled within Matilda, and the Name caught in her mind struggled against her hold. The stranger she'd called realized he didn't know her and pulled away, pouring out of her. Kāi burst into yellow light again, though now it deepened to a tarnished amber. His eyelids fluttered.

"Are you all right?" she asked again. "What happened?"

"What did you do?" He shook his head, and his eyes were anything but vacant now. Hot branding irons glared at her.

"Nothing."

"I *felt* it." His voice rose like she'd never heard it before and came down on her hard enough to break bone. "It was that magic from the journal. You were trying to control me!"

"Would you listen to me for a moment?" She backed away, but Kāi followed.

"I am my own man, not your servant." He didn't shout anymore, but his tone cut so deeply it barely made a difference. "So is Lucky."

Lucky growled uneasily—a child caught between angry parents.

"I know that," Matilda said as Kāi's anger threatened to smother her.

"Do you? Would you make Joseph Harrison eat supper on the floor?" Without breaking his eyes from her, Kāi thrust a finger toward the stairs. "Would you let any man sleep outside your room? You've been cruel and friendly to Lucky in ways you wouldn't with another man. He isn't human to you."

"Friendly? You know it isn't like that!"

"Not anymore," Kāi said, "because you couldn't get what you wanted from him."

Her blood sped through her body, hot and thin. "That's not fair."

"You don't know what you are doing! Whatever the magic or power is, it—" Kāi sucked in a slow breath, but it didn't seem to calm him. He trembled, and he scrubbed his arms as if the touch of Matilda's light had disgusted him. "It's probably why your brother was murdered. It changed Lucky, and I know it is changing you."

He might as well have kicked her in the stomach. The fiery retort she'd been planning fizzled on her tongue. "I'm trying to learn how to reverse the spell upon him," she said, but even to herself she didn't sound convinced.

"It isn't magic that confuses him anymore. It's you. How can Lucky believe he's a man if you refuse to treat him like one?" Kāi turned on his heels and headed for the door, stopping with his hand on the doorknob. "You might never have thought of me as more than a servant, but I've tried to be a friend. To you and to him. But I won't—I *can't* do it anymore."

Kāi stepped through the door and slammed it behind him.

— CHAPTER FORTY-FIVE —

MATILDA

Mîfä must have heard the shouting from the field. Shortly after Kāi had left, she'd come back to the house with the laundry and a worried gleam to her eyes. All afternoon and into the evening, Matilda had felt Mîfä's gaze upon her.

After changing into her nightclothes and brushing her hair, Matilda went to the hallway to make Lucky's bed. She dangled the patched blanket between both hands.

Would I let another man sleep here in my hall?

Lucky padded upstairs and waited for her to ready his blanket. She couldn't read the thoughts behind his eyes. They were too complex. Too human.

"Come with me." She tucked the blanket under her arm and walked down the hallway.

After a day of roasting in the heat, the air in Elliot's room felt warm and suffocating, and she opened the window to let in some fresh air. Stiff curtains hung open, leaving the glass bare, but Matilda left them. Lucky would want to watch the stars.

She folded the green-and-brown blanket and laid it across the empty bed. "This will have to do." When she backed out of the room, Lucky tried to follow, but she held up her hand and gave a firm *"No."*

He stood by the edge of the bed, held back by her command. His eyes seemed to wonder what he'd done wrong.

"Goodnight," she said as she closed the door, but she doubted it would be a good night for anyone.

Kāi didn't come to the farm the next Sunday. Matilda had left Lucky in Mîfä's care while she'd gone to church and visited Olive and Elliot, but even at the manor Kāi had kept his distance.

He needs time, that's all.

But another Sunday later he didn't come to the farm.

"He will come back," Mîfä assured Matilda, but even she gave up on waiting.

With the passing of summer, the sun fell lower in the sky. July moved into August. August drew close to its end. Still Kāi didn't return, and Matilda wondered if her mistake had broken the already shaky trust between them.

The farmhouse had never felt so quiet. Matilda focused on chores while Mîfä taught herself to read some of Olive's simpler books. Ever since Matilda had made Lucky sleep in Elliot's room, he'd been distant. Maybe he'd understood why she'd sent him there, or maybe he'd simply given up vying for her attention.

See? They were only flowers. It didn't mean anything.

Lucky was still in Elliot's room when Matilda got up that morning. The door stood closed, but his footsteps paced beyond it. It wasn't the frantic pacing he'd done in the barn; it was more like what Matilda did when she tried to sort her thoughts. Slow. Absentminded. His soft footsteps paused when she moved down the hall, but he didn't come out to greet her.

The farmhouse had never been so *lonely.*

Mîfä was a big help with the garden, as nurturing to the onions and carrots as she was to Lucky, but without Olive and Elliot's help, Matilda's morning routine made for a very long morning indeed. The sun soared high by the time she'd finished her tasks, and when she exited the chicken coop with a meagre basket of eggs, a dappled-grey horse grazed in front of the open barn. It whipped its tail wildly and wore a saddle with stirrups set for long legs.

"Richards." Matilda set her basket of eggs safely on the ground before she had a chance to find a target to throw them at. "What is he doing here?"

Her eyes darted toward the garden and about the meadow, but she saw no sign of either Mîfä or Lucky. *They'd better keep hidden!*

Rustles and clanks sounded from the barn, and a male voice uttered curses. Out of habit Matilda felt for her pistol, but she must have left it in the drawer.

You'll be fine. He's just a man. Just a vile monster of a man.

Another clang and a sputtered curse broke the late morning quiet, then Richards stamped out of the barn with a chain looped through his hand like a weapon. When he spied Matilda, he showed no embarrassment at being caught intruding on her land. Instead he looked *eager.* And malicious.

Without the comfort of her pistol, Matilda kept her distance. "I know you think this land belongs to you, Mr. Richards, but that's my barn you're turning into a mess."

The eager look on his face burned away in his bloodshot eyes.

"Where is he, girl?" he demanded with ire, collecting spittle on his moustache.

"I don't know who you mean."

Richards marched toward her and leaned forward, towering over her. "Don't lie to me! I found *this* on your property."

He raised the chain in his hand. Matilda flinched, but he merely held it in the air and waited for her to look. She followed the length of his chain down to the end where a leather dog collar dangled.

Oh no.

"You threatened my dogs; now one of 'em is missing. You did something to him. Or maybe you had those brats do it for you."

His liquor-drenched breath fell on her forehead. With his stench on her, she couldn't interpret his strange accusations. *Brats? Olive and Elliot?*

"They ran inside when I rode up," Richards's glare burned fiercer every second. "Looked guilty if you ask me."

Mîfä and Lucky! Matilda's heart climbed high into her chest. *He saw them. He saw both of them!*

"I didn't ask. Now, if you'll kindly leave." She made toward the house, but he stepped in her path. Her hand slipped behind her. She should have remembered her pistol!

Richards dragged his sleeve across his lip. Finally he grunted and stepped past Matilda, knocking her aside so hard she almost lost her footing.

"You have one day." He jangled the chain and collar for her benefit before struggling up into his saddle. "Tomorrow I go to my good-for-nothing nephew about this."

Matilda rubbed the spot where he'd elbowed her and kept her eye trained on him until the gelding loped out of sight. She abandoned the egg basket in the yard and ran for the farmhouse.

As she threw open the door, a commotion by the stairs overpowered the shriek of the hinges.

Lucky growled at the foot of the stairs and eyed the open door. Mîfä spread her arms to block his path, but he brushed her aside easily. She latched onto his arm, and he simply dragged her with him.

"No!" Mîfä shouted over his growls, and between strings of Chinese, she said, "No! Put it down!"

What's going on?

Matilda slammed the door and pressed her back into it. Lucky gave a disgruntled snarl and turned away like Elliot throwing a tantrum, and then Matilda noticed the pistol at his side. He gripped her weapon with an inexperienced hold, but his finger looped around the trigger surely.

"DROP IT!" Matilda shouted.

Lucky jumped as though she'd struck him, and the pistol clattered to the floor. He looked wide-eyed at his hand like he didn't understand where the gun had disappeared, and Mîfä dove for the weapon.

Matilda charged at Lucky. "What were you doing?" She jabbed a finger into his chest, demanding his attention. "*Never* touch that!"

Backing into the wall, he regarded her with his eyes stubborn, unapologetic, and strangely hurt.

"Upstairs." She thrust a finger toward Elliot's bedroom overhead. "*Go.*"

Lucky hung his head as he passed, but he stomped up every step angrily. Angry at *her?*

Matilda thought she might be angry too, beneath the terror. She put a hand over her throat and calmed herself with the feel of Nathaniel's coin.

What did he think he was doing?

With the weapon pointed toward the floor, Mîfä returned it to Matilda. Strands of black hair had escaped her braid after the struggle, but she left them loose. "He wants to protect you."

"Protect me?" Matilda snapped, unable to hold back the swell of emotion coursing through her. "He might have killed me. Or you. Or himself! He doesn't know how to handle a weapon."

That isn't true.

The first day he'd come into the house, Lucky had grabbed her rifle, but he hadn't held it like a weapon. This time he'd been close. Frighteningly close. He must have watched her. Learning. Imitating.

"That man is dangerous, like Mr. Võng." Mîfä's hand pressed against her cheek, the bruises gone but the memory ablaze behind her eyes. "He hit you. You are Lucky's family."

Family? The two of us?

Her hands felt relieved to hold the security of the pistol again, but that security now brought unease. "He needs to learn," Matilda said, her voice finally under control.

And I need to be more careful. Lucky isn't human enough to control his instincts.

She'd forgotten the vicious wild man she'd kept in her barn. Maybe that terrifying creature was closer to Sheridan than Lucky was, but at least she'd know what to expect from him. Lucky needed help, and he needed it before he killed someone.

If Matilda couldn't fix Lucky with magic, then she needed to take him to someone who could.

February 24th, 1884

It's Sunday morning. I should be singing hymns at church, but I pretended to feel unwell so I could slip away to the Fenians' meeting place unnoticed.

I told them a little of the information I'd gleaned from Joseph. Not much. A little about patrol routes in the city—enough to continue the lie that I am on the Fenians' side.

Right around now I'd ordinarily be telling Elliot to stop kicking the pew ahead of us. Olive might temper him. Matilda will try, bless her. She doesn't stand much hope of soothing Elliot when she's as hard-headed as he. But who am I to speak of stubbornness? That's why I'm writing this in the cold damp of the cellar, pretending my eyes are slivered with laughter at Gallagher's jokes and not from staring into the ether. Trying to snare his Name. Trying to imagine if the Power could make him choke to death on his own irksome puns.

The Power can turn a man into a killer strong enough to rip another's head from his shoulders, but it must be able to weaken them too. Make Gallagher brittle enough to shatter his ribs when he laughs at his own jokes.

My impatience is making it harder to pretend I'm one of them.

The longer I stay, the harder it is to pretend I'm not.

If I get Isaac alone to prey on his Name, I recognize his craving for retribution even before I reach for his scarlet light. Gallagher's jokes turn me as bitter as him. I see much of myself in Keith—the boy who let his regrets pull him too deeply into a fool's errand—but it's Sheridan's anger that speaks to me and frightens me the most.

When I'd let the Power sit beneath my skin, awake but barely a tingle within me, I used to sense Sheridan's approach before even my heightened senses let me see or hear him. He was a shadow that blocked the sun and sucked its warmth from the back of my neck. The brighter the day, the sharper those shadows, but now I can't sense Sheridan until he's upon me.

If you can't see the shadow, you're within it.

I don't know if it's the stain their sins leave on me when their Names brush mine or if I have myself to blame, but I can't tell myself from the dark anymore.

Spy or not, I'm twisted enough to belong here too.

— CHAPTER FORTY-SIX —

MATILDA

Duchess fought against the bit when Matilda stopped the wagon in front of Miss Kovacs's house. Matilda peered up and down the street. Evening hadn't fallen yet, but the only other souls were three young boys down the street playing with stick swords. The *clunk-clunk* of their weapons resounded, but the boys paid Matilda no heed.

"Hurry." She peeled back the canvas behind her and uncovered old horseshoes and Lucky's brooding face.

His rage simmered somewhere below his skin now, but he avoided looking at her as he climbed out of the wagon and followed her to the house. With a soft knock that wouldn't call attention from the boys down the street, Matilda cracked open the door and tiptoed down the hall with Lucky at her back.

"Miss Kovacs?" she called softly.

At the end of the hallway, a closed door muffled the sounds of an argument. As she drew closer, Matilda recognized Miss Kovacs's grouchy tones, but hers wasn't the only voice that sounded behind the door.

"But I need it," said the voice of a boy nearing manhood. It floated down the hall, airy like he'd meant to whisper but loud enough for all of New Westminster to hear.

A volley of muted insults followed. "I'm a mesmerist, not a sorceress," came Miss Kovacs's irritated voice. "I don't make love potions."

Footsteps thumped behind the door, and the handle twitched.

Matilda grabbed Lucky's wrist and flattened herself against the wall as the door opened to pin her beside him. The door crashed against his bare toes. He flinched, but Matilda flung her hand over his mouth to silence any protest.

"You must have something!"

The shuffle of footsteps moved past them. Matilda kept her hand over Lucky's mouth but felt better knowing his gasp of pain had gone unheard. Or she felt better until she recognized the voice of Miss Kovacs's customer.

Is that Junior Richards?

"I do," Miss Kovacs said. "I've a cane and half a mind to beat you with it."

Miss Kovacs seemed to be in a worse mood than usual. Matilda felt like she was stuck under the stairs in the cellar again, shoved into a corner and holding her breath.

"But I will have her!"

"Out, boy!"

A pair of feet shuffled down the hallway. Matilda heard Junior mutter something about witches having no hearts.

"They do have ears," Miss Kovacs snapped.

Junior yelped. His footsteps pounded down the hall, and the front door slammed shut.

Matilda felt darkly pleased to hear the boy put in his place. *Miss Kovacs should have a chat with his father too. Love potions! What a thought!* She made a mental note to warn Olive never to touch anything Junior gave her.

"I hope you haven't come for a potion too." Miss Kovacs's grumbling disrupted Matilda's secret thoughts. "The only brew

I make is applesauce. I can hear you breathing behind that door, whoever you are, so there's no use pretending you're not there."

"I'm Matilda." Caught like a girl with mud on her skirts, Matilda eyed the dangerous end of the cane in Miss Kovacs's hand. *She wouldn't really beat me with it, would she?*

"Miss O'Connor?" Miss Kovacs pulled back on the door and fully revealed Matilda in her embarrassment. Matilda felt suddenly glad for the woman's blindness. "You brought your cousin. And it seems he's *still* sick? You'd better come in before some other fool comes to buy a hex from me."

Matilda glanced up at Lucky. "How did you know it was him?"

"Never mind that. Into the room, now!"

Urging Lucky ahead of her, Matilda stepped into the room. The old woman shut the door behind them and motioned for them to sit.

Matilda had never been in this room before. It smelled woodsy, and walls, painted a muted greyish-brown, swallowed most of the light in the room. What light there was came from a window that reminded her of a porthole on a ship and from several fat candles that sat atop a low, black table. They dripped pale wax down their sides and made Matilda think of a witch's altar from a dark fairy tale. It was too much to hope Miss Kovacs would be a friendly witch, but with any luck she'd be a helpful one.

Four deep chairs gathered in a square around the table, standing so close together Matilda wondered if there'd be room for her legs. She took Lucky's wrist and pulled him to his seat, but he seemed more interested in the dance of candle flames than the women in the room.

"Let's not waste more time." Miss Kovacs set her cane against the wall and stood herself awkwardly close to Lucky.

"Actually…" Matilda settled into the seat next to Lucky and took a deep breath. *This is it. Be brave.* "I want you to teach me how to use Nathaniel's magic."

The lines around Miss Kovacs's frown deepened. Her chin rose high with seeming confidence, but her skin dotted with moisture. "So you know of the Power. And here I thought you'd changed the boy without realizing what you'd done. I should have known better than to trust an O'Connor to keep their nose out of trouble." She gestured to Lucky. He stayed turned toward the candles, but his eyes flicked to the old woman, keeping watch. "Tell me what you did to the boy so I can fix him properly and send you on your way."

Matilda clenched her skirt in her hands and glanced at the scar cutting into Lucky's hairline. The rashes, his wounds, they'd long since healed, but the idea that Miss Kovacs thought Matilda could have had anything to do with what had happened to Lucky set her insides aflame. "I didn't do anything to him," she said, her voice raised higher than she'd intended, "but if you teach me to use the Power, I can—"

"I absolutely will not *teach* you," Miss Kovacs said, her own voice raising. "I only taught your brother enough to fear the Power—and only because he stumbled upon it himself with his silly little tricks. You're the same, blundering with forces you don't understand. Tell me what you did to this boy. It should have worn off by now. Answer me! What are you playing at, girl?"

Matilda leaned farther back from the woman with each accusation. "I told you I didn't do this to him."

"Then who did? Who else knows of the Power?"

"There is...another." Matilda chose her words carefully. No need to give away everything she'd learned before even she understood it. "My brother wrote of a Mr. Wellington in his journals."

Miss Kovacs creased her brow. "Wellington? That name sounds familiar."

"You must help me use the magic." Matilda ignored the woman's angry musings and pressed her. "I need Lucky to— I need to help him."

Miss Kovacs shook her head. "You have not the slightest idea of the Power's evil. It corrupts the wielder as readily as the subject, as it did your brother. And my father." Miss Kovacs stepped on Matilda's toes as she leaned over her, her stare deadly sharp and so close to meeting Matilda's it was hard not to look away. "My father was a loving man once. In the end he used the Power to try to force his only daughter to marry a violent man for the wealth and prestige it would give him. When I felt my father twist my Name on his tongue, I vowed never to do it to anyone else. All these years I've kept that vow."

"If you won't teach me and you won't help Lucky," Matilda said, "then why did you tell me to bring him here?"

"I never said I wouldn't help him." Miss Kovacs crossed her arms, but instead of angry she seemed to be comforting herself from a difficult memory. "Someone must have stolen the boy's Name. I'll help him get it back."

Stolen?

That's why Lucky doesn't have a light. It was stolen from him!

"His Name is missing!" Matilda said. "Someone took his soul from him?"

Why would someone steal his Name? It wasn't as if there was a market for stolen Names. At least she hoped there wasn't.

"You're chirping like a preacher. Nathaniel was the only one who called them Soul Names." One finger tapped a rhythm on Miss Kovacs's sleeve. She pointed her nose toward the ceiling, seeming to search for the right explanation. "They are our protection. Like a conscience or, yes, even like a soul, if you must use your brother's terms. We shape them as we age, and they tell us who we are and, just as importantly, who we're not. But a person without a Name is an empty vessel without inhibition or semblance of their true self. One skilled in the Power can fill the Unnamed with any poison he chooses. Olive could become a murderer. You could live the rest of your life as a cricket."

Matilda recalled the feeling of taking Kāi's light from him and possessing it as her own. It had felt formidable. Wonderful.

Yet while she'd held that magical light within her, his body had been emptied of will or purpose. She'd taken away his Name and everything that had made him Kāi. No wonder he'd shouted at her.

"Someone planted a poison in this boy." Miss Kovacs shuffled sideways and put herself in front of Lucky once more. "It seems some has healed on its own, but he can't tell which parts of him are true and which are constructed. Even if he understands you, he won't answer. I doubt his body is aware it *can* speak."

Lucky's head tilted back from the woman in front of him, and his gaze flitted to Matilda as if asking permission to leave. Those lovely brown eyes punched her in the gut.

All those lessons she'd forced him through—all the frustration she'd heaped upon him—all for something he couldn't give.

"Then how can you help him?" Matilda asked. "Wouldn't you only fill him with your own poison?"

"I won't fill him with anything at all." Miss Kovacs uncrossed her arms and rubbed her hands so briskly together Matilda expected to see sparks. Lucky slid farther back in his chair and watched the old woman's hands with a guarded expression. "A stolen Name fights to return home. I'll help it struggle back on its own, but he won't like it. You must keep him calm."

Torn, Matilda chewed on her lower lip. What if this went horribly wrong? What if Miss Kovacs made a mistake and Lucky turned back into the beast? Or worse, what if he became Sheridan?

Even so, I can't keep him like this.

An hour ago Lucky had held her pistol, ready to fire. He was caught somewhere in the in-between—neither a man nor a wolf. She couldn't pretend that was any safer for him than it was for anyone else.

She placed her hand on Lucky's forearm, feeling the taut forms of muscle beneath his shirt as he gripped the chair. "Lucky, she's here to help you. Sit still and trust me."

It took a moment for her words to sink into him, but as they did his muscles relaxed beneath her hand. She felt him give her his trust like it was a physical thing she could touch.

"That's better." Miss Kovacs's hands found a hold on Lucky's head and turned his face toward her. Matilda kept her touch on his arm for reassurance.

Nothing happened at first. Miss Kovacs spoke no spells nor weaved them with her fingers, but sweat glistened on her forehead. For a moment, Matilda let her vision slip into her other sense. Lucky was his usual, lightless self, but Miss Kovacs burst into a silvery glow. She stretched arms of her light toward Lucky as if using it to see what her eyes could not.

And when that light brushed him, Lucky responded.

His eyes sharpened. A growl started low in his throat, then pushed upward, louder and more menacing. His lips pulled back over his teeth.

"No." Matilda grasped his arm with both hands. "I'm here. Calm down."

"He remembers this happening to him before." Miss Kovacs sounded more intrigued than frightened. She dug her fingers into his skin. "He's not letting me in easily."

The tendons in Miss Kovacs's wrinkled hands stood out as she held him tighter and slapped a heavy wave of her aura against him. Lucky's growl raised in pitch and ferocity.

"Quiet, boy," Miss Kovacs said. "Let me in—"

With a snarl, Lucky broke out of Matilda's grip and jumped to his feet. Matilda's vision returned to the mundane, and Miss Kovacs stumbled onto the table behind her, landing awkwardly on her hip and knocking over candles that snuffed out. Her eyes opened as though they stared into another world and looked upon a demon.

Matilda squeezed herself between them and pushed Lucky down into his chair, but she could do nothing to put out the violent spark in his eyes. "What happened?"

"It's like throwing myself into the side of a building." Miss Kovacs set the candles upright again then backed away to give Lucky space.

With the distance between him and the witch growing, Lucky's growls fell down his throat, more offended now than murderous.

"He's resistant," Miss Kovacs said, caressing her hip. "I should have realized it sooner. I thought he blocked me intentionally, but the shield in place is natural."

From the dark tone of the woman's voice, this shield wasn't a good thing. "What does that mean?"

"It means whoever did this to him put in a lot of effort to change him. A *lot* of effort, do you understand me? It would have taken a long time to break him, which means they wanted him for something. *Him*—not anyone else who would have been easier to control."

Horrifying possibilities passed through Matilda's thoughts, terrible things Lucky might have suffered. Her heart clenched so tightly she couldn't breathe, collapsing in on itself and twisting into a solid lump.

Not even a Fenian deserves that cruelty.

Lucky poised in his chair, ready to leap again at the first threat. Matilda's fingers reached to stroke his hair of their own accord.

He's a man, not a dog.

Her hands jerked back before they'd satisfied their whims. "You're safe now," she said, but the calming words didn't appease her hands. She set them in her lap to keep them proper.

"When I knew him," Miss Kovacs said under her breath, "Nathaniel wouldn't have been strong enough to do this."

The words stabbed deeply into Matilda's chest. "He didn't. My brother learned the Names, but Mr. Wellington is the one who stole them."

Miss Kovacs scratched her chin. "That name again. Wellington. He was the boy who died in the fire two years ago, wasn't he? Then he can't be the one who took your friend's Name. The Name would have returned to its host the moment the Wellington boy died."

Then he isn't dead.

The thought simply popped into Matilda's mind. She didn't know how it could be true, but if Lucas Wellington lived, it explained why Nathaniel's final journal entry described plans to confront his enemy. It explained why the Sceolan had thought Nathaniel was alive. Someone was controlling the wolf men—the one who'd stolen their Names in the beginning.

Mr. Wellington is alive!

As Lucky's growls finally faded, Miss Kovacs's back straightened. "You're the praying sort, aren't you? Then pray, girl, because whoever took your friend's Name is more skilled with the Power than I am, and he'll have felt my stumbling with the boy's Name. He might come here and do something about it." She waved her hands in the air. "Out, now. Both of you."

"But there must be something we can do!" Matilda said.

"Out!" Miss Kovacs herded Matilda out of her chair and toward the door, keeping her distance from Lucky as he followed behind them. "Frankly, I now think it a mercy to let the boy stay lost. As a dog he might forget his torments, but as a man he'll be haunted by them."

Matilda paused in the doorway and thought of the night Lucky'd been trapped in nightmares in the hall. "He already is haunted by them. I want him to be safe and...and I want him to be human again." She surprised even herself with her admission, but the moment she voiced the words, her whole being screamed they were true.

"Oh, dear girl." Miss Kovacs's lips pinched together in the first sympathetic look Matilda remembered the old woman ever sparing. "No matter what anyone else sees, he *is* human, but it might be kinder if he never remembers it."

— CHAPTER FORTY-SEVEN —

MATILDA

Sunset hadn't yet tinted the sky, but Matilda's skin crawled with the terrors of midnight as she hurried Duchess home.

She'd never thought anything could make Miss Kovacs's iron spirit cower.

Nathaniel, what did you get yourself into?

The wagon rattled through clouds of mosquitoes. Still and quiet, Lucky hid under the canvas in the back. Matilda wanted to crawl under there with him and hide from this nightmare, but when she neared the farm, she knew the nightmare wasn't over.

Horses and several men crowded the yard in front of the log house. From across the meadow, Matilda recognized Joseph on his white gelding. He wore his policeman's uniform and spoke with another constable, but two of the other men sat in the front seat of a covered black surrey. Matilda couldn't see their faces, but long tails of dark hair dangled down their backs.

Worst of all, Richards stood next to his horse and scratched at his moustache. He noticed Matilda's approach first.

Richards, you filthy liar! A day, he'd said, before he fetched the law. *Liar! He went straight to Joseph the moment he finished spitting in my face!*

"Lucky." Before Duchess carried them too close to the men, Matilda directed her voice through the canvas bundle behind her. "Don't move. No matter what happens you must not make a sound."

Please, don't let them see him.

With an ugly grin cracking open his face, Richards sauntered toward the wagon as Duchess crossed the meadow. Matilda's hands tightened into fists around the reins.

"Evening." Richards managed to make the greeting sound like an insult. He looked at her with the expression he probably used when he congratulated other gamblers for losing their money to him.

Matilda considered running him over but pulled back on the reins until the wagon stopped beside him. "You're as deaf as you are drunk. I've done nothing to your dog."

Richards's wretched smile widened until she thought his teeth would fall out. "The dog's only half of it. Did you think I'd mistake a Chinese wench for an O'Connor?"

"You hold your to—"

A roar cut Matilda off. Mîfä's father burst out of the farmhouse with a scowl, dragging Mîfä behind him.

Mîfä's eyes threw poisoned daggers. She'd tossed on her red silks in a rush, and they trailed in the dirt as Mr. Võng yanked her into the yard.

Not even a full step behind them, Kāi chased after Mr. Võng and argued with him in Chinese that even Matilda could tell was outraged.

"What are you doing to her?" Matilda sat straighter in her seat. "Let her go!"

Richards chuckled, but the laugh, like his smile, was a hideous thing. "I knew you couldn't afford a nanny for your brats, so I asked Joseph. Thought he'd lent you his, but it turns out the servant kidnapped the girl from the teahouse."

"No, he didn't."

Richards's shrugged. "I don't care." His grin vanished, and he slapped his hand on her seat. "Now, where's my dog?"

It was a tiny sound, so soft she wouldn't have noticed it if she hadn't already been listening for it, but when Richards leaned over the wagon and the scent of liquor poured off him, Lucky growled.

Had Richards heard? She couldn't help glancing at the back of her wagon.

"Get out of my way," Matilda said. Without waiting for Richards to comply, Matilda snapped the reins and pulled away from him before Lucky lost control. Richards muttered curses behind her. "Stay quiet," she whispered. "Lucky, stay quiet."

Joseph slipped out of his saddle and pressed a knuckle to his mouth, looking lost in thought, but the creak of Matilda's wagon drew his attention. He turned to her and lowered his hand, leaving a red impression on his lips. Once Matilda reined Duchess to a halt, Joseph strode up to her and dropped his voice low enough only she'd be able to hear. "What were you doing with this woman?"

"She wasn't kidnapped, if that's what you're asking." Matilda gave another silent prayer for Lucky to stay put.

"Of course that's not what I'm asking," Joseph said, "but Mr. Võng is a powerful man among his own here. Why on earth would you involve yourself in his marital problems?"

Marital problems? "There must be some mistake. He's her father, and she ran from him."

But she wasn't running now. Other than the threat in her eyes, Mîfä offered no resistance when Mr. Võng climbed into the back of the surrey and hauled her up beside him. Kāi argued until his face turned red, but Mîfä shook her head at him.

"Is that what they told you?" Joseph asked. "Mr. Võng is her husband. He paid the head tax to bring her from China."

"Married?" The word left a horrible aftertaste on her tongue. *Oh, Kāi. What were you thinking?*

Mr. Võng shouted an order, and his driver turned the surrey toward the city. Mîfä looked over her shoulder and gave one final, determined glance at Kāi, and then the wagon rolled around the bend in the road.

Matilda knew that look well. *Is that how I look whenever I'm told to give up on Nathaniel?*

"Now, what of my dog?" Richards asked.

His voice grated at Matilda. She'd hoped he'd disappeared while she'd been distracted.

"I'm not concerned for a lost dog at the moment," Joseph said as he returned to his mount.

"It's not *lost.* Your woman stole it."

His *woman?*

"That's enough." Joseph's words were aimed at Richards, but Matilda caught a warning look from him too. "Your dog isn't the first animal to go missing lately. Some boy probably took him home for a pet."

"My dogs aren't *playmates.*"

Matilda had to agree. She couldn't picture one of Richards's snarling mongrels playing fetch with a child, unless it was the child she imagined carried around in the dog's maw instead of a stick.

"But that girl has got something in her wagon," Richards said. "I saw the canvas move."

Alarm bolted through Matilda. "For the last time, your dog isn't here!"

"We'll see." Richards reached into the bed of the wagon.

She snatched the corner of the canvas as his stubby fingers grabbed for it. He gave an annoyed huff and seized Matilda's wrist, wrenching it away.

"Ah!" Matilda said, trying to tug herself out of his grasp.

"Jake Richards, you let her go," Joseph said with authority. He rushed to her and freed her from Richards's hold, his own, gentler hand replacing his uncle's at her wrist. "Touch her again, and I'll arrest you. Go home."

Richards hovered by the wagon and glared at his nephew, testing Joseph's resolve. Unspoken threats waited behind his mouth, but when Joseph returned his stare without blinking, Richards strode toward his mount and clambered into the saddle.

Matilda's heart fluttered with relief.

The moment Richards disappeared down the road, Joseph turned to her with concern across his features. "Did he hurt you?" He laid her hand in her lap like it was made of glass. "Are you all right?"

She rubbed her wrist. It'd probably bruise, but Joseph looked ready to fetch the physician for her. "It only stings a little."

Her lie seemed to relieve him. His stiff shoulders loosened as he released a long sigh, but as the worry left his face, a hesitant look replaced it. "You didn't have anything to do with his lost dog, did you? No, of course not. What use would you have for a wild beast?" Even as he made excuses for her, his expression darkened again. "You should have come to me about the girl."

It was all he said, but he might as well have shouted at her the way his reprimand tied her insides in knots. He retrieved his mount's reins, slipped his toe into a stirrup, and leapt gracefully into his saddle. Even disappointed with her, Joseph gave her a polite nod.

"Tomorrow, then," he said, but his gaze had moved past her.

"Yes," Kāi said. For all the noise he'd made only moments ago, she hadn't heard him approach.

Joseph nodded to the other constable and waited for him to mount up, then he clucked at his horse and both men turned for the city. As soon as Joseph disappeared from sight, Matilda climbed into the back of the wagon and tore away the canvas.

She didn't know why she'd expected something horrible, but when Lucky looked back at her, hair mussed but otherwise untouched, fear eased out of her in a whoosh of air.

Another secret I'm keeping from Joseph…

His face a mask of calm Matilda couldn't believe was real, Kāi walked up to the wagon and rested his arms across it. His shoulders sagged with what must have been heavy thoughts.

"I—" Matilda didn't know what to say. She barely had the energy to think at all. "I didn't know she was his wife."

"Mîfä is *my* wife!" Kāi's calm composure crumbled. He held his breath until he turned red, but when he released it, his temper subsided. A little. "It isn't easy to bring a wife to Gold Mountain. Mr. Võng and I made a deal: he would take care of her documents and pay the head tax, and she would work at his teashop until I could pay him back. But when he first saw her…he wanted her. The documents Mîfä used to come here were for his dead wife. I can't do anything except give him his money or run, and now that Mr. Harrison thinks I put you in danger, I'm out of work."

Oh, Joseph. "Let me speak to Mr. Harrison."

He shook his head. "You'll make it worse. We will take care of ourselves." Kāi surprised Matilda with a smile, tired but lit with hope. "I won't be able to watch our friend on Sundays anymore."

"*You* haven't been watching Lucky for some time," Matilda said. Lucky perked up at the sound of his name. Did he understand this was goodbye? Had he understood anything that had happened today? Matilda couldn't wrap her head around any of this. She wasn't ready to. If she'd known how little time she'd have left with Kāi, she wouldn't have chased him away. "Will we see you again? Lucky will miss you both."

It was a terrible apology, but Kāi chuckled. "Maybe we'll come back when I've earned enough money to pay the tax. Goodbye, Miss O'Connor." He gave a bow of his head. "Take care of Lucky."

"I'll try," she said, and then Kāi followed the wagon path back to the road and was gone.

Olive and Elliot were gone. Mîfä and Kāi were gone. It was her and Lucky now—just them against Fenians and the evil sorcerer who'd enslaved them.

Lucky must have sensed her unease, because he leaned into her as if to remind her he was there. He hadn't been so familiar in weeks. Maybe longer. She'd forgotten how it calmed and excited her at the same time.

"Good boy." She ran her fingers through his hair, and, for some reason, the simple touch untwisted the knots in her belly.

He's not a dog. You wouldn't do this to Joseph.

But neither had she ever wanted to ruffle Joseph's perfect hair. His kind words and sly smiles made her giddy, but even when he'd held her wrist moments ago, his touch hadn't stirred her. She couldn't remember if it ever had.

You wouldn't do it to a Fenian.

She jerked her hand back at the thought, but her fingers remembered the feel of Lucky's silken locks between them.

— CHAPTER FORTY-EIGHT —

MATILDA

On Sunday morning, Lucky didn't come out of Elliot's room until Matilda called him for breakfast. He shambled downstairs, blinking groggy eyes as he plopped into a chair at the table. His night terrors must have kept him awake again, but it was more than that. Matilda didn't bother explaining why Mîfä was gone or why Kāi hadn't arrived at the farm, even though it was almost time to leave for church. The way Lucky pushed his bread around his plate, he already knew.

He didn't try to follow her when she left. With how distant she'd made herself lately, maybe he thought she didn't care for him anymore. Sometimes *she* wondered if she didn't care, but when he didn't at least come to the door to see her off, she felt like she might sink through her wagon seat and plunge into the earth.

She hadn't realized how slowly Duchess had plodded toward the church until she arrived late to hear hymns pouring out into the street. After she found a place to tether Duchess, she hurried into the chapel and tried not to attract eyes as she found a seat next to Mother Harrison in the front pew. A soft hand patted her shoulder, and when Matilda turned to give Mother Harrison a polite glance in greeting, the woman beamed back at her with warmth that chased away Matilda's gloom.

Mother Harrison wore a cheery, rose-coloured dress that accentuated the healthy colour to her cheeks. It still hung too loose on her thin frame, but she no longer looked frail enough to break under the weight of her clothes. Her smile crinkled her bright eyes and lifted Matilda's heart.

She looks like a new person! Matilda tried to remember how Mother Harrison had looked last week but couldn't. Had she been too distracted to notice Mother Harrison's transformation? *How did this happen?*

Down the row, past Olive and Elliot, Joseph met Matilda's gaze with a jovial look of his own. As if in answer to her unspoken question, he shrugged a shoulder and looked one second away from a boyish laugh.

It was hard not to sneak peeks at Mother Harrison throughout the service. Matilda wanted to see what colour her aura glowed now that she sang the hymns as though she planned to hand-deliver their praises to heaven.

The reverend had barely brought the meeting to a close when Matilda turned toward the older woman. "You're looking well today!"

Mother Harrison almost bounced to her feet, and she gathered Olive and Elliot to her side like a mother hen. "I think the youth in these darlings is giving me new life. It's been some time since I've had a child to look after. I can't very well waste away on them." As she guided the children into the aisle, she fixed the crooked ribbon in Olive's hair, stroking her golden curtains, and offered Elliot a playful pinch of his ear. "And I feel much more at ease now that that frightful man is out of my house."

Matilda felt a muscle jump in her jaw. Those words weren't befitting the kindly woman she'd admired much of her life. "Mr. Kāi is a good man. You shouldn't say such things about him."

The disappointment in her voice stunned her, and immediately she feared she'd gone too far with her words, even if they were true. She didn't think she'd ever snapped at the woman before. To do it now—after Mother Harrison's fortitude had been withering for so long—might strike her too harshly.

But Mother Harrison simply rested a hand on Matilda's arm and gave her a sympathetic look. "I'm sorry, dear. I understand you had some peculiar sort of attachment to the boy, but there's no work left for him. I have strength enough to manage my own home now."

She does?

Joseph held the door open for them as they stepped out into the autumn sun, but nothing shone as brightly as his silver eyes. "Yesterday afternoon she pulled weeds out of her old flower gardens—after baking cookies all morning. I couldn't have stopped her if I'd tried."

Mother Harrison waved a hand through the air but gave an appreciative smile. "Nonsense. Olive did the hardest work. I think she'll be a fine cook one day. Elliot, too, if he can refrain from picking at the cookie dough long enough to put it in the oven."

Elliot hung his head and his cheeks flushed. They reminded Matilda of his scarlet aura. "I didn't eat that much."

Joseph let the door shut behind them and laughed. It was a robust sound that picked Matilda off the ground and danced her around the churchyard. When was the last time he'd laughed like that? "You ate until you made yourself sick."

"So did you," Elliot said, but then he joined Joseph with a laugh of his own.

Is this what life with the Harrisons looked like—cookies and colourful flower gardens and giddy laughter? If only Nathaniel would release his hold on Matilda so she could run to that life. To Joseph.

If only she could let go of Lucky.

"Your brother and sister helped me deliver what was left of the cookies to the widows in our congregation," Mother Harrison said. "I think those ladies were touched by the gesture."

She's even leaving the house without Joseph now?

How awkward for Olive and Elliot to put on a friendly face for the same ladies who'd called them "Fenian" and whispered about them behind their backs.

But maybe it was a good thing. Maybe Mother Harrison would change minds about the O'Connors yet.

"But don't worry. We saved a plate of cookies for you, dear." Mother Harrison squeezed Matilda's arm before letting Joseph help her into his polished buggy. "Why don't you come by and get them?"

Mother Harrison insisted Olive and Elliot ride with Matilda so they could visit without an "old lady eavesdropping" on their family time, and after Joseph climbed into the buggy beside her, she swiped the reins away from him and drove toward the manor herself, humming a joyful hymn. Matilda untethered Duchess and climbed into the wagon with her siblings.

"I don't believe it," Matilda said as she followed Joseph's red buggy at a private distance. "She looks more spry than me. Is she really well?"

"She started to improve after the lady from the asylum came. It was so sudden. Like a miracle." Olive was the picture of serenity as she soaked up the rare west-coast sun, but after a moment of bliss, the corners of her mouth tugged downward. "What if she's only pretending to be better to avoid having to go to that place?"

It stung Matilda that Olive couldn't trust happy moments to last long enough to enjoy them. *In time she'll learn.*

"And what if she is?" Elliot said. "Maybe she'll really get better if she pretends long enough."

I don't think it works that way.

Matilda thought of Lucky's sullen face back home. Pretending to be a dog to avoid being human hadn't slowed the changes in him. It couldn't erase that part of him deep down that waited to reclaim what had been stolen from him. It must be painful to live that lie. And lonesome.

She shook the thought aside. Now *she* wasn't putting any trust in the happiness they'd found.

When they arrived at the manor, Joseph waited for them by his buggy. He helped Olive and Matilda down from their seats, his hand clasping Matilda's slightly longer than necessary, and he took Duchess by the reins. "I'll see your horse gets a drink and some feed. You three go inside before Mother comes looking for you."

Mother Harrison bustled around the kitchen when they entered the house, and already Matilda smelled sage and melted butter and heard the sound of a knife chopping potatoes. Her stomach grumbled. Kāi was a talented cook, but nothing compared to Mother Harrison's mastery in the kitchen. Matilda and Olive sat on the chesterfield and revelled in the medley of scents wafting through the air while Elliot fetched a plate of cookies.

Instead of a plate, he returned with a glass platter, its floral pattern all but hidden under a heap of lightly-browned disks. He offered one to Matilda and Olive before setting the rest of the platter on the side table next to the chair.

"I made sure you got extra for..." He turned his ear toward the kitchen, but Mother Harrison's knife still busied itself with potatoes. He lowered his voice anyway. "You know."

Olive nibbled on the end of her cookie. "How is Lucky?"

He's a Fenian.

The thought soured Matilda's first bite of her treat, but she swallowed it down with a smile. "He misses the two of you."

"We miss him too," Olive said.

With three cookies in hand, Elliot squeezed onto the chesterfield beside Matilda. "Can we see him sometime?"

"See who?" Mother Harrison appeared in the parlour with a ruffly apron over her dress. Her eyes slivered at Matilda. "Matilda O'Connor, have you found yourself a young man?"

Elliot snickered.

Matilda shot him a glare. "No. There's, er...there's a stray dog that visits the farm sometimes."

A relieved look crossed Mother Harrison's face. "Oh, wonderful. I mean, I hoped you and—" She cleared her throat and settled in the plush cushions on her chair. "Never mind that. Be careful, dear. You never know what a stray's temperament will be like. They can surprise you."

If only Mother Harrison knew how true that was.

A mischievous light twinkled in Elliot's eye. "He's really strong, Mother Harrison. And he's enormous. When he stands on two legs he's…" Elliot raised himself from the chesterfield and set his hand a Lucky-sized height above his head, "…this tall."

"Oh, that's another of your tall tales, isn't it," Mother Harrison said with a playful tone. "He sounds monstrous!"

"He's not!" Olive protested. "He's very sweet."

"Olive was a baby, and you, Elliot, were still in your mother's belly, but Doctor Harrison and I used to keep a dog—a dear little thing with the softest brown eyes." Mother Harrison leaned her head back in her chair, and her gaze looked through the ceiling while her mind drifted far away. "She was my husband's dog, really. She'd follow him everywhere, and when he was at the hospital, she wouldn't budge from his study until he came home. It's strange. I don't remember what happened to her."

Matilda's cookie broke in her hand.

You couldn't bear the sight of the dog crying in the study after your husband's death.

She didn't remember she'd given the dog away? How could Mother Harrison forget something so closely tied to the horrifying memories she'd never been able to forget?

"Do you remember her, Matilda? You were so young then." Mother Harrison lowered her gaze from the ceiling, imploring Matilda. "Do you remember what happened to her?"

Matilda tensed in her seat. "I don't know." She stuffed a broken half of cookie in her mouth and swallowed it down too soon. "These are lovely," she said, stifling a cough. "Would you give me your recipe?"

Mother Harrison turned her gaze once more, squinting into the ashes in the fireplace. "In a moment dear. I don't know why, but it seems very important that I remember what happened to the dog. I can't even recall her name now. Isn't that strange?"

The longer she stared into the ashes, the more her brow creased in confusion and the quieter Olive and Elliot went.

"I don't think you should worry about that," Matilda said.

"No, I— Something happened to her. And..." Mother Harrison slapped a hand to her throat as her eyes widened with an emotional pain. "And something happened to my husband, didn't it! Why can't I remember?"

She can't remember what happened to Doctor Harrison either? Matilda slid to the edge of her seat and placed a hand on Mother Harrison's knee. "Why doesn't Elliot play us something on the piano?"

"No, I must remember!"

Mother Harrison slammed her hand on the side table with an explosion of cookies and shattered glass. A jagged shard of the platter sliced into her palm.

"Oh." Mother Harrison stared at the blood pooling on her table. "Oh dear."

Matilda hustled to the woman's side. She brushed glass off the arm of the chair and took her bleeding hand gently. "Elliot, fetch Joseph. Olive, I need a clean cloth."

The children dashed away without question. Matilda tended to Mother Harrison's hand, but she feared to remove the glass without knowing how deeply it pierced her. Blood dripped down Mother Harrison's wrist and blotted her sleeves.

Trying to blink an unending fog out of her eyes, Mother Harrison pressed her other hand to her head. "I feel dizzy."

"I know. Joseph will be here soon."

With the woman she admired in anguish once again, Matilda couldn't help but call to the Power. Mother Harrison's aura spread over her, dreary charcoal in colour and thick like a storm that blacked out the heavens. Maybe the clouds of her aura had something to do with the clouds in her memory.

The only thing Matilda knew was that she shouldn't have trusted this moment of happiness.

Blood stained the cuffs of Joseph's shirt as he attended to his mother's injury with tender care. He cleaned and wrapped the wound so expertly Matilda hated to think how many times he'd done it before. Olive and Elliot cleared up the broken glass and cookies then headed upstairs where they'd be out of the way, and once Joseph had helped his mother down a glass of brandy, he shut her soundly in her room to rest.

Matilda stood near him outside the closed door. She wondered if her presence comforted Joseph at all. Maybe he'd forgotten she was there.

"Do you believe in the judgement of God?"

It didn't sound like something Joseph would ask, but there was no mistaking the voice that always held so much power over Matilda. Now it sounded worn. Already she missed the lilt of his laugh.

Mother had taught her of heaven and hell. Matilda believed enough to read from the Bible and to meet Olive and Elliot at church, but that wasn't what he'd asked.

"You don't have to answer." He gestured down the hall, silently asking for her to follow him away from the door, and he led her back through the house at a wandering pace. "Would you think less of me if I told you I became a policeman because I didn't trust God to punish men like the ones who killed my father and left my mother with a broken heart?"

Joseph usually hid his struggles so well Matilda forgot he had them, but now she saw her angel without his wings, falling. Sometimes in her nightmares she tumbled endlessly into a void. Joseph walked upright on two feet, but inside she knew he spiralled downward with nothing on which to hold. His sparkling aura must be so anguished now. She didn't call the Power to her. She didn't ever want to see him like that.

"You know I could never think less of you," she said. "But times like this are when you need your faith. Or at least a friend."

"What I need is work. Those men you met in the woods, I need to find them."

The charm and good will Matilda had come to associate with Joseph were thin on his voice as he spoke. She feared to ask him what he'd do if he found the Sceolan. Could it be any worse than what she'd imagined doing herself?

Even as they sought to defend their motherland from English oppression and heal her wounds, the Fenians had injured only innocents. Hatred of them had turned Nathaniel into something frightening, and now even Joseph considered vengeance.

Something so dirty should never touch someone so pure, but how could Matilda warn Joseph not to take the same steps she'd taken all year—the same steps she *still* took toward a vengeance of her own?

"I know," she said.

And I need to find Mr. Wellington.

The only way for either of them to stop spiralling downward was to send that villain spiralling down in their stead.

April 30th, 1884

I found a doe in the woods yesterday. Even the beast's auras are plain to me now, the whispers of their Names like a song no manmade instrument could imitate.

Nor a man's tongue. I didn't have a hope of speaking the doe's Name. Through my experimenting, I've discovered the Names seem to respond only to a language the host understands. I sensed and absorbed some of the doe's hesitant curiosity when I stroked her Name with a thread of Power, but until I can learn to communicate through thought alone, her animal soul will remain safe from me.

The others have no idea how vulnerable they are to me now. They don't remember how I've toyed with them, but I remember the feel of their lights tainting mine, like filthy oil leaving a film behind on glass.

I know it's changing me, and I know I could stop it. All I need to do is give my partner the Names. I could be done with this. Little by little I could cleanse myself of the Fenians' taint, but there's a part of me that doesn't want to be clean, a voice that revels in the wicked hunger that festers in me and tells me I have more I must do. More I could have. More I deserve.

First, I planned to keep the Fenians' Soul Names secret until my Power was equal to my partner's, but now…now I don't recognize what's driving me anymore. That excites part of me.

And it frightens me.

It sobered me enough I sent a message to my partner. In a few days, we'll meet, and if I have any sense remaining, I'll give up the Names and be done with this.

Sheridan almost caught me reaching for Gallager's Name yesterday. I know his suspicion of me is growing. But so is the Power within me.

So is the hunger.

— CHAPTER FORTY-NINE —

MATILDA

For days the farmhouse felt still lonelier without Mîfä. Matilda wished she'd accepted more of her invitations to join her walks around the meadow while she'd had the chance, but Lucky helped with the feelings of solitude. With some convincing, Matilda had managed to get him to do a few chores, and as she worked around the farm, she listened to the *thwack* of his axe splitting logs for the woodshed. The meadow was so peaceful she could almost forget the Sceolan, but she hadn't been able to forget Lucas Wellington.

How do I find him?

And what would she ever do if she *did* find him?

As the sun fell over the trees, the moon appeared in the sky early, turning from a pewter crescent to a colour more blood-red than what coursed through Matilda's veins. Set against the darkened sky, the moon looked like a wound in the heavens. Matilda gathered in the last of the clothes drying on the line and called for Lucky.

After an afternoon of chopping wood under the assault of autumn sun, Lucky shone with sweat. She sent him to wash while she dumped the laundry on her bed and put her pistol in the nightstand drawer, then she shuffled downstairs and lit the stove for their supper. She fried a fat salmon and two of her biggest potatoes, setting the plate with the extra scoop in the spot across from hers. Lucky returned with damp hair and the scent of her lavender soap.

"Sit."

She gave thanks for the food, closing her eyes for a prayer that was briefer and less heartfelt than it should have been, but when she said her "Amen" and lifted her gaze, Lucky still had his eyes closed and his arms crossed the way she'd taught him.

It made her think of Joseph's admission. She wondered if Lucky understood anything as complex as God and prayer or if his supplication was only another imitation, but whatever faith Joseph had lost, Lucky seemed to have found.

After a moment of what looked like deep reflection, Lucky scooped up a mouthful of potatoes, remembering to use his fork without being reminded. He handled it with a proficiency that approached normal. If a stranger walked in on them, they'd find nothing peculiar except for Lucky's silence and bare feet.

"What would you sound like if you could speak?" She pushed her plate aside and rested her elbows on the table. "What would you say?"

For once she didn't wonder only about Nathaniel or Mr. Wellington—Lucky would have more to think of and say than that. He knew so much. She saw that knowledge hiding behind his eyes like flecks of gold hidden in red silt.

How wonderful it would be to talk with him as she did with Joseph—to hear him share his thoughts on the most profound of subjects or even the most mundane. Would he think only of chasing the gulls in the field, or would he marvel at their flight and feel a sense of longing as they soared overhead? What would he have to say about the rain or of angels? How would his voice sound when it cradled words like "home" or her name?

But what if he said her name with the spite Isaac and Keith said Nathaniel's? What if he hated the O'Connor in her as much as she hated the Fenian in him?

And what if he told her everything she wanted? What would happen to him when this was finally over?

Don't think about it. He'll never speak. He'll never change.

Never. It was a hard truth to face, but someone as gifted as Miss Kovacs couldn't help him. What could Matilda do?

She became aware of her unblinking gaze on Lucky about the same time he did. His eyes rose to hers with questions. He set his fork down and eyed the potatoes on his plate as though he thought he'd done something wrong.

If someone did this to him, someone can undo it. Miss Kovacs couldn't help him because he wouldn't let her, but maybe he'll let someone else in.

"Do you trust me?" she said.

She got up from her seat, rounded the table, and slipped into the chair next to him. Mindful of his bare feet, she inched her chair closer.

"You shielded yourself from Miss Kovacs, but you won't do that to me, will you?" she asked. "I know you don't like the way it feels, and I know we haven't been as close as we once were, but maybe I can help free you."

Lucky's eyes narrowed, uncertain. She couldn't tell whether it was because he didn't understand her or because he didn't trust her, but she chose to believe in the bond between them.

"I'm going to try…something. Let me in." *What am I doing? I don't know how to do this! How did the mesmerist do it?*

As Matilda took his face between her hands, Lucky didn't flinch from her the way he had from Miss Kovacs. It was a start.

The trance came to her readily.

No change in light or colour surrounded Lucky, but she felt the magic upon her as her hands burst into harmless burgundy flames. The Power reacted to her hold on Lucky, quivering through her skin like tiny earthquakes. It didn't shake the house or rattle Mother's photograph on the wall, but somewhere within her brewed great command. If she dug in deeply enough, she might be able to direct it into him.

A soft groan of protest escaped Lucky. His cheeks slipped under her palms as he tried to pull away.

"It's all right." She grew the Power around her until her skin tingled with the peak of an electrical storm. "Trust me."

Eyes nervous, Lucky closed them and slid his face back into her palms.

The Power rushed through Matilda's entire being, but Lucky was a dam too great to break down. He trembled under her hands as she threw waves of magic at him, but no sizzle of energy passed through him. It bounced back and returned to her.

He's resistant.

"Let me in. I know you can, and I need you to help me."

A crack emerged in the dam. It zigzagged through Lucky's resistance, but remained small. The dam held.

"More," she said. "I won't hurt you."

The crack widened. A small, lightless burst of Lucky's own energy collided with Matilda's and ignited the storm of power into something dangerous and wonderful. It thrilled through her body until her very being felt alive with it. She had to dig deeper. She wanted to feel more of this. *Needed* more of it.

Yes, a little more.

Already she felt Lucky patching up the hole in his shield, and the Power weakened in her. He pulled away again, closing off her link to the raw energy within him—to Nathaniel and to the answers she'd searched for too long.

"No!" She snared her fingers in his hair and pressed her head against his. "Let. Me. *In!*"

Something…clicked.

The dam broke down; she barged past it without interference, entering a new world unlike any other. She saw Lucky the way Miss Kovacs must see without sight, by feeling and impression. She heard him, but not by ear. The Power touched everything and told her everything. Somewhere so distant it seemed a half-forgotten dream, connected to him by a tiny thread, she felt Lucky's Name.

But something was in the way. Something trapped the Name and had all but severed forever the thread that connected it to him. She couldn't command the Name from here; it hid somewhere too far for her to hear its whispers. It seemed tainted, no longer pure, but she sensed a cloud of wit and cheer. She felt youth and playfulness. Goodness. Loyalty. Lucky's soul.

This must be the wrong Name. This can't be the Name of a Sceolan man.

Lucky jumped to his feet so fast Matilda yanked out strands of his hair. Pain shot up her knees as she tumbled to the floor. Her connection with Lucky gone, the Name flickered and went out. The Power vanished, leaving her dazed.

"Why did you—?"

Lucky stood over her, frozen but for the erratic heave of his chest. He peered at her with a look more betrayed than if she'd shot him with her pistol.

He remembers.

He remembered the chains in the cellar, and the mere memory of it tormented his dreams. Miss Kovacs had warned her that he remembered the feel of the Power on him too—the magic that had hurt him more than the chains and solitude.

Matilda had asked him for his trust and forced on him another terror.

"Oh, Lucky." She rolled onto one knee and poised to get up. "I don't know what came over me. I'm so sorry."

She reached for him, but Lucky broke from his stupor and dashed away. The door cracked against the wooden frame when it slammed behind him.

"No! Wait!"

Matilda rushed to the door, but when she opened it, Lucky was already gone.

— CHAPTER FIFTY —

MATILDA

Under twilight, the line of trees beyond the meadow was black and threatening. Matilda found a gap and plunged into them.

"Lucky!"

Her heart beat her insides into mush. *What if he never comes back?*

Even with a lantern, shadows clung to the ground and made it too hard to find a trail through the brush.

"Please come back!" She shouted into the woods and prayed he heard the regret in her voice.

A horrible stench assailed Matilda's senses as she called to Lucky. It overcame the scent of the trees and left an aftertaste of pain and death. As she moved, the stink deepened, staining her lungs until she thought she'd never smell anything else again.

The path curved to evade a fallen tree, its dead roots torn and brittle, and where the path returned to its original course, a creature lay over a patch of twigs and black earth. By the smell of rot, the beast had been dead at least a week or even two. It couldn't be Lucky, but still her knees weakened.

I told Richards I didn't steal his dog.

She pinched her nose but couldn't keep her eyes from the hound as she passed. She'd stumbled upon the scavenged carcasses of hares or birds in these woods many times before. They all looked the same—grotesque and deformed with bones sticking out like thistles and insects making homes in the flesh. But as Matilda's lantern poured light over the dog, it revealed something that made this creature different: the jaws of a hunter's trap clamped around one of its legs and buried metal teeth deep into the broken bone.

This is O'Connor land! Richards knows we walk through these woods!

Indeed, the trap had been set so far across the border between their farms she didn't doubt her neighbour had known. He didn't even care enough to keep an eye on the traps he'd set. His paranoia of strays had cost him his own animal.

How many other traps are there? What if Lucky steps in one?

"Lucky!"

Only the honking of geese flying overhead answered her. They hurried home with the last of the light.

"Lucky, please answer me!"

Matilda left the dead hound behind her and walked toward Richards's farm until the smell subsided, shuffling her feet with the hope she wouldn't step in a trap herself. Quickly the sun departed, and instead of cedar and fir there were only shadows and the crack of a twig.

"Lucky, is that you?" Matilda said softly, afraid to scare him away. She made herself small and nonthreatening. "Please come home."

The silhouette of a man parted from the trees and approached her. Another twig snapped, and the heel of a boot thudded on the earthen floor.

Boots?

The Sceolan? A wild man? Where's my pistol?

"Miss O'Connor?"

She jumped at the man's voice, but then its soothing tones brought her back down to earth.

"Mr. Harrison, what are you doing here?" Matilda squinted at the silhouette and tried to make out Joseph's face. He stood beyond the reach of her lantern, but she saw the outline of stiff shoulders and something hard in his right hand.

"I asked my mother that once. She said something about a stork." He sounded entirely polite as though they'd happened on each other at the general store, yet something strange ran beneath his voice.

"Why are you skulking around my farm?"

"Skulking? I've never skulked in my life!"

The joke sounded perfectly like Joseph but felt wrong. Did he sound hurried? No, that wasn't quite right. Withdrawn?

"Anyhow, you're in my uncle's part of the woods now," he said, his outline too rigid to complement his wit. "I can skulk as I please. What are you doing here?"

There it was again—a hint of hesitation before he spoke, as though he had to decide not only what to say but how to say it. It didn't feel natural or sincere.

She held her lantern higher to extend its reach. "Is something wrong? Are you hiding something from me?"

"All right," Joseph said with a sigh. As he stepped into the light, it revealed an anxious grin as taut as the rest of him and a silver revolver in his hand. "The truth is I'm hunting."

"Here and at this hour?" she asked. *With a pistol?* "What do you hunt?"

He slipped his revolver into the holster at his hip and covered it from her sight with his jacket. "Wild men. Or Fenians. I don't know anymore, but everything points to these woods."

Matilda's heart stumbled again. *What if he finds Lucky before I do?*

Joseph would misread him. He'd misunderstand Lucky's harmless growls of warning. With his strength so much less than it once was, Lucky might not survive another bullet.

"I told you I'd find them, and I meant it," Joseph said with eyes that were as firm as they were striking. "Whatever it is you're doing here, you should return home for tonight. It isn't safe."

Not without Lucky.

She didn't have time to argue, so she simply said, "Watch for traps. Your *uncle* has left them about."

"Wait." Joseph's hand slipped over hers to take the lantern from her. "I'll escort you."

"There's really no need—"

Matilda cut herself off as the night breeze shifted and a reeking smell invaded her nose again. She waved her hand in front of her face, but before she could get rid of the stench, a rumbling growl broke through the dark.

Lucky? Not now! Not here in front of Joseph!

He'd made no sound before the growl, approaching through the trees and brush without even a rustle. The growl came from so close, just out of the lantern's reach.

"Oh, wonderful," Joseph said with mock enthusiasm. "My uncle's dogs have come to play."

She slipped her hand out from Joseph's and stepped between him and the growl in the woods. "It's me, Lucky," she said low enough Joseph wouldn't hear. "Please go home."

Her whispers incited another snarl, but it sounded all wrong. The warnings were too deep. Too vicious. He sounded enormous, and the stink of rot grew in a cloud around her as it fell from his breath.

The skin on the back of Matilda's neck tightened. Her body begged to run.

It isn't Lucky.

She stumbled back into the lantern Joseph held aloft. It fell out of his hand and smashed to the earth, the flame smothered.

"Are you all right?" Joseph's hand gripped her shoulder. She heard him reaching for his revolver.

"Run!" Matilda said.

She grabbed Joseph's hand and pulled him away. He was too strong to drag behind her but shrewd enough to react. His long legs outpaced hers, and, his hand fastened to hers, he towed her behind him on paths she barely made out in the dark.

No sound of running feet chased them, but Matilda suffocated in their stalker's awful stench as she raced faster than her pounding heart could keep up. She clung to Joseph's hand and prayed he knew where he was going, but no matter how fast they ran or how many turns they made, the smell of the beast followed, thick and close. But why didn't he attack?

He's playing with his kill! she realized with horror.

"This way." Joseph said. He took her down another path, somehow keeping her safe from the reach of tree branches, but then he stopped so suddenly she crashed into his back.

"Get in."

Creeeak! Joseph pulled Matilda in front of him then steered her down wooden steps that groaned under her heels. They descended into darkness, and Joseph slammed the door shut over their heads.

Earth and dust fell upon Matilda. The air down here smelled as horrible as the wild man's breath, and Matilda didn't have to guess where she was. With a sick feeling in her stomach, she recognized instantly the smell of blood and the haunted feeling of the cellar.

Joseph said he burned this place…

A beast's disappointed growl thundered overhead. Matilda shrank back and stumbled over chains in the dark as the creature pawed at the rickety door.

That door won't hold him. Matilda covered her mouth and trembled, but the wild man huffed at the door. Then she heard nothing.

"He's gone," Joseph said, and for all his questions of God, it sounded like a prayer.

Matilda struggled to find her voice for a long moment and almost feared to use it once she had. "We should be dead. I can't see the end of my own nose."

"This should help with that."

The strike of a match sounded in the corner of the room, and a flame illuminated Joseph as he lit a lantern. Light flooded over the piles of Isaac's notes on the table, but before Joseph could set down the lantern, footsteps pounded overhead.

An ear-splitting *crack* tore the door off its hinges. Matilda ducked under a shower of splinters. Joseph pulled out his revolver.

The wild man loomed in the entrance to the cellar, but the beast merely sat at the top of the stairs and watched them. Watched her.

Light fell upon half of his face and body. He was colossal, and, unlike Lucky, this man hadn't been starved. Instead of fleshless bones, his skin rippled over sinewy muscle. He wore only threadbare trousers and the hair on his arms and chest, but Matilda realized she'd seen him before.

Last time he'd smelled of sweat and had pointed her own rifle at her. Now he didn't need one.

"Isaac?" Matilda barely recognized her own quivering voice.

At the sound of his name, no flicker of recognition crossed Isaac's eyes. Always with his gaze on Matilda, he stooped through the doorway and lowered himself into the cellar one thumping foot at a time. In the woods he'd moved without a sound. Now he wanted to intimidate her.

It worked.

Joseph pointed his gun at Isaac, but he hesitated. A gun wouldn't stop that man—a *cannon* might not stop him—but it would make him very, very angry. Joseph couldn't help them now, but maybe Matilda could.

I'm not going to die down here without a fight.

Energy crackled around Matilda the moment she called to the Power. She called more of it to her, and more, until her body hurt from the flow of it around her.

No aura surrounded Isaac. She couldn't take his face in her hands as she had with Lucky and try to return him to himself. All she had was the Power within her and a man who had no Name: an empty vessel to be commanded. If she was strong enough.

Isaac must have sensed the Power surrounding her. He snarled and lunged for her throat.

Please don't be resistant!

"STOP!"

The command tore from her chest and hurtled at Isaac in a blast of her own purplish light. He froze mid-leap, his snarl lost on the air.

When he landed on his feet again, he stood close enough to touch, his hands outstretched but still and his eyes vacant. The beast had left its shell.

"It worked?" Matilda said, gasping.

"What—?" Joseph's gun aimed for the ample target the wild man gave, but it looked forgotten in his hand. His aura flickered between a rainbow of colours before settling once again on her favourite deep emerald. The beautiful colour seemed out of place down here, but the distress in Joseph's eyes negated any comfort his aura might have given her. "What did you do?" he asked.

"Never mind that." She ducked under the beast's outstretched claws and hurried toward the stairs. "We must leave. Now."

She went up the stairs first, but she didn't dare turn her back to Isaac. Joseph climbed the stairs two at a time with the lantern in his hand, but behind him Isaac's fingers already twitched, breaking out from their spell. Isaac shook his head and looked over his shoulder. His eyes weren't playful anymore.

They were savage.

"Go!" Matilda hauled Joseph out of the cellar with all her strength. Isaac scrambled up the stairs behind him.

The Power surrounded Matilda instinctively. She reached an arm of it toward the wild man, but something pulled her back and broke her concentration. The Power slipped away from her.

Joseph clutched her hand and towed her away. "Run!"

"I can—"

Isaac leapt up the stairs. He bent his knees, about to pounce. It was too late. The Power was gone. She and Joseph were dead.

Zip. THUD!

A draft sped past Matilda, and something crashed into Isaac. Both fell to the ground, hard. Isaac roared.

"*Run,* I said!" The lantern swung under Joseph's hand as he pulled at Matilda. Shadows darted over the whites of his round eyes. "There's another!"

"Another...?" She tugged out of Joseph's grasp.

Two bodies locked together in combat and struggled for a hold on the ground. It was impossible to miss Isaac's hulking form, but the shape she recognized first was much smaller and dressed in Nathaniel's old clothes.

Lucky moved with more speed and strength than she'd thought he had left. He crushed Isaac into the ground. Isaac thrashed with bear-paw hands, looking for a kill. They were father and son, but Isaac couldn't even recognize Lucky anymore.

He came back.

Joseph caught Matilda's wrist and pulled her away from the scene before she could dig her heels in.

No! Isaac will kill him!

She twisted her hand out of Joseph's grip and raced back.

"What are you doing?" Joseph called from behind her.

She didn't pause to answer. Shapes moved through the dark ahead. Someone took a hit. She emerged from the trees as Lucky dropped to the ground.

Isaac stood with Lucky vulnerable at his feet.

"Don't touch him!" she yelled.

At the sound of her voice, Isaac charged at her. Energy zapped around her in a protective shield, but he was too fast. He lunged for her before she'd built enough power.

Lucky grabbed Isaac's legs and tripped him to the ground, but Isaac kicked Lucky in the chest with a sickening *crack.* Lucky grunted but held tight.

Isaac aimed another kick at Lucky, but his hands strained toward Matilda.

Why? He's only hunting me?

This wasn't a random attack. It was a job! Someone had sent Isaac to frighten her. Maybe to kill her.

Miss Kovacs warned me Mr. Wellington would protect his secrets!

"Keep him still!" she told Lucky. She whipped out her arm, guiding a sheet of energy over Isaac while Lucky kept him on the ground.

"Stop!" she ordered Isaac, but he was ready this time.

He steeled himself, and the Power bounced off him. Isaac slammed his heel into Lucky's chest again. Lucky yelped, and Isaac pulled free and leapt for Matilda.

She threw her arms over herself. *Be strong!* The Power thickened around her, and her arms *changed*. A little sturdier. Harder.

Isaac crashed into her with a brick-like shoulder. Pain burst through her arms and head, and the Power went out like a shattered lantern. She fell hard on her back and bit back a scream.

Every pulse of blood burned the veins in her arms. Every muscle felt torn. He'd hit her like a hammer, more than hard enough to break bone. She'd never felt such pain.

Yet her arms were impossibly whole. Swelling, but not broken.

Isaac recovered fast, raising himself from the ground. Matilda called to the Power, but it wouldn't come.

Where—? Why?

She sat up. Her head spun and a hot trickle of blood dripped down her forehead. Lucky crawled on his belly toward her, but Isaac already loomed over her with bared teeth.

BANG!

The sound of a pistol bellowed overhead.

"Don't you touch her," Joseph said. "The second one won't be a warning."

The light of Joseph's lantern enveloped Matilda. She knew his gun would be trained on Isaac. It wouldn't stop the beast, but perhaps if they all fought him together…

Isaac retreated a step. He puffed out his chest and growled a threat at Joseph, but as his eyes darted between the three of them, he yielded. Backing away from the light, he turned and limped into the woods.

The moment Isaac was gone, Matilda hugged her arms against herself and shuffled on her knees toward Lucky, her legs tangling in her skirts as she held back another cry of pain.

"Keep away from him," Joseph said. His hand touched her shoulder, and Lucky made a noise halfway between a growl and a whimper. It was a weak sound, short and quiet, but there was no doubt of his warning.

To Matilda the sound held more beauty than the songs of the first birds of spring.

"Hush. Mr. Harrison is a friend." She tried to shrug Joseph's hand away, but the movement jolted pain down her arms and fingers. "Let go. He won't hurt me."

Joseph repeated her last words with disbelief, but he released her. He stayed close, and she had no doubt he had his revolver at the ready.

Lucky cradled a rib, rolled onto his knees, and coughed. Enduring the throbbing in her arms, she reached for him to be sure he was real. Her numb, cold fingers couldn't feel the tears in Nathaniel's shirt or the sweat on Lucky's skin, but little shocks ran up her arms at the touch between them.

"You'll be all right, won't you?" Her voice wavered and fell. Her eyes stung, and her vision blurred. She was alive. Lucky was alive. He'd come back, and all the hurts and fears that had troubled her left her body in a rain of tears. "I'm sorry. I'm so sorry."

Forgetting Joseph and the Sceolan and all the rules she'd made to keep herself proper, she stroked Lucky's head. Through the pain she couldn't feel the tangles in his hair, but as she combed her fingers through it, Lucky leaned into her. He pressed his forehead to hers, and then she felt everything that mattered.

Shivers raced through her. He trembled with each tired breath, but his forgiveness streamed into her with a healing tenderness.

"I promise I won't push anymore," she said.

Joseph cleared his throat awkwardly, reminding Matilda he was there. "We should move before the wild man returns."

— CHAPTER FIFTY-ONE —

MATILDA

No one spoke on the way back to the farmhouse. No one wanted to attract another wild man, and Matilda worried she'd scream from the pain in her arms if she so much as opened her mouth. She clamped her teeth shut and let Joseph occupy himself with keeping watch. He led the way, and she lagged behind with Lucky, dragging her feet from sore exhaustion and a fear of Richards's traps.

When they reached the edge of the woods and the sleepy meadow sprawled before them, she wanted to cry again. The hens nestled in their coop and Duchess slumbered with the cows, oblivious. If not for the tears in her dress and the fire in her arms, she could almost imagine she'd woken from a nightmare.

They kept their silence even once they'd entered the farmhouse. Joseph set the lantern on the table and pulled chairs out for both Matilda and Lucky. He helped Matilda into her seat then attempted to help Lucky, but Lucky wouldn't have it. He backed out of Joseph's reach and sent him an indignant glare. Joseph raised his hands in surrender and gave him space.

With better light it was easier for Matilda to check Lucky's injuries. Where he wasn't a mess of blood and rent clothes, he was pale as the flesh of an apple, but his bare feet were shredded, and blood from a gash near his hairline stained a river down his cheek.

Yet the blood was dry, and already his breath stopped wheezing. Thankfully, his healing ability hadn't completely faded.

Once Lucky seated himself, Joseph knelt at Matilda's feet and took one of her arms into his hands. She winced as he massaged it through her sleeve, his careful touch igniting every nerve, but soon the pain dulled and feeling returned to her hand.

He massaged her other arm and reminded her of how he'd tended to his mother, but as he worked the pain out of her muscles, he focused his attention so fervently on his hands she knew he was angry.

"Thank you," she said meekly when he'd finished.

"First the runaway, and now a wild man." Joseph stood and turned his back to her. "Are you running a boarding house?"

"How did you know Lucky lives here? I never said a word."

Joseph pointed to Lucky's shoes by the door, too big to be an extra pair of Elliot's. *Oh.*

"You know what Lucky is, don't you?" she asked. "You told me you'd burned the cellar, but I saw the notes on the table. Someone's been reading them."

"I—" Joseph hung his head before turning to her again. "There are answers in that cellar. I didn't want to burn them away, but I didn't want to give you reason to return either. Yes, I know what this man is, and I know why you keep him here. You haven't given up on Nathaniel."

"How could I?" she admitted freely, too drained to keep any more secrets. "You haven't given up either."

"It's *my* duty to protect the city and the people here." Joseph's silver eyes darkened, never leaving Matilda, but his finger thrust toward Lucky like a sword. "That man might have died today. He still might, far as I can tell."

Lucky dug his nails into his chair. He didn't growl, but there was a dangerous edge to him as he watched Joseph.

"It's all right, Lucky." Matilda patted his knee until his eyes lost a little sharpness and Joseph's reprimand laid its full weight on her.

She'd made mistake after mistake, but each time someone else had paid the price. The wild man Joseph had killed. Olive and Elliot. Mîfä and Kāi. And Lucky. He could have died. Next time he might.

I can't afford any more mistakes.

Joseph found a third chair and set it in front of her. He sat down, leaned forward, and took her hand in his. She'd thought it would feel warmer. "You're the last of Olive and Elliot's family." His words felt harsh, but his tone was full of sympathy. "So help me, even if I must endure your hatred the rest of my days, I'll drag you from this house if it means those two won't lose you. I'd rather you chose to come with me."

Matilda's eyes fell to the tears in her skirt and the stains of blood and dirt, but she felt Joseph's hand on her chin. He took it in a steady but careful grip and turned her face toward him.

"Matilda," he said, his voice cradling her name with the same care he'd used to nurse her arms. "I want you, Olive, and Elliot to be my family. All *three* of you. Is that so wrong?"

Her eyes wandered to Lucky's. The light made them glow, but they looked cold. His gaze flicked between her and Joseph. She couldn't read his thoughts. Maybe it was time she stopped pretending she ever would.

I'm sorry, Lucky.

"Nothing I've tried has done a bit of good," she said. "This fixation of mine has changed me, and not for the better. It's only hurt those I care about most, and after tonight, I can't pretend otherwise. I know it's time for me to put it in someone else's hands."

"It is?" Joseph leaned back in his seat and looked at her with a puzzled expression. "To be honest, I expected you to contend with me."

Matilda pulled her hand out from Joseph's and felt the lump of her twenty-five-cent coin at her chest. She untied the strings around her neck and pulled the coin free, severing the bond, the obsession, that tied her to Nathaniel.

He'd chosen his path. Now she needed to choose hers.

She held the coin toward Joseph, and when he offered his hand she dropped it into his palm and forced a smile on her lips. It felt clumsy and strained, but one day it would feel right.

"Will you do something for me?" she asked.

He closed his fingers around the coin. "You know I will."

"Find Lucky the help he needs," she said. "And when that's done…we'll be married, Joseph Harrison."

— CHAPTER FIFTY-TWO —

LUCKY

Lucky doesn't like the big house. I— *I* don't like the big house. Matilda opens it and takes me inside. The floor feels like moss, but the air is dead and dark and feels like a fever. The other male's scent is everywhere. A strong, sweet scent Lucky hates.

The male closes the house behind him. His eyes are nervous when they pass over Lucky but change when they see Matilda. Lucky hates those eyes too. "They'll want to see you. I'll wake them and let you explain everything," the male says.

The male goes deeper into the house. Matilda watches him until he disappears up the stairs.

"Stop glaring at him." Matilda's voice is sad. It's my fault somehow, but I don't know what I did wrong. I protected her, but she looks tired. She sounds small. "He's a good man. You're going to stay with him at a hotel until— You… Just behave yourself."

Her voice dies, and her eyes are sadder now.

Footsteps thud overhead and down stairs. I hold in the pain and wait for another attack.

"Calm down. You're safe here." Matilda's face…lifts. Her eyes are brighter and her lips curl upward, but it's a lie. It's the lie she uses when she doesn't want *them* to see.

"Matilda!"

Olive and Elliot appear below the stairs. My heart thumps as they run closer. It hurts, but in a good way. The children collide with Matilda, tie her up in their arms, and bare their teeth happily.

"Joseph said you've come to stay," Olive says.

"Yes, it's true."

"Lucky?" Elliot is the first to notice me. His eyes bulge, and he runs like an excited pup. I brace for the impact. When it comes, Elliot traps me in his arms, and the burst of pain doesn't matter.

"Be careful!" Matilda pulls Elliot off me. "He's injured."

Olive pats my arm and pokes her finger through a hole in my shirt. "What happened?"

"Nothing you should worry yourself for." It's the male's voice now. I hadn't heard him approach, but I don't hear as much anymore. "Don't stay up too late. Your sister will still be here tomorrow."

Too soon Matilda sends the pups to bed. I try to follow Elliot, but Matilda blocks the way. She takes me to a seat that squishes. I wonder if it will swallow me whole.

"Stay," she says.

Matilda goes to the sweet-smelling stranger and takes him out of sight.

"Stop worrying," he says. His voice is low, but I hear him, barely. "I'll look after him."

"I know," Matilda says, "but…Olive and Elliot deserve a proper farewell, but I don't know how to tell them."

A proper farewell? Were the pups leaving again?

"He isn't moving to another country. They may visit him and write as many letters as they please."

No. They aren't leaving. The male is sending me away. Where? Matilda will stop him. She will stop him.

"Lucky doesn't read." I hear submission in Matilda's voice. Why doesn't she fight?

A moment later Matilda and the male reappear. She approaches me, but the male puts a hand on her shoulder. The muscles down my back go tight.

"You shouldn't stay up late either," the male says.

"I know."

"This is your home now, so feel at peace here. And keep Mother out of trouble, will you?"

"I will. Thank you, Joseph."

Joseph, Matilda calls him. *Jooooseff.* I hate that name.

"Good night," Joseph says. He peers at me from the corner of his eye then presses his lips to Matilda's cheek. A growl readies in my chest, but I stamp it down. I understand now.

That's why Matilda is sending me away. For *him.*

I don't like the big house at all.

— CHAPTER FIFTY-THREE —

MATILDA

Matilda woke to the sound of rain on glass and too much room in the bed. But for herself and Sable curled on the floor by the wardrobe, her bedroom was empty of life. The manor didn't creak like the farmhouse or let the wind whistle through the windows. It didn't echo with the sounds of children's laughter or arguing either. Olive and Elliot must already be at school.

Rainclouds shrouded the sun outside when she crawled out from her silken sheets and pulled the plum-coloured curtains back from the window. The beat of rain against the house made her think of ticking watches. Time passed too quickly. Her last day was wasting without her.

After scavenging an apple for her belly, Matilda harnessed Joseph's horse and hitched it to his surrey wagon. Despite the late hour of his arrival last week, Joseph had managed to get a room at one of the inns on Front Street—a grand-looking thing with tall, red walls of brick and windows so clean they reflected the skies perfectly. The rain eased as she neared the Fraser and the inn, but heavy mist bathed the windows in a woeful grey.

She didn't know what Joseph had said to the staff at the hotel, but they always smiled and let her upstairs without question. She climbed the carpeted steps and found the mahogany door marked *211* in golden numbers. Before Matilda opened the door, she prepared herself for a mess of sheets, flying pillow feathers, and falling curtains, but when she stepped inside, the room was immaculate.

The curtains sat open to the rivers of rain backlit by weak light on the glass. All pillows were in their violet satin cases and lined neatly on the made beds—wrinkle free except on the one where Lucky lay.

He curled up on his side with his knees bent, his head on a pillow made of his arm and his chin tilted toward his chest. His eyes closed in sleep, but his breath came unevenly, and his eyebrows twitched with another nightmare. Matilda shut the door and hurried to his side, but before she could touch him, her very presence seemed to startle him awake.

He flinched from her hand and swatted it away before recognition crept into his eyes. His expression shifted through a tempest of emotion, first afraid, then warm and welcoming, and finally cool and distant. He rolled off the bed, the nightmare clinging to him in the heave of his chest, but he turned from her to stare through the window into nothing.

Joseph had somehow gotten Lucky to wear his shoes again, and instead of Nathaniel's old rags, he wore a set of Joseph's clothes. From behind, the dark waistcoat almost made him look like Joseph. He stood a little too short, and his black hair had a disobedient ruffle never seen in Joseph's fair locks, but his shoulders cut the same shape. He clasped his hands behind his back in a way perfect for Joseph but too sophisticated for Lucky.

But for a bruise by the scar on his nose, his wounds had healed, at least outwardly. She knew his rib still pained him—sometimes his eyes twitched when he breathed—but he made no complaint. In fact, except for the moment of uncontrolled honesty in his eyes when she woke him each morning, he showed no emotion at all.

All he did was sleep the hours away or stare vacantly out that window.

Where was the Lucky who loved to run and to steal taffies from the jar? Where was the older brother who played with Olive and Elliot and stained his clothes with mud? And where was the man whose eyes sparkled whenever Matilda met his gaze?

I left him at the farm with Nathaniel.

Maybe that was the only place she could give him, both of them, the farewell they deserved. "Come," she said. "Let's go out."

For the last time.

Joseph had warned Matilda not to go to the farm without him, but by now he should have known she wouldn't make an obedient wife.

And as long as daylight accompanied her, Mr. Wellington couldn't risk exposing his secret by sending Isaac on the hunt, could he?

Could he?

The white gelding splashed down the road with prancing steps that made Duchess's beautiful strides look inelegant. A breeze much too cold for September swept over the land and chilled the mist on Matilda's skin. Or maybe it was her low spirits that let the cold in. When she looked next to her, Lucky turned his head aside and watched the rain fall from the surrey's canopy in swollen drops.

A gloom covered the sleeping meadow when they arrived. It was empty. Even the gulls had abandoned the field.

She'd known the cows and hens would be gone—Joseph had arranged for Richards to take in her animals, though she loathed the thought of that man touching them. But they weren't her responsibility anymore, and once she collected her things from the house, Richards would have her land as he'd always wanted.

Still, she hadn't expected her home to feel so lifeless.

"Here we are," she said in case Lucky had as much trouble recognizing the place as she did.

She reined back the horse in front of the house and took shelter on the porch with Lucky. He gazed forlornly toward the empty pasture, and Matilda left him to mourn the absence of his animal friends while she searched the house for a few things he could take with him when he…left.

There was little to find. Almost a year he'd stayed here. Memories of him lived in every wall, stone, and window, but what could she touch and hold in her hands? Once Richards took over this place, he'd tarnish even the memories.

She scooped the jar of taffies off the counter and fetched Lucky's patched blanket from Elliot's bed. In her room, Olive's sketches piled on the bedside table. Setting the jar and blanket on the cedar chest, she sat on the edge of the bed and picked up the drawings.

Lifelike depictions of Elliot and Matilda interspersed with sketches of Duchess, Sable, and Olive's favourite cow. Matilda found a drawing of a Musqueam camp by the Brunette River and swore she tasted the smoke of the camp's cooking fire on her tongue.

The last of the drawings showed the meadow resting under stars and a blanket of January snow. The farmhouse slept close to the barn, defended by Elliot and Lucky's snow wolves, and the cows huddled together for warmth. Matilda shivered when she looked at the snow but imagined herself gathered with Olive and Elliot around the fireplace. Lucky would sit over her feet as she mended Olive's apron and listened to Elliot's wishes that the next day would be too cold for school.

She blinked sore eyes and laid the winter scene with Lucky's blanket. Olive wouldn't mind, and maybe Lucky could pin it up in his new room. Maybe it would help with the solitude.

The rest of the drawings Matilda carried to Olive's desk under the window. She slid open the drawer but paused when she saw more drawings inside.

Two sheets of paper sat atop scattered pencils and an old schoolbook. Olive's signature and skilled inking marked the pages, but Matilda had never seen the drawings before.

On the first, Lucky stared back at Matilda. Unruly black locks haloed a handsome face and a lopsided smile. Matilda ran her fingers across the lines and felt her own mouth curl in turn, but there was a sting in her eyes. She flipped the page over and looked at the second drawing.

Another man's face marked the page. In so many ways this face was the opposite of Lucky's. Instead of black curls, fair locks swept back over his head. Dark eyes became light. Strong, lofty cheekbones smoothed down beneath a sprinkling of freckles. This man smiled too, but the smile spread more subtly than Lucky's. The only feature the two men shared was the gleam of wonder that brightened their gazes.

Nathaniel's face looked exactly as Matilda remembered it. The date scribbled in the corner next to Olive's name was only a few months old, but the details captured Nathaniel so perfectly anyone would have thought he'd posed for it himself. Perhaps he had. Perhaps he visited Olive's dreams too.

This was the Nathaniel Matilda wanted to remember. He was the *only* Nathaniel she wanted to remember.

Slipping the other sketches into the drawer, she folded the portraits together with the winter meadow and tucked them into her pocket. She gathered Lucky's things and took them downstairs.

He leaned into the porch railing precisely where she'd left him, closing his eyes and listening to the patter of rain on the roof.

With the clouds rolling over the daylight, Matilda could almost pretend the sun wasn't racing fast toward the west. She could pretend it had frozen in place and the end of the day would never come. Nathaniel didn't matter. Joseph didn't matter. Not even the farm mattered anymore. In this moment she and Lucky were here together, free.

I'm doing the right thing, aren't I? Then why do I feel…

The rain picked up again, but in the distance where the clouds were thinnest, a shaft of sunlight broke through their shield. The sun crossed toward the ocean, and too soon Joseph would return to the hotel for Lucky. A dreadful knot twisted in Matilda's stomach.

It was time to return, and it was time to tell Lucky what she should have told him days ago. It was time for them both to move on. Her with Joseph, so Olive and Elliot could have a better future than she could give them alone. Lucky, to a place where he'd be safe from wolf men and Mr. Wellington. It was for the best. Maybe one day they'd both understand that.

"Come here." She set the blanket and taffies by the door. "Sit for a moment."

She sat on the steps and fiddled with the high neckline of her dress, feeling the absence of Nathaniel's coin. Lucky settled next to her, but when Matilda looked into his eyes, beautiful like cocoa and cinnamon, the words she'd planned vanished from her thoughts. If she said them, they'd become true and Lucky would leave.

I can't.

She gathered the blanket and taffies in one arm and rushed into the rain, but warm fingers tangled in hers and sent tremors through her body. Lucky's touch was gentle, but the command it held over her was greater even than the Power. She let him take his blanket from her. He unfolded it, draping it around her like a raincoat.

"No."

The word sailed on a voice she'd yearned to hear for so long. It didn't even matter that it told her nothing of Nathaniel. She only craved the deep and candid sound of it.

Lucky's hand gripped hers and tempted her nearer, telling her to be brave.

"We must go back," she said. She relaxed the strain of their bodies pulling in opposite directions and let her eyes fall to the melding of their hands. "Whatever happens, you must understand this will be better for both of us."

And so must I.

"I can't help you anymore," she said. "Tonight Joseph is taking you to a place with people who can help you. Do you understand?"

Lucky's eyes narrowed but not with the confusion she'd expected. "No."

"You won't like it at first, but we both have to accept this now. I can't help you get your Name back, do you understand? I wish I could, but I have to look out for what family I have left." She tugged her hand out of his and marched toward the buggy. *I can't do this.*

"*No.*" Lucky threw himself into her path and stood so close she could smell his scent of earth and grass through the rain. He smelled real, not like a dog or a memory.

"Please don't make this harder for me than it already is." None of the words shattered as she spoke them, but the pitch of her voice climbed. "You're not a dog, and I can't keep you."

He slipped his hand behind her neck, tickling her skin so she felt it even down in her toes, and he pressed his forehead to hers as he'd done so many times before. While they touched, she floated, and only his hold on her kept her on the ground.

"Lucky." With all the willpower she could muster, she pushed against his chest but only accomplished losing her blanket as it fell to the mud. Where had her strength gone? "You can't do this anymore. It's not proper."

He made a sound through his teeth, but it wasn't a growl or sigh. She'd never heard this sound from him before. Her breath caught in her lungs.

"I—" His mouth struggled with a new sound. "I d— don't want to go, Matilda."

She must have been breathing, but she couldn't feel the air in her lungs. *Matilda. My name.* His inexperienced tongue embraced her name with a tenderness and intimacy she'd never known. For the first time, Lucky had more gift with words than she. "How—? Why?"

His forehead parted from hers with reluctance. She longed for his heat again, and he gave it.

He pressed his mouth softly to hers in a kiss that was chaste but flooded her with warmth.

Her heart raced, and before reason could stop her, she gave into him. The candy jar fell to her feet and flung taffies over the ground as her fingers tangled in Lucky's waistcoat. She knew only a need to pull him closer, then, too soon, he broke away.

His forehead found hers again, feverish against her skin as his breath sped alongside hers.

What are we doing?

Ice overpowered the heat in her body and frosted the blood in her veins. She shoved Lucky back hard.

His hand slipped from her neck, and he stumbled back, wide-eyed.

Matilda faltered on unsure legs. Words tipped out of her mouth without grace or destination. "You— Why—?" Only her heartbeat remained the same. It thrilled from what he'd done to her, betraying her. Betraying the good, kind man she'd promised herself to. What a weak, naive heart. "How dare you!" she said.

Lucky's face looked hurt and threatened. Tentatively, he stepped toward her.

"Don't." Her voice cracked. She backed toward the buggy, but he followed. "No! Go to the barn. Go *now!*"

Wounded, he dropped his eyes and shuffled through the rain. She didn't wait for the squeal of the barn door as he opened it and instead climbed into the buggy and whipped Joseph's horse toward the city.

Why would he do that? Why would he make me feel…? Why now?

Kāi had tried to convince her. No. She'd already known for some time but refused to admit it.

Lucky knew he wasn't a dog, and now, wholeheartedly, so did she.

— CHAPTER FIFTY-FOUR —

LUCKY

I back into the corner of the room that smells like oiled leather and Duchess and slide to the ground.

Bad! I hurt Matilda. I didn't mean to. I wanted her to understand what I've always tried to tell her, but she doesn't feel the way I do. I made her go. This time she won't come back.

Matilda chose the other man. Joseph. That pains me more than the cracked rib in my chest.

May 3rd, 1884

I underestimated him. My partner.

Sheridan left a note asking to meet me last night. Demanded, really. I was afraid he was going to confront me about his suspicions, maybe even try to kill me, but he didn't get a chance.

I met him at the edge of town after dark. As far as I knew, only he and I knew of the meeting time and place, but once I arrived, he barely had time to scowl at me before his face went slack. Dead, I thought. Dead but standing with his lantern in hand. My gaze slipped into the trance.

Sheridan had no light.

My amplified hearing caught a voice from the distance. "Come." Sheridan turned and plodded toward it until he and his lantern disappeared in the dark.

I recognized the voice. My partner's. But it had come from so far. I saw no hint of the master's light with my improved sight. Heard barely a crinkle of his footsteps on grass such a distance away the Power couldn't possibly have maintained a connecting thread strong enough to tie Sheridan to him. Yet Sheridan obeyed his command.

I gave him the Names too soon. Much too soon. I have nowhere near his Power. My only comfort is that we seek the same goal.

For now.

— CHAPTER FIFTY-FIVE —

MATILDA

Matilda buried her face in her satin pillow until Joseph called her downstairs. He told her with a terrified look on his face that Lucky had disappeared from the hotel, and she'd had no choice but to confess she'd left him on the farm.

I left him. How could I leave him there alone!

Even after hours, the memory of Lucky's kiss haunted her lips. Her heart hadn't forgotten how it had fluttered, but now it mostly hurt.

She didn't know how to look at Joseph. He didn't say anything, but somehow she felt he knew what had happened. He must have heard the skip of her heart or seen Lucky's embrace replaying in her eyes. What must he think of her?

Joseph had planned to fetch Lucky on his own, but when he hitched his horse back up to the surrey, Matilda climbed into the buggy before he could stop her.

I can't leave it like this.

Instead of arguing, Joseph saddled Duchess for Matilda's return to the manor.

The buggy rolled into the meadow. She turned in the seat and watched Duchess, trotting behind them at the end of her lead, perk her ears forward at the sight of home. When the buggy stopped in front of the house, Joseph slipped out of his seat and presented a hand to Matilda, but she stared at the barn, hesitant.

"Be brave," Joseph said. "Say your farewell."

Such a waste. I've wasted the last day!

Remembering the feel of Lucky's touch, she declined Joseph's hand as she stepped down from the buggy and left him with the horses.

The barn door creaked. Dimly she knew of the splintered wood at her fingers and the weight of the door against her palms, but it felt like the door opened of its own will and dragged her inside.

Part of her hoped Lucky had run into the woods to live free, but she found him in the tack room, slumped in the corner. His clothes and hair didn't drip from the rainfall anymore, but they hung heavily on him. He curled his arms around his body and raised his head, looking shocked to see her. That hammered another nail into her heart.

She knelt beside him on the hard, dirt floor and waited for the right words to come. "When you were hurt saving Elliot in that rainstorm, I told you to do whatever it took to make me understand you, and you did. I understand more deeply than I should, but I can't be selfish anymore. I have Olive and Elliot, and you can't provide for them any more than I can give you the help you need."

Lucky's chest rose and fell evenly, but his gaze swept to the corner of the room, avoiding her. She took his chin in her hand, pained and pleased by the feel of even that simple touch, and she drew him back.

"I'll remember you," she said, "and I want you to have something to remember too."

She slipped her hand into her pocket and retrieved the folded drawings she'd hidden there, untouched by the rain. Finding Olive's drawing of the sleepy farmhouse, she offered it to him. Lucky took it tenderly and held it open before his face.

"It makes me think of that snowball fight," she said. "Do you remember? I've never heard Elliot laugh so hard. Nor Olive. I bet they heard us halfway across the country."

For a long moment, Lucky stared at the stars and farmhouse Olive had captured on the page perfectly, then he took the other drawings from Matilda and unfolded the first with a soft crinkle. His own face opened up to him.

"Those are portraits Olive made of you and my brother, Nathaniel," she said. "I thought...well, I thought I might keep them."

He considered the drawing of himself with a gaze that seemed to appreciate the skill more than the subject, and Matilda wondered how she'd ever missed seeing this part of him. How had she ever dismissed the keen, discerning man beneath the spell?

With a rustle of paper, he unfolded the last of the drawings. His eyes fell upon the inked lines of the eldest O'Connor face, and the drawing shook in his hands. He stopped breathing.

"What is it?" she said.

In one sharp movement, Lucky scrambled to his feet and shoved the drawings away from him. They glided to the ground in three different directions.

Matilda rescued Nathaniel's portrait from the ground. "What's wrong?"

An unsettling groan escaped Lucky's lips. He backed into the wall and dug the heels of his hands into his eyes.

"Stop! You'll hurt yourself."

She touched his elbow, but he jerked away and, with his eyes full of pain, bolted out of the room.

"Lucky, where are you going? Why?" She glanced at the drawing open in her hand. A perfect resemblance of Nathaniel gazed back at her. Nathaniel—the man who'd delivered Lucky to his tormentor.

A man Lucky had heard her call brother.

— CHAPTER FIFTY-SIX —

LUCKY

N*o. No, no. The dreams. The dreams aren't dreams.*

I remember the nightmares. Blood and chains and hunger. I remember the dark and cold and the monsters. I remember the face with the blue eyes.

But they aren't dreams.

I close myself in Matilda's room and lock the door. I don't know why I go there, but these walls are the only ones that feel safe. But I still remember. I still feel…

Barely sensing my feet beneath me, I walk to the window. Then I walk to the door again. I run hands through my hair, but I can't stop the storm in my head. My fingers come back cold. Memories blaze through my mind like fire, but all of me shivers. I lean into the door, slump to my knees, and submit.

The doorknob turns. Jiggles.

"Lucky, let me in."

Matilda pounds on the door and shouts, but I can't face her now that I know. She's like him. *Nathaniel.* All this time I never knew.

The nightmares overtake me. I don't know how much time passes as Matilda shouts until she sounds ill and the cold fills me until I'd do anything to make it stop.

I can't relive those dreams again. I have to stop them. There must be...justice. Is that what it's called?

Yes. I need justice.

I grit my teeth and stare at the nightstand in both despair and desperation, but I need it—what Matilda hides there. She told me not to use it, but I need justice.

My hands shake, but I crawl toward my only way free of this nightmare.

— CHAPTER FIFTY-SEVEN —

MATILDA

After flying past a confused Joseph outside and barging into the house only to find a locked door between her and Lucky, Matilda collapsed to her knees in the hallway, depleted.

Time. He needs time to think.

On the other side of her bedroom door the room lay silent. With her fingers, she traced the solid wood barring her from Lucky, hoping for some secret way through.

Give him time.

But there was no time. It was the last day. The last hour. She couldn't let him go like this.

"Lucky, can you hear me?" Her voice was hoarse from shouting, but she knew he could hear it. She wasn't asking about his ears so much as his heart. She flattened her palm on the door. No answer came. "Nathaniel was wrong. He won't hurt you again. You know that, don't you?"

Feet scuffled in the room. She stood and waited for the door to open, but the noise moved away from her. She heard the grating sound of wood against wood, the sound she heard every time she put her journal away. What was he doing in her drawer? What was he looking for?

The only thing she could think of besides paper and ink made her gut wrench. *I need to get in there now!*

She didn't knock again. She flew downstairs for her heaviest pan. The doorknob surrendered to it in only two strikes, and the door flung open.

Lucky cast his eyes to his shoes and bared his teeth in a grimace. His arms fell limply at his sides, but the knuckles of his right hand turned white around Matilda's loaded pistol. He raised the weapon.

"No!" She shielded her body with her arms. Her heart ricocheted off her ribs. "Please, don't. You know I won't hurt you!"

His bloodshot eyes wouldn't meet hers, but his arm bent inward. He pressed the barrel sharply against his own temple.

Her pleas for her life froze in her chest. She went still, too afraid to move.

Why did he want to make her watch the life leave his eyes?

"Don't," she begged, more desperate than she'd ever been. "Please. I don't understand."

Lucky squeezed his eyes shut in pain and opened his mouth. "Th— they're not dreams."

The words fell clumsily, raw and heartbreakingly sincere but untested. Part of him was trying to connect to her. She'd have to reach the rest of the way before he gave up trying.

"The nightmares," she guessed. "They're memories? Put the pistol down, and you can tell me everything."

His eyes opened again, glistening with hurt and shame Matilda didn't know how to repair. "Why m— make me human?" he begged of her. "Now I know."

I should have listened to Miss Kovacs.

She'd only cared about that loathsome journal and its secrets, and now the cost would be deeper than she could bear to pay.

"Put the pistol down," she said. "I won't let anyone hurt you the way Nathaniel did."

Lucky's eyes welled with unshed tears. He shook his head.

"I k— killed Nathaniel."

Matilda's heart staggered. *No. No, it isn't true.*

"S— sorry."

Lucky closed his eyes. His finger tightened around the trigger.

PART IV

— AWAKENING —

Matilda, my dear sister, I can't bear the things I've done. The Fenians…I thought I was doing the right thing when I joined them, but I was as foolish as Father. No. I was more foolish, because I already knew the pain I could cause. I can't anymore.

God forgive me for what I've done; I can't ask you to do the same.

— CHAPTER FIFTY-EIGHT —

MATILDA

Drop it!"

Lucky started. Whatever dog remained in him answered Matilda's command, and the gun crashed to the floor. He stared at his empty hand, but the confusion only lasted a moment. He dove for the weapon.

For the first time she was faster. She kicked the weapon out of his reach. It skidded under the bed, and she barrelled into him. A tortured roar broke out of him as they tripped onto the bed and he struggled against her.

"Stop." She threw her arms around him and hugged him so tight she could barely breathe. "Please stop." She felt him break—felt every little piece of him crack and crumble. He hid his face in her neck and shuddered. She stroked his hair. "Everything will be all right."

In that moment she didn't think either of them believed it, but she held fast to him and stole away every pain she could.

Even after he'd stopped shaking, she hugged him close. She feared she'd lose him if she released him even for a moment, but as his pain turned inward, hers turned outward. Her throat ached as she tried to hold back the tears, and she'd caught his tremble.

He pulled away first, rolling his back to her. He spoke nothing more, and something in the air around him closed him from her. Warily, she got up from the bed, fetched the pistol from the floor, and searched the room for anything sharp or dangerous. Then she gave Lucky the distance he needed.

Joseph waited at the foot of the stairs when she came down. No surprise flickered across his face when he saw the weapon in her hand. He'd overheard.

"I'll watch him," he said.

She ran outside but didn't get far. The moment the door clicked behind her, her eyes flooded with tears. She stumbled down the porch steps and crumpled to the grass.

It isn't true. It can't be true!

Her head spun. The slightest movement made her stomach lurch, and she pitched forward. The pistol dug into her palm, cold and cruel.

He couldn't. He wouldn't!

It was a trick. A lie. Somehow Mr. Wellington must have altered Lucky's memory.

But there'd been a wolf in the woods the night she'd found Nathaniel's body. A wolf man. Lucky.

He wouldn't kill Nathaniel!

Lucky was no monster. Even if Sheridan lived somewhere beneath Lucky's skin, then Lucky's kind, gentle soul must have always been part of Sheridan too. Matilda couldn't believe for one moment that there was a murderer inside the man who'd brought her family life, light, and so much love.

Love.

Rocked by her sobs, she sat on her heels and lifted the pistol. She accessed the cylinder and shook every last bullet into her palm until the weapon was a harmless shell, then she hurled the bullets and pistol into the wicked sky. The rain washed away her tears, but it did nothing for the wound torn open inside her.

Love…

When she turned back, Joseph leaned against the porch railing and watched her. Underneath the pain, she felt a twinge of guilt. He didn't deserve to see her cry over another man, but she didn't disguise it. Now that she knew her heart, she couldn't hide it, not even for him.

"I'm sorry." Her voice strained from her shouting and tears, but her words were certain. "I can't marry you."

Josephs hands clasped each other tighter. "I know you're in pain, but that's why this isn't the time to change your mind. I pity him too."

"It isn't pity." She rubbed her chest to ease the agony beneath the skin and bone. "I know that now. I'm sorry."

Joseph controlled his expression carefully. "Matilda—"

"I've said the words I owe you, and I can't take them back. I'm sorry, Joseph. Truly." She climbed the steps, slipped past him and reached for the door.

"He's not there." Joseph's lips thinned. "He didn't like me in the house with him, so he went to the barn."

The *barn?* Matilda pictured the deadly tools and rope she kept in the barn and felt the ground falling out from under her. "You said you'd watch him!"

"He's safe—"

On numb legs she pushed past Joseph and ran to the barn, throwing the door open. "Lucky! Where are you?"

She rushed to the tack room and panicked when she saw Lucky wedged into the corner, his body limp and his eyes staring blankly ahead, but no injury marred his skin. No blood stained his clothes. He breathed, broken but alive.

"You shouldn't be here. You aren't in trouble." She knelt as close to him as she dared. He looked so fragile she thought even a brush of her aura might shatter what pieces of him still held together. "You don't have to leave tonight; I'll convince Joseph."

For a long moment Lucky didn't move. She wondered if he noticed her at all before the corner of his mouth twitched. He parted his lips, and those stumbling, full-hearted words came out once again.

"I owe you a life," he said slowly, more careful with each sound than he was with the hens' eggs. "Let me p— pay it."

"I won't. I know my brother did this to you. Or part of it. Nathaniel went after you that night in the woods, didn't he? You were protecting yourself from the man who gave your Name away."

Lucky squeezed his eyes shut in a grimace and caught his fingers in his hair. He took a long breath. "Nath..." He pinched his eyebrows together and abandoned the name. "He didn't."

Nathaniel didn't...?

"What do you mean?" Her stomach lurched again. "Are you telling me he didn't give your Name away?"

Lucky slid his hands out of his hair. He nodded.

"Then it was Lucas Wellington, wasn't it," she said. *He saw Mr. Wellington! He must know where he is. We can stop him. Joseph can stop him, and we can get Lucky's Name back!* "Where is he? Do you remember where to find him?"

"No." Lucky shook his head. "My name was Lucas."

— CHAPTER FIFTY-NINE —

LUCAS

I remember the nightmare.

Lucas Wellington. I am Lucas. I remember the name but not the man it belonged to. Matilda made me want to be a man. She made me believe I was human, but as far as I remember I've always been an animal.

I can't give her all the answers she wants, but if she won't take my life, then I'll give her what I can. I tell her everything.

My first clear memory is waking in chains and opening my eyes to dark and the smell of mould. I didn't know how I'd arrived in that cellar. Images came to my mind, fading memories, but all of them were too clouded to understand. And too frightening for me to want to.

As time passed those memories vanished altogether, but I knew I'd been in the cellar a long time. Iron around my wrists chewed through flesh. Blood both dry and fresh stained my skin and the walls. I stank of infection and sweat.

Other sets of chains surrounded me, but my only companions were the mice in the cellar. I'd shared this space with others before, but they'd been faster learners. Now each night they left to hunt in the woods above, and I was horribly alone.

I couldn't breathe in this place. Couldn't sleep. My stomach pained with the hunger of days, but there was no food, only filthy water leaking onto the floor from a rainstorm above.

Sometime after the rain stopped, the hinges of the cellar door whined and a man came to me. At the time I was curious. Hopeful. I didn't understand how dangerous he was.

He didn't come close. He seemed to despise me, but he visited every night. I couldn't see him in the dark, but I smelled blood on him and alcohol. The scent remained even after he'd left.

The man spoke to me. I think he'd been doing it even before I awakened, but after his visits I could never recall the sound of his voice. It was as unknown to me as his face in the dark. I think he made me forget it the way I'd forgotten myself.

I only remembered the feel of his speech as it crawled over me. It did something to me, something I didn't like. The feeling lasted only briefly at first. Shortly after the man left, I'd return to myself as though I'd woken from a dream, but over time his speech wore at me. It found a place to fester and spread.

I felt dizzy and confused after the man's visits. Sometimes I had bruises or lashes I didn't remember receiving. I might have done them to myself, but something else was happening to me too. My body changed. My hair grew long and matted. I thinned from lack of food and movement.

But the other changes were different. Unusual. I stopped feeling the cold. I should have been weak and dying, but my bones strengthened even though they felt lighter. I wanted to test them—to see how fast I could run and how tough I was, but the chains were always too strong to break.

My mind changed too. As time passed, the other wolves returned to the cellar only at the master's call, and the dark became a living thing to me. I feared and hated the walls and the sound of my chains on the floor. My hunger grew ravenous, and the dry bread the man brought me never satisfied. Before, the daytime sound of birds above me had been the only thing to soothe the pain of loneliness.

After, their tunes became the sounds that lure predators to prey. I *wanted* to prey on them as I had the mice in the cellar.

I tried to kill the man when he came, but a single word from him turned my vision black before I could touch him. He wasn't a man. He was a demon, and only three things were clear in my mind after he left me each night.

First: each visit, the demon spoke of another. My captor never showed me his own face, but his words summoned the image of this other man clearly in my mind. It was a young man, someone I felt I'd known once but couldn't remember. Fair of skin and hair, his blue eyes looked gentle but held the same darkness as the demon.

Second: I knew the scent of this new man—this second demon—as distinct to him as his face. I don't know how I knew it, but I did. And I knew one day it would lead me to him. I was sure because of the final thing I knew.

I hated this blue-eyed man.

When my captor left each night, my only company was the smell of alcohol he left behind and the knowledge that one day I'd kill the blue-eyed demon.

Then my captor set me free.

As always, I tried to kill my cruel master. I remember falling and waking sometime later. The hair on my face had been shaved smooth. I didn't understand it, but it didn't matter. My chains had been unbound and the door left open.

I should have embraced my freedom and lived wild, but I smelled demons. Both of them, somewhere close. I could no sooner have let the blue-eyed one live than I could have killed my master. I smelled the blue-eyed one. I heard him.

His voice carried power. Magic. I felt it in the way his voice fell upon my ears. The blue-eyed demon spoke to someone. A girl. I drew close, but he spied me and lured me away. I chased, and he gave good chase. He was fast.

I was faster, but he knew which thickets would slow me or dull my senses. He circled back, and his path crossed with another. The scents were so similar I didn't know which to follow. I chose one.

It belonged to the girl. Matilda.

She shouted, but her voice carried none of the magic then. She felt safe, but her scent was like the demon's. Was I was meant to kill her too? I didn't want to. I growled at her, warning her away.

Then a terrifying thunder roared through the heavens. A gunshot. I fled, and when I did, I caught the demon's scent again.

Not even the fright of the gunshot kept me away, and now the blue-eyed one tired. I didn't. I found him again easily.

He waited in a clearing with horses and barren corn stalks. Expecting me. In the dark I saw him with heightened vision. He saw me with the Power. His eyes widened with recognition and horror.

"Lucas? I thought you died in the fire. You weren't supposed to be there. You were supposed to be with…oh, I'm so sorry."

He sounded sad. He knew me, and I knew then why I'd been shaved. So he'd recognize me. So it would weaken his heart against me.

When I crept forward, he spoke again, louder. His magic slammed into me, but it never sank below the skin. Only one voice in the world could reach me, and that voice had ordered me to kill.

I remember what happened with more clarity than a beast should remember anything. I killed him. With teeth and bare hands, I killed him and left his husk.

Before my master could return for me, I ran farther from the cellar I hated so much, but never too far. Instinct kept me hidden in the woods.

Sometimes I could smell my master in those woods. He looked for me, but I stayed hidden until hunger drove me back into the clearing with horses and dogs.

That thunderous gunshot fired twice again, and I knew the agonizing fire of a bullet in my chest.

I ran, but my strength failed. I fell into water, drowning. The chill of enclosing death suppressed the fire and pain within my chest, and then the darkness I so hated and feared took me.

September 19th, 1885

I've dedicated a year to honing my skill, hiding south of the Fraser and readying to face him, living on little but rage and what I fish. My cheeks are hollow when I catch my reflection in the river's mirror. My trousers hang lower on my hips than before. "It's the fish," I thought. "They've been elusive."

Yesterday I hunted. If only I could have spoken the buck's Name and had it walk itself into my cookfire, but I can't mimic the whispers of the forest critters' Names. Even if I could, I'd have no way to communicate with the beast's shell in a language it could understand. "Walk." "Stop." "Die." I only know those words in my own speech.

The Names I take affect me too much already without imprisoning one within me while I slit its host's throat. I remained too close and felt the buck's Name wane and die, withering as its golden hues convulsed against my own sooty aura. Fear of death I understand in any speech.

My light used to be the colour of the blueberries Mother loved. Back before I'd first tried to harness the Power I'd secretly discovered. Now my Soul Name is blackened. Tarnished.

I suppose this is the price Miss Kovacs warned me about. The price of my arrogance. The Power in my veins corrupts me, turning me as hollow as the Names I've warped or snuffed out.

Skinning a buck has always been hard work, but yesterday I was only ten minutes into the work before I irritated the cough that's been bothering me all year. This time there was blood.

Mother. Even you are reaching out from the grave to punish me.

My cough turned into the first laugh I've had in over a year. The Power won't get to claim me for itself after all. God plans to strike me down first. I'm not ready to face him yet—him or God. I don't have the strength.

But now I also don't have the time to wait.

— CHAPTER SIXTY —

MATILDA

Matilda had no more tears, only a pang in her chest.

She'd had to do as much guessing as Lucky had done stumbling with speech, but with her help, he'd finished his story. Then he withdrew into himself and didn't speak more.

She supposed she should be angry. She should want justice for Nathaniel and for Lucky. Lucas. Far more than justice, she wanted to take him in her arms again until both of them healed.

He'd given her an answer she'd needed but one she'd never wanted. She'd already mourned for Nathaniel, so why did Lucas's confession stab her so deeply?

If Lucas wasn't the partner Nathaniel wrote of, then she only had two clues: blood and alcohol. The man who'd broken Lucas smelled of blood and alcohol.

A man like Richards.

She'd been right the first time. Richards was the true murderer. He was the one who'd had Joseph kill the wild man. He was the one who'd set traps in the woods, looking for prey. For Lucas.

When Nathaniel had decided to make things right, Richards had kept him quiet. It would have worked perfectly. As far as anyone in New Westminster knew, Nathaniel had already vanished. If

Matilda hadn't stumbled upon her brother's body, Richards would have gotten away with his terrible sins.

A knock at the tack room door drew her attention. Joseph stood in the doorway, his face solemn.

How long has he been here? How much has he heard?

"It isn't safe to linger," he said. "It will be dark before long. I need to take him now."

Matilda's toes curled uncomfortably. "Stay here a moment," she said to Lucas. Then to Joseph she gestured toward the door with a nod of her head.

He disappeared from the doorway, and she followed him outside the barn. The door groaned as she shut it and led Joseph farther away where she hoped Lucas's acute hearing wouldn't reach.

"You're angry," Joseph said.

"I'm bewildered." She kept her voice low despite the distance she'd put behind her. "I can't let him leave now. He needs stability."

"I agree, but don't mistake holding onto him with stability."

"I won't make him go!"

The squeal of the barn door distracted Matilda from anything else she might have said. Lucas marched toward them with purpose and cut between her and Joseph. He climbed into the surrey with his face stubbornly forward.

"It seems," Joseph said, "Mr. Wellington has made the decision for you."

So he did *overhear everything.*

"No, he hasn't," Matilda said. "Lucas, come down."

Joseph frowned and pulled Matilda away by her arm. He lowered his voice to a whisper, but it hit her as firm as a fist.

"I don't understand half of this, but whether he was compelled or not, that man admitted to—" Joseph looked over his shoulder. Lucas's face pointed away from them, but Matilda had no doubt he'd heard. "I'm a lawman, and I can't ignore his confession. He's dangerous like this."

"He's not dangerous to me."

"Let him go," he said. Strange how not so long ago a simple word from Joseph would have made her fly like a sparrow, but now his voice caged her away from the sky. "He wants to leave, and for his sake you must let him."

"Let go," she said. She yanked her arm out of Joseph's grasp. "Let go! Why must I always let go of everything I love?"

"Love isn't always healing," Joseph said. "Believe me, I know. I've held on to my mother for too long, and she's suffered for it. Don't make the same mistake."

"I—" No matter how she wanted to fight Joseph, one look at the pain in his eyes made her silent. He spoke truths she couldn't deny. The fight left her body, and regret seeped into its place.

Joseph's hands dropped to his sides, and he leaned back from her. "You should hurry to the manor. Olive and Elliot will wonder where you are."

He fetched Duchess and offered Matilda the reins, then he took his seat next to Lucas in the buggy.

Matilda held her breath as they drove away, but Lucas didn't look back once.

She returned to the manor with a bleeding heart. She couldn't remember the ride back, and she only vaguely recalled seeing Olive and Elliot in the parlour. They'd asked her something, but she'd wandered past them and down the hall without giving an answer.

Without meaning to, she ended up at Mother Harrison's door. She leaned her head against it, knowing she shouldn't add her burdens to the ones Mother Harrison already carried, but she longed for the comforts only a mother could give.

When her head touched the door, the door bounced open.

It revealed a messy room that once would have annoyed Mother Harrison. Clothes spilled from an open wardrobe and spread over the floor. Drawers hung out of the desk. The walls, once adorned with portraits and Joseph's childhood drawings, stood bare. Curtains hung open over a large bay window, but with the evening clouds, the room remained grey and cold.

Mother Harrison looked up from a book at her desk, the lines around her eyes and mouth giving her a tired but grandmotherly look.

"Oh, I didn't mean to bother you," Matilda said. She reached for the doorknob, but Mother Harrison shut her book and rose from her desk.

"Have you been crying, dear? Your face is a mess." Mother Harrison stepped over a pile of clothes and sat down on her bed, patting the space beside her. "Come here and sit down. Tell me what's happened to you."

Mother Harrison seemed more lucid today, sturdier, but the bandage wrapped around her hand reminded Matilda the woman's calm was fragile. "No, I'm all right. I shouldn't disturb your rest."

"Nonsense." Mother Harrison used the authoritative voice she'd utilized when she'd been a strict piano teacher. She patted the spot on the bed beside her once more. "Sit down."

Relenting, Matilda trudged across the room and fell into place beside Mother Harrison. Mother Harrison enclosed Matilda in her arms, building a protective wall around her. Matilda leaned into the older woman's embrace, and a few tears she'd thought she'd already spent leaked from her eyes and spilled onto Mother Harrison's dress.

"Today I had to bid farewell to a close friend." Matilda wrapped her arms around Mother Harrison and buried her face in the woman's shoulder. "I don't know if I'll ever see him again."

Mother Harrison squeezed her tighter and leaned her cheek against Matilda's head. "Darling, I'm sorry. Farewells are a painful business, I know."

Afraid she'd already led Mother Harrison too close to dangerous memories, Matilda pulled out of her guardian's embrace, regretting the loss of comfort. She wiped away her tears and brushed at the damp spots she'd left on Mother Harrison's shoulder. "I've made a mess of your clothes."

"Don't worry yourself about that. I've already got a wash to do, as you can see."

Mother Harrison gestured to the clothes blanketing her floor and to a man's shirt hanging from the chair at her desk. It was Joseph's shirt—the one he'd been wearing the night Mother Harrison had cut her hand. Spots of his mother's dried blood stained the sleeves.

"I don't think you'll get those stains out." Matilda rose from the bed and held the shirtsleeves to her eye for a closer look, but it was her nose that gave the best inspection.

A fruity aroma filled the air. Joseph must have spilled brandy on his shirt when he'd given his mother her medicine. But the scent was too strong, and when Matilda lowered her hands, a crystal glass on the desk caught the grey light from the window. Brandy filled the glass nearly to the brim.

"You didn't drink your medicine?" she asked.

"Oh, let me have that, will you?" Mother Harrison said. She stood up from the bed as Matilda offered her the glass, but instead of downing it, Mother Harrison cracked open her window and tossed the drink out. "I feel as though I've lost half of my life to that vile drink." She closed the window again and scowled at the empty glass in her hand with a vitriol she normally reserved for mice in her store of wheat. "Every time I drink it my memory gets foggier. Do you know I've forgotten how I knew your mother, dear? I can't recall why I invited her to move halfway across the country and live here." Mother Harrison gave the glass one last spiteful look before she set it back on the desk. "If only that were the worst part. I've kept every precious memory of my little Joseph locked away in my heart, but I can't remember who his father is. Maybe I'm getting old, but I'd swear someone is plucking the memories right out of my head."

Matilda suppressed a cheerless laugh. "It sounds like someone has bewitched—"

She paused in the middle of her words and stared at the glass on the desk. The drink's fruity scent made her head spin as pieces of the puzzle she'd been putting together for a year locked into place. Her hands wrenched Joseph's shirt.

Blood and alcohol.

Matilda shook the thought aside. Half of the men in New Westminster were heavy drinkers.

I met him a few times. Matilda recalled the words Joseph had said to her nearly a year ago when they'd stood in front of Lucas's grave. Nathaniel's journal had also written of the three men sharing each other's company. Surely Joseph should have recognized Lucas that night Isaac had attacked. Why didn't he say anything?

He must have his reasons. How could she consider for one moment that *Joseph* might have had anything to do with what happened to Lucas? How could a man with such a beautiful aura be so cruel?

His aura… Matilda's blood turned cold. *Joseph's aura!*

When she'd called Kāi's Name to her, his golden light had swirled amid her burgundy one. For a short time, Kāi had been without a light, but she'd held both colours within her. She'd stolen his Name, and it had become part of her.

Joseph's aura, his stunning and magnificent aura, shifted between grey, purple, red, and green.

But they weren't his colours. He'd stolen them.

One of those Names belonged to Lucas, and Matilda had just handed him over to the demon.

Matilda bolted down the hall to the parlour, ignoring Mother Harrison's alarmed shouts behind her. Elliot plunked haunting notes on the piano and Olive sat in the chair with a book in her lap, but she threw it to the floor when she saw Matilda.

"What's the matter?" Olive said.

"Listen to me," Matilda said, gasping. Where had her breath gone? She steadied herself with a hand on Olive's shoulder. "This place isn't safe. You and Elliot must leave. Now."

"Isn't safe? Why?" Elliot dropped his hand on the keys, sending a blow of discord into Matilda's ears.

"There isn't time! Don't bother packing. Leave now and go straight to—and go..." *Who would take them in?* She flipped through the names and faces of everyone she knew, but only one face gave any comfort. "Go to Miss Kovacs. Don't let her turn you away no matter what she says, do you understand me?" She raised her skirts in one hand and rushed toward the door.

"Matilda!" Olive's voice chased behind her. "What's happening?"

"Lucky is in trouble." She opened the door and leapt through it. "Go!"

She left the door hanging open and raced to the stable where Duchess had only now settled in for the evening. She saddled the mare in a rush, leapt onto her back, and kicked her heels in.

Halfway down Queens Avenue she pulled the mare to a stop when she realized she didn't know where she was headed.

Joseph never intended to take Lucas to the asylum.

He wanted his hunting dog back. He'd need a place to hide him. A secluded place already set up with chains.

"Haaa!" Matilda sent Duchess into a gallop through the twilight.

— CHAPTER SIXTY-ONE —

LUCAS

I didn't know what an asylum was or how it was supposed to look. Still I knew the building when I saw it looming over the hillside as Joseph turned his horse down a dirt road. In a wide clearing, private from the city and with a view of the Fraser, the building towered with corners of stone and dozens of windows like hollow eyes.

Even from a distance I sensed suffering. Overbearing isolation and pain stained the walls. Matilda thought this place could help me, but I knew all I'd find was more misery. Fair. I deserved it.

The rain kept the mosquitoes away, and but for the pattering sound on the buggy's canopy, the land lay in a hush as nightfall and rainclouds battled the last efforts of day. Joseph stopped the buggy short of the building, waiting. I didn't know why. It didn't matter.

He didn't speak. Out of the corner of my eye I noticed him watching me. Maybe he wondered if I deserved to be saved too.

We sat in the shadow of that menacing structure so long I thought for certain Matilda had passed us on the road and returned to the manor by now. Why was he waiting? I thought he knew I wanted this.

Then, without a word, Joseph clicked at his horse and flapped the reins. The buggy's wheels sploshed through mud as the horse turned the buggy around.

Back the way we'd come.

By the time we returned, the meadow was deserted—a graveyard of memories long passed. The buggy bounced as Joseph pulled us off the wagon tracks, passed the house, and carried toward the trees over bumpy terrain.

Again he stopped the buggy for no apparent reason. I kept my eyes ahead and watched the flick of the horse's ears like it was the only thing in the world that mattered. Joseph set down the reins, and a moment later a shock of metal pressed against my temple. The barrel of a revolver, cold and malicious and welcome, pressed into me.

"I've been searching for you," Joseph said. "I thought those rebels had hidden you away. I never imagined you'd become someone's pet."

Barely listening, I pressed my head into the weapon and trembled with a need for him to pull the trigger.

Joseph responded with a hard jab of the revolver into my temple. "You weren't supposed to remember anything. I thought I'd taken every last bit of Lucas out of you."

That I did hear, and it turned me colder than being barefoot in a blizzard. Finally, I turned my head, but no lie polluted his eyes. No remorse. I leaned away from the revolver, but he kept it unrelenting against me.

Matilda didn't know. She'd chosen him, and she didn't know. She *had* to know.

Then I had to survive to tell her.

Joseph tightened his grip on the revolver. "I'm afraid you'll never receive any of Matilda's letters."

I lunged for his throat.

He pulled the trigger.

— CHAPTER SIXTY-TWO —

MATILDA

Matilda leaned over Duchess as the mare's hooves pounded into the meadow. A gunshot bellowed through the field.

No!

Far across the field, two men struggled against each other in a buggy. One lunged at the other. Startled by the violence, Joseph's horse swerved. The buggy careened, and the men hit the grass in a tumult of fists and feet.

She'd seen this same scene two years ago but somewhere else—Mr. Gän pinning Joseph to the floor at the foot of the stairs while she watched.

This time Lucas fought against Joseph, and instead of using fists, Joseph pointed a revolver at Lucas's head.

No. She heeled Duchess faster.

Joseph wasn't going to make Lucas a dog again. He was going to take him from her forever.

— CHAPTER SIXTY-THREE —

LUCAS

I squirmed on my back, winded. My half-healed rib ached anew, but I fought against Joseph with everything in me. My everything wasn't enough anymore. He straddled my chest and aimed the weapon. I grabbed his wrist and pointed it away, but he tilted the barrel toward my head. He was stronger. How was he stronger?

"Lucas!"

A thunder of hooves replaced the rolling gunshot in the skies. Duchess. Matilda.

Joseph spat a curse and glanced her way. I took the opening.

Releasing his wrist, I cracked my knuckles against his jaw. Joseph rocked backward. The gun flew out of his hand.

Matilda dropped from the saddle and ran toward the weapon, but I was closer. From under Joseph I smashed my knee into his back and twisted out from under him. His fist slammed between my shoulders and forced the air out of my lungs. I collapsed. He beat Matilda to the weapon and pointed it at me.

"Matilda!" He wore a hunted look so convincing she'd be taken in easily. "Don't come any closer. He's gone mad!"

I clutched my rib so it wouldn't snap and struggled to my knees. She had to know. I opened my mouth, fumbling for words.

"He smells the blood on your hands." There was none of the gratitude or awe that usually chimed in Matilda's voice when she spoke to her mate. It was all fury now. "I know I do. I thought Richards was responsible, but it was you."

She knew?

Joseph eyed Matilda, scrutinizing her, then his panting stopped. His illusion of the victim dissolved, and he stood confident and intimidating. "Uncle Jake has the subtlety of a dancing pig. I've hidden this for years, and you and Nathaniel are the only ones who discovered me."

His voice darkened, full of unspoken threats. He turned the weapon from me. I rolled onto my toes, ready to lunge for him, but he pointed the revolver at Matilda.

"Congratulations," he said.

— CHAPTER SIXTY-FOUR —

MATILDA

Matilda patted her skirts, but her pistol was gone, its bullets emptied and lost in the meadow. She hadn't come with protection or a plan—only a will to save Lucas. Now they'd both die.

"I warned you many times," Joseph said. No kindness shone in his eyes. They were sickening, callous, and cold things. "I had every intention of being good to you, but you've made a mess of my plans yet again."

"Why?" Her question held so many other questions. Why had he doomed Nathaniel? Why had he hurt Lucas? Why had he toyed with her for so long?

"The Sceolan are a disease." Joseph's arm remained perfectly aligned as he held the gun. He was a rock with no care for the people he crushed. "My dogs are the cure."

"They're not dogs, and neither Lucas nor I are Sceolan," Matilda said.

"But both of you stand in my way."

He whistled, and the shrill sound vibrated in Matilda's ears. She didn't have to guess whom he called. She shivered, waiting for the approach of devils, and when two snarling faces emerged from the woods, she knew they'd come to drag her down to hell.

Two wild men snapped hungry teeth at Matilda and Lucas, licking their lips. She recognized Isaac, big as a mountain and twice as solid. Whatever damage Lucas had dealt at their last meeting was already gone, and the big man scowled at Lucas with a vengeful fire in his eyes.

The other wild man Matilda had never seen before, but she saw the resemblance to Isaac in his black hair and hooked nose. The real Sheridan. He was slighter than his father, but his appearance made her tremble like a child in the dark.

Naked but for mud and grime that turned his skin grey, the wolf man had a tangled beard and hair snaked down his chest and back in matted clumps. He didn't walk like a man who thought he was an animal; he prowled like he'd always *been* one.

Sheridan carried himself low to the ground, his sinewy arms dangling below him. Sometimes he supported himself on calloused knuckles, and sometimes his hands flexed with a need to tear an enemy's flesh. Human intelligence glittered in Isaac's eyes, if locked away, but Sheridan's stare held nothing but blood lust.

Both men stalked closer and parted around Joseph, who showed no fear of them. Matilda was armed only with her courage, and that dwindled with every step that brought the wild men closer.

She hurried to Lucas's side, and her fingers slid into his hand of their own will. She gripped him tightly, feeling both of their pulses race as she stared down her death.

Joseph spotted their clasped hands, but his expression never changed. Had he ever cared for her? Or had his words of affection been designed only to keep her docile?

"The sun is gone," he said with what would have been a handsome smile if not for the malice corrupting it. "I told you it was dangerous to go out at night. I'll be heartbroken when I learn your disobedience cost you your life." As though he'd forgotten Matilda and Lucas already, Joseph returned to his buggy and climbed into his seat. He clucked his horse into a trot across the meadow, and as he abandoned his victims to their fate, he called to the wild men almost cheerily. "Kill them both."

The wild men circled them slowly, drawing out the hunt. They herded their prey toward the woods and left them nowhere to run but into the domain of the wolves. Matilda had no intention of giving them sport. Her knees shook, but she planted her feet.

"Lucas, can you fight?"

He squeezed her hand reassuringly in answer. They wouldn't escape unharmed, but if he could give her time…

"I'm sorry, but I need your help. Keep them away from me."

Lucas gave her one more squeeze then leapt in front of her, poised for attack.

Please survive.

She cracked a dying branch from a cedar, gripped it like a club, and called to the Power.

It filled her with awareness. She knew each blade of grass under her shoes. She tasted the rank sweat and grime on the wild men and felt their ravenous hunger.

Isaac's hooked fingers sliced through the air toward Lucas's throat. Lucas ducked. He barrelled into Isaac's ribs.

The brute staggered backward, but Sheridan darted for Lucas's side, low. Lucas barely spun out of reach. Sheridan landed adeptly and turned back for another pass.

Power gushed through Matilda and out of her in a geyser. She slammed an arm of energy against Isaac as though the Power had physical weight, and Isaac reeled back from an attempt to crush Lucas's skull.

She *shook* Isaac with the Power. No other word described it—she shook him from the clutches of a nightmare. She needed him to awaken, to remember he was human and call his Name back to him.

Isaac, wake up!

She didn't know if she'd said the words aloud or had only felt them fly toward him on waves of her energy, but she felt a jerk of resistance from him, the tensing of muscles in the moment before waking.

Isaac shook his head and roared. The rope of Power between them snapped and threw Matilda back.

Both wild men charged Lucas at once. He accepted Isaac's fist in his side to avoid an arching blow from Sheridan that would have killed him. Lucas panted, suffering. Another blow would send him to the ground. Another blow might be the end.

She was going to watch him die in front of her.

His eyes on the bigger threat, Sheridan circled Lucas without any concern for Matilda. He looked for an opening. She found one first.

When Sheridan bent his knees, she threw a net of the Power over him before he could resist. The muscles in his body loosened. He stood suspended, a marionette dangling from her invisible threads.

She tried to remember the diagrams she'd studied in Nathaniel's journal. What was his Name?

"Take back your Name!" Her voice surged on the flow of energy with the command of a more powerful being. The demand sank into Sheridan's muddied skin. He was no longer a jar filled only with Joseph's murderous orders; her words filled him too. "Fight back!"

She felt a magnetic pull as something connected with Sheridan, and she heard the whispers of it as it soared, distant but coming ever closer. Then a light shot up over the trees and left a ghostly comet's tail behind it as it sailed their way. A Name. Sheridan's Name.

Weakened by years apart from its host, its violet colour looked muted and sick, but it searched for Sheridan like a child separated from his parent.

Yes! It's working!

The light flickered and strained against Matilda's call. Someone tugged on the other end. Someone stronger. The light followed a higher order and snapped back the way it had come.

This time the connection between Matilda and the wild man didn't sever. It shattered. Grains of the Power tossed in the wind, and every one returned to her like live coals burying into her skin. Pieces of Power flayed her mind and flesh and left invisible wounds that burned to her core.

Someone screamed. Her vision went dark. Her knees gave out from under her, but she didn't feel the ground when she hit. She felt only the excruciating burn of the Power recoiling into her.

The coals burned up and went out, and her vision returned, slowly. One foggy shape snapped teeth at her.

Instinct whipped her arms out. Her cedar club smacked Sheridan's jaw. He crashed into her and pinned her to the ground.

An arm wound around Sheridan's neck, lifting his weight from her. She scrambled out from beneath him.

Chest heaving, Lucas held Sheridan in a chokehold, but his grip slipped as Sheridan flailed at him. Isaac hounded Lucas from behind and reached for his vulnerable spine.

Matilda shouted and swung her branch at Isaac. He tore it from her and snapped it as easily as kindling. His fist flew toward her for a killing blow. She threw her arms in front of her face and closed her eyes.

BANG!

The sound echoed through the valley. Isaac yelped.

"Sorry, Isaac," said a rasping voice.

A hand enclosed Matilda's, and she recognized Lucas's touch. She opened her eyes.

Sheridan lay in the grass where Lucas had left him, as though sleeping.

He won't stay asleep for long.

Isaac turned away from them with an angry grunt and faced the one who'd attacked him.

Keith stood in the long grass with wide-set feet and aimed Matilda's rifle at his former leader. Isaac caressed his shoulder, his fingertips red with blood, and he shot Keith a murderous glare.

"Hope you don't mind if I borrow this." Keith raised the tip of the rifle just enough to draw Matilda's attention. The shaking boy she'd met in the cellar was gone. This man knew what he was doing as he faced down Isaac. "I know how it is to be one of you. You don't remember what this is, but you sure won't like it when I shoot again."

Isaac lunged. Keith fired.

BANG!

Isaac stumbled from another blow to the shoulder, and Keith reloaded the rifle with nimble fingers. When Isaac regained his footing, he studied Keith, angrier now but also cautious.

"Guess you found the real sorcerer, O'Connor." Keith didn't turn from Isaac, but he nodded toward the road. "I'll keep these two busy while I can. You and your pet go and batter that tricky little churl up for me."

Matilda nodded. "Don't kill them. I'm going to get their Names back."

"Then you'd better hurry," Keith said. "Isaac gets real grouchy when he's hungry."

She sprinted across the meadow with Lucas and swung herself into the saddle. She helped Lucas up behind her and heeled Duchess into a run.

Joseph hadn't gone far. Once around the bend, Matilda spotted the buggy paused down the road. Joseph leaned back in the seat and listened to the violence in the meadow with the same interest he'd given his mother's tunes on the piano. Matilda pulled back on the reins before they drew too close.

She had no weapon or plan. Worse, where she should have felt the Power flow in her, she felt numb and broken. All she had was guts. It would have to be enough.

"Get off," she said to Lucas.

Obediently he loosened his arms from around her and slid off Duchess. He winced when he landed on the ground, but he offered her his hand and waited for her to follow.

He'd suffered enough at Joseph's hands. If she had to face her death now, she refused to take him with her.

"Stay."

She kicked Duchess back into a run and left Lucas hobbling behind her.

— CHAPTER SIXTY-FIVE —

LUCAS

Stay?

Matilda deserted me in the middle of the road. I limped after her, but I couldn't keep up. I could barely breathe.

She left me to go and die alone at his hands.

Stay?

Not this time.

I stumbled into the cover of trees. Willpower alone gave me a second strength, and the fumble of my feet steadied. I ran faster but quieter. I forgot the pain in my chest and the blood draining from my wounds.

Matilda had soothed the beast in me until I'd almost forgotten it, but it hadn't disappeared. Now I called it back.

Joseph had made me a killer, and I would make him regret it.

— CHAPTER SIXTY-SIX —

MATILDA

Matilda's heart pulsed weakly as she approached Joseph, but her mind was strangely calm. As she slid from her saddle and tied Duchess to a tree, Joseph reclined in the buggy with his back to her.

"You're proving to be too much trouble. I heard the gunshots. Did you leave him there to fight? Or has the Sceolan brat returned for his comrades?" Joseph turned in his seat and draped an arm leisurely over the back, as though he'd chanced upon her at church.

But this wasn't the same man she met at church. This was the man her childhood bully had become. That charm that had once captivated her was only his mask. This was the real Joseph.

"A gun won't stop them the way it did your *Lucky*," he said. "I've made sure of it."

"No, it won't stop them." Matilda said. "Stopping you will."

He chuckled, and for a moment his laughter seemed real. "You have a gift with the Power to have taken to it so quickly, but you've only dipped your toes into it. You can't wield it as I can. Look at me."

"I am looking at you."

"*Look* at me."

Her weakened magic lay dormant in her, but she stirred it until she felt a sting where it had shattered before. She feared it wouldn't work, but as she looked at Joseph with her eyes aided by magic, she saw him as she had that day in the chapel.

Light swirled around him in many colours, first grey, then a weak but beautiful green, followed by vibrant gold. She saw a deep red and the violet she'd almost freed moments ago. The motley aura glowed around Joseph, both beautiful and disturbing. Stolen Names. People's souls swallowed by a monster. So many souls…

Oh, no.

"You understand," he said. "You can't control me unless you take away my Names. *All* of them. You might manage to steal one before I take yours, but you can't defeat me. Return and die with your lover."

She stood her ground. "I can't. I won't let you hurt anyone else."

"You're being foolish," Joseph said, shrugging. He stepped down from his buggy and slipped out of his waistcoat, folding it neatly and laying it across the seat. "You, of all people, should understand what I'm doing. The Fenians are nothing but animals. I have kept their kind out of our city. My methods mean no innocents are harmed."

"No innocents?" Her voice cracked as her body shook with rage. "What about Lucas? What about my brother?"

"Nathaniel was no innocent," Joseph said with a laugh. "He got the end he deserved. And your Lucas is the one who gave it to him."

With a shriek, Matilda lunged at him, but Joseph reached for the pistol at his hip. She halted, biting off the end of her shout, and thought quickly about how to avoid the bullet, but he simply set the weapon by his waistcoat.

"There's another thing you should know." Joseph loosened the collar of his shirt. "The Names I've taken do more than protect me."

He stripped his shirt from his body and placed it with care into the buggy. He cracked his fingers.

Then he *grew*.

Joseph was a reptile freeing itself from an old skin. Bones stretched and spread. Muscles hidden in a slim frame protruded from his back and chest, and veins popped out on his arms. He cracked his neck from side to side with startling pops and rolled his shoulders back to display more stony muscle than Isaac.

"You used the magic on yourself!" she said with horror.

"These Names let me be anything I desire." His voice was deep, gruff, and brutish, without any trace of his honey and silk. He flexed his fingers, and the muscles contracted all the way up his arm. "I'm faster than Sheridan and deadlier than Isaac. With Wellington's charm, I lured you to me." He approached her. His footsteps vibrated through the earth, and she shrank from him. "Now, should I kill you? I'd rather sculpt you into the perfect, obedient wife."

"It won't work. I'll never stop fighting you." Matilda clenched her skirts so he wouldn't see the quaking of her hands.

"I think not. If you were resistant to the magic, you wouldn't be able to use it. The fact you use it at all is also proof of your weakness to it."

"Then you're as weak as I am."

He took another step toward her, slowly, letting it build fear in her. She stepped aside, but he circled round her. "Do you think this is the first time I've used the Power on you?" he said.

He stepped forward. She stepped aside. He moved forward again, and she backed into his buggy, cornered. He trapped her against it, and his hand enclosed hers. It wasn't warm or gentle like Lucas's hand. The fingers dug painfully into her skin.

"Like this," he said.

Burgundy light flared around Matilda, and Joseph's aura touched it. Tainted it. A malicious fog of him surrounded her, corrupting her own being.

"Now you see how easy it is for me."

"No." Matilda fought the contagion that clouded her thoughts, but she wasn't strong enough on her own. Joseph twisted her wrist until she thought it'd break, but she let him have control while she threw her arm over the buggy seat and felt for what she needed. She jabbed Joseph's pistol into his stomach and fired.

BANG!

The horse spooked. Joseph staggered back with a grunt and dug his hand into the wound in his stomach. He claimed the bullet and pulled it out with his bloodstained claws, then tossed it by the road. "That won't kill me."

She rubbed her hand on her skirts to scrape the feel of him off her skin. "Maybe not, but I feel better."

Joseph growled and leapt for her. She pulled the trigger, but he caught her wrist with inhuman speed and yanked it above her head before the weapon fired into the sky. He dragged her into the secrecy of the woods and peeled her fingers from the revolver. He threw it away, deeper into the trees.

His aura took on a violent red. She reached toward it with the Power, but the moment her magic touched him, Joseph hid the colour from her sight. Yellow overtook the red before Matilda could discover its Name. She let the yellow speak to her instead, but as the beginnings of a Name formed in her mind, Joseph switched his light to emerald.

"You want to hear a Name?" Joseph pulled her wrist higher. She dangled from it, her toes barely skimming the ground. "How about yours? *Tenacity*."

His aura surrounded her again, dizzied her, spread through her as a poison. Her thoughts blurred. The Power drained from her and left her body prickling with the loss. Her own mind was fading. Her Name. It was leaving.

With her last drop of control, she kicked Joseph as hard as she could in the only place she knew would hurt. He howled and doubled over. Matilda fell to the ground and her Name poured back into her.

She ran. Something struck her hard in the back, and her legs gave out. She crashed on tree roots and rocks that cut into her palms.

Joseph stood over her and crushed her hand under the heel of his boot. She stifled a cry of pain as terrifying rage erupted across his face. He wouldn't keep her for a wife now. He'd kill her with as much suffering as he could.

Her free hand flung dirt and pebbles into his eyes. As he clawed at his face, she tore her hand out from under his foot, crawled through grass and needles, and found Joseph's revolver. She rolled onto her back and aimed at his chest.

Time. I need time to call the Names!

Joseph scrubbed dirt out of his eyes, and his light shifted from yellow to grey to green. She focused on the last colour with all of her desperate need.

Tell me who you are!

The green aura pulsed when she reached for it. It reached back, begging to be saved from the whirlpool it drowned in. It responded to her call and threw its Name at her.

Light.

"Light!" She called to it. The emerald glow flickered, but the flow of colours dragged it back into the pool of yellow and grey. Joseph recovered, and a sea of red swallowed the green from her sight.

"I won't let you have it!" he roared.

Just a little more time!

Matilda's finger hovered over the trigger. How many bullets did she have? How much time would they give her? She raised the weapon to Joseph's chest and readied herself for the blowback.

The snap of a branch sounded nearby. Joseph braced himself, but not against her.

A blur of a man vaulted over Matilda and collided into Joseph. They crashed to the earth and brush and struggled against each other with teeth and taloned fingers.

Matilda scurried back. Joseph tried to pin his attacker to the ground, but the man fought with everything in him. Feet kicked anything within reach. Hands grabbed and fingers cut into flesh and clothes.

"Lucas?"

His eyes stormed wilder than the day she'd found him. He struck viciously, brutally, and ignored Joseph's attacks. It was Lucas's body, but Matilda couldn't see Lucas in him at all. She didn't even see Lucky.

The two men broke apart and circled each other, breath heaving. Lucas focused. Joseph was stunned.

"What did you do to him?" Matilda demanded.

"Nothing!" Joseph spat blood on the ground and fixed his gaze on Lucas. "You made him weak—how can he do this?"

Joseph launched a fist at Lucas's injured rib, but Lucas spun out of the way. He grabbed Joseph's head and slammed his own into it. Joseph pummelled fists into Lucas's chest. The pounding should have killed him.

One of them *would* die. If she didn't act quickly, it might be Lucas.

She'd asked for time. Lucas had given it to her. Now she needed to find his Name before he really became a killer.

"Stop!" Joseph shouted. All of his concentration was on Lucas, but Lucas's resistance to the Power made him no easy prey. "STOP!"

Joseph's light burned a bloody red. That red wasn't the right aura—it didn't feel like Lucas at all. His Name was buried somewhere under it.

Lucas, show yourself to me. Now!

The red stirred. Other colours bubbled to the surface, but none answered her call. She ran the Power over them, sifting through violet, gold, and grey.

The emerald glow responded to the touch of her energy, flickering. A weak flame about to go out. She cradled it with tendrils of energy and listened again for its Name.

Light.

She closed the Power around it in a blanket, separating the Name from the colours that threatened to extinguish it.

Joseph gripped Lucas by the head and dug thumbs toward his eyes. Lucas snaked his hands around Joseph's throat.

"Light!"

Matilda pulled the green light free from the other flames. As soon as she'd called it, it answered the Power, breaking apart into embers and sifting free of Joseph's control. The emerald particles drifted away on an invisible current. They crashed into Lucas and surrounded him in his own shimmering light.

Lucas screamed.

Clutching his head, he tore out of Joseph's hold and collapsed on his back with his jaw clenched and lips drawn. His back arched, but then he went limp. He lay still, his gasps broken by a cough that speckled his lips with blood.

"Ha!" Joseph's wicked, triumphant laughter echoed through the night. "I should have thought of that."

Matilda pointed the pistol at Joseph. "What happened? What did I do?"

"You returned his Name." Joseph laughed again and brushed dirt and blood from his arms. He hovered like the reaper over Lucas's form. "Now the wolf is gone, and with it his strength and healing. Now he's only a weak, dying man."

— CHAPTER SIXTY-SEVEN —

MATILDA

Matilda ran toward Lucas, but Joseph leapt into her path, wagging a finger and clicking his tongue.

"Move," she said. She peered around him. Lucas grimaced and clutched his ribs. His chest rose and fell without rhythm.

"Are you going to save him?" Joseph asked in a mocking tone. He stepped closer, stretching to his full height as he leaned over her.

"Move out of my way!"

She dodged Joseph's body, but his hand snared her wrist. She whipped the pistol toward him. He snatched it from her, and, one-handed, he emptied the bullets into the brush.

"Let me go!" She struck him under his chin with a crack of her knuckles. He tossed the empty gun and grabbed that wrist too, whirling her around. He pressed her against his chest with her wrist contorted behind her back, unable to break free.

Tendons strained up her arm. With her back to him she couldn't see his aura or the stolen Names. But she saw Lucas. And she knew fear and the sting of Joseph's hold.

"Do you think you can take his Name back as easily as you gave it?" Joseph's voice rang with amused notes, but behind it she heard the boil of rage. "It won't hear you. It took me a year to pluck it from him, and it's struggled against me ever since. Now that it's returned, it won't go to you easily."

"Let go of her." Lucas said. He fought to stand and leaned his weight heavily into a tree. His back hunched, and an arm wrapped around his chest as if to keep his bones from falling out, but his eyes wrestled the pain back and kept a fierce watch on Joseph.

Don't move, Matilda begged him silently. *Stay still and stay alive.*

"I remember everything now." Agony laced Lucas's voice, but he no longer struggled with language. The words came through him without resistance. "Nathaniel planned to expose you. He asked for my help, but you were waiting for me when I came. You should have killed me."

"Why kill the perfect hound?" Joseph said. "Nathaniel betrayed me, but he had too much influence over my Fenian dogs for them to be of use. But you—with your resistance, Nathaniel's only hope was to kill you before you killed him, and I knew he was too fond of you to do it. That day Nathaniel sent you to me, when I learned of your resistance, I knew you would one day rid me of him. All it cost me was a fire and a servant to hide your disappearance. And Mother thought I had no use for that servant."

The servant? The body at the printing press—Matilda's stomach turned.

"But my memories..." she said. "I know I saw Mr. Gän attack you."

"It wasn't him you saw." Too many emotions for Matilda to count painted Lucas's voice. Fear. Anger. A longing sadness. His face paled as he shuddered with another breath. "Nathaniel sent me to get you out of the house. Remember!"

The memory of the night Mr. Gän had disappeared came to Matilda. Sounds of a struggle on the stairs. A fight. Shouting that was clear and desperate, yet she couldn't remember the words. A cloud fogged her memory. Distorted it.

Do you think this is the first time I've used the Power on you?

She remembered Joseph's own words to her, and then the illusion fell apart, the fog clearing.

She'd awoken that night, but not to the sounds of a struggle. To Lucas standing over her. He'd hushed her, given Nathaniel's letter to her, and displayed the coin at his neck. Undeniable proof her brother had sent him. Then he'd taken her by the hand and led her downstairs.

Where Joseph waited for them.

Frozen with terror, she'd watched as Joseph, muscular and monstrous, wrestled Lucas to the floor and shouted at him. *Light. Light!* But his calls did nothing. Lucas cried for Matilda to run, and Joseph beat him until he went still, his nose cracked and bleeding where now there was only a scar. Then Joseph had left him where he lay. He'd snatched Nathaniel's note from Matilda's hand and poisoned her memory.

Lucas had lost everything trying to help her, and she hadn't even had the courtesy to remember him.

"At first Nathaniel believed I brought you into my house out of compassion too." Joseph breathed the venomous words down her neck. "You were a hostage in my home and didn't know it. Now your brother and sister have taken your place."

"No, you snake. I sent them away." Matilda writhed against Joseph's hold. He forced her to her knees and twisted her wrist higher up her back. Waves of pain throbbed down her arm and shoulder. She stifled a cry.

"That makes no difference," Joseph said. "My latest hound has kept watch over them for some time. He already brings them to me. Can't your human ears hear them?"

Matilda heard nothing but the gasp of her breath, but then other sounds in the night pierced her ears. Sobbing. It came nearer. As it did she heard twigs snapping under feet and the grunts of a frightened boy struggling.

"Let us go!"

Elliot!

Four bodies emerged from the trees. Olive came first, her tear-stained face contorted in fear. Her aura flickered, thin and insecure, as she held onto an old woman's arm. Caught in one of their captor's hands, Miss Kovacs stumbled over brush and tree roots. Her mouth drew into its usual tight line, but mud soiled her dress and wayward twists of hair. The deep grey of her aura was still but not calm.

Elliot came next, his skin shining with sweat as he thrashed against the hound's hold on him.

This wild man was as slender as Elliot and not much taller, but his charcoal eyes, once cerebral and deep, now held only base instinct and hostility. His long, black hair had tugged free of its tail and draped around his shoulders.

"Kāi." Matilda called him by name, but he showed no recognition of it or of her.

"Fool! You weren't supposed to bring the witch too!" Joseph didn't hide his displeasure. He muttered something vile about Kāi's heritage, and his fingernails broke through Matilda's skin. "Never mind. Kill them now."

"Don't hurt them!" Matilda screamed.

Kāi twisted Elliot's arm. Elliot yelped, and Olive clawed at Kāi's face. He threw her to the ground. She fell hard in the brush and coughed.

"Don't you touch my sister!" Elliot shouted. He bit into Kāi's fingers. Kāi snarled and jerked away. Elliot wrestled free and ran to Olive, but Kāi seized him by the collar then grabbed him around the throat.

"Enough!" Miss Kovacs's voice rose above the tumult with command. Blind as she was, she grabbed Kāi by his ear and yanked it down like he was a schoolboy. Kāi didn't even flinch, but Miss Kovacs's voice came again like a volley of arrows. *"Bāo-vì jēh!"*

One of those arrows pierced Kāi. Matilda felt the rise of a Power that wasn't her own, and the air around Kāi burst into yellow flames. His eyes became his own again, and he released his hold on Elliot.

"Ah! Let go!" Kāi leaned toward the old woman to ease the pain in his ear.

Miss Kovacs liberated him with a jerk of her hand.

Kāi nursed his ear tenderly and winced at the bite and bruises Elliot had given him. Then he looked about the trees and people, confused. "Where—?"

Joseph squeezed Matilda's wrist behind her until she thought he'd tear it right off. "Witch!" he growled.

Miss Kovacs's walnut eyes glared in Joseph's direction. "Yes, you conceited, diabolical imp." She punched her wrinkled hands onto her hips. "I might be blind, but this close I can hear the call of this boy's Name through your tie to him. I only let him lead us here so I could discover the brute behind this madness and show him a thing or two about why frightened little boys and girls call me a witch."

Joseph's energy sparked with anger. Matilda felt it around her, boiling into her own aura. *He's losing control...*

"It seems I must break my vow tonight," Miss Kovacs said, the Power building within her and amplifying her voice until Matilda cringed from its intensity. When the Power hummed so forcefully Matilda felt the vibrations of Miss Kovacs's aura on her skin, the old woman released a surge of it that blasted outward.

A grey tidal wave of light slammed past Matilda, washing over her harmlessly even as it sought to drown Joseph. He jumped backward and dragged Matilda with him beyond the light's reach. Miss Kovacs extended her light farther, but it stretched too thin, tickling against Matilda and Joseph instead of engulfing them in Miss Kovacs's energy.

Miss Kovacs stepped closer. Her toe caught on a tree root, and as she stumbled to catch herself, her light shrank back into her.

She can't get close enough to hear the other Names!

Matilda twisted sharply in Joseph's hand, popping her wrist and tearing muscle. She cried out and let the pain fuel her as she whipped her head into his nose.

He howled.

She broke away and ran to Lucas. His hand felt cold in hers as she took it, but she turned to the rage of Joseph's red aura.

Come to me! Give me your Name!

Wiping blood from his mouth and chin, Joseph targeted her with his gaze and charged.

The red light pulsed. Violet tried to overcome it, but Matilda knocked it aside with a bolt of the Power. She dug fingers of energy into the mass and tore the red from the other colours. It resisted, tethered to Joseph.

Please, tell me who you are!

She called to it, but it slipped through her hold and fell back into a swell of purple.

Joseph reached for her. She ducked but knew he wouldn't miss.

Lucas shielded her with his body.

"Don't—"

Snap!

Joseph's hand turned aside. Elliot jumped in the way of danger, his own red light an inferno around him. He raised a heavy branch in his hands. "I said *don't touch my sister!*"

Joseph rubbed his chest where Elliot's attack had left tears in his skin.

"Give us room," Kāi said to Matilda. He, too, faced Joseph now, armed with a solid branch.

She wanted to tell them to run. "Be careful." She turned her back, and the sound of wood on flesh filled her ears. She wedged herself under Lucas's arm.

"Leave me," he said. "I can fight."

"Liar." She pulled him closer to her too easily.

They hurried away from the fighting and shouting, and she sat Lucas down against a tree under Olive and Miss Kovacs's watch.

He clutched the grass around him and tried to get up again, but Olive's mild hands held him back.

"Stay," Olive said.

Matilda lamented the loss of Lucas's touch, but she turned to Miss Kovacs. "Joseph is too strong. I can see the lights, but I can't call them."

"You can't paint a masterpiece when you've only held a brush once or twice." Miss Kovacs's arms swept the air for obstacles as she moved toward Matilda's voice. Matilda took the old woman's hand. "He's been painting much longer than you."

A crack and thud snagged Matilda's attention. Kāi rolled at the base of a tree, stunned and winded. As Elliot whipped his branch through the air, Joseph seized it and snapped it over his knee.

Kāi fought to his hands and knees. He took up his branch, scrambled after Joseph, and whacked him on the back of the head. Elliot dove for his broken branch. He came up wielding half in each hand, beating and stabbing.

"Then tell me how to master it," Matilda said, "before someone gets killed."

Miss Kovacs's age-spotted hand clasped Matilda with the strength of a younger woman. "*I* am a master. I can send the Names back if I know what to call them, but I need you to see them for me."

— CHAPTER SIXTY-EIGHT —

LUCAS

Humans are weak, fragile creatures.

Olive leaned over me. She called me by the dog's name and attempted to treat my injuries. Her hands felt like fire on my skin. Maybe I was cold.

"Help me up. I can fight!"

"No." Olive pressed down on my chest. She avoided my rib, but it still smarted. "Be still."

My strength abandoned me. Cracked bones and pain that wouldn't have slowed me as a monster now consumed me.

Matilda fought without me at her side. She faced a devil, but like me, she was hopelessly human.

— CHAPTER SIXTY-NINE —

MATILDA

Olive rustled behind Matilda, trying to keep Lucas still and making it hard for Matilda to concentrate. He needed her, but Elliot and Kāi couldn't fight Joseph with sticks alone. They needed Power.

She led Miss Kovacs as close to the fight as she dared and hid her behind a tree. The mesmerist's magic played against her own, fierce but controlled as she awaited Matilda's direction. Unable to stretch the Power as far as Miss Kovacs, Matilda crept dangerously close to the battle, reached out her arm, and watched the glow of her aura extend.

Tendrils of her magic stroked the edge of Joseph's aura, still a sickly purple. She beckoned to the light, but it didn't respond to her the way Lucas's Name had. It thought it belonged with the beast who'd corrupted it.

Miss Kovacs poked her head out from behind the tree. "What is taking so long? Give me a Name!"

"I'm trying," Matilda said, "but it won't be persuaded."

"You can't *persuade* a Name to come. You have to take it!"

How can I when it won't listen to me?

Kāi shuffled and weaved as he attacked Joseph, but his movements slowed dangerously. Elliot's attacks fell quick and hard, but he missed more often than he hit. With the enhanced sight the Power gave her, Matilda saw each drop of sweat on their faces and heard the strain of their hearts fighting for courage and strength.

Joseph didn't slow. His breath huffed, but his heart beat evenly, and his attacks came with deadly might. He crushed Elliot with a knee to the stomach. Elliot fell with a grunt and a wheezing cough. Kāi lunged with an overhead strike, but Joseph dodged it and swung Kāi into a tree. Kāi slumped to the ground and didn't get up. When Elliot struggled to his feet, Joseph grabbed him by the collar.

Matilda speared the violet light with daggers of the Power. *I have to steal it.* She raked the light with her own, shredding its bond with Joseph, and a river of voices rushed through her ears. Smoky letters formed a Name around Joseph.

Anger.

"I did it!" Matilda yelled into Miss Kovacs's ear. "I did it! *Anger!*"

The mesmerist inhaled, but to Matilda's heightened senses it was more than breath. Miss Kovacs's Power rose in a flood. Where her stormy grey light converged again with Matilda's burgundy, energy sparked. Each aura fed off of the other's and amassed into a daunting wave.

"Anger." Miss Kovacs spoke softly, but her voice could have carried to the other side of the world. "I release you."

Her voice poured over Joseph. Violet light burst around him in an explosion of particles. The light disappeared into the woods and fled to its true master. Now Joseph's colours swirled only between Isaac's red and his own grey.

A malicious scowl left nothing recognizable in Joseph's face.

"Do you think you're better at this than I?" He tightened his hold on Elliot and growled something so savage Matilda couldn't understand his voice. A flare of light erupted from Elliot's body.

Flames of his cherry light knotted with the deeper red around Joseph, and the aura around Elliot went out.

Her brother went limp and empty, a doll with his face but without his good soul.

"No!" Matilda screamed. "Let him go!"

Joseph whispered something to her brother. The poisonous spell filled him, and Elliot bared his teeth in the mask of a monster.

Joseph released his hand from Elliot but not his hold. "Get them."

Elliot skulked toward Matilda and Miss Kovacs, gaining speed.

"No, Elliot." Matilda hoped to touch some part of him that hadn't been tainted. "Stop this!"

"He doesn't hear you." A waver broke up Miss Kovacs's iron voice. "Keep your mind on your task. I need those Names!"

Elliot's eyes fell on Miss Kovacs. He leapt. So did Matilda. She roped her arms around her brother and dragged him to the ground.

A vicious snarl vibrated through his body. He had little inhuman strength yet, but he wielded every part of his own without thought for the harm it might do himself. His elbows beat Matilda's ribs, but she refused to let go.

"Let me feel for his Name!" Miss Kovacs hobbled out from behind the tree and bent toward Matilda as she wrestled with her brother. The old woman's hands searched the air for some hold on Elliot's skin. "Hold him still!"

"I'm trying!"

Miss Kovacs's hands found Elliot's face, but he threw his leg into her stomach. She crashed to the ground.

Matilda grunted at another blow from Elliot's elbow. "Miss Kovacs!" she called, but the woman lay on her side and clutched her hip.

"Ha!" Joseph's laugh spread through Matilda like an infection. As she grappled with Elliot, he watched her with an entertained grin and caught his breath.

Joseph's panting. Weakening. The Names—It's working!

Joseph hadn't simply lost Sheridan's *Name*. He'd also lost his speed and stamina, and his breath heaved with the absence of it.

He's weakening, but so am I.

A shuddering groan sounded, almost imperceptible over Elliot's growls. Rubbing the back of his head, Kāi lifted himself to his feet and got sick over the tree roots. His eyes caught Matilda's, and after a moment of confusion, he made as though to stumble to her aid.

"No!" she shouted through clenched teeth. Elliot's fingers tunnelled into her shoulder and tore through her sleeve. "Stay back!"

Joseph turned to Kāi as though he'd forgotten he existed.

"Run!" Miss Kovacs croaked. "All of you! You fools will only make him stronger!"

Kāi staggered toward Olive and Lucas, but he wasn't fast enough.

"Bāo-v—"

A stone struck Joseph's chin, and the Name died on his lips.

Quivering, Olive stood guard over Lucas as Kāi helped him to his feet. Her fist closed around pebbles, and her glare could have flayed skin.

I'm sorry, Elliot.

Matilda released her brother and elbowed him as hard as she could between his shoulders. He gasped and collapsed flat on the ground.

She ripped off the sleeve Elliot had torn at the shoulder and charged at Joseph. He opened his mouth to steal someone's Name, but Matilda sprang onto his back and strung the sleeve through his teeth.

Joseph lurched. She locked her legs around his waist. He grunted through the gag and wrenched her injured arm. Sparks of pain bolted through her, but she ground her teeth and held on. "Joseph Harrison," she said, "you keep your mouth shut!"

The sleeve stifled his snarl. She pulled it taut and searched his glow of red for a Name.

— CHAPTER SEVENTY —

LUCAS

Kāi wobbled on his feet but draped my arm over his shoulders, making my rib feel like it had snapped again. Someone groaned. I realized it had been me.

Olive stood guard over us with her fist clenched around stones.

Olive. Olive with *rocks*.

She launched one of them and struck Joseph.

"Hurry!" Kāi said in my ear.

With his support, my legs held my weight, but Kāi teetered as much as I did. I bit back the pain, and we hobbled through the trees.

It seemed so dark now. So quiet. I should have been able to hear the life in the woods and see the trees watching me in the night, but everything was black.

"This way!" A woman's voice called through the trees.

Mîfä?

She appeared on the path ahead in muddied silks and flapped her hand at us. "Hurry to the road! I fetched the cart."

I should have known she wouldn't let Kāi go far without her. She took him by the elbow and led us free of the trees where Joseph's horse waited, its ears laid back as it listened to the clamour in the woods. I leaned against the buggy as Mîfä helped Kāi to a seat, but then a distressed voice pierced the darkness.

"Joseph Harrison, you keep your mouth shut!"

"Matilda!" I turned my head, and a dizzying wave overcame me. *I can't leave her!*

"Get in!" Olive burst out of the woods but kept an eye toward the battle through the trees behind her. She scrambled up next to Kāi, who looked about to vomit again, and took hold of the reins. "Elliot is waking!"

Elliot clawed through brush and branches and emerged from the woods with a venomous glare.

I recognized the feral violence gleaming in his eyes. I'd felt it before; I knew what it would do to him.

I won't let that happen.

Mîfä tried to help me into the buggy, but I shrugged her off, my vision blurring with the pain and effort. I swayed on my feet.

"Go. Joseph knows Kāi's name. Probably Olive's too." I winced at another pang in my chest. "You have to get them far from here, or he'll use them against Matilda."

"What are you doing? You should come with us." Mîfä reached for me again.

I knocked her hand away. "Go!"

There must have been some defiance in my face she understood, because she gave a curt nod and climbed next to Olive.

"Lucky," Olive protested, but Mîfä took the reins from her and launched the buggy down the road without me.

I blocked Elliot's path and faced him alone, but the boy who prowled across the road wasn't the same boy I knew.

"Elliot." I hoped some part of him remained beneath the flashing teeth. He circled around me, and I turned to keep my back from him. "Don't let him turn you into me."

My warning went unheard. Elliot's knees bent, ready to spring. There'd be a fight, but it wouldn't last long.

Elliot vaulted. I let him come.

Hurry, Matilda. Before it's too late for both of us.

— CHAPTER SEVENTY-ONE —

MATILDA

Joseph tried to loosen Matilda's hold. He beat at her hands, and she choked back a cry.

The two red lights Joseph had stolen swam around each other. They were so alike, so bright and angry. They thrummed under Matilda's reach with a fierce energy, but she couldn't be sure which light belonged to her brother.

Elliot, where are you?

Joseph spun close to a tree. A branch whacked Matilda's shoulder and scratched lines down her bare arm. He backed toward a solid trunk to crush her against.

She yanked on his gag and shot energy into one of the red lights. She hoped it was Elliot's.

It wasn't, but it answered her.

"*Retribution!*" she shouted.

Miss Kovacs poked her head out from behind a fir, wearing the tree as a suit of armour and rubbing her hip. "*Retribution!*" she called.

The deeper red leapt out of the pool of light and shot into the woods with a tail of scarlet embers dying on the air behind it.

When the red abandoned him, Joseph shrank under Matilda, his body shortening, thinning. His muscles smoothed and popped back into a slender frame as Isaac's strength left him.

Joseph threw himself backward. The ground slammed into Matilda, and Joseph crushed her under his weight. She gasped for breath. Against her will, her fingers loosened from the gag.

Untangling himself, Joseph straddled her. She had no strength to fight as he pinned her wrists to the ground. He breathed on her, pouring the scent of blood and brandy over her face, and in the dark, his laugh of victory was worse than any nightmare.

"How will you stop me?" As he panted over her, Matilda felt the hot-cold sensation of his breath on her skin. "Go ahead. Try to take your brother's Name."

Joseph sat so close Elliot's light brushed over her. She wiggled her wrists in Joseph's grip and stroked the crimson aura with the Power. The beginning of a Name formed in the light.

Joseph squeezed her wrist until she screamed. The Name vanished.

He laughed again, a muffled sound both dark and mad. "Think of the sympathy I'll receive when my love is killed with her family in a farmhouse fire. You should have come to me. I'd have given you a life better than any you could have made for yourself."

She spat at him. "That life would have cost me my soul."

A dangerous heat flashed over Joseph. "An O'Connor soul is worth less than the breath it takes to Name it."

Matilda arched her back to unseat him, but he held all the control.

CRACK!

Joseph's eyes bulged. Splinters of wood fell on Matilda.

"And yours is worth less than that." Miss Kovacs stood over them with Kāi's abandoned branch. "Just like the strap," she mused.

Joseph released Matilda's wrist and swung at Miss Kovacs. He hit an old knee with a sickening sound. The mesmerist fell with a cry.

Hard as she could, Matilda thrust her palm into Joseph's bloodied nose. He yowled, and his hands cupped his face. She scuttled out from under him and grabbed for Elliot's Name.

The letters appeared. She took them. *Dreamer.*

She shouted the Name. Between grunts of pain, Miss Kovacs commanded the Name to leave the thief.

Colour drained from both Joseph and his aura. He tilted back, the pains of battle dawning on him as the last of his stolen strength vanished. The red light left only dull grey as it sailed in a cloud high above him.

"No!" In the last moments of the Name's flight, Joseph called after it desperately but couldn't claim it. Even in pain, Miss Kovacs was the better painter. "No!" Joseph shouted. *"Dreamer! NO!"*

The red light zipped through the trees. Matilda listened to the whispers as it burned past her, headed for Elliot.

He's safe now.

"No," Joseph said again, but his voice lacked the confidence it had held before. Fear shone in his eyes as they darted between Matilda and Miss Kovacs. "No, I won't give up!"

"I know." Matilda winced as she got to her feet. "So I must stop you. You're only Joseph Harrison now, and I'm not afraid."

The moment her Power touched him, Joseph darted into the woods toward the Richards's farm, kicking up mud as he fled.

Matilda started after him then came to a stumbling halt. Miss Kovacs slouched on the ground and rubbed at her knee, looking older than she ever had.

I need her.

"Go!" Miss Kovacs said as Matilda ran back to her side. She flapped a hand in the air, rejecting Matilda's attempts to help. "I can't keep up. Go!"

Joseph's light had already faded deep into the woods without her. Matilda bit her lip and left Miss Kovacs to fend for herself.

Her heels hammered into the ground, and her skirts tangled in her legs. Certain only that she couldn't allow Joseph to escape, she chased the grey light fleeing through the dark.

Joseph knew these woods, but Matilda knew them better. Under a clouded night sky, the grove lay burdened by dark, but with magic flowing through her, she knew every root and weed.

He weaved left and right, dodged trees, and bolted down strangled paths. He was faster than her, reckless. She raised her skirts above her knees, but Joseph's grey light got fainter as the distance between them grew. He was going to get away!

Snap!

A piercing, primal scream left Joseph. His light flared white and hot, and he crashed to the ground. Matilda slowed to a crawl, panting and watching him warily as she tiptoed toward him.

She smelled pain on him and a fear so strong it almost overwhelmed her, but there was a metallic scent too. Blood. One of Richards's rusting traps bit deeply into Joseph's ankle, snapping bone and tearing through clothes and flesh with its jagged teeth.

"Don't," Joseph said as he rolled onto his back and whimpered from the pain. His forehead glistened with sweat. "I protected us. Don't—*uhnn*—kill me."

"You'd deserve it," she said, but she crouched at his feet, wary. It took every drop of the strength left in her poor, beaten hands, but with a grimace and a flare of pain she pried back the trap's hold on his foot. Joseph dragged himself out of its reaches and choked on another scream.

He lay broken and vulnerable to her. *Miss Kovacs isn't here. I have to do this myself. One way or another.*

She took a deep breath to settle her nerves. "I'm going to make you forget. You'll forget the magic so you can't hurt anyone again."

Joseph's face turned paler than his pained, white light. "I…no! I only defended our country. I saved us from another raid." He scrambled back as his aura darkened to an agonized charcoal. Fighting with his pain, he couldn't resist the blanket of the Power she spread over him, but he felt it. He gasped in a sharp breath and shook his head as his eyes pleaded with her. "No. The Fenians will come back. They'll destroy everything you've built here. Nathaniel's sacrifice will be meaningless. You need me."

"Nathaniel sacrificed everything for his family," Matilda said. She was too drained even to feel anger toward Joseph for daring to speak her brother's name. She only felt grief that it had taken her so long to understand what she should have known the moment she read her brother's note to her. "It will have meaning when we move on and let ourselves be happy. I can only do that if I know you aren't a danger anymore."

"Don't do his," Joseph said. "Matilda, please."

Her blanket of Power thickened around him as she reached for the Name of his light. Only when she tugged at it did he push back, but it wasn't enough to stop her. He was weak, and she was desperate.

"Vengeance," she called.

His light spun around him in a whirlpool, and its waves left him and splashed down upon her. It filled her, *becoming* her.

Burgundy swirled with his gunmetal grey. The grudges that had stolen his humanity sharpened her own. Hatred, jealousy, and the longing for a father forever gone took root and bloomed—a hideous, thorny growth within her. His revenge became hers, dangerous and wonderful. She needed to exact it.

Upon anyone.

He was prone; it would be easy. He'd earned it, and she'd earned the right to give it to him. She *was* him.

No, I'm not.

Her light fought against Joseph's, a burgundy splash that threw itself at overwhelming grey until it beat the toxic wave down. She returned to herself, but Joseph's light rebelled within her. It wouldn't stay quiet for long.

She considered what poison to give him. What was a just punishment for someone who'd killed and caused so much hurt? She looked into his eyes, grey like his aura and staring hollowly back at her. As she prepared her spell, her body felt too heavy.

What is this feeling? Why?

After everything he'd done, he didn't deserve pity, but before her now she saw the unruly boy she'd known as a child—the boy who yearned for his father and worried for his mother.

Rage had crept into him slowly and changed him until he wasn't Joseph anymore. He was wrong, horribly wrong and unforgivable, but he'd been more alone with his pains than her.

I can't...

She released Joseph's light. The glow filled him from the inside, and his eyes took on awareness. She closed her connection to the Power, and as the energy vanished, so did the rest of her strength. She slumped on the ground, numb.

What am I doing?

"You...let it go?" Joseph asked.

"I want to heal." She strived for enough strength to sit upright. "I can't do that if I hold your Name captive for the rest of my life."

Joseph got to his knees, tender with his useless foot. "Good."

With a might that opposed his injuries, he threw himself at Matilda. Her body was made of mud as she landed on her back, and he pinned her easily.

"You'll die for that mistake," he snarled in her face.

Her heel rammed into his wounded leg. He howled. She dug herself out from under him, but he snared the hem of her skirt and crawled over her again, lit with a fury that demanded blood.

"Farewell, Miss O'Conn—"

Thunder echoed through the night, and Joseph fell in a heap on top of Matilda. Something slipped out of his pocket and thumped beside her as he released a slow breath against her neck and lay still.

"Joseph?" Matilda said. The unnatural calm that followed his breath drew on and filled her with disquiet. She shook Joseph's shoulder as she struggled to breathe under his weight, but he wouldn't stir.

When she pushed him harder, he rolled limply off her, lifeless. With the Power gone from her she saw nothing but his silhouette.

Matilda's shaky fists clenched around dirt and weeds and whatever had fallen from Joseph's pocket: a small, hard disc of metal that still held his body heat.

Nathaniel's coin. It lay on her palm when she opened it, and its return to her felt far, far too heavy to bear.

"Gotcha. Thought you strays could 'scape me?"

A drunken voice slurred. A lantern's weak flame and the slurp of feet through mud headed Matilda's way, and she recognized the incoherent string of curses and self-praise. Richards.

With one last glance to Joseph's motionless form, she crawled back the way she'd come.

Oh, Joseph, I'm so sorry.

"Thought you'd get away again, did ya?" Matilda listened to Richards ramble to himself as she moved through the trees. "I 'eard the other farmers out with their guns. Finally got— Jo— Joseph!"

Tears welled in Matilda's eyes. Once she'd clambered far enough away where she could barely hear Richards's panicked swearing, she fell in a wreck. Whimpers escaped her throat, but she didn't bother to hold them in anymore. She leaned over her knees and emptied herself of all her pain and fear.

What a wretched end for a foolish, miserable man. Years of pain and anger too mighty to overthrow were now, with the snap of a hunter's trap and the boom of a rifle, cut horribly short. It was done. It was over, but the wounds cut Matilda deeply. Maybe too deeply to heal.

Somehow, she wandered back to Miss Kovacs. The old woman stood on her feet again and supported herself with a cane made from a gnarled branch.

"By the sniffles you must be Matilda and not Mr. Harrison." Miss Kovacs's voice fell flat and tired. "I heard the gunshot. I won't ask what happened."

"Thank you." Matilda's remaining sleeve left rough scratches on her face, but she dabbed at her puffy eyes again.

"Come quickly," Miss Kovacs said. "There isn't time."

Miss Kovacs turned, and Matilda had to hurry to take her hand and guide her through the trees. She limped alongside the woman and heard someone sobbing as they neared the road. Olive? No.

Elliot.

Matilda bumped past Miss Kovacs and stumbled through the brush. Elliot's half naked form knelt by the road and rocked over another shape lying beneath him.

"Lucas!" The shriek made her throat raw. She ran to his side, and her swollen fingers felt his cold face and chest. Elliot cradled Lucas's head and pressed his shirt to a tear in Lucas's neck, but there was so much blood she smelled it even without the Power. Lucas's breath came in a shallow hiss.

"He wouldn't let go of me." Elliot's voice cracked. "I didn't mean to—I didn't—"

"Lucas." Matilda brushed his hair out of his eyes. "Lucas, look at me."

His eyes slivered open weakly; she didn't know if he saw her there beside him.

Miss Kovacs's cane thumped behind Matilda. "The wound is very serious."

Matilda had scarcely stopped the tears, but they streamed anew down her cheeks. "Lucky would have healed from this. He isn't all gone yet." She turned to Miss Kovacs. "Turn him back. Please, you must save him!"

Miss Kovacs felt her way to Lucas's side. "I've already tried. He won't let me in. It might be too late if he did."

"He'll let you in." Matilda sniffled back her tears. "He will if I ask him."

Taking Lucas's hand in hers, she pressed his icy fingers to her cheek and looked at him through the blur of tears. Without being called, the Power came to her.

Burgundy, red, and grey lights shone in the night, dark and clouded but strong, but Lucas's emerald light had lost its flicker, the flames almost spent.

"You told me you owed me a life." She prayed he still held enough of himself to hear her. "I want it—every long year until we're both old and wrinkled. Give me your Name for a while. I promise I'll care for it until you're strong enough to have it back."

Despite the frail glow of his aura, Lucas lay so still she wondered if he'd already vanished from his broken body, but then, gingerly, he tugged her hand. One weak finger brushed a tear from her cheek.

She feared to smother his aura, but she beckoned to his Name with tender wisps of energy. Faint letters formed and vanished almost before they'd appeared, but she already knew them. *Light.* She called to his Name with only a thought.

It came to her willingly.

Miss Kovacs didn't waste a breath. She dropped to her knees and clasped Lucas's face between her hands. "Now, Lucky, come back to this boy."

The mesmerist whispered many things to Lucas. Matilda kissed his fingers and prayed until his eyes closed and his hand fell limp in her palm. She cradled the last cinders of his Name and refused to let them fade.

Please don't leave.

September 30th, 1885

Lucas, I can't pretend I'm not still angry with your choice, though I know I asked a favour you had no hope of granting. I can't blame your fear of the Power. If I'd been more afraid, none of this would have happened.

Despite this lingering anger, I am sorry for your fate. Win or lose, my fate also draws near. I'd say I'll meet you in heaven soon, but I doubt any angel saved me a place.

Wherever your soul now rests, my friend, I hope you find more peace than I.

— CHAPTER SEVENTY-TWO —

MATILDA

The Vancouver air tasted salty like the ocean and danced with the calls of gulls, gossip, and a trumpet testing bold notes. Matilda felt the sun's caress on her back as she guided Mr. Gillie's black team along the edge of the crowd and pulled up behind the other buggies waiting for their passengers.

"I don't know if I'll find Elsie in this crowd." Olive said. She sat with Elliot in the back seat of the carriage and shaded her eyes from the sun, looking for her schoolmate in the throng. She'd dressed up today, wearing the hat Matilda had bought for her first birthday in their new home. With the wages Mr. Gillie gave Matilda for her work at his hotel, she'd been able to afford a matching dress for Olive too. "It feels, I don't know, important."

"It's the first passenger train to arrive; it's history." Elliot had grown a half head taller than Matilda now, and when he stood from his seat he had a good view over the decorated ladies' hats and bowlers in the crowd. He watched with interest as the woodwinds in the band pieced together their instruments and a drummer tapped a rhythm. "That's the biggest band I've ever seen!"

"When will the train come?" Olive asked.

"Soon," Matilda said.

Elliot sat in his seat again, but he watched the band hungrily. Matilda knew he must be imagining himself among them, blaring a horn like the one Mr. Gillie let him use. "What do you think Mr. Wellington looks like?" Elliot said. "Do you think he'll look like Lucas?"

Even after almost a year, a measure of guilt coloured Elliot's voice whenever he spoke of Lucas. Matilda leaned over her seat and patted her brother's arm. Maybe one day he'd forgive himself.

"I hear he looks more like their father," Olive offered with a wistful note. "The maids at the hotel say he's very handsome."

"You don't have to concern yourself with handsome gentlemen yet," Matilda said, and Olive blushed healthily. "Go. Find your friends, both of you. Don't buy too many pastries."

"We won't." Elliot slipped out of his seat and circled around the carriage to help Olive down. He grinned at Matilda in a way that left her no doubt he had every intention of disobeying her, then he and Olive dove into the crowd.

"Don't be late getting back to the hotel," Matilda called as they hurried away. The azure ribbon in Olive's hat bounced behind Elliot's dark head until the mass of people closed around them.

While she waited, Matilda enjoyed the glitter of the harbour under the bluest sky she'd ever seen. She remembered the photograph she'd once found in the newspaper of the British warships lying in wait for the Fenians, but the harbour was clear now. Matilda didn't fear the Sceolan anymore. They'd left long ago.

Excitement hummed around her as a whistle announced the train's arrival. Some in the crowd pointed fingers eastward, and others clapped cheerful hands together. Down the rail line, steam heralded the coming machine. It was such a strange beast of metal and oil, crawling toward the ocean with pistons thrusting. It was hardly the way anyone expected hope to travel, but Matilda felt its arrival thick on the air.

Train number 374 arrived at the station with a grand sound, bearing a banner with the face of the queen and tooting louder than any trumpet in the band. Its wheels squeaked on the rails as the great chariot slowed to a halt and the pipe released a sigh of steam. As the doors on the train opened, the band struck up a victorious tune.

Will he see the carriage through the crowd? Should I have gone closer?

Mr. Gillie had told Matilda their guest had insisted she be the one to collect him from the station, but she hadn't anticipated so many people. Some in the audience reunited with family or friends as they stepped off the train, but it seemed many had come simply to watch history roll in to the sound of a whistle.

From her seat, she gazed across the distance and searched the faces of the men who exited the train. Some belonged to men who were too old; a few belonged to men who were barely older than boys. Some exited with their wives, and others turned their heads so Matilda couldn't see their faces beneath their hats. Mr. Wellington might be anywhere.

I suppose he'll have to find me.

She waited patiently in the driver's seat and soaked in the spring air, closing her eyes and loving the breeze's salty caress.

"Is this the carriage for Felix Wellington?" said a deep voice.

"Oh, yes!" Matilda opened her eyes. A tall man stood beside the carriage and hefted two bulging trunks into the back. Had he brought his entire wardrobe with him?

I thought he was only staying a few days.

She resisted the urge to peer obviously at the face hidden under the brim of his black bowler, but she examined the rest of him. He was well-dressed in a crisp white shirt and a dark three-piece suit he'd kept magically free of wrinkles during his trip.

Beneath the shade of his hat, a satisfied smile found his lips as he finished loading his luggage, and Matilda couldn't help herself from wondering if the maids' gossip of his handsomeness was true. She leaned to the side for a peek beneath his hat, but he turned to her and revealed familiar russet eyes and the edge of a scar mostly hidden beneath his wing-tip collar.

Her heart almost jumped out of her chest. "Lucas!"

"Miss O'Connor." He tipped his hat and bowed much deeper than necessary. "I didn't mean to startle you."

"No, Lu— I mean Mr. Wellington," she said. "I was told your brother would meet me here. I haven't heard from you since you returned to your family. You…never responded to my letters."

"Ah, I should apologize." He scratched under his collar and looked guilty. "To tell the truth, I'm still reacquainting myself with words, and I needed—"

"Time," she finished for him. "We all did."

His hand dropped to his side. He looked at the space beside her and raised an eyebrow as though asking for permission to occupy it. When she made room for him, he swung gracefully up beside her, tipped his head back, and shut his eyes. She turned the team toward the hotel and sneaked private glances at him.

His skin had taken on a healthy glow. The cares in his face had softened, the wounds of his past lingering but no longer bleeding. A peaceful expression sat on his face as he breathed the sea air.

He seemed perfectly comfortable sitting beside her, but she jittered. "What did you tell your brother?" she said. "About your disappearance, I mean."

Once the words had left her mouth she regretted revisiting those dark times, but her question seemed only to amuse him. His eyes sparkled with mischief when he opened them. "I told him I'd followed after a beautiful woman. It wasn't really a lie, and he was too afraid to ask more. He doesn't know anything dangerous."

Beautiful. Matilda hoped he'd mistake the heat in her cheeks for sunburn.

Hearing his voice so open and natural made her feel like she was flying, but it was the feel of his presence beside her she revelled in the most. Too long she'd stubbornly endeavoured to make him speak. She hadn't appreciated how fulfilling it was simply to know he was near.

"Anyhow," he said, "the novelty of my resurrection wore off quickly. Felix has put me back to work and sent me to check on his investments. But how are Kāi and Mîfä? Have you been to the market?"

"I have." She thought of the busy store where Kāi and Mîfä had worked and lived since they'd mailed Mr. Võng the last payments of their debt—with no return address. "They've made friends here. Even if Mr. Võng finds them, he'll have to go through all of Chinatown to reach them. They told me to thank you for the gifts you sent the baby. It'll be any day now."

A little red flared in Lucas's cheeks, but he looked pleased. "It was nothing. I only wish Kāi would have let me do more to thank him." His voice dropped, turning serious as he looked at Matilda. "I'm sorry I could do nothing for Nathaniel. I know you wanted to clear his name."

She turned the team onto the hotel's street. Last year a great fire had razed most of Vancouver to the ground. With all of the city coming together to rebuild after a tragedy, it had felt like the right time for Matilda to rebuild her life and family surrounded by good neighbours as tenacious as she. Now rows of new, defiant buildings stood by the boardwalks as she drove past, and Mr. Gillie's hotel towered proudly over the road, lively and strong. It had been a much-needed beginning for her, Olive, and Elliot, healing so many hurts she'd thought were permanent. Perhaps it could help Lucas too.

"I still dream of him sometimes," she said, "but now my dreams are calm. There was no way to clear my brother's name without exposing both you and the magic. It's safer to keep it secret, and I don't want you to spend your life paying for a crime that was someone else's doing. Wherever he is, I know Nathaniel is pleased you were saved. So am I."

Lucas said nothing, but, though a shadow of guilt remained in his eyes, his silence was grateful.

Matilda stopped the carriage in front of the hotel's grand French doors, the symmetrical panels of windows sparkling in the daylight. A few patrons wandered in and out of the building, but with the celebration at the station, the street was serene enough to hear the song of the robins perched over the scarlet awning.

Matilda tethered the reins to the carriage. "Olive and Elliot will want to steal all of your time. Especially Elliot. He'll never admit it, but he's missed you."

"Only Elliot?" Lucas said, leaning toward her.

When she thought her heart might not survive another second of him being so close, looking at her like that, Lucas stepped down from the carriage and offered his hand to her. She accepted the warmth of his grasp and felt it more acutely than the sun. She held it perhaps a little too long before stepping down.

"How long will you stay at Mr. Gillie's hotel?" she asked.

"Not long."

Her lips pressed together. *He didn't have to say it so easily.*

"It won't be Mr. Gillie's hotel once the paperwork is done," he said. "Once he retires, it will belong to Felix."

"Is your brother moving to Vancouver?"

"No, he wants me to manage the hotel." Lucas collected his luggage from the back of the carriage and set it down at his heels. He turned to her, a playful gleam in his eyes she'd missed in the months they'd been apart. "And there's the matter of the life I owe you, if you still want it."

The ground seemed to fall away beneath her feet. Or maybe she was floating. "What do you mean?"

"When I met you I was Lucky, in more ways than one," Lucas said with a half-smile that was roguish but heartfelt. "Yet—though I'm certain I made an uncommonly handsome beast—I'd like the chance to meet you as Lucas from now on. Will you allow me the honour, Matilda?"

Pleasure shivered through her whole being to hear her name embraced by his voice. She'd never known her own name could sound so beautiful, and there was only one answer she could give him.

Without a care for any who might see, she stood on her toes, hooked Lucas by his lapels, and pressed her forehead to his. The touch sent tingles all the way to her toes. It felt right.

She didn't care if her name became part of the maids' gossip. Lucas had spoken it with reverence and heart, and that wonderful, blessed heart was all that mattered.

He cleared his throat. His voice sounded deeper and breathless, but he didn't pull away. "It's been a while since I've done this. Does this mean yes?"

"It means I missed you." She loosened her hold on him but never let go. "I'm glad you're back."

"So am I," he said, but he didn't cheapen the moment with more words. He simply widened that smile, full and warm, and let her lead him home.

July 12, 1887

We came back for the anniversary. All of us. It's just for a few days, but time seems to go still here.

The meadow was different. Livelier. Mother Harrison left the manor and now helps Junior manage the estate and the twins. She's got a handful, but the children have someone who loves them more than the bottle. They looked happier when we stopped by to see Olive's cow. Junior and Elliot didn't even make faces at each other.

This afternoon we visited the graves. So many of them, but I didn't cry as much as I thought I would. We laid a rose on each, even Joseph's. I miss him in a strange way, but now he has his father to keep him company.

Kāi gave his respects to Mr. Gän. I don't understand his customs, but the chrysanthemums and incense he placed after he'd swept the gravestone were beautiful. Lucas wanted to respect the man in his own tradition, so Kāi taught him the proper way to bow. Mîfä cradled her son in her arms and told me Kāi had finally tracked down a relative of Mr. Gän's. He'll have a nephew to sweep his grave now.

I returned Nathaniel's coin to him. That was the hardest, but it felt right after I did it. I felt lighter. When everyone else was distracted with their own prayers for him, Lucas took my hand in silent comfort. I hope my hand did the same for him.

It wasn't all sad. We visited Marta Kovacs, who must still be in good health the way she barked at us. She's been keeping Mother Harrison in better health too. They've become the most unlikely of friends, and I was pleased to find a little of Marta's fortitude has worn off on Mother Harrison.

Kāi and Mîfä took the kids back to the rooms we rented at the hotel on Front Street so Lucas and I could watch the sun set over the Fraser. I know you still read my journal, Elliot, so that's all I'm writing about that.

We leave for home early tomorrow. We thought about staying one more afternoon, but Olive doesn't want to miss Elsie's birthday party.

And I don't want to miss the looks on the hotel maids' faces when they see Lucas's emerald ring on my hand.

I might not write again for a while. We have a whole future to plan!

— ACKNOWLEDGMENTS —

Impostor syndrome has long been a companion of mine. I completed the first draft of *The Wolf's Name* nearly a decade ago, and though Matilda and Lucky have been good company, I kept their story on the shelf at Impostor's insistence. It wasn't until the fateful year of 2020 I decided to sneak *The Wolf's Name* into the query trenches while Impostor wasn't looking. 2020. What a strange time to first venture into the world of Twitter pitch events and query letters.

There are many people I need to thank for helping me bring Matilda and Lucky this far. First to Mum, who instilled in me a love of fairy tales and magic. To Dad, who performed as my scribe when I was too young to wield a pen. May you be well enough to do so again by the time this is printed. To my brothers Bryan, who kept telling me to kick Impostor to the curb, and Phil, lest I be accused of forgetting the middle sibling. Also, to my grandmothers, Joyce and Melva, who inspired a curiosity in my heritage. Love you all.

To Sommerville-sensei, who still doesn't know a conversation about war dogs during my first weeks of ninjutsu inspired Lucky's part in this story, thank you. To my Watson, Afton Aldridge, for being a springboard for my ideas and for being the first to read this book. I hope your Mary will permit me to borrow your talents when the game is next afoot. Also, to Candace Burt for helping me get this book on the right track when I sensed trouble in the early chapters.

Many thanks to Jana Rolls and Dr. Brittany Carr for your tips on west coast weather. I may have taken a teensy bit of creative license for the sake of atmosphere (pun intended), but it's much more accurate now.

I must thank Sam Leung as well as the people of Reddit for answering my Cantonese, Taishanese, and Irish questions, particularly WEN_QONHIUNG, Hussard, Moskau50, and holocene-tangerine. Your help was invaluable and so appreciated. Any errors are mine.

I owe thanks to Beth Phelan for hosting #DVpit, through which I found a home for this book. Ironically, I have impostor syndrome to thank as well. When I was sure those who showed interest in my pitch would lose it upon reading my manuscript, Impostor sadistically convinced me to send queries anyway to allow interested parties to personally reject me. I'm very grateful to those who didn't.

Which brings me to everyone at Outland Entertainment. First, to my editor Gwendolyn N. Nix for proving Impostor wrong. Your vision for Matilda's story was greater than I ever could have achieved on my own. She has been safe in your hands. To my copy editor Alana Joli Abbott for your reader's notes and for your patience when I had darlings I was reluctant to kill. To Tara Cloud Clark for catching my mistakes and for your kind comments on my story. To Mikael Brodu for making the interior so pretty. To Jeremy Mohler for the cover design and for putting up with my nagging. Artist authors are the worst. To all of you, thank you for believing in Matilda's story.

And because someone will have inevitably fallen through the cracks, thank you to any I may have missed but are owed appreciation. I'm scatterbrained, not ungrateful.

Before I wrap this up, I must also mention Denise Chong and her book *The Concubine's Children.* It was a tremendous help to me in researching the Chinese experience in Canada. Upon learning Denise's grandmother had the same occupation as Mîfä, I knew my decision to read her story had been wise.

The Chinese workers who came to Canada did far more for our nation than help build the Canadian Pacific Railway, and they were, to massively understate it, poorly treated for their efforts. It would have felt wrong to leave their presence unacknowledged while I wrote a novel set so close to the completion of the railway, but their story is ultimately not mine to tell. I found www.mhso.ca/tiesthatbind to be a useful resource. I hope you will as well.

And it is to you, fair reader, whom I offer my final thanks. Thank you for taking Matilda's journey with her. Thank you for supporting me in mine. And thank you for taking Impostor down a few pegs.

— ABOUT THE AUTHOR —

Born and raised in Canadian cowboy territory, Raelyn Teague started telling stories before she knew her alphabet. While at university, she turned her back on her love of writing in pursuit of a shinier, more "practical" career until she learned having her soul slowly rot away wasn't more practical after all. Luckily, writing (mostly) welcomed her back.

An artist and martial artist, when she isn't reading or working on her latest novel, she's doodling the characters from her favourite video games or reminding her cat she already fed him.